COLD
AS ICE

D1053868

OTHER BOOKS AND AUDIO BOOKS
BY STEPHANIE BLACK:

The Believer

Fool Me Twice

Methods of Madness

COLD
AS ICE

A NOVEL

STEPHANIE BLACK

Covenant Communications, Inc.

Cover image: *Face Behind Broken Glass* © FarukUlay, Courtesy of iStockphoto.com

Cover design © 2010 by Covenant Communications, Inc.

Published by Covenant Communications, Inc.
American Fork, Utah

Copyright © 2010 by Stephanie Black

All rights reserved. No part of this book may be reproduced in any format or in any medium without the written permission of the publisher, Covenant Communications, Inc., P.O. Box 416, American Fork, UT 84003. This work is not an official publication of The Church of Jesus Christ of Latter-day Saints. The views expressed within this work are the sole responsibility of the author and do not necessarily reflect the position of The Church of Jesus Christ of Latter-day Saints, Covenant Communications, Inc., or any other entity.

This is a work of fiction. The characters, names, incidents, places, and dialogue are either products of the author's imagination, and are not to be construed as real, or are used fictitiously.

Printed in the United States of America
First Printing: August 2010

16 15 14 13 12 11 10   10 9 8 7 6 5 4 3 2 1

ISBN: 978-1-60861-013-6

ACKNOWLEDGMENTS

For giving me feedback on the manuscript, thank you to my test readers: Anna Jones Buttimore, Jonathan Spell, Dianna Hall, Sue McConkie, Amy McConkie, Amy Black, and my husband, Brian. Thanks also to Brian for spotting a key mistake and giving me the way to fix it.

Another big thank you goes to all the people who took the time to answer my questions and share their expertise, with special thanks to Karlene Browning, Stanford McConkie, and Amy Black.

I'm grateful for the opportunity to work with the fantastic people at Covenant, including managing editor Kathryn Jenkins and publicist Kelly Smurthwaite. Thank you to Christina Marcano for designing another fantastic cover, and, as always, thank you to my editor, Kirk Shaw. Kirk, it's an honor to work with you.

CHAPTER 1

KAREN BRODIE SNATCHED HER BINOCULARS from the grubby upholstery of the passenger seat and focused the lenses on the couple emerging from Il Giardino. A couple on a date—it was always a couple or a group of friends or a family laughing together—and whom did Karen have? No one.

He should still be hers. He owed her that—owed her *everything*. Over the years, she'd tried to layer the pain of rejection with a protective shell, dulling sharp, gritty edges, but still the pain wore through, tearing at her insides until nothing whole remained.

The man exiting the restaurant had thinning gray hair and a paunch that pushed through his open coat. Karen slouched in her seat, lowering the binoculars. Philip would never let himself go like that. The older he got, the more attractive he got. Unlike her. She wasn't stupid enough to think she was pretty anymore. Black dye hid the hairs that had started to gray six years ago when she hit thirty—it figured that *she'd* get stuck graying early—but nothing from a drugstore shelf could give her the smooth, pretty face she'd had in college.

Back when Philip had noticed her.

At least she hadn't packed on the blubber. She was skinnier than she'd been fifteen years ago.

The doors opened, and Karen lifted the binoculars. *Not him.* What was taking him so long? He'd been in there for two hours, he and his darling chickie. How long could it take to eat a plate of spaghetti?

A long time, if you spent more time gazing into each other's eyes and holding hands in the candlelight than you did eating. What role had he chosen to play for her? He could be whatever he thought a particular woman would find most attractive. Sweet and shy? Suave and charming?

Witty and funny? Vulnerable and a little awkward? He could do them all. But only Karen knew *him,* the real Philip, the man she'd seen when fear had stripped away all the posing and he'd *needed* her. And she'd been there for him.

This was how he repaid her.

What would happen if she marched into the restaurant and told his girlfriend what he'd done to Leslie McIntyre?

The girl wouldn't believe her. Why would she? She'd view Karen as jealous and deranged, spewing lies. But *he'd* know she was telling the truth. And he'd be scared.

The thought of scaring him made her smile as she pressed the binoculars to her eyes. For years, she'd left him alone. She'd let him forget she existed. She'd let him forget what he owed her. He'd always been so cocky, so convinced she'd remain silent—first because she loved him, and then because to expose him was to condemn herself.

But what if she didn't care about any of that anymore?

Karen lowered the binoculars and switched on the engine to heat the car for a few minutes. Even with two layers of socks, a wool hat, insulated gloves, and a heavy coat, she got chilled from sitting still too long on this November night. Maybe she should stop cowering in the corner of the parking lot and stroll toward the restaurant—right when he was exiting. Watching him from a distance had been exhilarating at first, but now it wasn't enough.

It was time for him to notice her.

The warmth of excitement surged through Karen's stiff limbs as she watched another couple exit the restaurant. *Him.* And his sweetie pie. Hastily, she switched off the engine. She stuffed the binoculars under the seat, picked up her purse, and stepped out of the car.

Her knees trembled, making it difficult to maintain a steady, casual gait, but she managed it, approaching the couple as they neared his car. Clutching both her gloves in one hand, she pretended to search for something in her purse and let one of her gloves fall to the asphalt. She kept walking as though she hadn't noticed, until the cutesy soprano voice of the girl stopped her.

"Ma'am! You dropped your glove."

Ma'am. Like she was an old lady, another generation. "Oh—thank you." As Karen turned to take the glove from the girl, she let her gaze cross his.

And saw no response. Nothing. No recognition, no fear, no irritation. As though she were a stranger.

He and the girl moved on, leaving Karen standing there, gripping her gloves. For an instant, she wanted to whirl around and scream at him, but she held back. Making a fool of herself wasn't the way to get to him.

She heard the electronic beep as he unlocked his car. A new Acura. Not exactly a luxury car, but still much pricier than anything Karen had ever driven.

Maybe she hadn't managed to rattle him tonight. But she could hurt him in other ways.

* * *

"DON'T YOU HAVE NAPKINS?" ABIGAIL Wyatt scanned the contents of her brother's pantry.

"I didn't think to buy them." Derek Wyatt sat on the edge of the kitchen table, knocking one of the mismatched place settings askew. "I always wipe my hands on my shirt."

"That's not funny." Abigail tried to sound light, like it *was* funny, but she had to fight an urge to slam the pantry door. "Get off the table. You're messing everything up."

Derek poked the silverware back into alignment and grinned at her, the impish little-brother grin that had charmed Abigail from Derek's babyhood. Today, the smile didn't quite work; his cheek muscles were too stiff and his eyes too somber—olive-green eyes, half concealed by the dark brown hair that kept falling over his face. He pushed the hair back, absently rubbing the strands between his thumb and forefinger. Derek had a habit of fiddling with his shaggy hair when he was nervous, and the quirk always made her feel she was looking at a vulnerable child, not a six-foot-two-inch-tall man.

Realizing she was repeatedly pushing her own hair behind her ears, Abigail dropped her hands to her sides. "Buy some napkins," she said. "Cloth would be better, but given the . . ."

"Given that the rest of the place is decorated in contemporary dumpster, using cloth napkins would be like using crystal fingerbowls at McDonald's," Derek finished for her.

"I didn't mean that."

"Yeah, you did."

"Derek . . . I'm sorry. I'm not criticizing—"

He held up a hand. "It *is* junky, okay? My table is a cafeteria castoff that I bought for five bucks. I have one green plate, one red plate, and two plates with blue stripes. I would have borrowed Grandma's china for the event, but I hear Mom doesn't have it anymore." His dry tone sounded harsh. *Please don't let him use that tone with Mother and Dad.* Abigail felt like she'd been uttering variations on that prayer for three weeks straight.

"Sorry," he said, reading her expression. "That was stupid."

"You're nervous. I understand."

"I don't think this is going to work, Abby. They're not going to come."

"They'll come. And don't call me Abby in front of them. You know that bugs Mother."

"I shouldn't have written a note. I should have called. I'm a coward."

"We've been through this. The letter was a better approach. It gave you time to work out what you wanted to say and gave them time to think about their response. Plus, Mother likes the formality of handwritten notes."

"It wasn't much of a note. I just said it would be good to see them and would they come over for dinner."

"It was enough. You didn't need to write an elegant epistle. They *want* to see you."

"Do they?" Derek picked up a spoon and frowned at where the tip had been ground up in the disposal. "Then why did they let five years go by?"

"Why did *you* let five years go by?" Abigail turned away and picked up the Windex and cleaning rag. Five years—for Abigail, five long years of hammering alternately against the brick walls of Derek's bitterness and her parents' anger. She hadn't dared to hope Derek would send the note until she actually saw him drop it in the mailbox. Even then, she'd half expected that he'd jam his arm into the box, struggling to retrieve the letter before a postal worker could deliver a broken piece of his pride to the home where he hadn't set foot since the disastrous day of their grandmother's funeral.

She sprayed the front of Derek's fridge and started wiping.

"You already polished that," he said.

"Did I?" She kept wiping.

"You're mad at me. I'm sorry. I promise I'm not going to do the blame game. I'm trying to do this right."

"I know." She'd tried to coax Derek into going to their parents' home, but he'd insisted it would be better to invite them to his apartment, that he wanted to host them, to be the one to set the stage for the reconciliation. Abigail kept hearing her father's voice in her head, yelling to Derek that he wasn't welcome in their home and wouldn't be until he cleaned up his life. Derek either didn't think his life would yet pass muster, or he was too proud to ask for readmittance. Probably both, though Abigail had tried to convince him that their parents would welcome him the instant he made the first move.

Abigail set the glass cleaner aside and turned toward Derek. "I'd better go." She picked up her purse. "I need to go into work this afternoon."

"I'm scared," he said.

So am I, Abigail thought. "Don't worry. It'll be fine."

"I mean *really* scared—like, I-think-I'm-going-to-puke-right-now scared."

"In that case, you might need this." Abigail tossed him the cleaning rag.

Derek gave her a sour grin and flicked the rag like a whip. "It blows my mind when I think how few people in the world know what a brat you really are."

Abigail smiled. "Go ahead and spread the word."

"Who's going to believe me?"

Abigail moved to stand next to him. "Derek, it'll go fine tonight. They want this. You're their son. They want you back."

"Only because they can't trade me in for a different son."

"Derek."

"Sorry. But you know it's true."

She squeezed his shoulder. "They love you. You should have seen Mother's face when she told me she'd gotten your note. She was glowing."

Derek said nothing.

"Just—get some napkins, okay?" Abigail said. "Unless you want *all* of us to wipe our hands on your shirt."

"Sure. Napkins will make the difference."

"Little things that show you're being considerate *do* make a difference." Abigail regretted the lecture even as the words came out of her mouth. "Sorry. I'm slipping into bossy big-sister mode."

"It's okay. You packed peanut butter sandwiches in my Batman lunchbox and helped me with my homework so many times that you're entitled to some bossiness."

Abigail smiled, even as she ran through a mental checklist. Derek had already made the dinner; the chicken Kiev and twice-baked potatoes were in the fridge, needing only to be heated. The salad was in the fridge. The apple pie was on the counter. Everything had been prepared by Derek—he'd refused to let Abigail do any of the cooking. *"If I'm the host, I'm the host. If I wanted someone else to cook, I'd call Domino's."*

"See you tonight." Abigail started toward the door. Derek slid off the table and accompanied her.

Her hand was on the doorknob when he said, "You don't think they'll assume it's about the money, do you?"

"The money?" Abigail asked, even though she knew what he was talking about. The two hundred thousand dollars they'd given Abigail after she graduated from college, the money she'd used five years later to open her bookstore. They'd anticipated doing the same for Derek, but never had, since he'd left home at nineteen with no college degree and no skill at anything except drinking games.

"The money they set aside for . . ." Derek ran both hands through his hair. "I mean, I don't even know if they have it anymore. They probably spent it on something else. I just don't want them to think that's the reason I'm doing this. I don't expect anything from them now."

Abigail concentrated on buttoning her long wool coat, afraid to look Derek in the face lest he see the dismay in her eyes. Somehow, she hadn't even been thinking about the money.

But Derek was thinking about it.

Was that the reason he'd finally been willing to make a move to repair the breach between him and their parents? *Don't be so cynical,* Abigail berated herself. *He really wants to make things right. You know he's too proud to put on a show of apologizing just in hopes of getting cash.*

"I'm sure they won't think that," Abigail said, and added in what she hoped passed for a teasing tone, "Just be patient and try not to bring it up before dessert."

Derek chuckled. "Don't forget to bring the flowers. Without flowers, this thing is going to crash and burn."

* * *

HOT WITH EMBARRASSMENT, DEREK PEELED off his faded University of Rochester sweatshirt and flung it on the couch where Abigail had tried to scrub away both the stain and the smell that lingered from a spilled can of Coors.

"Idiot," he whispered. "You're a chronic bozo, Wyatt." Why had he mentioned the money to Abigail? He'd let his nervousness get the better of him. He'd wanted her reassurance that his parents wouldn't be suspicious of him, scrutinizing every leaf on the olive branch.

But it had been a mistake to say anything. Abigail had tried to joke about it, but he'd seen the anxiety in her face—and the buried questions. "*Is it about the money? Is that why you're finally doing this?*"

It wasn't hard to imagine his father asking the same thing. In fact, Derek would bet his new 24-inch diamond slab saw that his parents had already speculated on his motives in detail, and every one of their conclusions had cast him as greedy and conniving.

The too-familiar sense that his stomach was being squeezed between heated iron plates made Derek regret ever listening to Abigail. What made him think tonight would be anything but a disaster? A second-rate dinner at this hole-in-the-wall apartment. The arms of the couch were fraying. The rickety bookshelf would probably collapse the next time someone breathed on it. The only thing in the whole place that didn't look like he'd swiped it from a landfill was the heavy oak chair inlaid with pieces of polished agate arranged in intricate patterns. He was proud of the craftsmanship that chair displayed, but would his parents even notice it?

He hadn't seen his mother in five years, but he could easily picture Lillian Wyatt putting one gleaming shoe over the threshold and giving his apartment a bland look, like she disapproved but was attempting polite silence. She'd never been good at polite silences. Her silences radiated distaste and disapproval like corrosive fumes.

"*Just for a crazy change of pace, stop predicting the worst and give them a chance.*" He could almost hear the words coming from a white-robed angel sitting on his shoulder—an angel with Abigail's sweet face and sarcastic tongue. The halo would suit her.

He should have accepted her offer to hold the dinner at her house. It was a much better location—Abigail's cute little white wood-frame house with its cute green shutters, situated in the center of a tree-covered lot; Abigail's hardwood floors and braided rugs and cute country-style wicker baskets; Abigail's flagstone fireplace, all cozy and family-like—but he'd turned her down and insisted on inviting their parents to this dive. He should have at least hung a painting or two on the bare walls—

"You're not a kid anymore. You don't have to go all Martha Stewart to impress your mom." The sound of his voice made him feel a little better. When he talked to himself, his voice gave him a sense of objectivity, like someone outside of him was listening and giving him feedback—someone who might even approve of him. That was probably a symptom of schizophrenia, but he didn't care.

He flipped his hair out of his eyes. Abigail had hinted that he should get his hair cut, but he'd ignored her. He'd broken up with Catrina, and he'd quit the booze and weed. Wasn't that enough? He wasn't going to chop off his hair, trying to appear like some good-boy returned missionary. His parents knew he wasn't going to church, and they'd agreed to come to dinner anyway. They'd have to deal with the hair. It wasn't that long, anyway.

Scowling, Derek fingered the hair that hung to his jaw. He thought of Abigail's glossy brown hair, cut in a curving, shoulder-length bob. Everything about Abigail was neat and tailored, from her smooth hair to her subtle makeup to her conservative blouses and classic skirts. The only flamboyance she ever injected into her outfits came with the jewelry he'd made for her—a jade pendant caged in tangles of gold wire, a brooch of snowflake obsidian, a bracelet hung with chunky, triangular pieces of lapis lazuli. Dramatic, eye-catching pieces that he'd doubted she'd actually wear.

But she did. She wore everything he gave her, right along with her Marian-the-Librarian clothes and the flat-heeled shoes she favored so her five-foot-nine-inch frame wouldn't make her taller than any more men than necessary. He could fashion a necklace out of a chunk of concrete and Abigail would probably wear it, even if the weight of it broke her neck. And she'd make it look good.

From the kitchen counter, he picked up a white jewelry box tied with a gold ribbon. He yanked the ribbon loose. Inside the box lay a bracelet set with ovals of rose quartz, each cabochon polished to glossy perfection. The setting was intricate, antique-looking silver, and Derek had paid way too much for it, but it was perfect for his mother. She'd *have* to think it was beautiful. Even his father couldn't miss the beauty of what Derek had created.

Derek laid the bracelet back in the box. He shouldn't have opened it. He'd never be able to retie the ribbon in that fluffy, elegant way Abigail had. He tied a sloppy bow, grabbed his sweatshirt, and stalked out of his apartment. In three leaps, he was down the stairs and standing in the chilly basement.

As he breathed in the scent of lapidary cutting oil, the pain in his stomach began to ease. Enduring a landlady who probably rode a broom and boiled eye of newt on weekends was worth it, if it meant having his own space for his rock equipment. Not that this moldy basement was worth what she charged him for it.

Derek put on his work apron, turned on the water, and sat down at his cabbing machine. The comforting friction of the grinding wheel against the circle of onyx he was shaping helped ease the tension in his shoulders. *Stop panicking. Everything's going to be fine. Abigail said they're excited to see you. They don't hate you anymore, or they would have ripped up your invitation.*

Everything would work tonight. Abigail would play mediator; she knew how to speak their parents' language. She could bring them together. It's what she'd been fighting for, ever since the rift. It would work. Everything worked for Abigail.

Perfect Abigail, who did everything right. If their parents could have swapped Derek for another Abigail, they'd have done it in an eyeblink.

At least she'd botched *one* thing. After getting herself dumped by that Rowe guy a couple of years ago, she hadn't managed to find another man. Perfect Abigail was apparently a little slow at finding the perfect guy and producing perfect grandchildren, which must really bug their mother—with Lillian Wyatt, it was all about babies. She must be in shock that Abigail hadn't come through. Or maybe not. She probably figured no one was good enough for Abigail.

Derek methodically turned the stone to grind it evenly, trying not to think about how much easier it would be to reach for a twelve-pack and drink himself into oblivion than to face whatever was going to happen tonight when he talked to his parents for the first time in five years.

CHAPTER 2

"**H**ey, Karen." Philip's voice was friendly, and the sound of him speaking her name evoked a surge of excitement. Karen fought the response. Today, he wasn't going to play with her emotions.

Karen settled into the passenger seat of his car. He promptly accelerated out of the parking lot, as though he didn't want anyone to see them together. It figured. He'd been cool on the phone, but when she'd insisted it was urgent she talk to him in person, he'd agreed—though he'd insisted they meet in the parking lot of the Wegmans on Spruce Road rather than at his place or hers. His chickie-babe got a candlelit dinner at Il Giardino; Karen got a bustling grocery store parking lot on a Saturday afternoon.

She could tell he'd wanted to refuse to meet her altogether but hadn't dared. She liked that he was already a little afraid of her.

"So how are things?" he asked. "Obviously you're doing well. You look fantastic."

"Thanks." He was a good liar.

"You keep yourself in amazing shape." He grinned at her. "I'll bet you've got hordes of jealous women who'd love to force-feed you a platter of cheeseburgers just to make themselves feel better about their buffalo hips."

Karen had wondered if he'd try to charm her with that melted-butter voice he did so well. Even now, remembering the way he'd pretended not to know her when she'd approached him the other night, it was difficult not to drown in the warmth of his words. She *could* let herself believe everything he said, like she wanted to. They could enjoy a pleasant visit, maybe even go for a late lunch. She'd tell him she'd called because she was lonely; she'd wanted to get together with an old friend for old time's sake. Maybe it would be enough. Maybe she could live on it for another year or so. Maybe she wouldn't need to spend any more cold hours in her car, parked outside his house or outside restaurants.

But it *wasn't* enough. Despite the warmth of the car, she could feel the chill now, a coldness that passed all the way through her. "How's your girlfriend?" she asked.

He glanced at her. He was still smiling, but his eyes had turned flinty. "Is that what you wanted to talk about?"

"No." Karen waited for him to bring up their encounter in the parking lot of Il Giardino, but he said nothing. He kept driving, passing through the center of town where picturesque wood-shingled buildings and brass lampposts along brick sidewalks tried for a Norman Rockwell look that Karen had increasingly come to hate. Why had she come back to Ohneka, New York, of all places? Infested by boaters and vacationers in the summer, overrun by leaf peepers in the autumn, a gloomy deep freeze for the rest of the year. She should have sold her grandmother's monstrosity of a house and gone to Florida.

"*You're* sure doing well." Karen looked him over. Experienced only in discount-store shopping, she couldn't even identify if his coat and gloves were expensive items. They probably came from some high-end outdoor shop and cost as much as that loser tenant of hers had coughed up in the entire eighteen months he'd rented from her. "Life's been cushy for you, hasn't it? I'm surprised you haven't spent some of your money on a gorgeous wife and a handful of bratty kids."

"What do you want?" He wasn't pretending to be charming anymore. "My relationships are none of your business. We moved past this years ago."

"Yeah, you moved past it. Chucked me out of your life like a sack of rotten potatoes. And I left you alone like you wanted. *You're* the one who started parading yourself in front of me."

"That's a lie. You'd hardly have to see me at all if you weren't chasing me down. You were at the restaurant on Friday. And I've seen your car a few other times. You're following me."

"Why would I?"

Philip shifted his gloved hands on the steering wheel. "If you think you can get away with stalking me—"

"Maybe," Karen said, "you should call the police."

A horn blasted behind them. He jumped slightly and accelerated through a light that had been green for several seconds. Karen smiled, her heart pumping faster. She was making him nervous. It felt good.

He turned left into the parking lot of a bakery and parked near the bushes at the back of the lot. "Nice of you to bring me here," Karen said. "I'll take a pecan roll and a hot chocolate with caramel and whipped cream."

"What game are you playing? We laid all this to rest years ago."

"*Laid to rest* is a good way to put it." Karen enjoyed the way his jaw muscles tightened at her words. "Makes me think of funerals."

"You sick fool. Do you think you can threaten me? If I go down, you go down."

"Hmm. True." Karen stroked her chin with her index finger, creating a theatrical look of contemplation. She felt like an actress on the stage, footlights hot and bright, audience in the palm of her hand. "But what if I don't care anymore?"

"What do you mean you don't care? Do you *want* to get locked up?"

"Maybe it wouldn't be much worse than what I've got now. A ratty old house, falling apart piece by piece. No husband anymore. No kids. No one who cares about me. I don't even have any money. I hardly get by. Prison doesn't sound so bad some days. At least the state pays for it."

"You're being melodramatic. Save it for the soaps."

"Or maybe prison would be worth it to me, just to know that you were getting what you deserved."

His neck turned red. "You're bluffing."

"Maybe I could strike a deal with—oh, who's the person who does deals? The district attorney? After all, you're the one who—"

The malignant expression on his face dammed the words in her throat. Was she going too far? She wanted him scared, not furious. "Or maybe *we* could make a deal with each other," she said.

"A deal?"

"You don't want me around you. You *never* wanted me. You used me. And you owe me."

"What do you want?"

She gave a short, barky laugh. "What do you think I want? Money. I want to get out of Ohneka. I want to sell that junk-heap house. I want to go somewhere warm. California, maybe, or Florida. I want to start over, far away from you. Just think—you'd never have to see my ugly face again."

His expression tense and leery, Philip watched her. She hoped he would slide back into charming mode and tell her she wasn't ugly, she'd always underrated herself, but instead he said, "I don't owe you anything."

"Don't you?" Bitterness welled. "You lured me into helping you. I wasted my life loving you."

"That's not my fault."

"I hate you." It was a lie. Even now, she would have given anything to have him wrap his arms around her and tell her he'd been a fool, he'd loved her all along for her strength, her loyalty and devotion. But it wasn't going to happen. "Make a deal with me or I make a deal with the district attorney. I'm sick of you skating through life, getting everything you want, while I get stuck with nothing. I'm not saying I want either of us to go to prison. I'm saying I want a little something for keeping silent all these years. Give me the money and I'll never bother you again. You'll never see me again."

His face was immobile. "How much are we talking?"

"A hundred thousand."

"Get serious."

"Give me a break. I know you have money."

"I don't have a mountain of cash sitting in the bank. I don't have that much to give you."

"Maybe you'd better try. Really hard. Just because a case is old doesn't mean the police aren't interested anymore."

He laughed, a brittle laugh like a foot crunching through a layer of ice. "You're not very good at blackmail, Karen. Stop sounding like a bad movie. I don't mind helping you out. Even though things didn't work out between us, you know I appreciate what you've done for me. And if you want to make a new start somewhere else, I understand."

Relief and wariness mingled inside Karen as she studied his softening expression. "I want to leave," she said. "I just need money to do it."

"I can't do a hundred. I really can't. But I can do fifty."

Fifty! Karen had to bite the inside of her cheek to keep from smiling. She'd been hoping to walk away with twenty-five. "I don't know. It's . . . I have so many debts . . . I don't know if fifty would be enough to . . ."

"It'll take me a few days to get it, of course. I don't keep that much under my mattress." He chuckled. "But if you need money, why didn't you come to me earlier? You know I would have helped you. You didn't have to follow me around or threaten me."

Prince Charming was back in full royal regalia. Karen had to look away from him. She didn't want to get distracted by those mesmerizing eyes. "Okay, fifty."

"Deal." He held out a gloved hand. She shook it.

"I'll meet you right here. Let's say . . . Thursday night? Nine o'clock? I assume you want cash."

"Yes." Karen had to work hard not to sound triumphant. Why hadn't she stood up to him years ago? She'd been so spineless, always afraid of offending him, always wanting him to love her, even when she knew it was over. When she finally set aside that foul neediness, look what it got her! Fifty thousand dollars.

"I'm sorry things have been hard for you," he said.

She shrugged. "Just give me the money, and I'll keep my mouth shut, like I always have. And don't worry—I won't tell anyone where the cash came from."

He smiled. "I appreciate that."

* * *

SWEAT LAYERED PHILIP'S HANDS AND trickled down his sides. Finally, he stripped off his gloves, dropped them on the passenger seat, and unzipped his coat.

How *dare* she? Did she think she could manipulate him? Control him? Karen Brodie, of all people, ought to know him better than that.

He never should have gotten involved with her. It disgusted him to remember how panicked he'd been, so terrified of going to prison that taking Karen into his life for a while had seemed a small price to pay for freedom. But he'd paid far more than was necessary. Karen's fear of getting punished for her own role in Leslie's death would have been enough to impel her to lie for him. She hadn't needed his devotion on top of that—a fact proven true when he'd finally broken free of her and she'd done nothing.

But was it possible that now she *would* be willing to go to prison, just to see him punished?

It was possible. She'd certainly changed. She was only in her mid-thirties, but she looked older. She used to be passably pretty, but every line of her face had hardened, her wide, nervous smile had become tight and pinched, and bitterness poisoned her every word. She was still obsessed with him, but she hated him. Maybe enough to throw herself away to see him punished. As she'd pointed out, she didn't have much of a life to lose.

The thought of prison settled on his chest like a boulder. Maybe she was right—maybe he *was* the only one who'd end up behind bars. Maybe the district attorney would agree to a deal, and Karen would get off scot-free, or serve only a couple of years.

If she was to the point of stalking him, she was coming unhinged. She claimed that if he gave her the money, this would be the last he'd see of her, but it wasn't true. Once she'd tasted the satisfaction of making him bend to her demands, she'd want more. Given a year or so, she'd be back, more bitter and warped than ever, with another set of demands and another and another until she destroyed both of them.

How dare she threaten him? How dare she try to make a fool of him?

Leslie had made a fool of him.

A dizzying blast of memory left him both trembling and exhilarated. He'd taken care of Leslie. He could take care of Karen, if he had to. Didn't she realize that?

Probably not. She knew Leslie had been a mistake, unplanned. He'd told her over and over how much he regretted it, how awful he felt.

It was half true. He *had* been shaken. But beneath the horror of what he'd done, satisfaction flickered whenever he thought of the way Leslie's scathing fury and mockery had turned to terror.

He'd won. And now, Karen thought *she* could beat him and he'd be too cowardly to defend himself.

He'd thought she was smarter than that.

But he'd have to think things through carefully, very carefully. Last time he'd been lucky.

This time, he couldn't trust anything to chance.

* * *

"LOVE IT! YOU HAVE SUCH a good eye, Ellie." Abigail stepped back, the better to admire the swags of fake autumn leaves and ribbon that Ellie Stuart had draped across the top edge of the glass display case showcasing platters of chocolates. "I was afraid the plaid ribbon would look too busy, but it's perfect."

Ellie Stuart grinned and came to stand next to Abigail. "Next time you'll trust me."

Standing next to petite Ellie, with her flood of curly black hair and eyes the color of the lapis bracelet Derek had given Abigail on her last birthday, always made Abigail feel twice as tall and half as cute as her friend and business partner. Abigail had always wondered what it would feel like to be a delicate little thing, the girl the prince could sweep up onto his horse with one hand while wielding his lance with the other. Abigail figured if a prince tried to sweep her up, he'd overbalance and fall off his horse.

"You okay?" Ellie asked. "You look a little . . . anxious."

Abigail sighed and wandered over to straighten a shelf of books. She'd hoped that being at Words and Sweets in the hours leading up to dinner would calm her—that away from Derek, in a setting she loved, she'd gain more perspective and confidence. Instead, she increasingly wanted to rush back to Derek's apartment and vacuum cobwebs off the ceiling, or anything else constructive to prepare for tonight.

Hovering over Derek like that is not *constructive,* she reminded herself. *Back off and let him do this.*

"You *are* nervous," Ellie said. "Don't be. Everything will work out. They just needed you to nudge them in the right direction. You've done that, Abby, plus a lot more."

Don't call me Abby. Abigail held back the instinctive words. She'd never minded the nickname, but it irritated her mother. "*We didn't name you after your great-grandmother so her beautiful name could be butchered by people too lazy to speak three syllables.*"

"I'm not saying it'll be an easy thing," Ellie added. "I know there's a lot of pain on both sides. But it'll work out."

The door opened, and Abigail snapped her customer-service smile in place. A blond man carrying a cellophane-wrapped basket tied with a gold bow strode into the shop. "Good afternoon, ladies."

"Hi, Brendan," Abigail greeted him.

Brendan Rowe smiled, showing a boyish dimple in his cheek. He set the basket on the counter in front of Abigail. "Here's some early Thanksgiving cheer for my favorite tenants."

"I'll bet you say that to all your tenants," Ellie said.

"I do. But I mean it every time."

Ellie rolled her eyes. "Only you could get away with that."

Abigail laughed, wondering how many years would have to pass before the sight of Brendan Rowe meant nothing to her. It didn't hurt anymore, but there was always a sense of discomfort, like pressure against a new scar. "Thank you, Brendan," she said.

"Thank good old Bob. I'm just the delivery boy. He owns the property; I manage it. He buys the fruit; I deliver it."

"Does this mean we have to tip you?" Ellie asked.

"Only if you have class, Ellie."

Ellie grinned. "Well, that lets me off the hook. Seriously, we appreciate this. I can taste those mangoes now."

"Our pleasure. Everything going okay for you ladies? Anything you need?"

"We're good," Abigail said. "But thank you."

"In that case, I need a recommendation. I'm looking for a book for my mother for her birthday."

"Glad to help." Abigail walked toward Brendan.

"Books?" Ellie shook her head. "Who wants books? What she craves is two pounds of dark chocolate turtles."

"How about if I take both?"

"Sold," Abigail said. She thought back to what kinds of books Brendan's mother enjoyed. She was a big mystery fan. "She enjoys Diane Mott Davidson. Has she read her newest book?" Abigail picked up a copy from a display table and offered it to Brendan.

He studied the cover. "Yeah, she's reading this one right now."

"And she didn't buy it *here*?" Ellie teased.

"I think she picked it up at the airport. She just got back from Europe. How about something nonfiction? And make the book fat. Substantial. Bob will probably give her a yacht, so the book has to be big to compete."

"I'll see if I can find you a good word-per-dollar value. How about something historical?" Abigail led the way to the history shelves. "I know she likes American history."

"Wow, you've got a good memory."

Abigail's cheeks warmed a little. Maybe she should have pretended she *didn't* remember Melanie Chapman's reading tastes—pretended that anything remotely associated with Brendan Rowe wasn't important enough to stay in her mind.

Halfway through her first recommendation, he cut her off with a wave of his fingers. "Sounds good. I'll take it." He plucked the David

McCullough book out of her hand and smiled. "I knew I could count on you. Thanks."

Abigail smiled back. "You're welcome." She walked off as though she had some purpose in mind, but really she just wanted to get away from Brendan. Why was she so awkward around him? Her tears had dried a long time ago, replaced by the knowledge that Brendan wasn't right for her. But getting dumped was never fun, especially when you still had to interact professionally with your ex-boyfriend and see him at church.

"Mira told me I've got to try your new gingerbread–milk chocolate squares, Ellie," Brendan said, and Abigail felt a twinge of annoyance at the thought of Brendan's girlfriend, Mira Johansen, who couldn't be more than twenty-two. Where would Brendan look for a girlfriend next? The nearest high school?

What's wrong with you, girl? Abigail berated herself. *Crabby and catty—what business is it of yours how old Mira is? She's an adult; Brendan's an adult.*

It *wasn't* any of her business, and she didn't care whom Brendan dated. She was just feeling very . . . thirty.

Abigail glanced at her watch. Twenty past five. She was due at Derek's apartment at six. Their parents were coming at six thirty, and Abigail knew they'd be punctual to the minute.

Would Derek be ready? For an instant, Abigail envisioned herself walking into his apartment to find the oven cold and Derek in torn jeans and an oil-stained sweatshirt, sprawled on the couch, drunk out of his mind. It wasn't outside the realm of possibility that he might panic and decide to do the rejecting before he could get rejected.

Please soften their hearts tonight, Abigail prayed. *Please let them feel the love they have for each other.*

The whap of a book hitting the carpet startled her. She'd bumped a book with her elbow as she'd passed an end cap display.

"You break it, you buy it!" Ellie sang out.

Abigail laughed, but it sounded so flat that she was embarrassed. Ellie approached and wrapped her arm around Abigail's waist.

"You're really worried, aren't you?" She looked at Brendan, who was sampling the gingerbread squares. "Abigail's parents are coming to dinner at her brother's apartment tonight."

"Seriously? Wow, that's huge. Last you told me, they weren't even speaking to each other."

"They still haven't," Abigail said. "Derek sent them a letter inviting them, and they gave their answer through me. So . . . I'm hoping everything goes well tonight."

Ellie gave Abigail a squeeze. "It will. Don't worry so much."

"Are you going to be there?" Brendan asked.

"Yes," Abigail said.

"How's that apartment working out?"

"Great. He's got all his lapidary equipment in the basement—it's perfect for him."

"Glad to hear it. I'll take a pound of the gingerbread squares as well as the turtles." Brendan pulled out his wallet. "Want to know what I think, Abigail? You shouldn't be there tonight. Get your parents and your brother in a room together and walk away. Let them work it out. They're all adults. They don't need a referee."

"I can't bail out now," Abigail said. "My parents would view that as a breach of contract."

Ellie blinked her bright blue eyes. They were such a vivid color that people frequently asked her if she wore colored contacts—which she didn't. "Breach of contract?" she asked. "What—do you guys get your dinner invitations notarized?"

"Pretty much. If I said I'm going to be there, I'd better be there. And Derek would freak if I left him on his own. I'm not going to referee, but I think everyone will be a little calmer if I'm there."

"Good luck with using your mind powers on everyone," Ellie said.

When Brendan's transaction was complete, he headed toward the door. "You know where to find me if you need anything. I'm off to continue my deliveries. Have a good day, and Abigail, good luck to all of you tonight."

"Thanks."

"I think we lucked out with our landlord," Ellie remarked as the door swung shut behind Brendan. "I'm betting Derek's landlady doesn't give out fruit baskets. Plus, Brendan's awfully cute. I love the dimple."

Abigail winked at Ellie. "I think anyone fortunate enough to be dating Kyle Stratton ought to be satisfied with that and not spend time dimple-gazing at the property manager."

"Oh my gosh!" Ellie's cheeks went cherry-red. "I'm so sorry. That was way tactless. I forgot that you and Brendan used to . . ."

"No—really, Ellie, that's totally—" Abigail picked up a book on the fall of Rome and held it up "—ancient history."

"Nice visual aid. But you know, Brendan seems to be stopping by more often than he used to. I'm wondering if he's, uh, contemplating the study of . . . history."

"Please," Abigail said. "He just has a cute young girlfriend who likes chocolate."

CHAPTER 3

ABIGAIL CHECKED HER APPEARANCE IN the rearview mirror one last time and used the tips of her fingernails to slide a tiny clump of mascara off an eyelash. She knew she was being silly—it wasn't as though her appearance would make or break the evening—but she still wanted to look her best. Or maybe she was afraid of what she'd find when she walked into Derek's apartment and wanted to delay the moment a little longer.

A tap on her car window made her jump. A man with scraggly dark hair and a dirty coat was peering in at her. Abigail's first instinct was to start the car and speed away before she could be mugged or worse.

"Are you Abigail?" he shouted through the window, and Abigail hesitated. He wasn't a man—he was a kid, a teenager, his face speckled with acne and the childishly eager look in his eyes at odds with his big physique. Wasn't he the boy Derek's landlady hired to do yard work? Abigail had seen him around a few times, mowing the lawn or shoveling snow.

She rolled her window down a couple of inches. "Yes, I'm Abigail."

"I knew it. I know who you are, but I wanted to make sure. It would be bad to make a mistake, right?"

"Can I help you with something?"

"No, I'm supposed to help *you*. Derek said to wait for you and see if you needed help carrying things inside."

Bewildered, Abigail opened her door. "Well, I don't have a lot." She picked up the wrapped bouquet of peach roses, the box of chocolates, and the crystal vase that she'd set on the passenger seat.

"Here, I'll take all that." The boy snatched the chocolates from her hand. "I'll be careful with your fancy vase."

"Take the roses, and I'll hold the vase. You've got to let me carry something too." Abigail passed him the flowers. He cradled them in his arms like he was holding a baby.

"What's your name?" Abigail asked.

"Hunter, but I don't like it. I don't ever want to shoot an animal."

"Hunter's still a nice name."

"I hate it. It's really cold out here. You'd better come inside." Hunter led the way up the stairs to the front door of the gingerbread-trimmed Victorian house that housed Derek and another tenant on the first floor and the landlady on the second.

"I'll open the door for you." Hunter swung the door open with such enthusiasm that he nearly knocked Abigail backward. "You first."

"Thank you." Abigail stepped into the entryway. Derek's door was on the right. She knocked, refusing herself permission to sniff hard, testing the air for baking chicken Kiev.

Derek opened the door. Abigail goggled at him.

He grinned. "Does it look *that* bad?"

"I thought you weren't . . . wow!" She studied Derek's close-cropped hair. "You look great."

"It's only hair. Come on in. Hunter, you did good. Thanks, bud." He took the flowers and chocolates from Hunter and handed him a ten-dollar bill.

"Thanks." Hunter shoved the bill into his pocket. "You look weird with short hair. How come you cut it?"

"It's a special occasion," Derek said. "I trimmed my toenails too."

Hunter laughed. "Five years, right? You haven't talked to your parents in five years."

"That's right. So tonight's a big deal."

"Do they like short hair?"

"Yeah, they do."

"I wish I could not talk to *my* dad for five years. Do I have to go home now?"

"Yep, better run. See you later."

"Bye." Hunter turned and walked away, his shoulders hunched.

"Stand up straight, bud," Derek called.

"Okay, yeah." Hunter straightened his spine and marched out of the lobby.

Derek closed the door. The air in his apartment was savory with the scents of butter, garlic, and baking chicken. A piano sonata played softly in the background. Abigail couldn't hold back a smile of relief and excitement.

"I didn't know you had any Beethoven," she said.

"I didn't want to give Mom the satisfaction of knowing I liked it. You thought those earphones were always feeding heavy metal into my brain, didn't you?"

"As long as you're playing the gentleman, take my coat." Abigail held out her coat and purse. He bowed and took them to the coat closet.

"You really do look good, Derek. And thanks for sending Hunter to help me, though I'm not sure why you thought I needed ten dollars' worth of help carrying a vase and some flowers."

Derek chuckled. "Yeah, sorry, hope that didn't startle you too much. He was doing some homework here, and he was all but bouncing off the walls, he was so antsy to do something to help me tonight."

"You were helping him with his homework?"

Derek shrugged. "He kinda panics when he doesn't understand something, and he psyches himself out. He just needs someone to calm him down and tell him he can handle it."

"Does he have learning disabilities?"

"Yeah, he's in a special program. But his main disability is his jerk of a father who's always telling him he's stupid."

It was a jarring picture in Abigail's mind—Derek helping a struggling boy with his homework—and it embarrassed her to realize how surprised she was. She still pictured Derek as the kid getting chewed out for lousy grades. "He does yard work here, right?"

"Yeah. And he likes doing odd jobs for me when I can think something up. Needs the cash."

"How old is he?"

"Fifteen."

"He's a big kid."

"Yeah, no kidding. Six-three, maybe? I'm always bugging him to stand up straight. He hunches over like he's trying to make himself smaller—probably hopes if he gets small enough, people won't see him to make fun of him. He's a little different, as I'm sure you noticed. Carries a Beanie Baby turtle hidden up the sleeve of his coat and squeezes it when he's nervous, which is often."

"A Beanie Baby?" Abigail thought of the social toll a habit like that would take on a fifteen-year-old boy.

"He keeps it hidden. If he ever takes it out in front of you, you'll know he trusts you."

A rap came at the door. Derek's face spasmed with a panicky expression that made him appear about the same age as Hunter. "They can't be here already!" he whispered. "They're early! I've changed my mind. I can't do this. You talk to them—I'm climbing out the window."

Abigail tried for a reassuring smile, but panic had gripped her as well, and she had a wild mental image of the two of them pushing and shoving each other aside in an effort to be the first to escape out the window.

"It's going to be fine," she whispered. "Open the door." Not wanting to look like she was hovering, Abigail walked into the kitchen area and started unwrapping the cellophane from the stems of the roses. Derek shot her a desperate look.

"Do it," Abigail whispered.

Derek pulled the door open.

"Hey, Wyatt—whoa, what happened to your hair?"

Abigail's shoulders dropped with a release of tension. She didn't recognize the male voice of the visitor; it certainly wasn't her father.

"Got a haircut," Derek said, an undercurrent of laughter in his voice that Abigail recognized as the giddiness of relief. "What's up?"

"It's your sister I need to see. She's here, isn't she? I saw her walking in with that geeky kid."

"Uh—yeah, she's here. But that 'geeky kid' is a friend of mine. His name is Hunter Conley."

"Sure, sorry, no offense intended. Let me talk to your sister."

Derek stepped back from the door and looked at Abigail. She raised her eyebrows at him. He shrugged.

Abigail laid the roses on the table and went to stand by Derek. The man at the door looked to be in his late twenties or early thirties, with a square face and somewhat thick features.

"There you are." He grinned at Abigail. "Knew you had to be Derek's sister—he'd never snag such a pretty girlfriend, eh, Wyatt?" He jabbed Derek in the ribs. "I'm Chase McCoy. I'm a friend of Derek's. I live right across the lobby there." He aimed his thumb over his shoulder.

"It's nice to meet you," Abigail said, hoping Chase McCoy wasn't planning to ask her out. She got pushed into enough blind dates by her parents, and the last thing she wanted to do was go out on yet another date with a stranger.

"Derek told me you own the bookstore on Main Street," Chase said.

"Yes."

"And you sell stuff besides books, right? And candy, I mean. I know you sell some of Derek's rocks."

"We sell some of his bookends, yes," Abigail said cautiously.

"I've got something that'll interest you. Can I come in for a minute?"

"Now's not a great time," Derek said. "I've got guests coming for dinner."

"No problem. We can hammer out details later." Chase stepped forward so he was halfway over the threshold and held up the three-ring black leather binder he was carrying. "I'm an artist. Oil paintings. I'm offering to let you sell them in your store. I guarantee they'll sell like wildfire."

Sell like wildfire? Abigail pictured herself passing a bucket of flames across the counter of Words and Sweets.

"This'll be a great thing for you and me both," Chase continued. "Big local angle. You know—'Come meet Ohneka artist Chase McCoy.' We could do some big events, bring tons of people into your store. Ka-ching!" He mimed opening and closing a cash register. "Towns love having their own celebrities. And I want to help local business owners, you know?"

Abigail glanced at Derek, wishing she had some idea of what he'd said to Chase about her store. Derek was grinning at his shoes.

"Mr. McCoy, I appreciate your interest in my store, but I don't usually take things on consignment—"

"Oh, yeah, I understand all that, but you'll want these paintings because they'll make you money. We can hammer out a deal that works for both of us. You do some advertising for me—posters, you know—flyers—"

This was getting out of control. "Mr. McCoy—"

"Chase. Don't be so formal, girl! You sound like someone's granny. Now what I've got for you here are photos of some of my paintings. You'll want to see the originals, of course, but the photos will give you an idea of what you want to display first. I've also listed the selling price and the cut I'll give you." He thrust the binder at Abigail.

Not knowing what else to do, Abigail took it. "I'll have a look, but I can tell you right now that it's unlikely—"

"It's powerful stuff. Metaphorical, you know, cutting right through the pain of life like a steel blade. This will put your bookstore on the map. I'll check back with you next week so we can sign on the dotted line."

"Gotta go, Chase," Derek said. "I think the chicken is burning. See you later." He shut the door.

As soon as Chase's heavy footsteps faded, Abigail said, "You didn't tell him I'd sell his paintings, did you?"

Derek lifted his hands, eyes wide, mouth twisting as he fought an obvious battle not to ruin the innocent look with an evil grin. "I didn't, I swear. I just mentioned you owned the bookstore, and he jumped on it."

"If he's half as good as he is pushy, maybe he's the next Andrew Wyeth." She flipped open the binder. In the first picture, overlapping slashes of orange and black ringed a gray circle flecked with red. The painting was entitled *Death in Autumn*. Chase McCoy wanted twenty-five hundred dollars for it.

Derek reached over and turned the page. The next painting had a hailstorm of red X's raining down on a coiling red river. It was entitled *Storm of Pain*.

"I kind of like his style," Derek said. "I think I'll get Mom one of his paintings for Christmas." He pointed to a single black X amidst the red ones. "What do you think this represents? The death of his dreams after you tell him you'd rather get eaten by piranhas than sell his paintings?"

Abigail slammed the binder on his hand.

* * *

FIFTY THOUSAND DOLLARS! WHY HADN'T she done this years ago? Karen hummed to herself as she swished around the rooms she occupied on the second floor of her home, dusting, vacuuming, spritzing mirrors with ammonia water. There was no real point to this housekeeping frenzy—it wasn't as though she ever had visitors—but her energy was bubbling over, and she might as well channel it in a useful way.

And who knows? Maybe Philip *would* stop by at some point. Maybe he'd come here after he gave her the money. She could say it was a cold night and suggest a hot drink and some of that Danish pastry he loved. She'd be sure to bake one next Thursday before she went to meet him.

He *had* looked at her differently after she'd stood up for herself and demanded the money. Like he respected her at last.

Karen lowered her cleaning rag and stared hard into the mirror. The bony, sallow face staring back at her made her stomach bunch into a tiny ball. Who was she kidding?

But then again . . . she ran her hands over her straight black hair. Maybe at the right salon . . . a softer color . . . maybe some layers, or a little bit of curl . . . different makeup . . . She'd seen those before-and-after pictures in *Good Housekeeping*. The right makeup, hairstyle, and clothes could make an amazing difference. She'd gotten so lazy after the divorce—didn't even try to look pretty anymore. Maybe if she tried . . .

But that took money. Expensive salons, manicures, new clothes from some nice store at the mall. If her deadbeat tenant would just pay everything he owed her, she'd have plenty of cash to fix herself up before Thursday.

She smiled at her reflection. She'd gotten money out of *him*. She could certainly wring it out of Derek Wyatt. Adrenaline pumped through her bloodstream, and the flush of pink in her cheeks made her look ten years younger. She could take on anyone tonight.

She slid the phone book off the shelf and flipped through it, looking for a good salon. First, she'd make some appointments. Then she'd go bill collecting.

CHAPTER 4

ABIGAIL TRIED TO EAT AT a natural pace, but nervousness and excitement rendered her mouth dry, and she had to reach for her water glass after every couple of bites.

It was happening. At last it was happening. When Derek had opened the door to her parents, a few seconds of awkward silence had yielded to awkward greetings, and now, halfway through the meal, the atmosphere was warm. Seated at Derek's kitchen table, Lillian and Paul Wyatt looked a little stiff, and conversation dragged in spots, but overall, Abigail couldn't have asked for anything better. How strange—and how beautiful—it was to see her parents and Derek at the same table: Derek looking boyish and shy in his button-down shirt; Lillian elegant as always, salon-blonde hair curling gently around her face, her pastel sweater complemented by a teardrop pearl pendant that had been her mother's; Paul, husky and broad shouldered in a white shirt and a blue blazer.

"That chair is quite remarkable," Lillian said, gesturing at the heavy oak chair inlaid with pieces of polished agate. "How did you make it?"

Derek beamed. "One of my customers is a furniture maker. I described the kind of chair I wanted, he made it for me, and I added the stone." As Derek explained the process of cutting and polishing the agate, Abigail sneaked a glance at her father. Paul was looking intently at Derek, obviously fascinated by what he was saying, and Abigail wondered if he was thinking of offering his own woodworking skills to Derek on a future project.

"What a unique skill," Lillian said. "It must take a long time to create such lovely patterns with bits of stone."

"It takes a while, yeah."

"How did you get started working with rocks?"

"Well, the girl I used to—my old girlfriend—her older brother was a rock hound, and had a bunch of equipment in her parents' basement. He taught me some basics, but he wasn't really into it anymore, and when he moved to Arizona, he sold me his stuff."

"So you've got an Internet business up and running, eh?" Paul Wyatt jiggled the ice in his glass. Abigail reached for the pitcher, but Paul got to it first. He refilled Abigail's glass before refilling his own.

"Thanks, Dad," she said. He smiled at her.

"A small business," Derek said. "I sell jewelry, bookends, things like that. I'd like to do more furniture."

"Must be hard to make a living that way," Paul remarked.

Abigail tensed, but Derek said simply, "That's why I haven't quit my day job. But my goal is to make a living at it eventually. I'd like to open a brick-and-mortar store. With the summer tourist traffic, I think I could do pretty well."

"Where do you work now?" Paul asked.

"At Janssen's Hardware," Derek said, and Abigail realized her father was as nervous as she was, asking questions to which he already knew the answers in an effort to make conversation. Abigail had already told him about Derek's job.

"Have you thought about school?" Paul asked.

Abigail crossed her fingers under the table, hoping Derek wouldn't interpret the question as criticism and get defensive.

"Yeah, I have," he said. "In the spring, I was thinking of taking a couple of business classes at the community college."

Lillian smiled. Her sweater set was pink, and Abigail thought how pretty Derek's bracelet would look with it. She couldn't wait to see her mother's face when Derek gave her the gift.

"More chicken, Dad?" Derek rose to fetch the platter from the stove; the table was too small to hold it.

"Thank you, son."

Son. Abigail held back a smile. Derek slid another golden-brown roll of chicken onto Paul's plate.

"So do you have any fun holiday events coming up at the store, Abigail?" Lillian asked.

"We'll be having a visit with Santa in the first week of December. All children's books will be on sale, and Ellie will be outdoing herself handing out samples of peppermint fudge and almond bark. We've got a

couple of local authors doing an event the week before Thanksgiving—"
Catching Derek's grin, she knew he was thinking of Chase McCoy and
his talk of being a local celebrity. She flicked Derek a dirty look before
continuing. "One author has done a photographic book about the four
seasons of the Finger Lakes. The photos are breathtaking."

"How lovely," Lillian said. "Aunt Patricia might enjoy a book like
that. Let me know the details of the event, and I'll plan to be there."

"That would be wonderful. Thank you."

"Dating anyone?" Paul asked abruptly.

Too accustomed to the question to get embarrassed, Abigail said,
"Not at the moment, unfortunately."

"That handsome young man you introduced to me last time I was
at your store, the one who moved to the area not long ago," Lillian
supplied. "What was his name?"

"Kyle Stratton."

"Didn't you say he's LDS? We thought maybe . . ."

Now Abigail *did* blush, and she was ashamed of the jealousy that bit
her heart. "He's dating Ellie."

"Oh." The expression on Lillian's face made Abigail wonder whether
she or her mother was more disappointed at this fact.

I don't think anyone could be more disappointed than you are, girl.
Annoyed at her thoughts, Abigail picked up the water pitcher and refilled
Derek's and her mother's glasses. Kyle Stratton might be handsome, with
wavy chestnut hair and a classically sculptured face that would have
made him a perfect leading man in a 1940s movie, but he was Ellie's
boyfriend, and Abigail would sooner dive into Lake Ohneka in the
middle of an ice storm than steal her best friend's guy.

He wasn't even Abigail's type—something she'd repeated to herself a
thousand times since Kyle had come to Ohneka.

And who *was* her type? Not Brendan Rowe.

"Is Kyle in your ward, dear?" Lillian asked.

"No. I mean, he would be, and he's come a couple of times, but his
dad is in a care center about an hour and a half away, and Kyle goes there
every Sunday to go to church with his mother and visit his father. His
father has cancer; he probably won't last much longer."

"I'm so sorry to hear that."

"That's why Kyle moved here—his dad's health, I mean. His parents
own a beautiful resort on Lake Ohneka, and his dad was devastated

when he had to retire from the business. Kyle was living in Manhattan but quit his job to come here and take over."

"That's wonderful that he was able to help his family at such a difficult time," Lillian said. "He sounds like a very kind man."

"Yes, he is." And why couldn't he be a self-centered jerk—which would make things a lot easier for Abigail—and why were they talking so much about Kyle anyway, when he was off limits? Hoping they were finished with this evening's relationship quiz, Abigail spread a little more butter on the last fragment of her dinner roll.

"Now that I think of it, Christine Peterson mentioned that her nephew just moved to the area. Joseph Peterson." Lillian's words sounded more rehearsed than casual. "He's a physical therapist, I believe. He's in the Canandaigua Ward—"

"Oops!" Derek said. "The dessert. I was going to warm the apple pie. Excuse me." He stood up. Abigail gave him a grateful look.

A knock came at the door. "Excuse me again," Derek said, moving toward the door. Abigail wondered if Chase had returned to ask if she'd decided to take his paintings yet.

Derek opened the door a few inches, standing so his body blocked the view of the visitor.

"My goodness!" A female voice pierced the air. "Whatever have you done to yourself? No more druggie hippie, eh? I had no idea you knew how to work a shirt with buttons."

"What can I do for you?" Derek's voice was friendly, but a little too tight. Abigail recognized the voice of the visitor—Karen Brodie, Derek's landlady. Abigail had never known her to be in a good mood.

"My goodness," Karen said. "I'm surprised you had the money for haircuts and clothes."

"I'm in the middle of dinner. I'd be happy to come see you as soon as—"

"Oh, do you have company?" The door flew open, slipping out of Derek's hand. Karen Brodie stepped over the threshold. "I wondered who that spiffy Jaguar in the driveway belonged to. Are you Derek's parents?"

Abigail jumped to her feet. "Mrs. Brodie, these are Derek's and my parents, Lillian and Paul Wyatt."

"It's not *Mrs.*," Karen said acidly. "Do you see a husband anywhere near me?"

Abigail's cheeks went hot. "I'm sorry, I didn't mean to—"

Paul rose to his feet, and Karen strode forward to shake his hand. "My goodness, Derek's not exactly a chip off the old block, is he? Though he's dressed up like one tonight."

"Excuse me, but this is not a convenient time," Abigail said. Given Karen's aggressive entrance into the room, she figured anything short of bluntness wasn't going to make an impression.

"Oh, quit worrying. I'm not going to pull up a chair and spoil your party." Karen turned toward Derek. "I just need the rent."

Redness crawled up Derek's face. "Sure. I'll bring it by tonight when I'm done."

"Like heck you will. You're already six days late for November—not to mention that you never paid me in October."

"Look—I haven't deposited my paycheck yet. I'll do it first thing Monday morning—"

"Write the check now. I won't deposit it until Tuesday, so you'll be okay."

"I'll bring it later tonight," Derek snapped. "You're interrupting a dinner party."

"Oh, I'm *sorry*. How can I be so rude? Interrupting a party to insist you meet your *legal* financial obligations? You paid me—let's see—" Karen pulled a scrap of paper from her pocket. "—July's rent on July 21st. Half of August's rent on August 12th, and I didn't get the other half from you until September 24th. Then half of September's rent on October 17th, and you still haven't paid the other half, or anything for October. And now November's rent is six days late. I'm not putting up with this. You claim you don't have what you owe me, then you go on a shopping spree?" She gestured at his clothes. "And pricey candy too, eh?"

Abigail glanced at the box of chocolate-covered macadamia nuts sitting on the counter. "The chocolates are a gift from a friend of mine."

"Oh, well, excuse *me*. I suppose your friend also donated that big hunk of machinery Derek just hauled into my basement."

Frown lines cut deeper into Paul's face. Lillian kept her gaze focused on her dinner plate. Her cheeks were pink.

Panic surged through Abigail. "Ms. Brodie, Derek told you he'll be by later tonight. If you'll excuse us, please—"

"If you'll excuse us, please," Karen mimicked. "My, aren't you the proper one."

Derek drew an angry breath, but Karen cut off his response with a wave of her hand. "Never mind. Stop by tonight, then, but if you don't,

I'm starting eviction proceedings, and that junk of yours will be rusting in the street." She glanced at Paul and Lillian. "Maybe your parents could lend you some cash. Apparently not everyone in the family is broke and irresponsible." She swung around and exited the apartment, leaving the door gaping open.

Derek closed it, his hand moving slowly. He was standing with his back to Abigail, but she didn't need to see his face to discern his emotions. His muscles were as rigid as the rocks he polished.

Abigail met her mother's uncomfortable gaze and mustered a smile. "She'd make a good character in a Dickens novel, wouldn't she?"

Lillian's lips trembled like she wanted to speak, but she said nothing.

Abigail hoped Derek would say something to reduce the impact of Karen's words—maybe explaining that Karen was a bitter, nasty woman who was exaggerating the situation—but Derek offered no explanations as he returned to the table. That meant Karen *hadn't* misstated anything, and Derek wouldn't sink to pretending she had.

Why didn't you tell me you were short on cash? Abigail knew it was a stupid question—Derek hadn't told her because he was too proud to ask her for help.

Abigail struggled to revive the conversation, even resorting to talking about a couple of guys she'd met at a singles dance last month and repeating Ellie's teasing comment about Brendan Rowe stopping by the store more often than he used to, bypassing the facts that Brendan already had a girlfriend, and even if he hadn't, Abigail wasn't interested in rekindling the relationship. But this time, even the diversion of potential romance didn't work. Lillian gave polite answers, but it was like trying to discuss the drapes and wallpaper while the roof was falling in. It was almost a relief when Paul finally looked up from his apple pie and gave voice to the silent weight crushing all of them.

"So you're having some financial troubles, are you?"

"It's nothing." Derek cut himself a second slab of pie. "I'm on top of it."

Abigail wished Derek hadn't tried to dismiss it like that. Being behind on his rent was not what their father would consider being "on top" of anything.

"What was that woman saying about your buying new equipment?" Paul asked.

"Just stuff for my rock business," Derek mumbled, his mouth full of pie and ice cream.

"You recently bought something big?"

Derek swilled half the water from his glass to wash down what must have been a colossal chunk of pie. "If I'm going to cut rocks, I need saws. It takes money to get any business off the ground."

Under the table, Abigail dug her fingernails into her palms. Derek sounded too defensive. "Funny how it takes money to make money," she said lightly. "I found that out in a hurry with Words and Sweets."

Paul glanced at Abigail, and Abigail immediately wished she hadn't said anything. Referring to her bookstore would remind her father of where she got the money to get started—and make him wonder if Derek was after the same. "Spending so much money that you can't pay your rent is no way to get a business off the ground."

Red patches showed on Derek's neck. "When a chance comes, you grab it or you miss it. This is a 24-inch diamond slab saw, new condition, for half the price of a new saw. If I'd passed this one up, I wouldn't have been able to afford another one this good for years."

Lillian ran her thumbnail along the handle of her fork, her gaze lowered.

"With all your Christmas orders coming in, you'll be in the black before you know it," Abigail said. Derek didn't look at her. Neither did her parents.

"You meet your obligations first," Paul said. "Then, if there's money left over, you buy the extras."

Abigail nudged Derek's foot under the table, hoping to send a message: *Don't get angry. Don't get defensive. Admit you messed up. Tell him you'll set it right as fast as you can.*

"This wasn't an extra," Derek said. "It was something I needed."

"What happened to all the money you make at Janssen's? This place can't cost much to rent."

"They don't pay a lot, all right?" Derek snapped, and Abigail felt as though she were watching a marionette show—Derek and her father, yanked about by the strings of old behavior patterns, strings that she'd fervently prayed would break.

"They must pay more than this," Paul said.

Abigail took the pitcher and started refilling glasses, even though they were all at least three-fourths full. "Maybe we should talk about something else. Derek's an adult. He can manage his own business."

Paul glanced at Lillian. No one said anything.

Abigail snatched at the only topic that came to mind. "I met Derek's neighbor tonight. He's an artist."

"Is he?" Lillian responded with mechanical courtesy.

"He'd like me to sell his paintings at the bookstore."

"I imagine a local artist would be of interest to customers." Lillian lifted a miniscule bite of ice cream to her lips.

"Yes, but unfortunately, from what I've seen of his work, it wouldn't suit Words and Sweets. It's very modern and . . . strange. I hate to turn him down, but I really can't sell it."

Lillian nodded. "I imagine that must be awkward turning him down, with his being Derek's friend."

"Is your paycheck going for drugs?"

Paul's question was so abrupt that for a moment Abigail couldn't figure out what he meant—until she realized he wasn't looking at her, but at Derek.

Derek's jaw clenched. "You always have to think the worst of me, don't you?"

"I'm speaking from past experience."

"I messed up in high school. I'm not like that anymore."

"That woman called you a druggie."

"Karen Brodie is an idiot. I'm clean. I don't even drink anymore. I grew up, okay?"

"Adults meet their obligations."

Derek's voice rose. "It's none of your business! I've never walked away from a debt. I'll take care of it."

"With a little help from us? Is that what you were hoping? Haircut and a clean shirt and we'd think we could trust you now?"

Lillian sat like she'd frozen solid.

"Dad, it's not fair to—" Abigail began, but Derek cut across her.

"Yeah, you nailed it. I invited you here to pick your pocket. It's not like there's anything else I could want from you."

Paul's face flushed in the same pattern as Derek's—scarlet along the jawline, forehead and cheekbones, with the middle of his face pale.

"If we all calm down—" Abigail tried again, but Paul shoved his chair back and stood up.

"You tore our lives apart for years," he boomed, his voice so loud Abigail was sure Chase McCoy could hear it across the lobby. "You broke your mother's heart and insulted the memory of your grandmother in a way no one will ever be able to forget. We're not setting ourselves up for another round of grief. Lillian, let's go."

"Mother," Abigail whispered. Lillian sat motionless, her expression stoic to the point of blankness.

Derek pushed back from the table so violently that his chair tipped and crashed onto the floor. "Don't let my scummy presence interrupt your dessert. Finish your pie. Here are some chocolates." He flung the box into the middle of the table, knocking over two water glasses. "Don't worry—I didn't spend any money on them. I bashed Abby's friend over the head and stole them. And robbed the cash register. And shot out the windows of a couple of churches. Good to see you again."

He wheeled around, snatched his keys off the top of the microwave, and stalked out of the apartment.

CHAPTER 5

EYES FOGGED WITH TEARS, ABIGAIL dried the salad bowl and stowed it in Derek's cupboard. She'd worked slowly, hoping Derek would return before she finished, but the dishes were done now, and Derek was still gone. The apartment felt chilly and empty, and the overhead light in the kitchen and the lamps in the living room area didn't give enough illumination to rid the apartment of shadows.

Her parents had departed immediately after Derek, saying little to Abigail. Words had crowded in Abigail's throat—pleas to see that they weren't being fair to Derek, that he *had* changed, that they couldn't backslide over the progress they'd made—but the look on her father's face had kept her silent. Now was not the time to confront him. He was raw with the sense that he'd been manipulated into meeting with Derek, when Derek's only motive for suggesting the reunion was dollars and cents.

And what was Derek's motive? Abigail was ashamed of her own thoughts, but Karen Brodie's voice replayed in her head, detailing Derek's rent history. Abigail had had no idea Derek was financially underwater. And he *had* mentioned the money earlier this afternoon.

But he's not like that. He wouldn't play a role to get cash. He wants to repair the relationship.

Or he *had* wanted to repair it, before their father's accusations started flying. And before their mother's silence told the story—Lillian shared Paul's fears that Derek wanted to use them.

No point remained in lingering at Derek's apartment. He had probably driven past the house several times to check for her car. He wouldn't come in until she was gone.

Abigail swiped tears off her cheeks with the dishtowel. Had she pushed too hard for this? Had she urged her parents and Derek to meet before they were ready? For the first part of the evening, things had gone so well. If it hadn't been for Karen Brodie's untimely visit . . .

Fighting a furious urge to go hammer on Karen's door and scream out her anger and frustration, Abigail folded the damp dishtowel and hung it up. Karen had the right to expect Derek to pay his rent on time, but she'd confronted him in the nastiest way possible, plainly seeking to humiliate him in front of his parents. Why did she hate Derek so much? Or was she that way with everyone? Whenever Abigail had crossed her path, she'd been rude.

Time to go. She'd talk to Derek tomorrow—if he'd take her calls. Would her parents and Derek blame her for urging them to come together? For a moment, Abigail pictured the family in permanently broken fragments—Derek and her leading their own lives, Lillian and Paul alone with neither children nor grandchildren. She forced the picture out of her mind. If she started thinking that way, she'd be bawling the whole way home, and she needed to get control of herself.

Abigail headed into Derek's bathroom, washed her face, and touched up her makeup. It was silly pride to not want her face revealing that she'd been crying, but she wouldn't put it past Chase McCoy or Karen Brodie to pounce the instant she opened the door—Karen on the hunt for Derek and Chase eager to launch another sales pitch. She didn't want either of them seeing that she was upset. Especially not Karen.

She took her coat and purse from the closet and picked up the crystal vase of roses and the water-stained box of chocolates. There was no point in leaving the chocolates. Derek wasn't a big chocolate fan, and if Abigail left Ellie's gift with him, it would end up in the trash—probably with the box crushed and twisted. The chocolates had been aimed at Paul's sweet tooth.

Halfway out the door, she remembered Chase McCoy's binder and went to retrieve it from the magazine rack where she'd stashed it.

With her hands full, Abigail fumbled to pull Derek's door closed behind her. Her purse slipped off her shoulder and the vase tipped, spilling water down her coat. Annoyed, she righted the vase and reached for the doorknob.

"Do you need help?"

The male voice behind her made her jump. The vase tipped again, and she grabbed for it, but in her frustration, her fingers slipped. The vase hit the tile floor of the entryway and shattered.

The man leaped to her side; a brief glance told her it wasn't Chase McCoy. "I'm sorry, that was my fault," he said. "I startled you. I'll replace the vase."

"It's not your fault," Abigail said, glad that at least she hadn't been caught crying by this stranger. "I'm just clumsy. I'll grab a broom and take care of it." She gathered up the spilled roses.

"Can I help you?"

"No. I'm fine. Thanks." A couple of roses fell to the floor as Abigail reached for the doorknob. The man picked them up.

Knowing it would be rude not to meet his gaze, Abigail forced herself to look at him as she took the flowers. Black hair, a handsome face with a rugged, outdoorsy quality—maybe it was the tan that lingered in his skin in a month when most of the population had already gone winter pale. His earth-brown eyes were somehow both attentive and remote, as though his conversation with her was not the real topic of his thoughts.

"You sure you're all right?" he asked. They were almost eye-to-eye; he had maybe two inches on her.

"I'm fine," she said. "Thank you for your help." She retreated into Derek's apartment, stuffed the peach roses—Lillian's favorite—into the trash, and swiped a broom, dustpan, and a roll of paper towels.

The stranger was still in the lobby when she emerged. Hands in his pockets, he stood by the staircase that led up to the second-floor apartment occupied by Karen Brodie.

"I'll replace the vase," he said. "That must have been expensive."

"No—truly, it wasn't valuable. Closeout sale . . . I didn't pay more than thirty bucks for it. Please, forget about it. It's nothing, and it's not your fault I dropped it." Abigail began sweeping wet shards of glass into a pile.

"I'm sorry to bother you," he said. "But can I ask you a couple of questions?"

Under other circumstances, she might have been glad to spend a couple of minutes answering questions asked by a good-looking man, but right then she just wanted to be left alone. She tried—not very hard—to sound pleasant as she said, "What about?"

"The house."

"I don't live here. This is my brother's apartment." Discomfort crawled along her nerves, and the entryway seemed suddenly very isolated. Attractive or not, this man was a total stranger. But Chase

McCoy was probably in his apartment, and Karen was probably upstairs. Abigail wasn't totally alone—she hoped.

The stranger shifted his weight but didn't move any closer to her. "Is your brother around?"

"Is there a point to these questions?" Abigail made her voice cool. If he didn't take the hint and go away, she'd retreat into Derek's apartment and lock the door. *Lock the door with that flimsy lock that a junior high school student could spring with a credit card.*

"I'm sorry," he said. "I'm not doing this very well. My name is Ethan Hanberg. Karen—the owner—called me saying the house needed some repairs, and I came out to have a look."

"Then you should talk to Karen."

"Karen's not here."

"Perhaps you should come back when she is."

He gave a small, gruff laugh. "That wouldn't go very well. Has your brother complained about any problems with the house or his apartment? Leaks, problems with the heating system, anything else?"

"He hasn't mentioned anything."

"Okay. Thanks. Sorry to bother you." He drew his gloves out of his pocket. "This is . . . going to sound strange, but if it's all the same to you, I'd appreciate it if you didn't tell Karen you talked to me. We aren't on the best of terms."

Abigail swept the chunks of crystal into the dustpan. "I thought she hired you to do repairs."

"It's a long story."

"I don't have any reason to say anything to Karen Brodie. We aren't on the best of terms either." She spotted a shard of crystal near the wall. Impatiently, she reached for the fragment. It sliced the tip of her finger. With a gasp, Abigail pulled her hand back.

Hanberg hurried to her side. "Are you hurt?"

"No," Abigail said, as blood welled in the cut. "I mean it's nothing, just a nick." With her other hand, she fumbled in her pocket, hoping for a Kleenex, and came up empty. A drop of blood broke loose and hit the floor. This was so *stupid*. Couldn't she do anything right tonight?

"Let me finish here. You'd better go take care of that." Hanberg took the broom and dustpan before she could protest.

Abigail mumbled a thank you, hurried into Derek's apartment, and locked the door behind her.

A few minutes of pressure from a folded paper towel, some antibacterial ointment, and a Band-Aid took care of the minor cut. When Abigail opened the door to the lobby, Hanberg was gone. The broom and dustpan were leaning against the wall near Derek's door, next to the roll of paper towels.

Abigail picked up the paper towels. Sticking out of the cardboard tube in the center of the roll were two folded twenty-dollar bills.

Abigail stood holding the money, not sure what to do. Obviously, Hanberg was unwilling to accept that the broken vase was not his fault. She didn't want his money, but what was she supposed to do now? Track him down and force the cash into his hand?

Reluctantly, she slid the bills into her pocket. She returned the cleaning supplies to Derek's apartment, retrieved her belongings, and locked the door behind her.

At least her mother hadn't been there to witness the demise of the vase. Smashed glass would have been exactly the reminder Lillian didn't need tonight.

Not that things could have gone much worse.

Icy rain fell steadily from the night sky. Abigail pulled her hood up and hurried to her car, wondering bleakly where Derek was now.

* * *

"I AM *SO* SORRY." ELLIE leaned forward, arms resting on the countertop, her bell-shaped jacquard sleeves spreading gracefully around her wrists. The blouse was the same blue as her eyes, and Abigail thought absently of how good Ellie looked in a vivid shade that would make Abigail look washed out. "Oh, Abby, I can't believe it. What awful timing! Did you want to jump up and strangle that woman?"

"Pretty much. She had a legitimate gripe, but—"

"That kind of harassment isn't how you collect a debt. She was *way* out of line. You should file a complaint."

Abigail sighed. "That wouldn't fix anything."

"I'd have socked her in the jaw."

"You can't even reach her jaw, shorty."

Ellie laughed. "You'd be surprised at how high I can jump. What has Derek said about everything?"

"Nothing. Not to me. He didn't come back to his apartment Saturday night while I was there. I tried to call him several times yesterday, but he won't answer."

"He's gotta be feeling horrible. Your parents don't really think he was after their money, do they?"

"I . . ." Abigail rubbed her fingertip along the spine of a book sitting near the cash register. "I'm not sure. And I don't think *they're* sure. I think they're scared."

"So they reject him before he has a chance to hurt them again."

Abigail thought of her parents' reactions Saturday night—her mother's silent withdrawal and her father's refusal to cut Derek any slack or assume anything but total irresponsibility on his part. "Yes. I think Dad wants incontrovertible proof that Derek has changed before he'll be willing to let him back into their lives. It's mainly for Mother's sake, I think. He worries so much about her that he's very protective of her. Any shadow of trouble, and he'll be up swinging his sword."

"Why is he so jumpy?"

"I think it's . . . well, she's had some struggles. More than just with Derek, I mean." Abigail checked her watch. Seven minutes until she needed to unlock the door of Words and Sweets and begin the process of interacting with customers, making herself smiley, chatty, and helpful, when what she wanted was to lie down on the floor and stay there. Discouragement made her feel like her limbs were encased in stone.

"What kind of struggles?" Ellie asked. "Whoops, that's a nosy question. Tell me to be quiet whenever you feel like it."

"No, it's fine." It was a relief to vent a little of the pressure and pain. "She . . . well, she always wanted a big family, and they tried, over and over, but she kept miscarrying."

"I'm so sorry. That must have been terrible for her."

"Yes . . . When I was a teenager and Derek was finishing up elementary school, it got really bad. She felt like she was running out of time, and became almost . . . obsessive."

"Obsessive?"

"Baby magazines and books everywhere . . . She was always crocheting blankets or booties; she was so hopeful that each pregnancy—and there were five while I was in high school—would be successful. She'd be in bed for weeks—she got really sick in the early part of her pregnancies—then she'd miscarry, and she'd be depressed for months . . . It was awful. Dad was so worried about her. I know he didn't want to keep trying for another baby when it took that kind of toll on her, but she wanted it *so* badly. Since she'd been able to have me and Derek, she knew she could carry a pregnancy to term, so she was always convinced that the next pregnancy would be viable. I think Dad told himself that if she could stay totally still and quiet for the first few months, maybe that would make the difference, so we got a constant refrain of 'leave your mother alone, don't bother her' . . . After that last miscarriage, the doctor and Dad finally said no more, and then the depression . . . Anyway, it was bad."

"Which left *you* taking care of Derek," Ellie said.

"Yes, I did a lot of that. Dad finally got her to a therapist and on some medication, and she was much better after that, but since then, Dad's always regarded her as fragile, whether she is or not—and I don't think she is."

"When did Derek start having trouble?"

"End of junior high. I was off at college by then—I'd better unlock the door." Abigail picked up her keys and headed for the door to begin the business day. Two girls who were apparently late to school giggled their way into the store. After ordering hot chocolate heaped with cinnamon whipped cream and sampling Ellie's pecan fudge, they bought a copy of *Walden* and giggled their way out the door. Abigail watched them go, wishing she could laugh like that. Maybe you had to be sixteen for it to work.

You didn't giggle like that even when you were sixteen. You were born dull. No wonder you're still unmarried at thirty.

No wonder Kyle prefers Ellie to you.

"You know," Ellie said when they were alone again, "I think maybe your parents and Derek aren't the only ones stuck in the past. You're still feeling like the caretaker, aren't you? Like it's your job to mother Derek and keep the family functioning."

"I think you've spent too much time browsing the Psychology/Self-Help section," Abigail said dryly.

Ellie chuckled. "I'm saying maybe Brendan was right—maybe you need to back away and let your parents and Derek work things out."

The door opened. For the rest of the morning, a steady trickle of customers kept the conversation between Abigail and Ellie on hold, for which Abigail was grateful. She didn't want to talk about her family anymore.

Maybe Ellie was right. But it had been five years since the break. Even with her prodding and pleading and reasoning it had taken *five years*. Without her urging, how long would it have taken before they even agreed to talk?

And you made great progress Saturday night, Abigail thought sourly. *Lucky for them that they have you around.*

Where was Derek? Abigail slipped her cell phone out of her pocket and checked in the hope that she might have missed a call.

Nothing. No calls from Derek. None from her parents. Not that she would have missed the calls—she'd left her ringer on, something she never did while interacting with customers.

What would Derek do about his rent? Obviously, he'd been lying when he'd told Karen he just needed to deposit his paycheck. How deep of a financial hole had he dug for himself?

Abigail *had* to talk to him.

She slipped the useless cell phone back into her pocket and forced herself to walk over and offer help to a customer peering uncertainly at the Classic Literature shelf.

By the time her part-time employee, Melissa, showed up at four to begin her shift, Abigail's frustration had solidified into a plan. If Derek wouldn't take her calls, she'd go to his apartment and see if she could catch him home. If he was there, he'd open the door to her. He wouldn't leave her standing in the hallway.

At seven, Abigail left the store and drove to Derek's. The evening air held a chill that skewered her bones as she approached the Victorian house with its peeling gingerbread trim. She hurried into the warmth of the entryway. Whispering a prayer under her breath, she rapped on Derek's door.

No answer. Abigail hesitated, wishing she'd thought to peek inside the garage to see if Derek's Jeep was there. That way she'd know whether to hold her ground and knock until he opened the door or to give up and come back later. He was probably in his rock room—

At the sound of footsteps behind her, Abigail whirled, hoping to see Derek.

Karen Brodie grinned at her. "He's not here, sweetums, and he's not in the basement either. He's avoiding me. Didn't come by on Saturday night like he said he would, not that I expected him to. I can spot a liar. I was trained by one of the best liars in the business."

The pain of decimated hopes brought sharp words from Abigail's lips. "You were unconscionably rude Saturday night."

Karen laughed. "Unconscionably. Bet they taught you that big word in librarian school."

"I own a bookstore. Not a library."

"A bookstore? Really? From all that cleavage and that tiny leather miniskirt, I figured you owned a bar."

Involuntarily, Abigail glanced down at her turtleneck sweater and ankle-length skirt.

"So your brother lies and cheats me, but I'm the bad guy for embarrassing him," Karen said. "Is that how you see it?"

"I know Derek owes you money. I'm not excusing that."

"And he's never going to cough it up. I know the drill. First the rent is late. Then it's late and incomplete. Pretty soon, it's no rent at all, and I get the hassle of kicking another loser into the street."

"Derek is not a loser."

"So what's his story, anyway? Here are you and your parents looking like churchy little cookie cutter people, and then there's Derek, the stringy-haired, dope-smoking—"

"Have you ever actually witnessed him using drugs?" Abigail interrupted, struggling against her anger. "Or do you just assume he does?"

Karen shrugged. "I don't pay enough attention to him to know what he does."

That was a lie, Abigail thought. Especially when he'd first moved in, Derek had complained that Karen seemed to enjoy watching him. She'd linger in the doorway of the rock room while he worked, or show up at his apartment wanting to conduct alleged "maintenance surveys" and then take a ridiculous amount of time examining every square inch of his apartment.

Behind that prickly facade, Karen must be a very lonely woman. Abigail studied her, trying to get a better feel for her opponent. She'd thought of Karen as being a lot older than she was, but looking into her face, she realized Karen was probably only a few years her senior. Tall and thin, as tall as Abigail—if there had been any grace in her movements, she would have been what Lillian called "willowy," but the hardness of her face and posture made her look stringy. Her hair was dyed a flat black and hung straight on either side of her face, a style that made her cheekbones appear too prominent and her neck too long. Her eyes were deep blue with rings of gold around the irises, and Abigail realized that if Karen would smile—a genuine smile, not that tight, mocking grin—it would completely transform her harsh appearance. Was there a way

Abigail could reach out to her, make some kind of connection, get her to give Derek a little more time?

"I know it must make things difficult for you when your tenants fall behind on their rent," Abigail began. "You have expenses—"

Karen snorted. "Yeah, yeah. Soften her up with sympathy. Let me guess—you got an A in Psych 101. So what's up? Your brother must want something from your parents pretty badly to whack off his hair and get all spit-polished. Cash, right? Good. Maybe he'll get it and he can pay me."

Abigail wanted to snap at Karen, but she restrained the curt words. "I know Derek hasn't been the most reliable tenant. You have good reason to be frustrated with him. But at heart he—"

"Heart of gold. Sure. Cut it out and melt it down and maybe it'll pay his back rent."

This was a waste of time. "Good night, Ms. Brodie."

"I've done well for Derek," Karen said. "Where else would he find a rental that includes a big basement area for his rock junk? If I kick him out, he doesn't have a prayer of finding a situation this good, not for the reasonable rent I charge. Plus you can bet that when a new landlord calls me for a recommendation, I'll give her an earful. He'll be living out of the back of his Jeep. I hope those rocks make a comfy bed."

"I'm sure he'll get the money to you as quickly as he can," Abigail said coldly.

"Which won't be quick enough to stop me from advertising for a new tenant." She looked Abigail up and down. Uncomfortable, Abigail started to turn away, but Karen prodded her arm.

"You know, princess, it doesn't matter to me where the money comes from. If someone pays, that's all I care about. Derek's got rocks in the head, but you look like a sharp girl. Have a bit socked away, don't you? Yeah, you do. You're that type. Follow the prophet, stay out of debt, and cram a year's worth of wheat in your closet."

The references caught Abigail by surprise. Karen obviously noted the confusion in her face. She laughed.

"Yeah, I'm LDS, or used to be. Got tired of all the goody-goody hypocrites. Look, I'm willing to let bygones be bygones. Let Derek start over. Clean slate and all that. Truth is I don't want to throw him out. Except for the rent issue, he's a good tenant. Takes care of his place. No loud partying. Given a choice, I'd rather not evict him."

Abigail gripped her purse. Derek would hate it if she interfered.

Karen grinned. "Not fair, is it? Trust me, I know how it feels to shield a creep who doesn't deserve it. But it still kills you to see your cute brother in trouble, doesn't it? Cough up, and we can all be happy."

Derek *didn't* have the money and probably had no way to get it anytime soon. Karen would delight in making his life miserable. And Karen was right—it *would* be a miracle if Derek could find another setup that suited his rock business as well as this one did.

"How . . . much does he owe?" Abigail asked.

CHAPTER 6

BY MIDNIGHT, DEREK FIGURED HE was safe. Staying up late was stupid—he had to be at Janssen's at six in the morning—but the corner of the bar where he'd spent the evening was a refuge from two stubborn women who wanted something he didn't have.

Karen Brodie wanted money.

Abigail wanted character.

Stiffly, Derek stood and zipped his coat. A dozen times that night, he'd nearly ordered a beer, telling himself it didn't matter—drink or don't drink; his parents would hate him either way. But each time he'd opened his mouth to speak, that sore place inside him had torn open a little wider, and he'd turned back to the stupid glass of ginger ale that had long since grown warm on the table in front of him. Catrina's mockery still bounced around in his head. Maybe she was right—maybe he *was* a freak or a fanatic to care so much, but no child would suffer because of him. And stopping had been so rough that no way did he want to start again, not even with one drink.

Absently, he started to push his fingers through his hair but jerked his hand away in disgust at the feel of the short strands. Why had he cut his hair? It had only made him look desperate. A pathetic, nerdy idiot.

The house with its perversely cheerful gingerbread trim was dark and silent as Derek pulled into the driveway. He parked his Jeep in the portion of the detached garage reserved for him, grimacing at the loud grinding of the garage door opener. He wouldn't put it past Karen to spring from her bed and gallop downstairs to confront him.

She'd enjoyed humiliating him at dinner. With a few ugly words, she'd destroyed everything and convinced his parents he was the same sack of scum they'd always despised.

What now? Everything he had in the bank wouldn't cover what he owed her, and sooner or later, she'd catch him home—or he'd return to find his stuff cleared out. He wasn't sure what legal hoops she'd have to jump through to evict him—couldn't even remember what his contract said. But if she threw him out, where would he go?

Move in with Mom and Dad. They'll kill the fatted calf for you and serve it up laced with rat poison.

Derek opened the outer door. On the table near the mailboxes, one low-wattage lamp with a fringed pink shade provided enough light for him to make it silently to his door.

Tucked between the doorknob and the frame was a folded piece of paper. Derek scowled as he picked it up. He was tempted to tear it up without reading it—it was either an official notice from Karen that he was in violation of his contract, or it was a note from Abigail, who'd already left multiple messages on his phone.

Once he was inside his apartment, Derek's curiosity took hold, and he unfolded the note to see a message written in blocky handwriting.

Kid—

Sorry I missed you. Should have called first, but my cell's AWOL. The wife's birthday is coming up, and I want you to make something spectacular. Hush-hush—I don't think I've surprised Nosy Nelly once, but this time I'm going to pull it off. Can you meet me Thursday night, 9:00, in the Henning picnic area at Kemper Park? I've doodled some ideas that will blow your circuits. Don't call me—you'll tip off the wife. If you don't show, I'll stalk you and we'll reschedule.

Bob Chapman

Derek blinked at the odd note and reread it twice. Then relief swept through him in a wave that warmed his cold fingers and toes. From anyone else, he would have thought this was an odd practical joke, but Robert Chapman was the definition of eccentric. Derek wouldn't be surprised if he showed up to the meeting in pajamas—or a tuxedo. *Must be nice to have enough money to do whatever you want, without caring what anyone else thinks.*

Money. Derek grinned at the paper. Something spectacular. Six months ago, Chapman had commissioned Derek to make an elaborate malachite and jade necklace for his ancient mother-in-law, and he'd been so pleased with Derek's work that he'd paid Derek twice what they'd agreed upon. *Eccentric and rich.* If Chapman wanted something spectacular, that meant big money, and Chapman would pay half in advance. Derek was willing to bet that Chapman's half-payment would cover everything Derek owed Karen.

Nine o'clock Saturday night at Kemper Park. Fine. Weird place to meet, but whatever it took to keep Chapman happy was fine with Derek, and Chapman specialized in offbeat meetings. The first time he'd met Derek had been at a bowling alley. The second time had been at a sushi joint where Chapman had demanded his sushi be cooked and served with ketchup. Too bad Abigail hadn't ended up marrying Brendan Rowe. Watching her deal with wacky Chapman as a stepfather-in-law would have been great entertainment.

Relieved that a solution had appeared for at least one of his problems, Derek unlaced his boots, chucked his coat on the floor, and went to bed.

* * *

FOR MUCH OF THURSDAY AFTERNOON, Karen lingered in front of the mirror, checking her appearance from a variety of angles. She giggled—a strange sound to her ears, like an echo from long ago. She liked the way her chocolate-brown hair curved a few inches below her jawline, framing her face with graceful tendrils. Professionally applied rose-pink blush brought warmth to her skin. And with the concealer and foundation the salon woman had applied so deftly—her face looked so smooth! She could pass for twenty-five, or even younger. Philip would hardly recognize her.

With pleasure, Karen pictured the scene. He'd look at her. His eyebrows would shoot upward. He'd stare. *"Karen . . . you look amazing. I'd forgotten how pretty you are."*

Karen pivoted, admiring the stylish blue-and-cream wool jacket and the silk shirt underneath. The cut of the pants flattered her, making her appear sleek and toned, like a model.

She looked good. And he would notice.

Karen touched up her lipstick with the tube she'd purchased at the salon for an exorbitant price. She'd blown through nearly all the money she'd gotten off Abigail Wyatt, but the investment was worth it.

Last week, Philip had met the new Karen Brodie, the woman not afraid to stand up to him and get what he owed her. This week, he'd begin to see that the new Karen wasn't just assertive—she was intriguing. Alluring.

"Listen, Karen, I know you were planning to go to Florida or California, but are you sure you want to leave? Maybe we ought to spend a little time together. We don't even know each other anymore. Maybe it's time to start over."

Karen smiled as she imagined his voice. She'd have to be careful not to agree too quickly. If she did, he'd revert to thinking of her as a pushover. She'd say it was too late; she was leaving. Then bit by bit, she'd let him persuade her.

Maybe he'd even kiss her.

The phone rang. Karen hurried to answer it. Maybe it was him, calling to confirm their plans for tonight.

She didn't recognize the number on the caller ID—it wasn't his home or work number, but it might be his cell phone number. She didn't know that number. "Hello?"

"Hey, Karen. It's me."

It *was* him! Carefully nonchalant, Karen said, "Oh, hi."

"About tonight—don't worry, I haven't forgotten. I'll be there. I'm all set. But could we change the location? The bakery parking lot is so public. Tacky. I'd rather have a place where we can talk in peace."

Karen was glad he wasn't there to see the huge smile on her face. "Should I come to your house?"

"No, I won't be home. I'm coming straight from work. Can you meet me at Kemper Park?"

"Kemper Park! It's November!"

He chuckled like she'd said something witty. "I'm not suggesting we have a picnic. It's just a private place to meet. A private place to . . . talk."

The park. Moonlight glittering gold on Lake Ohneka. Towering trees all around. The two of them—

The two of them freezing to death. Karen changed her fantasy to a picture of them alone in his warm car, huddling close, no one else around . . .

"Sure, I can meet you there," she said.

"Let's make it eight thirty, okay? Henning picnic area. If you don't see my car in the lot, check near the tables. My engine is acting up, and I may have a friend drop me. Maybe I can hitch a ride home with you."

Karen spoke flatly to hide the thrill surging through her. "Sure, whatever. Just make sure you bring the money." *Give him a ride home . . . and maybe he'd invite her inside . . .*

"Don't worry. I have the cash. See you at 8:30. Don't be late."

"See you." Suppressing a girlish giggle, Karen hung up.

* * *

CAREFUL NOT TO DISTURB PAUL, Lillian Wyatt slipped out of bed and lifted her velour bathrobe from where she'd draped it over the back of her recliner. At three o'clock in the morning, she'd had her fill of lying in bed, unable to sleep.

Without turning on any lights, she tiptoed to her sewing room. She eased the door shut and switched on the brass gooseneck lamp next to her sewing machine.

Standing on her stepstool, she reached to the back of the top closet shelf, fumbling behind the roll of quilt batting until her hands closed on a cardboard shoebox. Paul would never have reason to rummage through her sewing closet, so she didn't worry about his finding the box by accident.

The thought of what he'd say if he saw the box brought heat to Lillian's cheeks. He'd only be concerned about her, of course, worried that keeping it wasn't healthy, but she'd rather avoid that humiliating conversation.

Her chair creaked slightly as she sat down, the box on her lap. The noise was too soft for Paul to overhear, but still, she tensed. After a long moment of quiet, she lifted the lid and removed the folded piece of white felt that lay on top. She spread the felt over the desk next to her sewing machine.

One by one, she removed shards of china and laid them on the felt. The lamplight glimmered on the lacey gold pattern that rimmed the edge pieces. Delicately, she lifted two pieces and held them together, their broken edges aligning. Like a puzzle. If she could reassemble the broken platter, would everything in her life be whole again?

She laid the two pieces down and picked up two others, careful not to cut her fingers. She'd never tried gluing any of the shards together. It was pointless; Derek's foot had shattered the platter—along with the door of the china hutch and a stack of plates—into hundreds of fragments. Any attempt at repair would create not her mother's lovely bone china, but a scarred patchwork.

Her heart had catapulted into her throat at the sight of Derek opening his apartment door. Handsome, his hair neatly trimmed, his clothes crisp and pressed, an uncertain little smile of welcome on his lips. *My son.* How she'd dreamed of that meeting. Derek back in her life. Derek with his troubled past behind him.

And then everything had shattered.

Lillian let the tears trickle down her face; it was easy to cry when no one could see her. She should have realized it was too perfect. A humble Derek seeking a reunion. A clean-cut Derek, rid of that shaggy hair Lillian had always hated, serving them a dinner he'd cooked himself.

Derek as the son she'd always hoped to have.

If it hadn't been for the intrusion of that sneering scarecrow woman, Lillian would have been willing to accept Derek at face value. On the drive to Derek's house, she'd even imagined them all together around the dining room table on Thanksgiving. Derek would be telling jokes like he had when he was six years old and had a new joke for every occasion. The candlelight would reflect in Abigail's eyes as she smiled at her brother. Paul would beam with pride.

While those pictures had formed in her mind, Lillian had even praised herself for keeping the dream rooted in current reality—for not imagining a man sitting next to Abigail with his arm around her and a ring on Abigail's finger, for not populating the table with grandchildren yet unborn. Just Paul, Lillian, Abigail, and Derek, a family once again.

Hadn't she learned anything? Dreaming only led to broken dreams.

Paul had apologized all the way home. *"I'm sorry, honey. This is my fault. I should have known it was fishy. I should have known he was after money. I can't tell you how sorry I am you had to go through this."*

And she'd kept insisting it was all right, that she was fine, as if she'd *ever* been fine from the day that anger and pain had gouged a seemingly unbridgeable chasm between her and her only son.

She'd thought Derek was building a bridge at last. Instead, he'd been looking to drag Paul and her down into the chasm with him. He didn't want a relationship. He wanted the money to get himself out of trouble.

Didn't he?

Lillian pieced two of the largest fragments together, watching the light play on the gleaming white surface of the china. What a failure she was, a shadow of a mother.

The nightmares came almost every night now—a knocking at her bedroom door, a thin, little-boy voice calling, "Mom?" And she'd try to respond, but she couldn't—she couldn't move, she couldn't call out to him, she couldn't do anything but lie paralyzed as the boy's voice turned to sobs. And then silence.

She'd *tried*. In every way she knew how, she'd tried to reach out to him, but her efforts came too late. Derek had pushed her away, bent on destroying himself and trampling everything she valued. How many nights—how many years—had she spent pacing the floor and crying, watching the clock, frantic with fear that a knock would come at the door and police officers would report that Derek had been killed with his drunken friends in a car crash, or had died from an alcohol or drug overdose?

Finally, the pain had been too intense. After the disaster at the funeral, reeling with grief over the loss of her mother, she'd taken refuge in Paul's decision to ban Derek from the house. Derek was an adult. They no longer had any control over him—if they ever had. They'd tried to help him and they'd failed.

Failed, failed, failed. That's all Lillian had ever done where children were concerned. Fail. She'd failed Derek. She'd failed Abigail too, cheating her out of her high school years, burdening her with adult responsibilities that Lillian should have carried. No wonder Abigail was still so protective of Derek. She'd been more of a mother to him than Lillian had.

Lillian rearranged the china fragments, large pieces on the left side of the square of felt, small pieces on the right. She knew what Paul would say if she told him she wanted to talk to Derek. *"You know you'll regret it. Behind the short hair and the smile, he's the same Derek who ripped our lives apart. Don't let him get his claws into you again."*

But what if they'd been too hasty in judging him?

She thought of the comment Karen Brodie had made, implying that Derek used drugs. As his landlady, she probably knew a lot about him. Like whether he'd taken up with some trashy new girlfriend—or girlfriends—after he'd broken up with that actress he'd been living with in Ithaca. Abigail had claimed he wasn't involved with anyone, that Derek realized shacking up with that girl had been a bad choice, that he wanted to get his life on track. But Abigail was so devoted to Derek that she might be a bit blind. Karen Brodie, on the other hand, seemed the kind of woman who would delight in hunting up and sharing every bit of dirt on Derek that she could find.

Maybe Lillian should talk to Karen Brodie. Better to know the straight truth and face it than to let uncertainty gnaw at her. If Karen confirmed Abigail's version of the story—that Derek *was* cleaning up his life, even if he was making poor financial choices—maybe there was hope. And if Lillian hinted to Karen that she was willing to pay for her help, she suspected that not only would Karen reveal everything she knew about Derek, but she would let Lillian into Derek's apartment for a look around. After living through Derek's teen years, Lillian knew exactly where to look and what to look for. If Derek was drinking or using drugs, the evidence would be there.

Relieved at having a definite plan in mind, Lillian returned the china fragments to the box, one by one. Tomorrow, she would call Karen.

CHAPTER 7

KAREN KEPT THE ENGINE RUNNING as she waited in the parking lot at Kemper Park. She wanted the car toasty warm when Philip joined her, a cozy haven from the wind. She'd splurged on the priciest car wash in town, and both the interior and exterior of the car were spotless. She couldn't do anything about the tear in the passenger-seat upholstery, but she'd draped a fleece throw over the seat to hide it. A collection of love ballads—ones that would remind him of their college days—played softly on the stereo.

She couldn't remember the last time she'd been this excited.

Maybe she wouldn't take the money at all. Maybe she'd just let him hand her the envelope and she'd finger it gracefully for a few moments before offering it to him. *"I can't take it. I could never turn you in. I was just feeling so desperate that I got a little crazy. We're in this together. I could never blackmail you."*

He'd be so grateful. What man wouldn't be grateful to have fifty grand handed back to him? He'd realize how generous she was. How much she cared. He'd lean over and touch her cheek and whisper . . .

Karen frowned. Maybe it *wouldn't* work that way. Maybe if she handed the money back, he'd chalk it up to cowardice and revert to viewing her with contempt. She had to think carefully about the best way to handle this.

Where *was* he? It was 8:37. He was usually very punctual.

Could he be here already? He'd said if she didn't see his car to check the picnic area. She'd assumed if he was here, he would have heard her car and come out to meet her, but maybe he'd been talking on the phone and had missed the sound of her engine.

Karen scowled at the picnic enclosure. It was open on three sides, but the one solid wall faced the parking lot. She'd better go check to see if he was there, though the idea of meeting him in that chill, dark enclosure was hardly the romantic start to the evening that she'd wanted. If he tried to shove the money at her and walk away, she'd demand they go sit in her car to work out the "details." Whatever those were.

Reluctantly, Karen switched off the engine and stepped out into the coldness of the night. At least this would give her a chance to better show off her new ivory dress coat and silk scarf.

Her expensive leather pumps clacked loudly on the sidewalk as she came around the side of the enclosure. Though the parking lot was illuminated, the picnic area was not, and Karen couldn't imagine she'd be able to see a thing in there. What kind of a nitwit suggested meeting at a place like this in November? She'd been too wussy on the phone. She should have told him this was absurd and insisted he come to her house.

Wind rattled the trees and Karen shivered, pulling her coat more tightly around her. The coat was more elegant than it was warm. She was an idiot to think he might be waiting in the picnic area, freezing his keister off, but he *had* said to check if she didn't see his car. And it was ten minutes past the rendezvous time, and it was unlike him to be late.

Maybe he'd been stringing her along. Maybe he wasn't coming at all.

No, he wouldn't dare not show. If he made a fool of her tonight, he knew he'd pay a lot more than fifty grand.

In the darkness, a tiny light flickering on a picnic table drew her gaze. A votive candle? For an instant, Karen imagined a candlelit dinner in the deserted pavilion—maybe he'd brought a gas-powered heater, and a takeout meal—or wasn't that a fireplace she could barely see on the back wall, near the tiny light? He'd build a fire and they'd huddle close to it, the two of them . . .

But he wasn't there. Karen squinted in all directions, but saw only darkness—darkness broken only by that tiny light. A manila envelope sat next to the candle.

Curse him. Karen strode forward to where the light flickered. It was a plastic tea light, not even a real candle. She picked up the envelope, feeling the weight of it. The money. He was handing the money over without even having the courtesy to face her. He'd probably left town. The coward.

What a fool she'd been to think he cared about her—had *ever* cared about her. He'd used her from the beginning.

How could he have been idiot enough to leave fifty thousand dollars lying unattended in a park? Even though it was highly unlikely anyone would wander past, if anyone had, the tea light would have piqued their curiosity.

Karen lifted the flap of the envelope and reached inside. Her gloved fingers withdrew a stack of bills, bound together with a rubber band.

Bills? Karen swiped up the tea light and held it over the bundle in her hand. It was a stack of newspaper pieces, cut to the size of bills.

That *snake.*

A scraping noise behind her made her jump. The tea light fell out of her hand. She started to turn, his name on her lips, but a jolting burst of light inside her skull made her stagger and fall.

* * *

A CAR WAS PARKED IN the lot near the picnic pavilion, but Derek knew instantly it wasn't Bob Chapman's vehicle. This car was an old Ford Escort, the same kind of car Karen Brodie drove. Chapman drove an assortment of vehicles—everything from a Hummer to a Mini Cooper—and they were always new and eye-catching. This car must belong to some park service guy or security guard.

Derek glanced at the clock on the dashboard of his Jeep. 8:51. Chapman would be here any minute—he was always early.

As the minutes passed, Derek squirmed restlessly in his seat and stared at the back wall of the picnic pavilion and the stone chimney rising in the center of it. The parking lot lights cast dim illumination on the back of the pavilion and threw shadows over a few feet of dead grass, but the rest of the park was dark. Trees loomed overhead, shaking in the wind. What a weird place to meet. He wished Chapman had chosen a good, warm restaurant instead.

When he couldn't stand the tension of sitting and staring, Derek started fiddling with his iPod, searching for some music to distract him. Settling on Brahms's Symphony No. 4, he settled back in his seat and breathed deeply, trying to banish tension.

He might as well have tried to banish winter and order the trees to leaf and the flowers to bloom.

This meeting with Chapman *had* to go well. Derek had no idea what he'd do if this commission fell through.

He'd run into Karen Brodie tonight when he was arriving home from work. She'd been in the entryway getting her mail, clutching a couple of department store shopping bags. He'd braced himself for her to start ranting about the rent, but instead she'd grinned at him. She'd looked completely different—her hair had been cut and dyed brown, and she'd done something with her makeup that made her look a lot younger and prettier. She was even wearing a long dress coat instead of that Michelin Man number she usually wore. Derek hoped this makeover meant she had a boyfriend now. Anything that might distract Karen from haranguing Derek was welcome.

He twisted the dial to turn the heater to high. He'd been unable to find his heavy coat tonight—couldn't imagine where he would have left it. Maybe it was in the rock room. He hadn't wanted to take time to look for it and risk being late to Kemper Park. Chapman hated it when people kept him waiting.

In an effort to moisten his dry mouth, Derek started chewing a stick of gum, then remembered Chapman thought chewing gum made people look like cows chewing their cud. He spit the piece back into the foil wrapper. *Settle down. You don't have to put on a show for Chapman. Just let him crack his jokes and go on his crazy tangents and then you agree to do whatever he asks. And tell him you can't get started without money up front.*

The instant he had the money in hand, he'd call Abigail, apologize for ignoring her, and tell her it was all right—he was in the black again. For a fragment of an instant, he thought of calling his father and telling him about Chapman's commission—that, once again, Derek was the craftsman of choice for a man who could afford anything he wanted—but there was no need for that. Abigail would relay the news to their parents. *So what are you hoping for? That they'll decide you're worth something after all? Not going to happen.*

When it was 9:10, a burst of panic made Derek yank the keys from the ignition and swing the door open. Chapman had said to meet him in the picnic area. What if the eccentric multimillionaire had meant *in* the pavilion—not in the parking lot—and was even now sitting at a picnic table in the cold, waiting for Derek? It would be just like Chapman to do something kooky like ride his bike through the park on a November night instead of driving one of his cars.

Derek sprinted toward the pavilion. Was he too late? Chapman might have already assumed he wasn't coming and pedaled away. And Derek needed that money *now.*

The interior of the pavilion was dark except for a tiny light flickering on the floor near the back wall. Derek scanned the area but saw no sign of Chapman. What was that light? Was Chapman crouching in a corner, planning to leap out and startle Derek when Derek came to investigate? Derek wouldn't put it past him to pull a practical joke like that.

"Hello?" Derek called. This cold, dark picnic area surrounded by skeletal trees gave him the creeps, and that tiny light flickered like an eerie beacon. He wanted to return to his Jeep, but disrupting Chapman's joke was a bad idea.

Shoving his fists into his pockets to control the impulse to punch anyone who leaped out at him, Derek stepped carefully between the picnic tables, moving toward the light obviously meant to lure him in. *Your calendar is off, Chapman. Halloween was last month.*

In the near-darkness, Derek made out a light-colored bulk on the ground near the fireplace. It seemed to be shaped like—Derek stopped in his tracks, his heart thudding like crazy. Was that a person? He couldn't tell what it was, but it was about the right size for—

"Mr. Chapman, this isn't funny." Derek spoke before he could stop himself, his voice too harsh. "Mr. Chapman?"

No answer. No rustle of clothes, no footsteps. Swearing under his breath, Derek edged toward the flickering light that illuminated only a small circle of ground.

It was a small plastic light made to look like a candle. A plastic flame glowed orange-yellow, giving a feeble impression of fire.

Fighting the urge to turn and run, Derek picked up the plastic candle. He shuffled a few cautious steps closer to the object lying in front of the fireplace, bent, and held the tiny light above it.

It was a woman, dressed in an ivory coat.

The light jiggled as Derek's shaking hand moved it the length of her body. She lay on her stomach, facing away from him. The collar of her coat and her blue scarf were spattered with red, and when the light shone on her head, Derek choked back nausea. Her skull was misshapen, her brown hair matted with blood.

Derek straightened up, yanking the light away so he couldn't see that horrible wound. This wasn't a joke. She was dead, her skull crushed. He could smell the blood.

Paralyzed, Derek stood in the blackness, the light of the candle hidden by his curled fingers. That coat—the brown hair—

He forced himself to lean over the body and hold the light where it would illuminate her face.

Karen Brodie.

Derek dropped the light and retreated, stepping backward until he banged into a picnic bench. Who had done this to her? And what was she *doing* here? Had she followed him? No, she'd been here before him—that car in the parking lot *was* hers.

Who had killed her?

Chapman—

No. Derek couldn't fathom cheerful, wacky Bob Chapman hurting anyone, and why would he want to attack Derek's landlady? That was nuts.

Derek dug into his pocket for his cell phone, but as he went to dial 911, his finger hovered over the first number. How had Karen and he both ended up here tonight? Had she seen the note Bob Chapman left on his door? She was nosy enough to read it. Had she planned to disrupt his meeting with Chapman the same way she'd destroyed the meeting with his parents? Was that why she'd looked so gleeful when he'd seen her earlier tonight?

Teeth chattering, Derek hurried to his Jeep. Sitting inside with the engine running, he tried to sort through the tumult in his head.

It was 9:15. Where was Chapman? He was the kind of guy who thought he was late if he wasn't early. If he was coming, he'd be here by now—unless he'd come earlier, encountered Karen, and—what? In a burst of insanity, he'd murdered her? *Yeah, right.* What kind of motive could Chapman have for killing Karen? Did he even *know* Karen? His stepson did; he was Abby's ex-boyfriend/realtor who'd brought Derek to Karen's house. But Derek had no idea if Chapman knew Karen personally, and even if he did, why would he care about her one way or the other?

Chapman hadn't killed Karen. Either he hadn't come tonight, or more likely, he'd biked up to the pavilion, seen no sign of Derek, and pedaled off, unaware that a woman lay dead on the ground.

Derek fidgeted with the phone, his stomach churning. Karen's murder must have been a random crime. Maybe while waiting for Derek and Chapman, she'd chanced upon a drug dealer making a sale, or seen something else she shouldn't have. Lousy luck. He'd hated Karen, but he never would have wished this on her, or on anyone.

He'd hated her . . .

The horror in Derek's chest twisted into fear. The police would figure out in half a heartbeat that Derek and Karen had been in conflict.

They'd find out about the overdue rent and about Karen's threat to evict him. They'd find out about the dinner party—Derek imagined his father telling the police what a loser Derek was, a drunk and a drug addict who'd hoped to weasel money out of them and had been enraged when Karen messed up his scheming. *"It wouldn't surprise me if he killed her. The kid's a mess."*

Did Derek really want to call the cops and place himself at the scene of Karen's murder?

They'd blame him. Landlady murdered. Her deadbeat tenant at the scene. The police would think Derek, already infuriated by Karen's ruining things with his parents, had seen her in the picnic pavilion and realized she was trying to ruin things with Chapman as well. They'd think he lost his temper and bashed her on the head.

Who would stand up to defend him? No one—except Abigail. And the police wouldn't listen to his sister, especially not with his own parents condemning him.

Derek crammed his phone back into his pocket. No one had seen him here. If he left, the police would never know he'd found her body. They'd question him eventually, but they'd question a lot of other people too. A woman like Karen Brodie would have more enemies than friends, and the police would have no particular evidence against Derek.

Karen was already dead. He couldn't help her. Why invite trouble?

Derek shifted his Jeep into gear and sped out of the parking lot.

* * *

IT WAS NEARLY TWO O'CLOCK in the morning when Derek remembered the fake candle. He'd touched it with his bare hands, putting fingerprints all over it.

Then he'd dropped it next to Karen's body.

CHAPTER 8

"**H**EY, ABIGAIL. THERE'S A GUY here who wants to see you." Abigail looked up from the purchase order displayed on her computer screen. "Tell him unless he's six-foot-four, has biceps to die for, and is heir to the throne, I'm not interested."

Melissa Barry laughed, eyes sparkling behind retro cat-eye glasses. "His arms are pretty big. Is that enough? He says he has an important business deal going with you."

"A business deal?"

"Says he's an artist."

Wonderful. Chase McCoy. She might as well deal with him now. "Fine, send him on back."

Melissa disappeared. A moment later, Chase strode through the open door of the office. "Good to see you, Abby."

Abigail concealed her irritation. The nickname seemed overfamiliar coming from a man who barely knew her. "Hello, Chase."

Chase shrugged out of his coat. He was dressed in a striped Oxford shirt and Dockers. He looked—Abigail hoped—like he was on his lunch hour and was due back at the office very soon. "Nice store," he said. "Has that country-ish, hometown appeal."

"Thank you."

Chase settled in the chair facing her desk. "So have you had a chance to look at my paintings?"

"Yes." She stood and took the binder from where she'd stowed it on top of the filing cabinet. "Your work is very unique, and I appreciate your thinking of our store. But as I said, I don't usually take things on consignment, and—"

"You can make an exception. You're the boss lady, right?"

"I'm afraid I can't sell your paintings."

"What do you mean you *can't* sell them? Is it a space issue? We can work that out. Rearrange a few things—we could go out there right now, and I'll show you exactly where we could—"

"Your paintings are too modern for the tone of the store. You said yourself we have a 'country-ish' feel."

"They're landscapes! What could be more country than landscapes?"

Abigail hunted for a tactful way to say she never would have guessed the dark slashes of paint were landscapes, but for the title next to each picture. "They're a very modern approach."

"Are you crackers? I'm giving you first shot at this! Even when I'm famous, I'll still sell at your store. Think of the money you could make!"

Abigail opened her mouth to ask why he hadn't approached the local art gallery instead of the local bookstore then clamped her lips shut. Of course Chase McCoy would have approached the gallery first. And they'd turned him down.

She extended the binder to him. "I'm sorry, but I don't think—"

He took the binder and laid it on the desk. "How much do you know about art?"

"I don't claim to be an art expert. But I know my store."

"So you don't know squat about art, but you think you can judge what sells? I'll bet you're one of those people who stands in front of a Picasso and whines, 'Why is it all weird? I don't get it.'"

If Chase McCoy thought insulting her was a good way to get her to her stock his paintings, he was an even bigger oaf than she'd thought. "Your style is not something that meshes with the atmosphere in our store, and your prices are far beyond what a customer would come in here expecting to pay."

"Is that what this is about? Price? Don't freak out so easily, girl. I can be flexible on price."

"It's not just the pricing."

"Give it a try. Do one event. I'll provide the refreshments. You pass out the flyers and do some advertising. We'll set up my paintings, gather a big crowd—you just watch the money fly into your cash register."

Abigail shuddered inwardly at the thought of all of Ohneka thinking she endorsed Chase's creepy work.

"I'm not asking you to sign a long-term contract," Chase said. "I'm talking about one event."

Abigail drew a deep breath and tried to draw calm vibes from the painting of a grassy, sunlit meadow Ellie had hung on the wall, joking, *"It'll remind us that somewhere, far away, summer exists."*

"I won't be selling your paintings," she said, knowing she had to be completely clear or Chase would jump through a perceived loophole. "I will not be advertising them or holding any events. I'm sorry, but I'm simply not interested in what you're selling. Your style is too dark, too severe, and too modern for Words and Sweets."

Chase folded his thick arms. He *did* have big biceps, and Abigail wondered if he lifted weights in addition to wielding a paintbrush.

"I wish you the best of luck," she said. "I need to get back to work now."

To her surprise, the anger left his eyes, and he smiled at her. "Derek recommended you."

"Derek told you I sometimes sell paintings. That wasn't meant to be construed as any kind of guarantee."

McCoy linked his hands behind his neck and leaned back in his chair. "Too bad Derek's dinner party was a wreck the other night."

Caught off guard, Abigail fought to keep her expression cool. Had Chase overheard the argument—or had Derek talked to him? Much as she wanted to order Chase out of her office, she wanted even more to know if Derek had confided in him. "What did Derek say?"

"Derek didn't say anything. Derek's full of secrets, isn't he? Bet your parents don't know the half of what he does, and he'd like to keep it that way. Sucking up to them for money . . . he must be desperate."

Abigail's skin went clammy. "You don't know what you're talking about."

Chase laughed. "Maybe you ought to ask Derek what he was doing in the middle of the night last night, speeding away and then coming home all pale and panicked. Karen Brodie's not the only one he owes money to, is she?"

Abigail resisted the urge to tell him the rent had been paid. Derek would be mortified if Chase knew Abigail had bailed him out. "What are you talking about?"

"Getting leaned on, isn't he?"

"I don't know what you mean."

"See, here's the thing, Abby. I'm sure you don't want to make things harder for your brother. Maybe we ought to work together to make sure your parents—and the police—don't learn things about Derek that they shouldn't. That could really foul up Derek's plans. Your parents have a lot of dough, don't they? I heard they gave you the money that got you started in the book business. And I think Derek's got more on the line than just his bank account. Some not-so-nice people have their own ways of collecting debts, you know?"

He stood and shoved his arms into his coat sleeves. "Hang onto that binder and have another look at it. My business card is in the front. Give me a call in a couple of days."

He sauntered out of the office, leaving Abigail dumbstruck.

* * *

EYES BURNING AND HEAD THROBBING from lack of sleep, Derek slumped on his couch and stared at the ceiling, knowing within a few minutes he'd be on his feet again, pacing around the apartment, muscles twitching with nervous energy. He ought to get ready for work—it was already eleven, and he was scheduled to work from noon to eight today—but he couldn't seem to force himself to go through the practical motions of dressing and shaving.

He'd netted maybe an hour of off-and-on dozing until he'd given up trying to sleep around nine thirty this morning. Every time he'd closed his eyes, he'd seen Karen's body sprawled on the concrete, her hair sticky with blood, her coat collar spattered with red. Every time he'd started to drift off, he'd jerked awake again, sure he'd heard footsteps, sure the police were about to pound on his door.

He was an idiot, a complete *idiot*. How could he have forgotten he'd touched that stupid candle? Derek started shaking whenever he thought of driving through silent streets at two in the morning—the biting chill of the picnic pavilion—trying not to look at Karen's body as he snatched the candle and fled.

He shouldn't have stolen evidence from the site of a murder, but he'd been too scared to stand there and try to wipe the candle clean. It was easier to grab it and run.

Had anyone seen his Jeep, either then or earlier in the evening when he found Karen? Had Karen told anyone she was going to Kemper Park to harass Derek? Derek could picture himself admitting to the cops that yeah, he'd been there; yeah, he'd seen her, but she was already dead, and he'd left her lying there and gone home. *"I didn't hurt her. Honest, officer."* No one would ever believe that. No innocent person would leave a dead woman stiffening in the cold.

What about Bob Chapman? Karen might have mentioned Chapman's note to someone. If the police got Chapman's name and talked to him, he'd be another voice reporting Derek had been there last night.

But Chapman couldn't know that. He hadn't seen Derek.

Derek's heart thumped faster. He should call Chapman and pretend he hadn't made the meeting last night. He could apologize for missing it and ask to reschedule. He could say he'd been feeling sick, so he'd stayed home—no, that wouldn't work. Chase or Karen might be able to testify that his Jeep hadn't been here—

Derek's mind jerked to a halt in mid-thought. Karen couldn't tell anyone anything. Karen was dead, and he'd walked away from her body like it was a piece of roadkill.

Don't think about it. What else could you do? And it's not like you made her suffer.

He couldn't claim he'd been sick. He'd say Chapman's note had fallen to the floor and he hadn't noticed it until too late to make the meeting. It was a decent excuse, given how Chapman had left the note balanced between the doorknob and frame.

Chapman's note had said he'd lost his cell phone, so Derek would have to call his home phone. He leaped from the couch and hurried into his bedroom to the two-drawer filing cabinet where he kept all work-related papers. He snatched the folder of special orders and flipped through the sheets until he found the one with Bob Chapman's information.

Fingers so clumsy that he kept punching the wrong buttons on his phone, Derek had to try three times before he got the number right. His throat constricted as he listened to the phone ring. Chapman probably wasn't there, but at least Derek could leave a message.

"Hello, Chapman residence," a female voice said on the other end.

Having expected voice mail, he now found himself fumbling to speak coherently. "Hi, uh—yeah, hi. This is Derek Wyatt. I was supposed to—uh—Mr. Chapman wanted to meet with me, but I didn't get his message until too late, and I need to talk to him to, uh, reschedule."

"Oh, Derek! You're Abigail's brother, the boy who makes the beautiful jewelry from polished rocks. Bob raves about you."

"Uh—thank you, yes, that's me." Apparently he was talking to Mrs. Chapman. He'd expected a maid or a butler or some housekeeper to answer the phone.

"The necklace you made, the one Bob gave my mother—it's so striking. So original. She gets compliments whenever she wears it."

"Thanks." Despite the situation, Derek grinned—and promptly realized he'd blown it. Bob Chapman had wanted this birthday gift he was commissioning from Derek to be a surprise for his wife—hence the super-spy meeting at Kemper Park. He'd told Derek not to call him at home. And now Derek had called his home phone and spoken to his wife. Melanie Chapman would know exactly what her husband was planning. *Another stroke of brilliance, Captain Clod. Why don't you shoot yourself and put yourself out of everyone's misery?*

"I'm sorry Bob isn't here," Melanie Chapman said. "He's in Europe right now—Denmark today, I think, or was it Finland? I can never remember his itinerary. At any rate, he'll be home on Monday."

"He's—in Europe?"

"Yes. At least he'll have the trip out of the way before the holidays."

Cold prickles across his skin made Derek shiver. "Uh . . . sorry . . . I just wondered . . . when did he leave?"

"We left together . . . oh . . . was it two weeks ago? We did some touring before he started his work. Business and pleasure, you know—Bob likes to mix them." She laughed. "I came home last week and left him to his work. Can I help you, Derek? Or pass along a message?"

Derek groped for an answer, but the only words that came out of his mouth were a nonsensical, "You're sure he's been gone the whole time?"

"What do you mean? We were on vacation together, and now he's finishing up with a business trip. Is something wrong?"

Derek swallowed. "No, nothing's wrong. I was—up too late last night; my brain's on snooze. Uh . . . stupid question . . . has he by chance lost his cell phone?"

"No, he has it. It's one that works both in Europe and at home. If you tried to call him and he didn't answer, he's just busy—he'll get back to you. He loves your work. He always talks about what a talented young man you are." She chuckled. "Brendan's gotten a lot of bragging mileage over being the one who brought you to Bob's attention."

"Glad it worked out." Derek's mouth formed the words automatically.

"You—don't need to give him a message. I'll talk to him after he gets home."

"Okay. Keep up the good work. You've got a real gift."

"Thank you. Bye." Derek hung up, his heart pounding so violently that he could feel the vibrations all along his limbs.

Bob Chapman hadn't left that note. He'd been thousands of miles away.

So who had?

Who knew Bob Chapman was his most treasured customer and that Derek would respond to any note from him, no matter how bizarre?

Anyone with an Internet connection could have figured it out. An endorsement from Chapman featured prominently on Derek's website. And Chapman's genial, eccentric personality was well known to Ohneka residents. Anyone could have forged that note.

Karen? Had *she* left the note? She was clever enough to use Chapman's name to manipulate him. But why would Karen want him at the park? Some kind of spiteful joke? Derek tried to envision it: first "Bob Chapman" would summon him to the park, then to some other crazy location, and on and on while Karen watched and laughed, seeing how long she could keep him running, so desperate for money that he'd crawl into the sewer if that's what "Chapman" wanted. If it had started as a joke, it had gone hideously wrong when Karen's stakeout at the park had taken her into the path of a murderer. Derek imagined a serial killer stalking the park, with Karen as his first victim.

No, none of that made sense. If Karen had wanted to spy on him so she could laugh at what a sucker he was she wouldn't have left her car in plain sight.

But *somebody* had wanted him at the park.

Wanted him at the park at the time Karen was murdered? What if her murder wasn't random?

That was too crazy to believe. Did he really think someone had plotted to kill Karen and frame him for it?

The note. At least he'd saved the note. If the police learned he'd been there, he could show them the note summoning him. Experts could analyze the handwriting and maybe figure out who wrote it.

Where had he put the note? The drawer where he kept his mail.

Derek jerked open the kitchen drawer containing a stack of bills and a few pens and pencils. He scooped the papers onto the counter and scrabbled through them.

The note wasn't there. Had he left it on his dresser?

He checked his dresser, the tables in the living room, the magazine rack, and the kitchen counters. Unable to think of anywhere else he would have set the note, he grabbed his keys and headed out to his Jeep. He must have brought the note with him when he drove to Kemper Park to meet Chapman.

The note wasn't in his Jeep.

Sweaty with fear and frustration, Derek returned to his apartment. What had he done with that note?

CHAPTER 9

Lillian Wyatt stepped out of her car and cast an edgy look at the old Victorian home comprising Derek's apartment. When she'd been here the other night, she'd thought the exterior attractive, but daylight exposed it as shabby. The gingerbread trim needed a fresh coat of paint. The shutters were charming, but overall the house looked in need of refurbishment.

Derek was at work. She had called Janssen's Hardware, pretending to be a customer, and had asked when he'd be in. He was scheduled from twelve o'clock to eight o'clock today. She didn't have to worry about running into him here, but still, nervousness dogged her as she walked into the entryway.

Karen Brodie had laughed when Lillian had called her yesterday afternoon to ask for an appointment. *"I don't see what's so secret that we can't say it over the phone, but sure, come on over."*

Remembering Karen's directions, Lillian climbed the staircase, trailing her fingers along the carved railing. She hadn't wanted to have this discussion over the phone. She wanted to be where she could see Karen's face, probe a little more, take a little more time, and read gestures and body language as well as words. She didn't doubt that Karen would initially say anything she could to make Derek look bad, but Lillian didn't think it would be difficult to corner her and compel her to separate facts from animosity.

Lillian clutched her purse a little closer to her body. A bit of cash and a hint that more would be forthcoming if Karen would keep a discreet eye on Derek would go a long way toward keeping Karen from telling Derek that Lillian had visited her.

Between Abigail's endless optimism and Karen Brodie's sour pessimism, maybe Lillian could get a realistic picture of her son. And

Paul would never notice any missing money. He dealt with the big things—stocks, other investments, things Lillian didn't know much about. She dealt with the day-to-day cash flow, paying bills and transferring money into the checking account as needed.

Lillian steadied herself, firmed her expression to hide her apprehension, and tapped on Karen's door.

Karen didn't answer the door, and Lillian heard no footfalls within the apartment. She waited a minute then knocked again.

Nothing. Frowning, Lillian rapped loudly. Karen had chosen the time for the appointment, so there was no excuse for her not being here. Was she rude enough to stand Lillian up?

Behind her, she heard the rattle and swish of the front door opening. She turned and looked down the staircase, expecting to see Karen Brodie. Instead, two men entered the lobby.

Disappointed, Lillian turned back and knocked one more time on Karen's door, not expecting her to answer. The vile woman didn't even have the courtesy to keep her appointments—and after Lillian had driven all the way from Syracuse.

Footsteps thumped on the stairs, and Lillian pivoted to face one of the visitors. A rounded paunch gave him a soft look, but the keen way he assessed her made her think he was here on some unpleasant official business—or maybe the fact that he bore a strong resemblance to Supreme Court Justice Clarence Thomas made Lillian read authority into his demeanor.

"If you're looking for Karen Brodie, she isn't home," Lillian told him as he reached the upper floor. "We had an appointment, but apparently she's broken it."

The man reached inside his coat and pulled out a wallet, which he flipped open, displaying a badge. "I'm Detective Jeffrey Turner, Ohneka Police. You're here to see Karen Brodie, ma'am?"

Discomfort brought slight warmth to her cheeks, and Lillian wished she hadn't said anything about having an appointment with Karen. How humiliating to be associated with a woman who had drawn the attention of the police! But she couldn't erase her words now.

"Yes, I came to see her, but I'm afraid she's not here. If you'll excuse me—" Lillian started toward the stairs.

"Just a minute, ma'am." Detective Turner pulled a notebook and pen out of his pocket. "Could I get your name, please?"

The warmth in Lillian's cheeks heated to a scorching blush as she imagined her name typed in a police report. "Whatever business the police have with Miss Brodie has nothing to do with me, I assure you."

"Are you a friend of Karen Brodie's?"

"No, I am not. I've only met her once."

"Your name, please, ma'am, and some ID, if you don't mind."

She did mind, but she knew Turner was painting politeness on the surface of an order.

"Lillian Wyatt," she said. She took her driver's license out of her purse and handed it to Turner. He scribbled in his notebook and passed the card back to her.

"Why were you coming to meet with Ms. Brodie?" he asked.

Horrified at the prospect of admitting she'd planned to ask Karen about Derek's activities, Lillian parried the question with one of her own. "Why are the police asking questions about her? I told you, I hardly know her. I'm sure I can't tell you anything helpful."

"I'm afraid Karen Brodie is dead."

Lillian recoiled. "Dead! What happened?"

"It's our job to figure that out, Ms. Wyatt."

Clearly Karen hadn't died of natural causes or in an accident, or the police wouldn't be here asking questions. She must have been murdered. Murdered!

Where had she died? Not here, or her apartment would be a crime scene, with all that yellow tape and specialists in latex gloves rushing around putting evidence in envelopes. Probably she'd been at some sleazy club, or another place that invited trouble. The stupid woman. Why had Lillian ever thought meeting with her was a good idea?

"I'm sorry to hear of her unfortunate death." Lillian took a baby step toward the stairs. "But as I told you, I didn't know her. I'm afraid I can't help you." Turner would surely have the good sense to realize there was no point in detaining her. She took another baby step.

He held up a hand. "A moment, please, ma'am. You said you'd met Karen Brodie once before. When was that?"

Lillian hunted for words to make the meeting sound as uninteresting as possible. "On . . . oh, let me see. Last Saturday evening. I was visiting one of her tenants, and Miss Brodie knocked on the door. I didn't even speak to her."

"Which tenant was that?"

The hallway seemed suddenly dark and claustrophobic. "Detective Turner, nothing about a chance meeting has any bearing on whatever happened to Karen Brodie. If you would allow me to go about my business, you could focus your attention on people who might actually be able to give you information."

Turner's deep brown eyes scrutinized her with intensified interest, and Lillian realized she was handling this completely wrong. Her balking at answering routine questions had piqued Turner's curiosity.

"Sorry for the inconvenience," he said. "Which tenant were you visiting?"

Knowing her cheeks must be crimson, Lillian said, "Derek Wyatt." It was patently foolish to wait for Turner to ask about the name connection, so she added, "My son."

"Why did you have an appointment with Karen Brodie today?"

If she had to admit the truth, she would wither with humiliation. Lillian floundered mentally for a moment, but her voice was smooth when she said, "I wanted to discuss the rental market in Ohneka. My husband and I live in Syracuse, but we've been thinking of investing in some rental properties in this area. I was hoping Miss Brodie could give me some advice."

"When did you last talk to her?"

"I called her yesterday, early in the afternoon—perhaps around two? She told me to come over today at three." Lillian hoped Turner wouldn't ask why she hadn't simply sought Karen's counsel in a phone call.

"Is your son home right now?"

"He's at work."

"Where does he work?"

"At Janssen's Hardware."

Turner jotted on his pad. "Thank you, ma'am. May I have your phone number, please, in case I need to speak to you again?"

Lillian gave it, and at Turner's nod of dismissal, she hurried down the stairs on watery knees, wanting to get away before he changed his mind and thought of something else to ask her. It had been wrong to lie about her meeting with Karen, but what was she supposed to say? That she'd wanted to talk to Karen to see if Derek was a drug-addicted womanizer and to offer Karen a little cash to spy on him? Should she have admitted that Karen had come to Derek's apartment on Saturday to berate him over unpaid rent and it had been a distasteful and humiliating scene?

She couldn't possibly have shared such sordid information with Turner, and it had no bearing on the murder anyway.

Not until Lillian was nearly home did her relief at getting away from Turner begin to chill into apprehension. Detective Turner would talk to Derek. Would he tell Derek about Lillian trying to visit Karen? Derek would never believe she'd wanted to ask Karen about rental properties, not after that mortifying scene at the dinner party. Derek would know she'd lied. Would he tell Turner so? Sometimes Derek was appallingly forthright when tact was needed, and Lillian had a hard time imagining he'd keep his mouth shut to protect her. More likely he'd enjoy the prospect of her being caught in a lie by a police detective. What were the penalties for lying to the police? Was it considered perjury, or was that only if you lied in court?

Lillian blinked tears out of her eyes. How could she ever explain this disaster to Paul? He'd told her to keep away from Derek, that getting involved with him would only lead to pain.

Why hadn't she listened to him?

* * *

THE INSTANT DEREK CAUGHT SIGHT of the two men in ties and overcoats, he knew why they were here. He returned his gaze to the length of PVC pipe he was cutting for a customer and kept up a silent drumbeat in his head. *Don't panic, don't panic, don't panic. You knew they'd want to talk to you. Keep your cool.*

He had no reason to be scared. Even if some psycho *had* tried to frame him by tricking him into going to the park at the time Karen was murdered, that scheme had failed—Derek hadn't called the police, and no one had seen him there. There was no evidence to place him at the scene of the crime.

Who had found Karen's body—and when? The icy lump inside him felt a little smaller and a little less cold at the knowledge that Karen's body was no longer freezing on the ground in Kemper Park. Not that it mattered to Karen, but at least her body would now be treated with respect. No thanks to Derek.

The men disappeared down another aisle. Maybe he'd guessed wrong. Maybe no one had found Karen yet. Maybe the men were here on their lunch breaks, seeking a Brita filter and a windshield scraper. *Yeah, so they came together in a cute little herd, like teenage girls going to the restroom.*

His customer departed. Derek moved busily along the aisles, a friendly smile on his face, seeking out someone else who might need help. *Don't panic.*

"Hey, Derek."

Derek swung around to see his manager standing with the two men.

"These gentlemen need a few words with you," she said. "You can use the break room."

"Uh—okay, sure. Thanks, Sal." Derek hoped he sounded casual and a little puzzled. His heart was doing running long jumps inside his chest as he strolled toward the break room with the men in his wake. Should he say something small-talky, like mention what a cold November it had been so far? No, too cheesy.

Once they were in the break room, Derek nearly reached to shut the door but stopped himself. Shutting it would imply that he knew these men were here to talk to him about something he didn't want overheard. He had to act completely clueless about the reason for their visit.

"What can I do for you guys?" These cops looked like they'd been partnered by someone obsessed with contrasts: one of them was a little heavy around the middle, black, bespectacled, and reminded Derek of the math teacher who'd flunked him in precalculus; the other was pale, beanpole lean and tall, and didn't look too many years older than Derek.

The older guy flipped open a wallet, displaying his badge. "I'm Detective Jeffrey Turner, Ohneka Police. This is Detective Abe Bartholomew. We need to ask you a few questions."

"Sure, no problem. What about?" Was he overdoing the innocent-ignorant charade? He should have let himself sound more worried. Most people *would* be worried at being confronted by two police detectives. "Nothing's happened to my family, has it?" *Dumb,* Derek berated himself. If the cops were here to deliver bad news, they wouldn't start off with *"We need to ask you a few questions."*

"We're not here about your family, Mr. Wyatt. Unfortunately, Karen Brodie, your landlady, was found dead this morning."

Derek let his mouth fall open. "Karen is *dead*? What happened?" He tried to block out thoughts of her corpse lying in the picnic pavilion all night, blood freezing on her scalp.

"When did you last see Ms. Brodie?" Turner asked.

"Uh . . . hang on, let me . . . man, this is crazy." Derek sank into one of the molded plastic chairs. "Uh . . . I saw her last night, actually.

I ran into her in the lobby around . . . I guess it was around six. She was getting her mail."

"Did she say anything about her plans for yesterday evening?"

"Uh . . . no. She didn't say anything. Just kind of smiled at me. She looked really different—" Memory flickered. He'd been so distracted by everything else that he'd forgotten Karen's fixed-up appearance. This was something the cops might be interested in. "She was all dressed up. She even had a new haircut and dye job—looked a lot better than her last one. I noticed she was wearing makeup. I don't think she usually wore it. She looked really nice and kind of excited. I remember wondering if she had a new boyfriend."

"You have no idea who she might have been planning to meet?"

"Not a clue. I didn't know her that well. I mean, she was my landlady, and I've lived there for a year and a half, but I didn't know her on a personal level."

"You said you thought she might have a new boyfriend. Can you think of any names? Anyone she'd talked about or anyone you'd seen her with?"

Derek wracked his brain, wishing he could come up with someone for Turner, but he couldn't remember seeing Karen have visitors at all. "Sorry, I can't think of anyone."

"Do you know of anyone she might have been seeing in the past?"

"Uh . . . well, I know she's divorced. I don't know her ex's name, but I know it's not Brodie. She seemed pretty bitter about it all."

"Did she seem to be in conflict with anyone in particular?"

"I have no idea."

"Was she a difficult landlady?"

"Uh . . . well, she wasn't the friendliest woman on the planet. Kind of an angry person."

Turner's tone was matter-of-fact. "Did you have any problems with her?"

Derek would have traded everything he owned for the ability to control the flow of blood through his vessels. His neck must be blotchy red from nervousness, and heat seeped into his face. Should he admit to his clashes with Karen? His mind jumped back and forth between his options. The police would inevitably learn about his poor payment history from Karen's records—or maybe they already had, and that was why Turner was asking if he'd had trouble with Karen. Better to come clean now than to let the police think he was hiding things.

Derek shifted in his seat, fighting an impulse to get up and close the door. The thought of his coworkers hearing what a loser he was made him cringe.

Either lanky and silent Detective Bartholomew had ESP, or he didn't want the conversation overheard either. He walked over and clicked the door shut.

"We argued over the rent," Derek admitted. "I've been strapped for cash lately, and I was behind on my payments. But I was going to pay her everything I owed as soon as I got my next paycheck."

No particular interest showed in either Turner's or Bartholomew's face, and Derek was relieved for the five seconds it took him to figure out that the detectives might just be adept at keeping their interest hidden when they sensed the tug of a fish on the line.

"How behind were you, Mr. Wyatt?" Bartholomew asked. He had a much deeper voice than his skinny stature and young face seemed to indicate.

"Not too far behind." Derek realized to his dismay that he'd been absentmindedly crumpling and flattening a napkin someone had left on the break room table. He pushed the napkin aside. "Just a month or so. Like I said, I was going to pay up very soon. Karen knew I always paid up eventually."

"So you'd had this trouble before," Turner said.

The temperature of Derek's face notched up a few more degrees. "I've been late now and then, but like I said, I always paid up."

"Ms. Brodie confronted you about the late rent?" No hint of accusation sounded in Turner's voice, but Derek was certain both Turner and Bartholomew were watching him with increased intensity.

"Yeah, come on, of course she confronted me, but it was no big deal. She was always crabby. And it's not like she would've thrown me out."

As soon as he spoke the words, he knew he'd made a mistake. He could have mouthed Turner's next line right along with him as Turner said, "Did she threaten to evict you?"

"She threw a few threats around, but I could tell she wasn't serious." Derek fervently hoped that when they'd searched Karen's apartment they hadn't found paperwork indicating she'd started eviction proceedings.

"Where were you last night between the hours of seven and midnight?" Turner asked.

The question he'd dreaded. Derek had thought carefully about how to answer this. "I was home until around . . . uh . . . I guess I left at maybe 8:30? Or a little earlier? I was going to see the new James Bond movie, but it was sold out, so I grabbed a burger at the Onion Bowl and went home. I got home . . . let's see, it was before ten. I was home for the rest of the night." Derek hoped that sounded credible. He'd learned about the sold-out showing from a coworker, and the Onion Bowl was always packed, so the police couldn't reasonably expect anyone there to remember seeing him. It was a lousy alibi—actually not an alibi at all, since no one could testify as to where he'd been—but at least it gave him an excuse for being out of the house.

"Was anyone with you?" Turner asked.

"Nah. I'm between girlfriends."

"Is there anyone who could confirm your whereabouts? Did you talk to anyone?"

Something about the way Turner looked at him made Derek feel as though he were under his father's gaze. Turner was built a lot like Paul too, with those broad shoulders and that paunch.

Derek's tongue felt pasted to the roof of his mouth. He swallowed hard. "I didn't talk to anyone at the theater, and the restaurant was a zoo. No way would they remember me." Were these still routine questions, or was he now a suspect?

"Why was your mother going to meet with Karen Brodie this afternoon?" Turner asked.

So astounded that it took him a moment to realize his mouth was hanging open, Derek scrounged for an intelligent reply, but the best he could manage was, "Uh—what makes you think she was going to meet with Karen?"

"I met her at Karen Brodie's door a couple of hours ago," Turner said.

She was at Karen's door? What was she doing there? She didn't even know Karen. The only time she'd seen her had been when Karen had crashed the dinner party.

"Maybe she was . . . uh . . . looking for me," Derek said. Could that be true? Could his mother have regretted the way things had turned out the other night?

"She said she had an appointment with Ms. Brodie," Turner said. "She'd set the appointment yesterday."

An appointment? Completely bewildered, Derek stammered out, "Are—are you *sure* it was my mother? Lillian Wyatt?"

"That's right. She didn't say anything to you about the appointment?"

"No . . . uh . . . no." Could she have come to offer to pay Derek's overdue rent? *Dream on, sucker. She probably came to warn Karen to throw you out now and cut her losses.*

"Did your mother have any interest in investing in the Ohneka rental market?"

Derek tried not to look too boggled, even as his mind tied itself in knots. Investing in Ohneka? Whether or not his parents were hatching some financial scheme, Derek would have bet his new saw, his Jeep, and his left hand that Lillian would never have gotten involved with Karen Brodie on any kind of business deal. Lillian would be so humiliated by the fact that her son owed Karen money that she'd shrink from the thought of facing her. Besides, Derek was sure Lillian would find a rude, abrasive woman like Karen detestable.

Turner and Bartholomew both stood watching him, waiting for him to answer the question. He straightened up in his chair. *Get a grip, bozo.* "I have no idea why my mother wanted to talk to Karen Brodie. She didn't say anything to me about it. You'll have to ask her." Even as he said the words, he realized if Turner had run into Lillian at Karen's door, he'd already asked her why she was there, and apparently Lillian had offered some explanation about investing in the rental market—which Turner hadn't believed, or he wouldn't be pushing the same questions at Derek.

Part of Derek wanted to burst out laughing. The police investigating what Lillian Wyatt had been doing knocking on the door of a murdered woman? The police suspecting she was a liar? He pictured Turner and Bartholomew knocking on the Wyatts' door—the grim displeasure on Paul's face as he realized the police suspected his wife—Lillian sitting in a bare little room at the police station, struggling to maintain her dignity and her hairdo throughout an interrogation . . .

"Thank you for your time, Mr. Wyatt." Turner's voice jounced Derek out of his thoughts. He handed Derek a business card. "If you think of anything at all that might help us determine what happened to Karen Brodie, call me immediately."

"Sure, yeah, I will." The amusement inside him faded to cold misery. Whatever Lillian's reason for visiting Karen, one thing was certain—it was all about Derek. *He* was the cause of whatever embarrassment she would suffer at the hands of the police. She'd let Derek back into her life for one brief dinner, and he'd immediately started carving chunks out of her peace of mind. Even when he didn't try to hurt her, he was a disaster.

No wonder she hated him. He wondered how many times she'd wished *he* had been one of her miscarriages and she'd given birth to a different child—*any* other child but Derek.

"Do you have any idea why Karen Brodie would have been at Kemper Park last night?" Turner asked.

Jolted by this question when he'd thought questioning had ended, Derek tried to sound wryly puzzled. "Kemper Park? No idea. It's not exactly picnic season, is it?"

"No, it's not," Turner said. "Thank you, Mr. Wyatt."

Derek rose to his feet as the detectives walked out of the room, but the instant they were out of sight, he crumpled back into his chair. *Idiot!* He'd blundered big time, making that crack about picnics. Yeah, people associated picnics with Kemper Park, but they also associated the park with baseball fields, swimming, sailing, that big new children's playground, and, at this time of year, ice skating.

Derek would bet that as Turner and Bartholomew walked to their car, they were speculating on the coincidence that Derek Wyatt would happen to refer to the very area of the park where Karen Brodie's body had been found.

CHAPTER 10

FOR THE REST OF THE afternoon, Chase McCoy's words gnawed at Abigail. *Was* Derek in debt to someone dangerous? A drug dealer? A loan shark? *Had* Derek done something that would interest the police? Or was Chase bluffing, gambling that Abigail would rather stock his paintings than delve into information she'd rather not have? Bleakly, Abigail imagined the results if she hung those atrocities on the wall of the store. Ellie would be appalled, certain Abigail had lost her mind. Their customers would be put off. And Abigail could imagine Chase stomping into her office a month from now, demanding to know why she hadn't managed to sell a single one of his masterpieces and insisting she hand-deliver ad flyers to every address in town or Derek's sordid secrets would hit the headlines.

But Derek had been doing so well—or at least he seemed to be. How much did she really know about how he spent his time? Since he'd moved to Ohneka, she usually saw him about twice a week—she would invite him over for Sunday dinner most weeks; he'd stop by the bookstore or stop by her house to show her some sketches of a possible new project; she'd drop by his apartment and take him cookies or a pie; occasionally they'd catch a movie or go mini-golfing. She'd never seen any signs that he was using drugs, and since he'd told her he was quitting alcohol altogether, she'd never seen signs that he was drinking. Her biggest concern had been that he seemed socially isolated—he was almost always home when she stopped by spontaneously, even on weekends—either busy in his rock room or buried in his website. She'd invited him to church and town activities, but he usually declined both. She'd had the impression he was pouring all his spare time into his rock business and was content with that for the moment.

But what had he been doing last night when Chase had seen him heading out somewhere, looking panicked?

Or was Chase lying?

She'd expected Derek to call her—if only to chew her out—after she'd left him a note explaining that she'd paid his rent, but she hadn't heard from him all week.

Having finished ringing up a sale of a pound of cream-filled chocolates and two mystery novels, Abigail bid her customer good-bye and looked over to greet the customer now approaching the cash register.

Her heart did an annoying little jump that made her want to slap herself. "Hi, Kyle."

"Abigail." Kyle Stratton smiled at her in a way that made her want to forget everything else and stare at him for as long as he was willing to stand there—which wouldn't be long if she unnerved him with a dreamy, vacant gaze. The wind had disarranged his chestnut hair, and Abigail involuntarily imagined how it would feel to smooth the stray strands back in place for him—as Ellie would have done had she been here.

"Good day in the world of literature?" he asked.

"Yes, actually. People are starting their Christmas shopping. I'm sorry, but Ellie's not here. She had today off."

"That's okay. I'm just looking for a birthday gift for my secretary. She's going on a Mediterranean cruise over Christmas, and I want to get her a travel guide."

"Lucky her," Abigail said. "Though I can't imagine what the Mediterranean has to offer in December that Ohneka doesn't."

Kyle laughed, while Abigail tried not to wonder if her pearl-gray sweater and navy slacks made her look frumpy. Something about Kyle's presence always gave her the feeling that clothes that had looked fashionable when she put them on this morning now looked like something she'd raided from her grandmother's closet, and the classic shoulder-length bob that had seemed to flatter her face when she styled her hair that morning was now an exercise in blandness. If Kyle blinked, Abigail's dullness would probably make her blend right in with the wall.

"Great necklace." Kyle gestured at the blue agate Abigail wore on a gold chain. "Derek's work, right? Almost looks like a flower, but more abstract."

Abigail touched the curving edge of the glossy stone. "I told him it looks like something you'd see if you put a drop of pond water under a microscope. That's when he gave it to me."

Kyle laughed. "I like it." He leaned over the counter and spoke quietly. "How are you holding up? Ellie told me the dinner with Derek and your parents was . . . disappointing."

Abigail glanced around the store. Melissa was helping an elderly woman in the children's section, and the other customers all looked intent on their browsing. No one was close enough to overhear words spoken softly, so Abigail said, "*Disappointing* is one word for it. And all the other words for it—well, I'm not permitted to say them in polite company."

Kyle smiled ruefully. "I'm sorry to hear it went badly. I know you worked hard to set it up."

Abigail looked down and straightened a stack of flyers advertising upcoming holiday events. "Maybe the time wasn't right."

"And maybe you had the bad luck to have the Wicked Witch drop in on you."

Abigail's cheeks warmed at the thought that Kyle knew of Derek's financial problems. Ellie had apparently filled him in on the entire story. Not that there was any point to being embarrassed on Derek's behalf—it wasn't as though Kyle hadn't already heard worse about him. He'd been around enough to learn the whole Derek saga.

"Bad luck," Abigail said. "Bad timing. And bad judgment on Derek's part to get himself in that pickle."

"That doesn't excuse what his landlady did."

"I know. She's . . . well, she seems to enjoy embarrassing people."

"Maybe Derek would be better off if she did throw him out," Kyle said.

"No matter where he goes, they'll want him to pay his rent." Abigail tried to make it sound joking, and Kyle responded with a sympathetic smile.

"Whatever you do, don't blame yourself for what happened," he said. "You did everything right."

"Thank you. But you're the only one who thinks so. Derek hasn't returned my calls all week, and I'm too scared to call my parents. And as if things weren't bad enough—" Abigail stopped herself. She'd just about spilled her problem with Chase McCoy. What was she thinking?

"How are things getting worse?"

"I'm exaggerating. Ignore me. It's been a stressful few days."

Kyle frowned, giving Abigail such a long look that she broke eye contact and started rearranging the pens in the Words and Sweets mug next to the register.

"Honest girls like you are horrible liars," he said.

Abigail blushed, wishing a customer would approach the cash register and put an end to this conversation.

Kyle chuckled. "That was a compliment, by the way. I like people who can't lie to me. What's wrong?"

"Truly, Kyle, I don't think you came here to listen to me whine. Why don't we find that book you wanted?" She came out from behind the counter.

"Thanks. But first—I left my jacket in the office. Would you mind grabbing it for me?"

Abigail couldn't remember seeing a man's jacket in the office, but she said, "Sure," and started toward the back of the store. Kyle followed her.

The coat tree held only her heavy coat and a jacket of Ellie's that had been there since September. "I don't see it," Abigail said. "Are you sure—"

Kyle closed the door. "Never mind. I didn't leave my jacket here."

Flustered, Abigail offered a feeble smile. "So what are you up to?"

"I want to know what you were going to say. You started to tell me something and then stopped."

Abigail's gaze went automatically to the leather binder sitting on her desk. "I have customers. I can't hide out in here."

"Melissa can handle things for a moment."

Why was he so concerned about her? Was he the kind of guy who went out of his way to help anyone in need? *I hope you appreciate what you've got, Ellie.* "I'm just worried about Derek . . ." She lost her nerve and let her voice trail off.

"You mean beyond the financial mess and the trouble with your parents?"

"Well . . ." Why was she such a coward? Here was Kyle Stratton, worried about her, wanting to help. Why not confide in him? He wouldn't be shocked at the thought that Derek might be in trouble.

Abigail looked Kyle straight in the eyes. "May I ask your candid opinion on something? I want an honest opinion with absolutely no sugar-coating."

"All right, I'm game."

"I want you to take a look at this artwork." She handed him the binder. "Then I want your blunt opinion. No holds barred." The silvery door chime signaled a new customer. "Excuse me," Abigail said. "I'll be back in a few minutes."

When she finished assisting the woman who wanted "anything with princesses or magic" for her ten-year-old niece, she returned to the office to find Kyle sitting on the edge of the desk, the binder next to him.

"Well?" Abigail said.

"Would it be unsporting if I asked you if Derek painted these?"

"That's cheating. Just tell me what you think, good or bad."

Kyle drummed his long fingers against the portfolio. "You want the truth?"

"I told you I did."

"It looks like fourth-grade art class meets Stephen King. If it were better executed, it might be powerful, but it just comes across as tacky and creepy. Candid enough?"

"Yes. Thank you."

"Did Derek paint them?"

"No. His neighbor did." Already feeling better for having shown the paintings to Kyle, Abigail quickly told him the rest of the story.

"When you paint that badly, I guess extortion is the only way to get anyone to sell your work," Kyle remarked. He didn't look shocked—just disgusted and amused. "You're not letting this clown get to you, are you? He doesn't have anything on your brother. He's just observant enough to know you're protective of Derek, so he thought he could push your buttons. Laugh in his face."

"I'd better not laugh. He's a lot bigger than I am. But you're right. I shouldn't let him get to me."

"Don't worry about him. What you ought to worry about is what Ellie would do if you started trying to sell those paintings here."

Abigail laughed, picturing Ellie with fists on hips and sapphire eyes ablaze. "You're right. That's a scary thought. And don't worry. I never planned to take his paintings. I do have *some* taste."

Kyle gaze flicked from her head to her feet. "You have fantastic taste. You always look classy."

"Oh, please." Abigail tried for an air of amused skepticism but knew the blush in her cheeks would ruin the effect. *He's Ellie's boyfriend,* she berated herself. *The fact that he knows how to flatter you and any other woman doesn't mean he really thinks you look good, or anything else.* Determined to repair her businesslike facade, she said briskly, "Let's go find that travel guide. And thank you for your help. I feel better."

"Glad to help."

Kyle's contemptuous dismissal of Chase McCoy *did* make her feel better. Even though she wouldn't let Chase manipulate her into selling his paintings, letting him manipulate her into feeling pressured, worried, and paranoid was nearly as bad.

If Chase's words held any shred of truth, she'd find out. As soon as she got off work, she'd go to Derek's apartment. She'd park her car around the corner where he wouldn't see it, and then wait in his apartment until he arrived—even if that meant waiting until midnight.

Abigail glanced around the store with a grim smile. She'd make sure to bring a few good books to read.

* * *

PREPARED WITH A FLASHLIGHT IN hand, Abigail approached the darkened garage where Derek parked his Jeep. She shone the light through one of the small, square windows. The Jeep was gone.

It didn't matter. Derek would come home eventually, and when he did, they'd talk. He'd avoided her calls long enough. She needed to know what he was thinking in the aftermath of that disastrous dinner. She needed to know his reaction to the note she'd left him confessing she'd paid his rent. And *he* needed to know what Chase McCoy had hinted about him and how Chase was attempting to pressure Abigail. It was time to get everything out in the open.

Abigail walked up the porch steps and opened the door to the entryway. A large figure jumped toward her, startling her into a yelp of fear.

"Sorry! Sorry, I'm really sorry!" Hunter Conley backpedaled, moving away from her. "I scared you. I didn't mean to scare you. You think I'm the killer. That's what my dad said. He asked me if I creamed the ugly witch, but he didn't say *witch*, but Derek said not to say the other word because swearing makes people sound stupid. But he swears sometimes, I've heard him, but he tries not to."

Drowning under this incomprehensible waterfall of words, Abigail attempted to start the conversation over. "Hi, Hunter. Do you know when Derek will be home?"

Hunter grabbed his left forearm with his right hand and squeezed hard, kneading the fabric of his dirty coat. Abigail was about to ask him if he'd hurt his arm, when she remembered what Derek had said about the stuffed turtle Hunter carried in his sleeve, the turtle he squeezed when he was nervous. He looked worse than nervous now—he looked frantic.

"I thought you were Derek, so that's why I jumped up, because I've been waiting for him," he said. "But you don't look like him, even though you're his sister except you both have brown hair but his is darker and it was dumb to be confused. Do you think I killed her?"

Abigail fought an urge to edge away from Hunter. Derek had said he was a nice kid, but this babbling about murder gave her the creeps. Should she ask him what he was talking about, or would that only push him deeper into a fantasy world? "Of course I don't think you killed anyone," she said cautiously.

"Good." Hunter's face relaxed. "I didn't like her, but I wouldn't ever kill anyone, or any animals either. I don't like my name. I wish I had a dog."

Abigail moistened her lips. "Who didn't you like?"

"Karen. She paid me, but she was a jerk. Did you know her? She owns this whole house. Derek didn't like her either."

Chills tingled along Abigail's spine. "Hunter . . . did something happen to Karen Brodie?"

"Yeah, didn't you hear? It was on the news. My dad saw it. I saw it, too. She's dead. Killed."

Abigail gasped. "She was murdered?"

"Yeah. But they didn't say how, if she was shot or stabbed with a knife or what."

Abigail felt sick to her stomach. The fact that she'd disliked Karen was irrelevant; Karen was a human being, and someone had cut her life short.

"My dad says I killed her because she was a cheapskate and didn't pay me enough, and he's going to call the cops and tell them I did it. He says they'll lock me up. I didn't do it! I swear! I've got to talk to Derek. He'll talk to the cops for me. He'll tell them I didn't do it."

Abigail flicked a glance toward the stairway that led up to Karen's apartment. "Was it—did it happen here?"

"No. At that big park on the lake, Kemper Park. They found her body there. I haven't even *been* to Kemper Park since summer, I rode my bike there, but my dad said the cops won't care, they'll lock me up anyway 'cause I have psycho eyes."

What he had, Abigail thought, were the eyes of a terrified, gullible child. Derek hadn't exaggerated when he'd said Hunter's father was a jerk. "Hunter, your dad is . . . your dad is just pretending with you. The police will know you didn't hurt Karen. You don't have to be scared."

He plucked frenetically at his sleeve. "I don't want to go to prison."

"You won't." She touched his elbow. "Your dad won't tell the police you killed Karen, because people who tell lies to the police get in trouble, and he won't want to get in trouble. Do you understand?"

"Yeah. He doesn't like the cops anyway."

Surprise, Abigail thought. "Then he definitely won't call them. You don't have to worry."

"I wish Derek was home."

"I know. So do I. But he might be out late tonight." *Avoiding me.* "Will you get in trouble with your dad if you're out too late?"

"Yeah."

"You'd better go home. I'm going to wait for Derek, and when he gets here, I'll tell him you need to talk to him. He'll talk to you tomorrow. And don't worry—the police aren't going to arrest you."

"Okay." Hunter's shoulders drooped and he finally drew his hand away from the hidden turtle. "You're smart, Derek told me you were. You're pretty too. I went to a farm once and I got to touch a horse and it was all shiny brown and pretty like your hair but I was too scared to ride it. My mom was pretty, I mean I think she was pretty, but I don't have any pictures. She left a long time ago."

"I'm sorry."

"You better be careful. Someone killed Karen and it wasn't me, so it was someone else, which means there's a *killer* around. Lock your door."

"I will."

Hunter pulled his stocking cap lower over his straggling hair and headed out the front door, walking with his shoulders hunched like he wanted to knock a few inches off his height.

As Abigail unlocked Derek's door with the key he'd given her a few months ago, she found her hands were shaking. Karen Brodie murdered! Why? Had it been a random crime, with Karen in the wrong place at the wrong time? What had she been doing at Kemper Park?

Too distracted to read the novel she'd brought with her, Abigail looked around Derek's apartment for something to occupy her while she waited for him. A few dishes were stacked in the sink. She washed them, taking up all of five minutes, and wiped the counters and table, though they didn't need it.

What else could she do? A couple of books had fallen over on Derek's battered old bookshelf in the living room. Abigail went to stand them up and realized the problem—one of the green marble bookends was missing. Derek must have taken it down to the rock room for some reason. Abigail tilted the books slightly to the right so they'd lean on each other and remain upright without the bookend. She dusted a few shelves then gave up on housework and sat on the couch with her book in her lap.

Two hours passed before she heard the rattle of the outer door opening. Abigail sprang to her feet, ears attuned to the tread of footsteps in the lobby. At the clack of Derek's key unlocking the door, relief flooded her.

Realizing Derek wouldn't enjoy opening the door to find her poised to pounce on him, she settled back on the couch.

The door opened and Derek walked inside. As he swung the door closed, he caught sight of Abigail, a startled, guilty expression making him look like a little kid. "Hey, Abby. I—didn't see your car."

"Maybe you didn't look in the right place," Abigail said. "I parked around the corner."

"Uh . . . okay." Derek opened the coat closet and took off the jacket he'd been wearing. The short hair looked oddly unfamiliar on him, like he was masquerading as someone else.

"Strangest thing . . . I lost my heavy coat," he said. "Can't figure out where I left it . . . I thought it might be downstairs, but it wasn't . . ."

"It'll turn up," Abigail said. Derek's too-casual mutterings were a sign of strain, as was the hollow-eyed look on his face. Derek wasn't good at hiding his feelings.

"I'm sorry to break in." Abigail kept her voice calm but didn't attempt to match Derek's offhand attitude. "I would have called, but I figured your voice mail had enough messages from me."

"Yeah . . . sorry . . . listen, I'm starving. I'm going to nuke a potpie. Do you want one?"

"No, thank you."

Derek opened the freezer and took, what seemed to Abigail, an inordinate amount of time to locate the correct box, open it, and punch a few holes in the pie's crust. She knew he was stalling, not wanting to sit down and talk to her, but after five days of trying to get in touch with him and now two hours of sitting here waiting for him to return home, she was tired of delay.

"Did you hear about your landlady?" she asked.

Derek shot Abigail a glance before returning his gaze to the pie he was placing inside the microwave. "Yeah, I heard. How did you find out?"

"Hunter Conley."

Derek punched buttons on the microwave, punched more buttons, and punched again, frustration tightening his face. If he was messing up the simple sequence required to cook a frozen potpie, he was even more tired and rattled than he appeared. "When did you see Hunter?" he asked.

"He was in the lobby waiting for you when I arrived." Abigail related what Hunter had told her.

Fury flamed in Derek's eyes. "Someone ought to shoot that—"

Abigail cut off what she feared would be a scorching burst of profanity describing Hunter's father. "At least Hunter knows he can come to you for help. Obviously he looks up to you."

Derek sighed and shoved his fingers through his short hair. "I'll talk to him tomorrow." He took a plate out of the cupboard.

"So do you know anything about what happened to Karen? I haven't seen the news report. Hunter just said she'd been murdered and her body was found in Kemper Park."

Derek slammed the plate onto the counter so hard that if the plate hadn't been made of plastic, it would have shattered. "How would I know what happened to her? Do you think I killed her?"

Startled at his reaction, Abigail fought down the fatigue and stress that made her want to lash back in kind. "You know I wasn't implying anything," she said quietly. "Don't be an idiot."

"Sorry." He gave her a weak smile. "I've just never been questioned in a murder investigation before.

"Did the police talk to you?"

"Of course they talked to me." Derek's voice went harsh again. "They'll talk to everyone who knew Karen. Why wouldn't they talk to me? I'm just the kind of guy who could take a rock and smash Karen's head in—"

"Derek!"

"Sorry. This is just too weird. I'm not going to pretend I liked Karen, but it makes me sick to think of someone . . ." His voice faded. His skin was gray-white, his jaw muscles so rigid they looked like stone he'd shaped down in his rock room.

Abigail rose to her feet and walked toward him across the worn braided rug. "Are you okay?"

"Yeah. I guess."

"What did the police ask you?"

Derek gave an explosive little laugh. "Go ahead and say it. Do they think I killed her?"

"It would never even occur to me to think they might suspect you. I only met Karen a few times, but considering the way she . . . well, she seemed like a person who would make enemies easily."

"Yeah, well, maybe her other enemies weren't about to get chucked into the street for nonpayment of rent."

"She was *still* giving you a hard time?" Karen had sworn that if Abigail brought Derek's rent up-to-date, she'd give him a clean slate.

Derek gave Abigail a strange look. "Why would she stop hounding me? I don't have the money I owe her. You didn't think I was telling the truth about just needing to deposit my paycheck, did you? You can't be *that* convinced I'm a good guy."

"Derek . . . you got my note, didn't you?"

"What note?"

"About the rent. The note I left you, right there on the table."

"*What* note?"

"I paid your rent. Everything you owed."

Derek gaped at her. "You paid?"

Abigail blushed. She hadn't expected to have to explain this while Derek stared at her in disbelief.

"I came to visit you on Monday," she said. "You weren't here. Karen saw me and pounced. She said she didn't care who paid, that as long as someone did, she'd give you a fresh start. I know this situation works well for you, with your rock equipment in the basement. You'd never find something else this good for this price. I didn't want her to evict you." Abigail offered an apologetic smile. "We're family. You were in a tight spot. I wanted to help. You're not mad, are you? Just pay me back whenever you can."

"You left me a note?"

"I put it right here." Abigail tapped the center of the kitchen table. "I don't know how you could have missed seeing it. Maybe a draft blew it to the floor."

Derek scanned the floor. With a sudden motion that made Abigail jump, he shoved the table to the side and looked at the spot where the table's pedestal base had rested. No note—just a couple of Cheerios.

"It doesn't matter," Abigail said. "Anyway, you know now."

"I wish I'd known before." There was a rough edge on Derek's voice. "I would have been a lot less nervous talking to the police."

Abigail scrutinized her brother. He looked more than tense—he looked scared. "Derek, what *did* the police say to you?"

He started to run his fingers through his hair, paused, scowled, and scrubbed his scalp with both hands until his cropped hair stood on end. "I look like such an *idiot*."

"You *are* an idiot if you think the police would suspect you of murder just because of some late rent."

"Someone bashed Karen over the head," Derek snapped. "So what's the first thing the police will want to know? Who had it in for her. Let's see . . . how about the deadbeat tenant she was about to evict—the guy she'd made a fool of a few days earlier when she destroyed any chance that he might be able to mooch big bucks off his rich folks."

The microwave beeped. Derek opened the door, snatched the potpie, and dumped it onto the plate.

"Is that why you wanted to meet with Mom and Dad?" Abigail asked flatly.

Derek whacked at the piecrust with a fork, breaking it into small pieces. "That's what the police will think."

He'd dodged the question, but under the circumstances, Abigail didn't want to press it. "Did you tell the police about the dinner?"

"No. But someone will. Probably Dad. He'd love to see me in prison for murder."

"Don't be ridiculous," Abigail said, but a chill made her shiver. Chase McCoy knew about the dinner party. Had Karen told him? It was easy to imagine Karen bragging about how she'd humiliated Derek.

What else did Chase know? Or had it all been a bluff? "*Derek's full of secrets . . . maybe you ought to ask him what he was doing last night, racing around all pale and panicked . . .*"

Last night . . . When did Karen Brodie die?

"Evidence that you had a reason to be angry with Karen isn't evidence that you murdered her," Abigail said, the words awkward and unreal on her tongue. Derek *couldn't* be paranoid enough to think he'd get accused of murder simply because he'd been angry with Karen. Something else was bothering him, something he hadn't told her. What if he *had* been out last night like Chase McCoy had said, doing things he didn't want the police to know about? Was that why the police interview had shaken him so badly?

She filled a glass with ice and water and brought it to Derek as he sat at the table, shoveling chunks of carrot and turkey into his mouth.

"Thanks," he mumbled.

"Derek . . . you're not in trouble, are you?" she asked. "I don't mean about Karen. Is there—anything you need help with?"

He kept his head bent over his plate. "So you're with Dad now? You think I'm on drugs?"

"No. I didn't say that."

"Then what would I need help with?"

"Like . . . debts, maybe?"

"The only person I owed money to was Karen, and you took care of that."

Abigail moistened her lips. "Chase McCoy is trying to pressure me into selling his paintings."

Derek gulped water and set his half-empty glass on the table. "Not surprised." He sounded relieved at this apparent change of subject. "But I figure you can handle him. And I swear I never told him you'd sell his paintings."

Abigail kept her tone matter-of-fact. "Apparently, he thinks blackmail is good business practice."

"Blackmail!"

"He hinted that he knew some things about you that you wouldn't want Mom and Dad or the police to know about, with the implication that if I wanted him to keep your secrets, I'd stock his paintings."

"*What?*"

At the incredulity and confusion on Derek's face, Abigail felt buoyant with relief. Derek plainly had no idea what "secrets" he was supposedly keeping. Chase *had* been bluffing.

"Don't worry," Abigail said. "I didn't cave in."

"That dirty little . . . what garbage did he make up about me?"

"He didn't get specific. He implied you were in debt to some scary types and that was why you were sucking up to our parents, trying to get money."

Derek snorted. "Proof?"

"None that he offered."

"The guy's a buffoon." Derek turned his attention back to his dinner. "Did you call the cops on him?"

"He caught me so off guard that I stood there staring while he walked out. And I'm sure if I did tell the police, he'd claim I completely misinterpreted his meaning. It's not like I've got any proof."

"Yeah, you and him both. He just said 'Derek's into shady stuff' and thought that was enough?"

"More or less. The best he could come up with was something about you running around in the middle of the night last night looking scared."

Instantly, Derek's countenance changed. Mockery fled, fear returned, so naked in his eyes that Abigail couldn't misread it.

"What did he say about last night?" Derek asked.

Mouth paper-dry, Abigail reached for Derek's water glass and took a few swallows.

"Abby!" Derek snatched the glass out of her hand. "What did he say?"

"Just what I told you. That you were running around in the middle of the night looking—he said something like 'pale and panicky.' Derek, what's wrong?"

He didn't answer, but the fear in his eyes told more than a mouthful of words.

Abigail pulled out a chair and sat down before her knees buckled and sent her to the floor. "You *were* out last night, doing something you're worried about. What's wrong? You've got to tell me. Did you . . . did you lie to the police about what you were doing last night?"

"I didn't kill Karen," he whispered. "I swear I didn't kill her."

"For heaven's sake, I *know* you didn't kill her. Why do you keep thinking you'll get blamed? What were you doing last night?"

A raspy laugh scratched its way out of Derek's throat. "I was at Kemper Park. I found Karen's body."

"You found—*you're* the one who found her? That's awful! Why didn't you tell me? Is that why you're afraid they'll blame you—because you're the one who called to say she'd been murdered?"

"I didn't call," Derek said. "I drove home and left her there."

CHAPTER 11

"**Y**OU'RE POSITIVE IT WASN'T BOB Chapman who left the note?" It was difficult to maintain a calm facade after the story Derek had told her, but Abigail gave it her best effort. "Brendan always says he's—quirky." That wasn't an exact quote; Brendan Rowe usually referred to his stepfather as a "half genius, half raving lunatic."

Derek took a piece of popcorn from the bowl in Abigail's lap. She'd learned years ago that Derek found talking much easier if he had something to occupy his gaze and his fingers while he spilled his guts. After a lot of experimentation, Abigail had settled, at the age of sixteen, on popcorn. Derek would take it from the bowl one piece at a time, rotate it in his fingers, examine it, and toss it into his mouth. And he'd talk, in a way she could never get him to open up otherwise.

"Chapman is quirky, but he's not crazy or vicious," Derek said. "And he's *not* a murderer."

Abigail pictured Bob Chapman with his cheery grin, wiry body, and white hair that flew in every direction. Derek called it "conductor hair"—Chapman looked like an eccentric maestro who'd finished leading a wild rendition of Tchaikovsky's 1812 Overture, cannons and all. "I'm not suggesting he killed Karen. I'm just wondering if he *did* write the note that inadvertently got her to Kemper Park."

"And he flew back from Europe for a few hours to post it on my door? He's been overseas for the past two weeks—unless you think his wife lied to me."

Abigail had to admit it didn't make sense. She could picture Chapman pulling a practical joke on Derek, but he'd want to be here to enjoy it—he wouldn't arrange for someone else to leave the note while he was thousands of miles away.

"Someone left that note knowing I'd jump to meet with Chapman, no matter how crazy the circumstances." Derek squeezed a piece of popcorn between his thumb and forefinger. "I should have realized it was a hoax when the note made this big point about not calling him, but I was so excited at the thought of another commission from Chapman . . . thought it could save my neck . . . wasn't thinking . . ."

"Whoever left the note must have known you were desperate enough to act without thinking it through."

"I did wonder if it was Karen. She'd have thought it was funny to trick me into going to the park and waiting there in the cold for a guy who would never show up."

"Then what was *she* doing there?"

"She . . . wanted to see the joke in action? But some psycho or drug dealer found her first?" Derek frowned at an unpopped kernel. "Never mind. I know it doesn't make sense. Besides, she was dressed up. Fancy new coat, dressy shoes, all that. She'd gotten her hair cut and dyed. I—noticed it when I saw her earlier that evening."

At the lurch in Derek's voice, Abigail knew what he was thinking. He'd noticed the haircut earlier, but at the park, all he'd noticed about her hair was the blood soaking it.

"A haircut," Abigail murmured.

"Yeah, and you know, she actually looked good. I always thought she was an ugly hag—sorry," he added at Abigail's reproachful glance. "But with her hair done differently and those nice clothes, she looked kind of pretty."

"She must have had a date, or some other big event last night."

"Yeah, I know. I told the police that."

"So when they figure out who she was seeing, they'll probably know who killed her," Abigail said.

"Pure genius, Holmes. But what were they doing at Kemper Park? You think their hot date involved hanging out in a freezing picnic pavilion in order to torment her deadbeat tenant?"

"No. It makes no sense at all."

"There's only one answer that does make sense. Someone lured me there to try to frame me for killing Karen."

"That's crazy!"

"Do you have a better explanation?"

"Did you keep the note? I'd like to see it."

Derek broke bits off his next piece of popcorn, using tiny, meticulous movements. "I kept it, but I can't find it. Can't figure out what I did with it."

Abigail hid her dismay. "This apartment is a black hole when it comes to notes. You'd better find it. It could be important evidence. And you've got to give the police that tea light."

Derek tensed. "How stupid would I be to give the police evidence that I was at the park?"

"You can't hide the truth."

"You don't get it, do you? You think if I 'fess up they'll shake my hand and thank me for the evidence. I found her dead and I *walked away*, then I ran back and stole evidence because it had my fingerprints on it. Does that sound like something an innocent man would do?"

"You panicked. They'll understand that, especially since you were afraid someone was trying to frame you." Abigail bit the inside of her lip, hoping they *would* understand. Why did Derek have such a knack for dealing with trouble by making it worse?

"If our roles were flipped, they'd believe *you*. Who could accuse doe-eyed, soapy-clean Abigail Wyatt of murder? But me—"

Abigail cut him off, her voice hard. She wasn't going to let him wallow in self-condemnation. "The fact that you were once a dope-smoking dolt isn't evidence of murder."

"Fine," Derek snapped. "But—"

"They don't have any evidence that you killed her—because you *didn't*. Stop making assumptions about what they'll think, and give them a little credit. And *find that note*. Maybe Karen did write it. Maybe for some reason she wanted to trick you into going to the park, but something went horribly wrong with whatever she was scheming. The note will help the police unravel what else she did that evening and maybe lead them to who killed her."

"I'll find the note, okay?" Derek pressed the heels of his hands against his eyes. "Do you have any idea why Mom was here this afternoon wanting to talk to Karen?"

"*What?*"

"The cops told me they met her at Karen's door."

"At Karen's—did you—did you see her?"

"No. I was at work. Apparently, she claimed she was interested in investing in Ohneka real estate and wanted to consult Karen about the market."

"That's absurd. She would never have gone to Karen Brodie for advice. And she never said anything to me about buying property here."

"She lied, obviously. But why was she here?"

"I have no idea. No idea at all." Abigail's thoughts whirled. Could Lillian possibly have come to offer to pay Derek's rent but had been too embarrassed to admit to the police that her son had fallen behind on his obligations? Had she been worrying about Derek ever since that wreck of a dinner party and had finally come here to see what she could do?

"I'll talk to her." She turned to face Derek. His eyes were bloodshot and his shoulders rigid.

"You need to tell the police the truth," she said. "You can't withhold information."

Derek's expression was immobile. "If you were the cops and got handed a story like the one I told you, what would *you* think?"

"I would think Karen was up to something on a couple of levels. This whole thing is completely bizarre, but maybe the police will find evidence in her apartment and everything will click into place. And, Derek, I wouldn't rule out the possibility that her fixed-up appearance was for *you*. Yes, she was nasty to you, but you told me how she used to watch you. Maybe she was interested and thought that with you being in trouble with your rent, she had enough leverage to manipulate you."

"Manipulate me into *what*? Marrying her?"

"I don't know know how her mind worked. But from what you told me, she seemed like a lonely, bitter person. Maybe she was unstable as well. Maybe whatever she was up to wasn't even rational."

"And how did she end up dead?"

"I don't know. Maybe it was random. Maybe it was a robbery. Did you notice if her purse was on the ground next to her?"

"The Eiffel Tower could have been next to her and I wouldn't have noticed. I was too freaked out."

"Okay. But you've got to tell the police everything. Promise me you will. Trying to hide the fact that you were at the park is idiotic. For one thing, Chase knows you were out last night."

"That's not proof of anything. So he saw me leave at two in the morning. When they examine Karen's body, they'll figure out she died a lot earlier than that."

"You still need to tell them everything."

"Sure, I'll tell them. If I ever get the urge to go to prison for murder,

I'll tell them." Derek crushed two pieces of popcorn against each other. "So when you talk to Mom, are you going to blast *her* for fibbing to the cops? Or do lies only count if they come from me?"

* * *

BEFORE WORDS AND SWEETS OPENED the following morning, Abigail called Chase and told him she needed to meet with him. Chase was friendly—almost jovial—on the phone, told her to bring his binder, and insisted on treating her to lunch at a soup-and-sandwich cafe. Abigail didn't want a lunch date, business or otherwise, with Chase McCoy, but neither did she want him in her store or her home. Meeting him in a neutral public setting seemed like a good idea. She needed to know exactly what Chase had seen Derek doing the night Karen Brodie died. Whatever Chase knew, the police knew by now.

Worried and distracted, Abigail went through the motions of helping customers, while trying to avoid the reproachful looks Ellie kept firing at her. Ellie had tried to talk her out of meeting with Chase—"*The guy is scary, Abby. He tried to blackmail you into selling his creep-o-rama pictures—who knows what else he's willing to try? What if he's the one who killed Karen Brodie?*"

A hand on her shoulder made Abigail jump.

"Sorry. I didn't mean to startle you."

Abigail turned at the familiar sound of Brendan's voice. "You're fine. I'm just jumpy."

"Yeah, I'll bet." He lowered his voice. "You heard about your brother's landlady, I take it."

"Yes."

"Talk to you for a minute?"

"Sure." Abigail led the way to her office.

"You okay?" he asked when they were alone.

"I'm shaken," she said.

"I can tell. So am I. I've known Karen for years." He held out a bakery bag. "Brought you a muffin. If you can steal a few minutes away, let's go for a walk. I'm betting you could use a little time out."

Trying not to show her surprise, Abigail said, "Thank you, but I really shouldn't leave Ellie."

"I think she can handle things for fifteen minutes."

True. The store hadn't been particularly busy this morning. Why not go on a walk with him? Brendan just wanted to discuss business. "All right. Let me tell her."

A few minutes later, they were strolling along Main Street. Sun shone between clouds, and the temperature was mild enough that Abigail wished she'd worn her lighter coat.

"Thanks for the muffin," she said, flattered that Brendan remembered she loved the lemon-blueberry muffins from the bakery near Words and Sweets.

"My pleasure. So how's Derek doing? Is he okay?"

"He's—pretty rattled."

Brendan shook his head. "I can't imagine who would have killed Karen. You don't expect that kind of thing in Ohneka."

"No, you don't." With new perspective, Abigail took in the familiar sights of downtown—the polished storefront windows, the wooden planter boxes that held geraniums and begonias in summertime, the wrought-iron benches beneath brass lampposts. Who would ever expect murder in a peaceful place like Ohneka?

"Does Derek have any idea what happened?" Brendan asked. "Had he seen Karen doing anything weird lately?"

"No. He really didn't know her that well."

"Yeah, she wasn't an easy person to get friendly with." Brendan slid his coat off his shoulders.

"Do *you* know anything she was up to that might have put her in danger?" Abigail asked.

"No." Brendan looked thoughtful. "She never seemed the type to get mixed up in anything illegal."

"Did you know her well?"

"Not anymore. I knew her better when we were younger. Her mom worked for Bob for a while."

"She grew up in Ohneka?"

"Yeah."

Abigail took a bite of muffin. She hadn't eaten much breakfast this morning, and the tang of blueberry and lemon tasted even more delicious than usual.

"Listen, is Derek okay staying at the house?" Brendan asked. "I know that would give some people the creeps. Does he want to go somewhere else temporarily, or move out for good? I could find him a place."

"Thanks, Brendan. I'll tell him you offered, but I think he's okay."

"I haven't heard what's going to happen to Karen's house, but if Derek does end up needing to move, just call me."

"Thanks. I will."

"So how did things go with your parents and Derek the other night? I've been wanting to ask you."

Abigail sighed. "It was a little rocky." The last thing she wanted was to tell Brendan the role Karen had played in the destruction of the evening and the mess Derek was in.

"At least they talked," Brendan said. "That's good, right?"

"Something like that," Abigail said. "So how are you doing? Is Bob running you ragged?"

Half an hour later, Brendan walked her to the back door of Words and Sweets, gave her a hug and left with the farewell words "Hang in there."

Abigail hung up her coat and headed out to the sales floor. Ellie was ringing up a transaction and a pair who looked like mother and daughter were browsing the new releases table.

After her customer left, Ellie sidled up to Abigail.

"I thought you said fifteen minutes?" she whispered. "So your watch is broken, huh?"

"Sorry."

"Sure you are." Ellie grinned. "You leave me doing all the work while you go for a little chat and a little cuddle with the property manager."

"Ellie! He was here offering to help find Derek a new place, if he needs one."

"That took half an hour?"

"We were just chatting. He was telling me about his work."

"Did he or did he not hug you?" Ellie whispered.

"Were you or were you not spying on me?" Abigail whispered back.

"He did! I told you so, Abby. I think Mira's history."

Abigail bent so she could hiss in Ellie's ear. "This is the most juvenile conversation we've ever had. He gave me a brief, completely platonic brother-hug. He's a *friend.*"

Ellie smiled and walked off. Abigail didn't want to smile in response, but she couldn't help it. Even though Brendan's visit had been business-related, it cheered her that he'd come to see her personally rather than calling—and that she'd gotten through an entire conversation with him without feeling flustered. Even though she had zero romantic interest in Brendan Rowe, it was nice to feel comfortable with him as a friend.

Zero interest.

When the time arrived for her appointment with Chase, Abigail left the store in Ellie's hands and drove to the café. She sat at a table near the window and waited, Chase's leather binder on the table in front of her.

"Hey, Abby. You're looking good." Chase pulled out the other chair and sat down across from her. "You've got amazing eyes. Like dark chocolate."

Abigail didn't respond. After the things he'd said yesterday, did he really think this was a good time to make a lame attempt at flirting?

"What's good here?" Chase opened his menu. Abigail stole a glance at him over the top of her menu as she pretended to skim the list of sandwiches. His too-wide smile didn't match the flat expression in his eyes. His good humor was faked.

After they placed their lunch orders and the server departed, Abigail handed the binder across the table. "Blackmail is a crime," she said, keeping her voice low.

"Whoa, girl!" Chase stuffed the binder under his chair. "I don't know what you're talking about."

"Would it be clearer if I had the police talk to you?"

"You've got screws loose. I haven't done anything wrong. Since when is offering a business owner a chance to sell my paintings illegal?"

"I won't be selling your paintings."

"Fine, no problem. Your loss. I'll take them to someone who appreciates real art."

It wasn't difficult to figure out why Chase was retreating from his amateurish attempt to pressure her. It had been a spur-of-the-moment tactic—maybe he'd imagined Abigail would be easy to manipulate. But with the police all over the place asking questions about Karen, Chase had probably gotten cold feet, realizing his actions could land him in prison.

"I want to know exactly what you saw Derek doing in the middle of the night, on the night you mentioned," Abigail said.

"Since we're not working together, I don't see why I should tell you anything."

"Maybe it would help me forget what happened yesterday. And it won't hurt you to tell me."

Chase got a strange look on his face, as though someone had thrown fragments of excitement, interest, and fear into a bag and shaken them up. "Derek sent you." He dropped his voice to a whisper. "Wow, he killed Karen, didn't he? I didn't think he'd have the guts."

For a moment, Abigail couldn't find breath to respond. She'd wanted to think Derek's fear that he'd be accused of killing Karen was mostly paranoia, and it rattled her to have Chase jump so rapidly to the conclusion that Derek was a killer.

"He's afraid I know something, so he sent you to scope me out," Chase said. "You go tell him it's no good trying to scare me, because I already told the police everything. If anything happens to me, he's cutting his own throat. Got it?"

Chilled, Abigail drew her coat around her shoulders. "Derek didn't kill her. And he didn't send me. Tell me what you saw that night."

"Oh, I get it." He grinned. "Oh, yeah, I had you pegged right. The little mama, trying to mop up her brother's messes. You want to know how much trouble he's in so you can try to fix it."

"This is a waste of time." Abigail stood up. "I'll talk to the police and find out what they—"

"Sit down, girl. I didn't say I wouldn't tell you."

Abigail sat.

"It was about, oh, maybe two in the morning? I was up late, painting. I do some of my best work after midnight."

If he was painting while half asleep, that would explain a lot.

"I heard Derek's door open, then loud, fast footsteps, like he was in a big hurry. Thought it was weird, of course. I heard his Jeep drive away. Went back to painting. Not too long later—maybe half an hour?—I heard him coming back. Gotta admit, I was curious, so I cracked my door open so I could have a peek. He came through the front door—I couldn't see him real well; the night-light in the foyer is pretty dim, but man, I could see enough to know he was scared. He raced inside and shut his door. I thought he was in trouble with some loan shark or drug dealer." He leaned close to Abigail and whispered, "So what was the deal? Karen was bragging about how he was trying to get money off your parents and she woke them up to what a loser he is, but it wasn't just about the money, was it? Derek never seemed like a guy who cared that much about money. Was it some romancey thing that went bad? I know she was older than him, but some guys like that, and when he first moved in, Karen was always yakking about him—"

"Derek was not in a relationship with Karen," Abigail whispered back angrily. "And what makes you think she was killed at two in the morning?"

Chase shrugged his broad shoulders. "How would I know when she died? Maybe you ought to ask Derek."

* * *

HE WASHED THE HEAVY MARBLE bookend, but not too well. Traces of blood would remain in the more porous, unpolished portions of the stone.

He didn't like handling the bookend. It was a crude, repulsive weapon, and he felt nauseated whenever he thought of the way bone had fractured and droplets of blood had spattered as he brought it down again and again on Karen's skull. Given a choice, he would have preferred to strangle her, but a rock would be the obvious weapon for Derek Wyatt to wield. Besides, he didn't want any similarities between this crime and Leslie's death. With sixteen years and a couple thousand miles between Leslie's death and Karen's, he hoped no one would make any connections, but still, it would be foolish to take that chance.

Stupid Karen. Wherever she was now, he hoped she was sorry. All that talk about "owing" her—he hadn't forced her to help him. He hadn't forced her to steal that key to Leslie's apartment. She'd *wanted* to help—she'd been all giggling and gleeful at what he planned to do.

If only there were a way to bring her back for a few minutes, he'd like to watch her grovel and cry and tell him she never should have tried to make a fool of him. Then he'd kick her back to the flames of hell and she could roast for eternity, knowing he was the one who'd sent her there.

Not that he *liked* killing. He hated it. He'd fantasized about hurting Leslie, of course, after the way she'd rejected him, yelling at him in the middle of the student center, telling everyone in earshot that he was a controlling jerk and she was sick of him. All the eyes focused on him—the twisted, sneering smiles—the humiliation so intense that it burned like being drenched in acid. He'd wanted to grab her right there and—

But he hadn't. Leslie *would* pay, but if he'd lashed out at her then, he would have paid with a prison sentence. He'd always been smart enough and strong enough to plan. So he'd waited patiently, letting her think she'd won—waited until everyone thought he'd handled her rejection with humor and good grace. And then—

He *still* hadn't meant to kill her. The vandalism would have been triumph enough, and he'd gloried in the thought of her horror and rage when she found her precious designer clothes slashed to pieces and everything she owned splashed with paint. He could have smiled at her every time they crossed paths on campus, knowing *she* knew he'd gotten his revenge, but she was helpless to prove it.

Humiliation for humiliation. An eye for an eye.

It wasn't his fault she'd changed her plans and come home early that night. What was he supposed to do when she caught him there? Let her win? Let her strut around bragging about how she'd put her pathetic ex-boyfriend in jail? Before he'd stopped to consider what he was doing, he'd picked up that silvery belt hanging from a rack in her closet, and looped it around her neck and pulled it tight. He'd thought about stopping before it was too late, but he couldn't. He couldn't let her tell anyone.

Maybe he liked killing a *little*. The terror in her face had been delicious payback, balm that soothed the wound she'd carved inside of him. Maybe he *was* garbage, not good enough for her or anyone. But he'd won.

Next time he was in the area he ought to go put flowers on Leslie's grave. It had been too long, and she deserved that mark of respect from him. She knew he'd won; he could be kind now. But he'd better not go near her grave until Derek Wyatt was convicted of murdering Karen Brodie.

He'd leave some flowers for Karen too, but nothing too nice—maybe a few carnations. Maybe she'd see them from hell and compare them to the bouquet of roses on Leslie's grave. She'd know he still loved Leslie, not her. That would sting, and it would serve Karen right for putting him to all this trouble.

Carefully, he set the bookend on a folded towel to dry.

* * *

ABIGAIL DIDN'T CALL HER PARENTS to tell them she was coming. She didn't want to give them a chance to claim it wasn't a convenient night for a visit. Better to just show up. If they were out for the evening, she'd have wasted a lot of time driving to Syracuse and back, but that didn't annoy her like it normally would. At least driving made her feel she was doing something, as opposed to pacing around her house, fighting the urge to go grab Derek and shake sense into him. Couldn't he see how he was digging himself into a hole? Sooner or later, the police would figure out he'd lied to them. Through Chase McCoy, they already knew he'd been acting strange the night Karen died. At least Derek's two o'clock venture to retrieve the tea light had been many hours removed from the time of Karen's death, but still, it looked odd.

Chase made Abigail's skin crawl. What had *he* been doing at the time of Karen's death?

Probably painting warped pictures. If Chase had killed Karen, she doubted he'd have had the sangfroid to waltz into her store the next afternoon and try to bully her into selling his paintings. He wouldn't have wanted to do anything to risk attracting the attention of the police.

Abigail pushed Chase out of her thoughts. Figuring out who killed Karen wasn't her job, and the police would have already determined whether or not Chase was a suspect. Her concern was her own family.

Couldn't Derek see how much better it would be if told the truth voluntarily, rather than waiting for the police to uncover his lies? If he was candid with them, they'd be a lot more likely to trust him. But Derek had always assumed people would think the worst of him—assumed and acted on that assumption, which inevitably made things worse.

She'd wanted to push Derek harder last night and make him realize the futility of keeping secrets, but she could tell from his expression and that gritty tone in his voice that if she pushed, he'd start erecting a wall between them. She'd spent too much time scraping her fingertips bloody tearing down his walls to want to provoke him into building a new one. It was wiser to give him some time to think about it, and then talk to him in a couple of days.

Abigail decelerated along the exit ramp. How best should she approach her mother tonight? The thought of Lillian going to talk to Karen Brodie—and then, when confronted by the police, making up some excuse about wanting advice on real estate—both bewildered and excited Abigail.

Lillian had wanted to talk to Karen about Derek—no other explanation even began to make sense—and regardless of what she'd planned to say, the fact that she'd *done* something regarding Derek stirred new hope inside Abigail. She'd finally stepped out of that passive, protective shell where she'd hidden for the past five years and had taken action.

Derek's words echoed in her thoughts. *"Are you going to blast her for fibbing to the cops?"* Not a good approach. If she wanted to find out what her mother had been doing at Karen's, she needed to approach the subject with gentleness and tact.

Lights glowed in the windows of the Wyatts' handsome colonial home. *Good.* They were home. Abigail parked in the driveway, whispered a quick prayer, and walked to the front door.

She gave a courtesy knock and opened the door. The spicy scent of pumpkin bread wafted pleasantly through the air, and some of the tension eased out of her back muscles. Pumpkin bread was one of Lillian's specialties, and the smell of it would always mean autumn to Abigail.

"Hello, it's me," she called out.

"Come on in, honey," her father called from the direction of the family room. Pleased—and relieved—that his tone had no edge to it, Abigail hung her coat in the closet and headed for the family room.

He was sitting in his recliner near the fireplace, dressed in his favorite relaxation clothes—old blue sweats and a faded forest-green velour bathrobe that Abigail had given him for Christmas many years ago. The sight of it made her add an item to her mental Christmas list: *new bathrobe for Dad.* The television was on with the sound turned low and a copy of *Scientific American* lay open on his lap.

"Hi, Dad." She kissed his cheek.

"Didn't know you were coming. Mother must have forgotten to mention it."

"I didn't forewarn her. It was—an impulse trip."

He looked down and flipped a page in his magazine. "Have some pumpkin bread. It's on the counter."

"Thanks, I will." Dinner had been a bowl of canned soup and a handful of baby carrots, and the sweet scent of the bread made her stomach growl.

She cut a thick slice from the loaf on the cutting board, put it on a napkin, and returned to the family room. Paul had turned off the TV, a mark of respect that she appreciated. He knew she wanted to talk.

Abigail sat on the couch. "Where's Mother?"

"Movie. Girls' night out. Her book club wanted to see the movie version of—can't remember which book, but they read it a few months ago."

"Oh." Abigail's hopes deflated. "What showing did they go to, do you know?"

"They were meeting at seven thirty. Why?"

"I was hoping to talk to her." But meeting at seven thirty meant a later showing, which meant a late arrival home, which meant Abigail wouldn't be able to talk to her about Karen Brodie tonight. Lillian preferred an early bedtime, and wouldn't want to hold a weighty conversation at ten thirty at night.

Abigail took a bite of rich, cinnamon-laced bread and had the odd thought of wondering what Karen Brodie had eaten for her last meal. Something delicious? Something prepackaged and hurried? What kind of food had she enjoyed?

And why was Abigail thinking like this? What did it matter now whether Karen had been a frozen-dinners woman or a gourmet cook who concocted a new dish every day of the week?

It matters because she was a real person, with real emotions and real preferences. A couple of days ago she was eating and working and moving forward, and now she's dead.

"I've got something for you. I was going to bring it to you last week, but it wasn't finished yet." Paul stood. "Come into the garage."

Carrying her pumpkin bread, Abigail followed him into the chilly garage.

Paul switched on the space heater he kept near his woodworking tools. "There it is. Is that what you had in mind?"

"It's beautiful!" Abigail set her pumpkin bread on the workbench and picked up the umbrella stand. When she'd mentioned offhandedly a few weeks ago that she planned to buy an umbrella stand, her father had instantly offered to make one for her.

"Walnut," he said. "The whitewashed finish should match that bench you have in your entryway."

"It's perfect." Abigail ran her hand over one of the panels. "Thank you, Dad."

He shrugged and took it out of her hands. "I'll set it near the front door so you don't forget it when you leave."

Abigail glanced at the boards propped against the table saw and recognized the pieces of the same style of bookshelf Paul had made for her when she bought her house. "Oh, you're making a new bookshelf. For whom?"

Paul averted his eyes. "Don't know yet," he said gruffly, heading for the door.

Surprised at his obvious discomfort, Abigail picked up her pumpkin bread and followed him. He didn't know? Her father always planned things in advance.

A bookshelf. Derek desperately needed a new bookshelf; the one he had was scratched, ancient, and leaned to one side. Abigail had mentioned that to her mother when Lillian had asked about Derek's living situation prior to the dinner.

Could her father have been planning . . . ? Abigail didn't dare ask.

She sat on the couch and Paul resumed his favorite seat near the fireplace. "I hope you know we don't blame you for what happened at Derek's," he said.

Able to finally set that fear aside, Abigail relaxed against the comfortable couch. "Dad, it didn't have to end like it did. He deserves more of a chance than that."

"I'm willing to give him all the chances in the world if he shows he really wants to change. But what I saw was the same old Derek, only this time playing a role to try to wring money out of us."

"He's not the Derek you remember. I'm not saying he's perfect, but when he came to Ohneka a year and a half ago, I could tell something had changed inside him. I don't know what happened, but he was . . . different. He'd broken up with the girl he was living with, and within a couple of months he quit drinking—which was *not* easy for him—"

"I'm not disputing that he's made some progress."

"So . . . as soon as he's perfect, he's welcome to check in with you again?"

"Smart-mouthed kid," Paul muttered, looking away. Like Derek—and unlike Lillian—he had little skill at hiding his emotions. Confusion and unhappiness showed in his face. "I can't risk letting Derek into a position where he can break your mother's heart again. She's suffered enough because of his choices."

"How will you know whether or not he's trustworthy unless you give yourself a chance to get to know him? He never *asked* for money. You only assumed that's what he wanted."

"Considering his financial problems and the fact that he's trying to start a business, it's not hard to nail his motives."

"That's not fair."

Paul's shoulders twitched in an irritable shrug. "Maybe I didn't give him enough of a chance the other night. But all the signs pointed to the same old Derek. Sober, maybe, but the same old Derek who used to have your mother crying every night of the week."

Abigail wanted to ask what signs he'd seen, besides Derek's financial troubles, but she could tell he was getting angry. Time to try a new tactic. "Why did Mother go to visit Derek's landlady yesterday?"

Paul's brow creased. "The woman who barged in demanding the rent?"

"Yes. Karen Brodie."

"Why in heaven's name would Mother go talk to her?"

He looked so bewildered that Abigail realized she'd blundered. Lillian hadn't told Paul she was going to see Karen. Why not? Because she feared he'd disapprove?

At Abigail's silence, Paul asked, "Who told you she was visiting that Brodie woman? Derek?"

"Yes. He didn't see her, but he heard . . ." Did Paul know Karen Brodie was dead? Even if he hadn't heard anything about it on the news, surely Lillian would have told him. But if she hadn't told him she'd gone to Karen's . . .

"Heard what?" Paul frowned at her. "Derek heard what?"

Abigail stalled by taking a bite of pumpkin bread. She should have waited until she could talk to Lillian directly, like she'd planned.

"Abigail, what did Derek say?"

She couldn't evade it now. "I don't know if you heard, but Karen Brodie was murdered Thursday night."

Paul's eyes widened behind his bifocals. "She was murdered!"

"Yes. They found her body yesterday in Kemper Park—that's a big park on the shore of Lake Ohneka. The police have been talking to people who knew her, looking for information. Naturally they talked to Derek, since he's one of her tenants."

Paul sat up straight. "They questioned Derek?"

"Of course they did. They'll want to talk to anyone who saw her recently."

"What did Derek say about it?"

Abigail set her half-eaten pumpkin bread aside, her heart pounding. She couldn't possibly tell her father that Derek had found Karen's body and walked away, rather than risk police attention. "He . . . he said the police had asked him if he had any idea of her plans for Thursday night, if she was seeing anybody, that kind of thing. Derek didn't know anything about her personal life, so he couldn't help them."

"Do they think it was some boyfriend who killed her?"

"I don't think they said anything to indicate one way or the other. They were just asking questions. Maybe it was a random crime."

"What did Derek say about your mother?"

Realizing she was repeatedly pushing her hair behind her ear, Abigail lowered her hands to her lap. "He . . . apparently when the police came to Karen's house to look around and talk to the tenants, Mother was there, at Karen's door. She told the police she'd had an appointment with Karen."

"An appointment!" Paul rose halfway out of his chair and sank back again. "What would she want with Miss Brodie?"

"She told the police that you two were interested in investing in the rental market in Ohneka and she'd come to consult Karen."

Paul frowned deeply, carving creases from the corners of his mouth all the way to his jaw. His expression confirmed what Abigail had already known: Lillian had lied.

Paul stood. He lumbered to the fireplace and twisted the dial to lower the level of the gas flames. "You heard this from Derek?"

"Yes."

"He's got his story messed up. We have no plans to invest in Ohneka."

Abigail traced her fingernail over the dusky blue fabric of the couch cushion. "He was telling me what the police told him. He didn't see Mother or know she was there until they told him."

"Sounds like a bunch of malarkey."

"Maybe she didn't tell you what she was doing. Isn't it possible she wanted to . . . well, maybe offer to help pay some of Derek's rent?"

"Your mother knows that the way to help someone is not by enabling their irresponsible behavior."

Abigail's cheeks warmed at the thought of the check she'd handed to Karen.

"And if she wanted to bail him out financially—which she wouldn't—she'd talk to Derek directly." Paul slid his hands into the pockets of his bathrobe and stood staring at Abigail. His gaze would have made her uncomfortable, but he didn't seem to be seeing her. "How did she die?" he asked. "The landlady. What did the police say?"

Abigail started to speak but choked back the words as she realized she didn't know if the police had told Derek how Karen died or if he knew that fact only through his own observation. "I don't know," she said. "I didn't talk to them myself. Maybe there was something about it on the news."

"Abigail."

His tone evoked the same surge of guilt it had when she was a child. Hadn't Kyle told her yesterday what a bad liar she was? Why did she think she could get away with lying to her father?

"I want to know what Derek said to you." His voice was gravelly.

She'd blundered again. If she'd told him straight out how Karen died, he would have assumed the information came from the police or the news, but now her discomfort and hesitation had marked this fact as incriminating. *Incriminating? Derek didn't kill her!*

But he did lie to the police about what he'd done that night.

Knowing silence would make things worse, Abigail spoke carefully. "He said she'd been hit on the head."

Paul stood so rigidly that he looked as though he was bracing himself. "What was Derek doing Thursday night?"

"You can't possibly think Derek had anything to do with what happened to Karen."

"I didn't say he did. I asked what he was doing on Thursday."

Paul *was* worried that Derek might be involved, or he wouldn't have asked the question. How could he think that of his own son? If Derek ever found out—

For a moment, she almost repeated Derek's lie about the movie and the hamburger place, but she couldn't do it. She wouldn't lie for him. "You'll have to ask Derek," she said quietly.

CHAPTER 12

PAUL OPENED THE FRIDGE. "Would you like strawberry jam, love?"

"No, thank you, just a touch of butter." Lillian made her words casual, like this was any other Sunday morning, like her head wasn't throbbing from tension and her stomach contracting in queasy spasms that made her sure she wouldn't be able to eat a bite. Paul brought the buttered toast and set it in front of her.

"Thank you, dear."

"A pleasure." As Paul sat down, Lillian's gaze flicked involuntarily toward the newspaper. She'd checked while Paul was in the shower and had found another article about Karen Brodie. Paul hadn't seen the report of her murder in yesterday's paper; on Saturdays, he started early with household tasks and kept himself so busy that he rarely did more than glance at the sports section. But today, he would read most of the paper.

This new article repeated a few facts from yesterday's report: a woman walking her dog had discovered Karen's body in Kemper Park, and the police were investigating. The article gave a little of Karen's background, relating how she'd grown up in Ohneka and had returned there after graduating from college. It quoted an old high school teacher who remembered her as "a sharp girl, extremely bright." Given the scarcity of personal comments about her, Lillian suspected that Karen had been a very isolated person. If she always behaved the way she had at Derek's the other night, it wasn't surprising that no one had been close to her.

Though the article was not prominently placed, the words *Ohneka Stunned by Brutal Murder* would catch Paul's eye, and once he brought up the subject, she knew she'd have to confess that the police had confronted her at Karen Brodie's door. She should have told him yesterday, or the day before, but hadn't been able to make herself do it. Last night, she'd lingered at Theresa's house after the movie, chatting over dessert, counting on Paul's going to bed without her. But when she'd returned home, he'd been in the family room, reading a magazine. She'd made a show of exhaustion and had hurried to bed before he could do much more than greet her. *I'll tell him tomorrow,* she'd promised herself.

Now it was tomorrow, and the words were as firmly lodged in her throat as they'd been last night.

Paul picked up the newspaper and scanned the front page as he spooned oatmeal into his mouth. Lillian watched him out of the corner of her eye. Any moment now he'd see the article, recognize the name . . .

He set the paper down. "How are you this morning, dear?"

"Fine. Just a little tired." He had to have seen the article. He'd scanned the entire front page.

Paul stirred the oatmeal in his bowl, not looking at her. He appeared pallid and tired, Lillian realized. No wonder—he'd stayed up far past his usual bedtime. But it was more than that. He looked worried. Maybe she shouldn't tell him this morning. If he already had something on his mind, then adding to his stress wouldn't be a kind thing to do. She could tell him this afternoon, after church.

Or maybe she'd never have to tell him at all. Why worry him? Probably nothing would come of the coincidence that she'd been at Karen's door when the police arrived. Even if they did mention her visit to Derek and Derek questioned her tale about rental properties, what would it matter? Would the police give his word more credibility than hers? Unlikely.

Lillian blinked away the wetness in her eyes. Was she glad that the police might think her son was unreliable, when *she* was the one who had fudged the truth?

This was all so ridiculous. She was worrying too much. By now, the police would be finished with routine questioning and moving on to focus on genuine suspects. They wouldn't even be interested enough in Lillian to ask Derek about her. Feeling better, she took a bite of toast.

By the time she'd finished her toast, Paul still hadn't turned a page in the paper, nor did he seem to be really reading it.

"Dear, you look under the weather," Lillian remarked. "Are you feeling all right?"

Paul set his spoon in his empty bowl and faced her. From the seriousness in his expression and the way he straightened his shoulders, Lillian knew he was about to say something important. She prepared herself to act shocked if he told her he'd just read an article about Derek's landlady being murdered.

"Abigail came to visit last night," he said.

"Oh, she did? I'm sorry I missed her. I've been wanting to call her but thought it might be better to wait a bit until we'd all had time to . . . recover."

Paul laid his hand on top of hers. "Honey . . . apparently Derek fed her some strange tale about you going over there a couple of days ago to visit his landlady."

"Oh." Lillian focused on the toast crumbs on her plate, too uncomfortable to meet Paul's gaze. Obviously the police *had* told Derek and Derek had told Abigail. "I'm sorry. I should have told you."

Paul squeezed her hand. "You *were* there?"

"I . . . oh, I know it was a poor idea. I wanted to talk to Karen Brodie about Derek. I wanted to know what he was really doing, what she'd seen."

"Lillian! Why would you do that?"

Lillian patted her cheeks with her napkin, absently wishing she could wipe away the heat of embarrassment. "I could tell she was the type of woman who liked making hurtful remarks, but I thought if I spoke to her face-to-face, I could elicit a more accurate picture of Derek."

Paul kept squeezing her hand. "I wish you'd told me."

"I know. But I didn't think you'd like the idea. I know Abigail keeps us up to date on Derek, but she seems overly optimistic, doesn't she? And Miss Brodie seemed the opposite. I thought perhaps her perspective would balance Abigail's." She looked up at him. "I want to know what our son is doing, Paul."

"You're inviting pain."

"Sometimes ignorance hurts worse than anything."

Paul sandwiched her hand between both of his. "Honey, you know Karen Brodie was killed two nights ago."

Lillian nodded. "I was there when the police came to check her apartment."

"Did they say anything about Derek?"

"No. Well, I told them I'd met Karen Brodie once when I was visiting him, and I told them where he worked."

Paul's face was colorless, and he held her hand so tightly that fear surged through Lillian. Whatever was troubling him, he hadn't yet hit the worst of it. "Honey, I'm afraid the police might be interested in Derek. Last night, Abigail got very strange when I asked her if she knew how Miss Brodie died."

"Strange in what way?"

"She started to say something, stopped herself, then gave some excuse about how maybe the news would have some information on it. I pressed her and she said Miss Brodie had been hit on the head. Then I asked her what Derek was doing the night of the murder and she wouldn't tell me."

"Perhaps she didn't know."

"She did. You know the look Abigail gets when she doesn't want to say something? That stiff, blank look?"

Lillian's heartbeat accelerated. "But just because she wouldn't tell you doesn't mean it relates to Miss Brodie. Maybe he was . . . out drinking."

"Maybe."

"You can't think Derek would . . . would . . . kill Miss Brodie over a rent dispute!"

"I don't want to think it's possible. But . . . ." His gaze flicked to the dining room where the mended china hutch stood against the wall. "We know he has the capacity to lose control of himself when he's furious."

* * *

A MORNING SPENT CUTTING AND shaping pieces of lace agate for a new bracelet worked enough of the tension out of Derek's system to leave him feeling a little ridiculous at his panic over the visit from the cops. How could he have been so paranoid? Those questions had been routine. Only his guilt over having been at Kemper Park had led him to think the police were interested in him as a suspect. His flub about referring to the picnic area wasn't a flub at all. What was so suspicious about associating a park with picnics? Let Turner and Bartholomew try to make something out of *that* in front of a jury. And so what if Chase had seen Derek run out in the middle of the night? Chase couldn't know where he'd gone, and that was hours after Karen's murder.

What would happen to Karen's house now? Who was her heir? Derek's stomach sank at the thought of the house being sold by whichever sibling or niece or nephew inherited it and the new owner tossing him out. It would be tough finding a new place.

Too bad for you. At least you're still alive. The image of Karen's bloodied skull and her body sprawled on the concrete floor of the picnic pavilion made Derek feel small and queasy. Any decent person would have immediately reported her death.

But since when had he ever been a decent person?

He wished he hadn't told Abigail about finding Karen. She'd caught him off guard with the news that Chase had seen him rushing off to retrieve the tea light, and it had seemed easier to tell her than to evade her questions. But he should have known how she'd react. *"Tell the police. You've got to tell the police."* She didn't get it. She thought justice would always win. It would probably never occur to her that the police could arrest the wrong guy. It must be nice to go through life with that kind of buttercups-and-sunshine perspective, but why *wouldn't* she view the world that way? Things always worked for Abigail.

"Mr. Wyatt?"

The voice behind Derek made him jump. He jerked the agate away from the grinding wheel before he damaged it and turned to face his visitor. Over the noise of the machinery, he hadn't heard footsteps.

Detectives Turner and Bartholomew stood near the doorway of the rock room. Derek's heart lurched again. *Stay calm, bozo. Routine, remember? Or maybe they're here to tell you they nailed the killer.*

Derek flipped the switch to stop the grinding wheels. "Hi. Sorry. Didn't hear you coming."

The two men approached him. "What are you working on?" Turner asked.

"Bracelet." Derek showed him the piece of agate stuck to a wooden dowel with green dop wax. *Routine. It's routine.* "One of these big ones, two medium ones, six small ones, copper setting. What do you guys need?"

"What kind of car do you drive?" Turner asked.

Derek's mental song of *"routine"* went suddenly out-of-tune. "Uh . . . it's a 2004 Jeep Liberty."

"Color?"

"White. Used to be white, anyway. I need to wash it." *He already knows what I drive,* Derek thought. *All that info is in his cop database. Why the questions?*

To give me a chance to get spooked?

"Were you driving your Jeep last Thursday evening?" Turner asked.

Derek's palms went sweaty, right on cue. "Sure. I only have one car. Why?"

"Were you at Kemper Park on Thursday evening, Mr. Wyatt?"

A string of profanities that would have permanently damaged Abigail's eardrums circled in Derek's brain. Someone had seen him there?

"Listen, if you guys want to chat, come upstairs. It's a lot more comfortable." Derek hung his work apron on a hook and went to the sink to wash his hands. Was there a witness? If there was, and Derek denied being there . . .

But how reliable could the witness be? Someone called the cops and said, "I saw a white Jeep at Kemper Park the night Karen Brodie died"—so what? His wasn't the only Jeep in town. No way would a witness—if there even *was* a witness—be observant enough to remember the license plate number. And Turner hadn't actually *said* there was a witness. He'd only asked Derek what kind of car he drove then jumped to asking him if he'd been at the park. He was guessing and trying to fluster Derek into admitting something.

Derek worked the suds higher up his arms, cleaning off the tiny balls of oil that clung to the hairs on his forearms. Turner didn't have anything on him. Yeah, he was suspicious. No way around that. But suspicion wasn't enough. He was fishing, hoping Derek would chomp down on the hook.

Derek dried his arms and led the way upstairs to his apartment. "Have a seat," he said. He didn't want to extend the visit, but after moving up here on the pretext that it would be more comfortable, it would be awkward if he didn't invite them to sit.

They sat on the couch. Derek took the chair with its leather cushion and inlays of polished agate. "I don't know what the story is about my Jeep," he plunged in, "but I wasn't at Kemper Park. I already told you where I was that night—theater, burger joint, home. That's it." He spread his hands in a gesture of bewilderment, feeling the wetness along his sides and back where his shirt stuck to his sweaty skin. Should he make up some excuse for where he'd gone when Chase saw him leaving in the middle of the night? No. Better not to bring it up. If they mentioned it, he'd shrug and say he hadn't thought it mattered because they'd only asked him where he'd been between seven and midnight.

Turner and Bartholomew remained silent for a few beats. Though they didn't exchange any glances, Derek was certain they were communicating via telepathy: *The kid's a liar.*

Bartholomew spoke in that deep voice that sounded like he'd pilfered it from some fat-guy opera singer. "May we have a look at your Jeep?"

If they were asking permission, they didn't have a warrant. If they didn't have a warrant, they didn't have enough evidence to get one. Derek had no idea what they thought they could gain by just looking at his Jeep—did they think he had a bloodied tire iron sitting on the front seat?—but he wasn't taking chances. "I don't think there's any point to looking at it. It has nothing to do with your case."

"Do you have a license plate holder from the Grand Canyon?"

Sweat dribbled down Derek's sides. That stupid license plate holder. He'd never bothered to change it when he'd bought the used Jeep. "What does that have to do with anything?" he snapped. *Wrong attitude. Too defensive.* "Look, sorry, guys. I know you're just doing your job, but you're wasting my time. I told you before that I didn't know anything about Karen's personal life. I don't know what she was doing the night she died, and I have no idea who killed her."

"At about ten past nine last Thursday night," Turner said, "a white Jeep Liberty was parked outside the picnic pavilion at Kemper Park, a few slots to the right of Karen Brodie's Ford Escort."

Derek wondered if it were possible for fear alone to crush his lungs. There *was* a witness. Or was Turner still bluffing? *Sure, idiot. He just managed to guess where you parked in relation to Karen's car.*

Derek could hear Abigail whispering *"I told you so"* in his ear. It would have been better to tell them the truth at first than to let them find out from a witness, but he'd been so sure no one had seen him there. What kind of eagle-eyed kook wandered around the park on a cold November night, taking mental snapshots of old Jeeps?

"Was that your car, Mr. Wyatt?" Turner asked.

Derek licked his lips. What else did they have? A partial license plate number? If the witness had noticed his license plate holder, he might have noticed the numbers. Should Derek stonewall and say the Jeep wasn't his? If all the police could ever get on him was the fact that he'd fought with Karen over the rent and one witness had seen a car that looked like Derek's at Kemper Park, that wouldn't be enough for a conviction. Why admit to anything? It would just open the door to—

"I'm guessing you don't play poker," Turner said. "And if you do, I'm guessing you usually lose."

Anger and embarrassment brought a new rush of blood to Derek's face.

"What were you doing at Kemper Park on Thursday night?" Turner asked.

Derek's mind raced. *Admit it—don't admit it—*

Turner shifted his large body on the couch and Derek knew the wooden bar that ran behind the thin foam cushions was pressing uncomfortably against his spine. No one lasted long on that couch unless they used the throw pillows for extra padding.

"I wasn't at Kemper Park." Derek made his decision. "I don't know whose car your witness saw, but it wasn't mine."

"One week ago, Karen Brodie interrupted you during a family dinner," Turner said.

"Yeah, she demanded the rent, dropped a few insults, and left. That was it. The rent got paid, by the way. My sister helped me out."

"Who was there at the dinner?"

"Just my parents and my sister."

"What's your relationship with your parents like?"

Derek's neck burned. Turner knew the answer already, or it wouldn't have occurred to him to open the subject. He was prodding Derek into a position where he'd have to admit that Karen's appearance at dinner had smashed the budding reconciliation to pulp. He wasn't going to let Turner drag the story out question by painful question.

"It's rotten," Derek said. "And yeah, things were going well at the dinner and we were making some headway in being nice to each other until Karen barged in. Now we're back to not speaking to each other, which is fine with me."

"What prompted your decision to try to reconcile with your parents?"

Who had given them all this information? Abigail thought Karen might have talked to Chase and told him what she'd done to Derek. Or had his parents told the police he was a slimy, conniving loser? "What do you mean what prompted it? Maybe I was sick of being the black sheep."

"Understandable," Turner said. "I believe you're in the process of starting up a business selling polished rock jewelry and so on."

"Yeah."

"It takes a hunk of money to get a business off the ground, doesn't it?"

"It's not free," Derek said.

"You must need money badly right now," Turner said. "That's tough that Karen Brodie wrecked your chances with your parents."

CHAPTER 13

"Morning, Abby." Ellie Stuart's usual greeting sounded a little flat as she passed Abigail on the way to the office at the back of Words and Sweets. She returned a few minutes later and started arranging chocolates on a platter in the display case.

"More gingerbread–milk chocolate squares," she reported. "We sold out yesterday."

"I'm not surprised." Abigail found it difficult not to sound flat herself. Between worrying about Derek and worrying what her mother's reaction would be when her father reported on Abigail's visit, Abigail hadn't slept much.

"So is there anything new on that horrible situation with Derek's landlady?" Ellie asked.

"Not that I know of."

"I tried to squeeze some info out of Kyle—he grew up in Ohneka, so I thought he might have known her, and might have heard if she was, you know, messed up in anything bad, like drugs or an abusive relationship. He said her name sounds familiar, and he thinks she might have worked a summer at his parents' resort, but he never really knew her. That's it. Real helpful source of gossip, huh? Men! Did Derek say anything about it? Do the police have any idea what happened?"

Abigail debated how to answer that question. She hadn't told Ellie that Derek was at Kemper Park the night Karen died. That was too heavy a burden to put on Ellie. Plus, Ellie wasn't good at keeping her mouth shut. "No new developments, at least as far as I know."

"Could have been some crazy meth addict," Ellie suggested. "She might have been in the wrong place at the wrong time. But then again, if she's as nasty as you described, she might have made someone pretty mad."

Abigail scrutinized Ellie's face, wondering if she was hinting at the fact that Derek had been angry with Karen. But Ellie just looked tired—as tired as Abigail felt. Her eyelids were puffy and there was a small smudge of mascara under one eye.

"Are you all right?" Abigail asked, flattening a box she'd emptied of books.

"Yeah." Ellie sighed deeply and slid the glass door on the display case shut. "I had a bad night. Kyle and I broke up."

"Oh, Ellie! I'm so sorry."

She must have overdone the sympathy. Ellie arched her eyebrows and smiled crookedly. "It's not *that* tragic. Yeah, it hurt, but you know . . . for a while now . . ." She shrugged. "I wasn't sure Kyle and I were the greatest match. And he hadn't been calling as much, and seemed kind of distant—I could tell he was pulling back."

The fact that normally talkative Ellie hadn't mentioned the growing distance between her and Kyle told Abigail it was a painful topic. "I'm sorry."

Ellie fluffed one of the Thanksgiving-plaid bows on the front of the display case. "He said he really liked me and all the usual compliments, but he wasn't sure we had a future." She smiled. "He said he was too old for me, which I suppose means I'm too young for him, which is a nice way of saying he thinks I'm immature."

"Ellie, you are *not* immature. How old is he?"

"Oh, I'm not sure. Mid-thirties, maybe? A few years—or a decade—older than me, yeah." She giggled. "You know, it hurts to get dumped, but deep down, I think I'm relieved. Sure, I bawled for a while, but I think it was mainly crying for lost dreams, if that makes sense."

"It does." Abigail hid her relief that Ellie wasn't devastated about the breakup. "You wanted him to be the right one for you, but you don't think he was, and you're not excited at the prospect of starting over."

"Yep. That's it." She sighed. "And you gotta admit—the guy is one handsome hunk, even if he is an old fogy."

Abigail was tempted to say *I hadn't noticed,* but figured that would be pushing credibility too far. "Mid-thirties isn't exactly old fogy material to some of us," she said instead, and felt her cheeks burn. She'd meant it as a joke about her age, but it came out sounding like she'd set her sights on Kyle.

Ellie smiled. "Well, you're welcome to the old geezer, but I don't know, Abby . . . I'm not sure he's your type." Despite the smile, her eyes looked troubled.

Mortified, Abigail stammered, "I—I didn't mean to imply—"

Ellie's face went hot pink. "Oh no, seriously, I'm not being possessive or jealous or whatever. Like I said, I've been wondering for a while if he's right for me, and last night clinched it—he isn't. If you want him, he's yours. I just have a hard time imagining . . ." Her voice faded. "Let's change the subject. I'm through with Kyle Stratton and don't want to talk about him anymore. Snack?" She held out a chocolate. "Dark chocolate and orange fondant."

"I'll take it," Abigail plucked the candy from Ellie's plastic-gloved fingers, glad for the change of subject, but unable to stop herself from wondering what Ellie would have put after *"I have a hard time imagining"* if she hadn't censored herself. *"I have a hard time imagining Kyle could ever be interested in someone as dull as you"*? Ellie would never say something so cutting, but would she be able to prevent herself from thinking it?

The chime sounded. Abigail hastily swallowed her last bite of chocolate and focused on the two men entering the store, glad for something to think about besides Kyle and Ellie.

"Good morning," Abigail said. "Can I help you find something?"

Both men glanced around the store. Behind the chocolate display case, Ellie smiled a greeting.

"Ms. Wyatt." The older man spoke as both of them moved toward Abigail. "I'm Detective Jeffrey Turner, Ohneka Police. This is Detective Abe Bartholomew." Turner showed her a badge. Abigail studied it, not because she doubted his identity, but because she wanted to delay the moment when she had to look him in the face. *Derek.* These must be the two detectives who had questioned him at Janssen's on Friday. What could they possibly want with her?

"Is there a private place we could speak with you for a few minutes?" Turner asked.

Abigail's throat was dry. "Yes, of course. Come into the office." She glanced at Ellie. Ellie offered a supportive smile, but her eyes were worried.

"May I take your coats?" Abigail asked as they entered the office.

"No, thank you, ma'am, we're fine." Detective Bartholomew spoke in a rich, deep voice that caught Abigail by surprise. She grabbed a folding chair from where it leaned against the wall and set it up next to the chair already facing her desk.

"Have a seat," she invited, closing the door. The two men sat down. She pulled her own chair out from behind the desk, wondering if her heart could beat any faster without her going into cardiac arrest.

"How can I help you?" she asked.

"I'm sure you're aware of the murder of Ms. Karen Brodie last Thursday night," Turner said.

Abigail nodded.

Turner's gaze was intense, but somehow opaque, as though he were reading her thoughts without exposing any of his own. "How well did you know Ms. Brodie?"

"Not well at all. I met her a few times when I was visiting my brother."

"On the eighth of November, you paid Ms. Brodie the rent that your brother owed," Turner said.

"Derek had fallen a little behind. It's not easy getting a new business off the ground, and I wanted to help him out."

"Why did you give the money directly to Ms. Brodie instead of to Derek?" Turner asked.

How did Turner know that? Maybe Derek had told him. "I . . . hadn't really planned to . . . I'd tried to talk to Derek, but . . ." Abigail swallowed and tried to organize her thoughts, clipping out the memories she'd rather not share with the police. "I'd come to try to talk to Derek, but he wasn't home. I ran into Karen Brodie and . . . and I agreed to pay Derek's back rent."

"Ms. Brodie asked *you* for the money?"

"She didn't care who paid it, as long as she got paid, and I knew cash was tight for Derek."

"Why didn't you tell Derek you'd paid it?"

"I tried. I left him a note, but it must have fallen to the floor and gotten lost, because he didn't see it." Why was Turner making an issue of this? Was he implying that Abigail had paid Karen directly because Derek was so flaky he would have squandered the money elsewhere if she'd given it directly to him? She hadn't stopped to think how strange it looked that she'd dealt directly with Derek's landlady, as though Derek were a child. Or an unreliable loser. Why had she let Karen manipulate her into writing a check on the spot?

"Did you call Derek about the rent?" Turner asked.

"I tried. He . . . doesn't always answer his phone."

"Usually? Or specifically following the dinner party with your parents that Karen Brodie interrupted?"

Abigail gripped her hands together in her lap, her palms wet. She wanted to claim Derek was always careless about answering her calls, but that hadn't been true for a long time. "He needed a little down time after that dinner, I think."

"He was upset."

"The evening didn't end well."

"Thanks to Ms. Brodie's interruption."

"That was the catalyst, but Derek and my parents have always argued."

Turner was silent for a moment, dark eyes studying Abigail. Abigail couldn't decide where to look. If she kept her gaze locked with his, did that appear aggressive, like she was expecting trouble? If she looked away, did that make it seem she had something to hide?

"Derek's relationship with your parents," Turner said. "I believe they hadn't spoken to each other in some time?"

Where was he getting his information? "That's right. They—things had been tense between them for many years. Derek wasn't an . . . easy teenager."

"How so?"

"He—always was one for learning things the hard way. He got into some trouble in high school." Abigail bit the inside of her lip, wishing she hadn't said that.

"What kind of trouble?" Turner asked.

Was this an attempt to gather information or a test to see if Abigail would be candid? She'd be candid; she had nothing to hide. All these problems of Derek's were history. "Alcohol. Drugs—mainly marijuana, but he tried a few other things. But he's cleaned up his life. He's doing fine now."

"Your parents had cut off contact with him?" Turner's voice was soft, tinted with sympathy. She couldn't discern any accusation or suspicion in his face.

"Yes—well, it had been a long time coming. This was five years ago—Derek had moved out; he was living with a friend and doing everything he could to trample on my family's religious beliefs, so it was very hard on my parents, and there was a lot of tension whenever we got together. Then my grandmother passed away, my mother's mother—it was a difficult time for her, and at the funeral . . ." Abigail stopped. Did she have to go into this?

"What happened at the funeral?"

Abigail fingered the metallic black hematite beads that hung from the heavy bracelet she wore and tried to think of a way to detour the conversation. How had questions about Karen Brodie's murder turned into a tell-all about the rift between Derek and their parents?

"Ms. Wyatt?"

She could either answer Turner's question or state flatly that she didn't want to discuss it. The latter choice would make Turner think she was hiding something. "Derek came late." Abigail twisted one of the beads. "And he came drunk."

It still made her sick, remembering Derek swaying up the aisle in the chapel, his tie loose around his neck, his white shirt untucked and stained on one sleeve, his bleary eyes searching the pews for his family. When he'd spotted them, he'd pushed his way toward them, stepping on toes, falling into the lap of Lillian's older sister, elbowing a five-year-old cousin in the face. *Sorry, sorry. Sorry I'm late. Got lost.* Every word carrying to every corner of the chapel, every gaze glued to Derek, the nine-year-old granddaughter singing a solo at the microphone losing her place and falling silent.

Bartholomew stood. The motion startled Abigail; the younger officer had been so silent that she'd hardly noticed him. He walked to the water cooler in the corner, filled a cup, and brought it to Abigail.

"Thank you," she murmured. She took a few sips. "A couple of my cousins escorted Derek out of there." *Escorted.* What a polite word for it. *Dragged* was a better word, dragged Derek out while he shouted profanity-laced orders for them to get their hands off him.

"I'm sorry," Turner said. "That must have been a painful experience for your family. What happened after the funeral?"

The compassion in his voice made it easier for her to go on. "That night, when Derek came to the house, there was a huge fight. My father told him it was over, they no longer considered him their son, to get out and not come back. Derek said that was fine by him, they'd never cared about him anyway. On his way out, Derek put his foot through my mother's china hutch, smashing my grandmother's china—" Abigail would never forget Lillian's wail of anguish as Derek destroyed this treasured memento of the mother Lillian had buried that day.

Abigail took another sip of water, moistening her dry mouth. "It was over a year before I could even get my parents to talk about him, and

Derek was just as bitter, but over the last couple of years, there's been a lot of softening, and Derek took a huge step forward when he invited them to dinner. That was the first time they'd spoken in five years."

"Your parents gave you the money that you used to start this bookstore?" Turner asked.

Abigail felt like she'd been yanked into a pool of frigid water. What was the matter with her? Was she sleep-deprived or just an idiot? These were police officers, and she'd rattled on about Derek's problems like she was confiding in Ellie.

Turner was waiting for an answer, so Abigail said, "Yes. They gave it to me when I graduated from college."

"It was a sizeable sum, I believe?"

Did she have to tell him the amount? He watched her in silence, waiting for her to speak. Not wanting him to think she was holding anything back, she said, "Two hundred thousand dollars."

"Had they promised the same financial assistance to your brother?"

"They'd always planned to assist him when the time was right."

"What would make the time right?"

"When he got his life on track and could make good use of it. And he *has* gotten his life on track. He doesn't use drugs anymore, he doesn't even drink at all. He works hard. All these problems I told you about, all of that is past. He's not like that anymore."

"The night of the dinner party, was Derek hoping your parents would decide he was ready for the money?"

Abigail's fingers felt stiff and cold as she clutched the half-empty cup of water and tried to think how to deflect these questions. She knew what Turner was doing—trying to elicit confirmation that Derek's goal had been to convince their parents he was ready for the money—and Karen Brodie's obnoxious interference had cost him two hundred thousand dollars. "I don't know. He didn't say."

"What was your impression?"

"I don't know. I can't read his mind."

Turner's voice was still gentle, still touched with sympathy. "Ms. Wyatt, was Derek at Kemper Park last Thursday night?"

From the icy tingling that spread over her skin, she knew her face must have turned white. "He—I don't—you'll have to ask Derek about his activities that night. I wasn't with him."

"Ms. Wyatt. Was Derek at Kemper Park last Thursday night?"

Why was Turner asking *her* this? Why wasn't he asking Derek? *Because he tried asking Derek, and Derek wouldn't admit anything. Turner probably talked to your parents, and they referred the police to you.* Abigail could imagine her father's voice: *"We haven't had anything to do with him for years. We have no idea what he's up to. Talk to our daughter, Abigail. She knows something. When she was here the other night, I could tell she was hiding something."*

Turner and Bartholomew both waited, watching her. From outside, she heard the chime of the door and the muffled sound of Ellie's cheerful voice talking to a customer.

"Talk to Derek," Abigail said. "If you have questions about his activities, talk to him. I can't speak for him."

"I understand. Let me rephrase my question. Did Derek tell you he was at Kemper Park last Thursday night?"

Cold water slopped into her lap; she'd forgotten she was holding the cup. Her heartbeat thundered in her ears.

She couldn't betray Derek's confidence.

She couldn't lie to the police.

She couldn't do anything but sit in paralyzed silence, uncertainty ripping her in half. But silence *was* a confession; she knew Turner and Bartholomew had already read the truth in her face.

Turner reached over and took the empty cup out of her hand. "Abigail," he said softly. "If you deliberately withhold information, you are obstructing a homicide investigation. Do you understand me?"

"Please—Derek wouldn't—" Tears blurred her vision. How could this be happening? "He would never have hurt Karen Brodie no matter how angry he was. I *know* him. He's not a murderer."

"I didn't say Derek killed her. But it wasn't a coincidence that he and Karen were both at Kemper Park, at the Henning picnic pavilion."

"You need to ask Derek—"

"A witness saw his car there. Derek knows something, and he told it to you. What is it?"

The note. That crazy note that had lured Derek to the park. Had Karen written it? Or had she received something similar? Could the note have been the work of Karen's killer? *Was* someone trying to frame Derek? Who?

This doesn't make sense. None of it makes sense.

If she exposed Derek's lies to Detective Turner, Derek would never trust her again. "Please don't put me in the middle of this. Talk to Derek."

"This isn't about putting you in the middle. This isn't about you at all. This is about justice for a woman who was brutally murdered. This is about getting a killer off the streets. What was Derek doing at Kemper Park?"

Tears spilled down Abigail's cheeks. She couldn't stand in Turner's way. She couldn't collude with Derek in hiding information he should have given the police. *Obstructing a homicide investigation.* Her voice shook as she said, "Someone left a note on his door, claiming to be a client and asking Derek to meet him there."

CHAPTER 14

Abigail parked in front of Janssen's Hardware. The instant Detectives Turner and Bartholomew had left Words and Sweets, Abigail had, with Ellie's approval, rushed out of there to find Derek. She had to talk to him immediately. She wouldn't let Turner be the one to tell him Abigail had betrayed him.

Hastily, she wiped the smeared makeup from under her eyes. Derek wouldn't appreciate it if she came staggering into his workplace looking like a train wreck.

"Hey, Abigail!" Manager Sally Hamilton greeted her with a wave as she walked in the door. "How's business?"

"It's good. You?"

"We're selling a lot of ice melt. That sky looks ready to unload the first snowfall of the season any minute now. Ugh!" She laughed and flipped her blonde ponytail over her shoulder. "Can I help you find something?"

"I need a word with Derek."

"Sure, let me call him up for you."

"Don't bother. I'll ferret him out."

Distracted by a customer, Sally turned away and Abigail walked swiftly out of sight.

She found Derek mixing paint for a customer. Abigail grabbed a couple of paint sample cards at random and pretended to examine them while she waited.

When the customer left, Derek approached Abigail. "Thinking of redoing your bathroom?"

He wasn't smiling. Abigail didn't bother to smile either. This was only going to get worse from here, so there was no point in feigning good humor.

"I need to talk to you in private," she said in a low voice. "Can you take a minute?"

"This can't wait until after work?"

"If it could, would I be here?"

"Let me ask Sal if I can skip out for a little while. I'll tell her it's a family matter. She'll buy it. She doesn't know my family thinks I'm scum."

"Derek—" But Derek strode away.

When they were seated in Abigail's car, she turned to him, ready to speak, but he cut her off. "Drive somewhere. We're supposed to be dealing with a family emergency."

"Fine. Where?"

"I don't care."

Abigail drove to a nearby bagel shop and parked. "Two police detectives came to talk to me today."

Derek stared at her. "Turner and Bartholomew?"

"Yes. They were asking about you."

"Why would they go to you?"

"Why do you *think*? They came to you already, didn't they? To tell you they had a witness who saw your Jeep at Kemper Park the night Karen died. And you denied everything." Stress and guilt honed sharp edges on Abigail's voice. "What is *wrong* with you? You didn't kill Karen—why do you keep acting like you did? You couldn't look any more guilty if you stood on the roof of town hall and shouted a confession."

Derek seized her wrist. "Did you tell them I was there?"

She shook off his hand. "What was I supposed to do? They asked me point-blank. Repeatedly. I tried to evade the question. I tried to tell them to talk to you. None of it worked. I had the choice of either lying through my teeth, remaining silent—which would have only made them *more* suspicious—or telling them the truth."

The horror and betrayal in his eyes hurt so much that it was all she could do to restrain her tears, but she held his gaze. "I'm sorry. I didn't want to tell them anything. But they already had a witness who saw your Jeep, and I wasn't going to add my lies to yours. You've got to trust them to do the right thing. Stop panicking and making things worse."

Derek slouched in his seat and closed his eyes. For a long, agonizing moment, he was silent. Abigail tried to keep her breathing steady as she focused on the lead-gray sky. She would wait for him to speak first.

"I trusted you," he said hollowly. "And the first chance you get you spill everything to the police. I should have known angel-girl Abigail would rather see her brother go to prison for murder than tell a little lie."

Abigail flushed. "You're not *guilty*, Derek. And obstructing a homicide investigation is not like telling someone their pants don't make them look fat."

"A witness." He spit the words out. "How can you be so gullible? Maybe someone saw my car, but I guarantee you they didn't get a license plate number, or Turner would have arrested me. The cops were fishing, and you swallowed the hook. Nice job. Did you tell them everything? About the note claiming to be from Chapman? About me finding Karen's body?"

"No," Abigail said. "I told them you hated Karen so much that you lured her to the park and murdered her with a baseball bat."

"I'm surprised sarcasm fits in your sanctimonious value system."

"I'm surprised you're able to recognize it as sarcasm. Since you're so sure everyone will think the worst of you, I thought you'd take it seriously."

"Yeah, well, I'm usually right in my predictions. When was the last time someone gave me a break?"

"How about Sally Hamilton?"

"Sal hired me because I'm your brother and you vouched for me."

Abigail slapped her forehead. "Oh, I was supposed to RSVP to your pity party. Is it too late?"

Derek scowled and turned his gaze toward the snowflakes starting to dance around the car. "This is a total mess. What am I supposed to say when Turner comes after me?"

"Tell him you canceled your membership in Club Stupid and are ready to be honest with him."

Derek laughed, a brief, harsh sound. "Everything's so easy for you, isn't it?"

Fury swept through Abigail like a sheet of flame. "Don't you *dare* say that to me." She didn't mean to shout, but her voice kept getting louder. "Do you have any idea what it felt like getting stuck between a police detective and my own brother? This is *your* mess. *You're* the idiot who found a body in the park and walked away, because you're so convinced that the world hates you, that your only cope-with-danger mechanism is to hide under a rock."

Derek gawked at her, his eyes bulging. "Abby—"

"You had chance after chance to tell the truth, and all you could do was *lie*. And now you're angry because I wouldn't help you lie yourself into deeper trouble. I'm so *sorry*. How could I be stupid enough to tell the truth when lying was obviously such a *good* strategy, and was working so well—"

"*Abby.*" Derek gripped her shoulder. "You're losing it. Stop yelling."

Abigail knocked his hand away, rested her forehead on the steering wheel, and lost her battle to keep tears from spilling over. *Calm down,* she told herself. *Calm down. At least it's out in the open now. He'll deal with it.*

Derek slumped in his seat, silent, while Abigail fought to regain control of herself.

"I don't know how anyone could reach thirty and still be naive enough to think that a mess like this could have a happy ending." Derek's voice broke into her thoughts, his tone less rough than it had been.

"Just call me a walking miracle," Abigail mumbled.

"I'm calling you a freak. So what now?"

Abigail swiped her tears away and sat up straight. "Find the Chapman note, even if it means going through garbage cans. Detective Turner needs to see it. Did you check your pockets? Maybe you put the note in the pocket of whatever clothes you were wearing when you found it."

"Hey, that could be right." Relief brightened Derek's face. "Yeah, I could have done that. Run me home, would you? I want to check right now, seeing as how Turner and his sidekick will be arresting me any minute."

"They won't arrest you. They'd need more than knowing you were at Kemper Park."

"They've got more than that. They've got a motive."

Chilled at the memory of Turner's questions about the money Derek had hoped to get from their parents, Abigail said, "You can't be the only one who hated Karen Brodie."

"Yeah, I guess," Derek said. "But how many of her other enemies were at Kemper Park the night she died?"

CHAPTER 15

"JUST PARK IN MY GARAGE. I'll go open the door for you," Derek said. "Karen doesn't like it when—" He stopped himself. "Okay, that was dumb. I'm on autopilot."

Abigail nodded. Karen's death still seemed unreal.

They were nearly to the top of the front steps when the door swung inward and a dark-haired man strode from the house—the handyman who had startled her in the hallway after the dinner party and had left her the money for the broken vase. She tried to think of his name, but to her surprise, she couldn't remember it. Usually, she had a good memory, but with all the stress of the past week, it was a wonder she could remember her own name.

The man didn't even glance in her direction as he hurried down the stairs. When he was out of earshot, Abigail asked, "Who's that guy?"

"Uh . . . I think he does—did—odd jobs for Karen. I've seen him around a few times." Derek unlocked the door to his apartment. "Why? Want his phone number?"

"Ha ha. I saw him the night of the dinner. Ran into him in the hall. He was asking questions about the house."

"He probably doesn't know Karen is dead and he's here finishing a job," Derek said. "It's not like the police would have called to let him know, and maybe he doesn't read the paper."

"He'd have to be living in a cave not to know about Karen."

"Fine, you're right. I have no idea what he's doing here."

"He's a little strange." Abigail took off her coat. "When I talked to him before, he didn't want Karen to know he'd been here. He said they weren't on the best of terms."

"*That's* strange? I'm betting she wasn't on good terms with anyone who worked for her. She treated Hunter Conley like dirt."

"I wonder if the police have questioned him."

"The handyman? I'll bet they have. They talked to Hunter."

"How did Hunter handle it?"

"Okay. He was terrified before they came because his dad fed him a lot of garbage about how cruel the police were and how they were going to haul him off to prison, but afterward, he came over here and rattled on for an hour about how nice they were." Derek tossed his jacket onto the couch. "All right, let's find that note. I'm going to check the laundry hamper for the clothes I was wearing when I found it. *You* check the garbage. Enjoy."

"Thanks." Abigail made her voice sour, but she was glad to hear Derek teasing her. He'd handled this a lot better than she'd feared. She wondered if he was secretly relieved that she'd forced him out of his shaky haven of lies.

Derek disappeared into the bathroom. Wishing Derek had some rubber gloves, Abigail spread newspaper on the kitchen floor and began the distasteful process of searching through the kitchen garbage can. Ten minutes of searching through greasy microwave-dinner trays, wadded-up napkins, and orange peels brought no results. Abigail rolled up the newspaper, dumped everything back in the can, and washed her hands with an abundance of soap.

"Want me to check your bedroom and bathroom trash baskets?" she asked. "And it's the pure definition of love that I can even stand to ask you that."

"Already checked the bathroom," Derek called. He was in his bedroom. "Have a look in here."

She checked the trash basket in Derek's bedroom and found only a crumpled Kleenex, a few papers where Derek had doodled ideas for new jewelry, and a sock with a hole in it. "You must have emptied your trash since you got the note."

Derek was rifling through his closet. "Uh . . . no, I'm pretty sure I haven't, because I took it out that day. I remember, because I was trying to avoid Karen." He slammed his closet shut and spit out a few words that made Abigail wince.

"Sorry," he said. "But this is driving me crazy. I checked the pockets of every pair of pants I ever wear."

"Shirts?"

"Most of mine don't have pockets, and even if they do, I never put anything in them."

"Coat?"

"Hey, maybe. Except I can't find my heavy coat."

"I'll check all your jacket pockets." Abigail hurried back to the living room. She opened the coat closet and searched every pocket of the jackets and sweatshirts hanging there.

On the floor at the back of the closet lay a light brown mound of insulated fabric. Abigail grabbed it.

"Here's your heavy coat," she called. "It was on the floor of the closet." She dug into the pockets and found nothing but gloves.

"In the coat closet?" Frowning, Derek approached her. "I looked there."

"It was way at the back."

"I *looked* there." Derek took the coat. "Weird. Things keep disappearing—" With a sharp motion he held the coat away from him.

Puzzled at the shocked expression on Derek's face, Abigail reached for the coat. "What's wrong?"

Derek made a choking sound—either the failed beginning of a laugh or words collapsing in his throat. "I get it now. I get it. I'm such an *idiot*."

"What are you talking about? Do you remember where you put the note?" Abigail snatched the coat and turned it so she could see what he'd been staring at. She couldn't see anything wrong with the coat except for a few brownish blotches on the cuff and back of the right sleeve and a few more spots on the front of the coat.

"What is it?" she asked.

"Those stains weren't there before. I ran it through the wash just a couple of weeks ago. The coat was clean."

"I don't understand what—" Abigail lifted the sleeve for a closer look at the marks on the tan fabric. Brownish-red circles, like something had spattered the sleeve. It looked like—

Abigail looked into Derek's ashen face. "Derek . . ."

"It's blood. Karen's blood. Abby, someone *is* setting me up. First they tricked me into going to the park. Now they're planting evidence."

Abigail carried the coat into the kitchen where the light was stronger and examined the sleeve again. Derek followed her.

"I *knew* I hadn't thrown the note away. We can't find it because the killer took it back. He didn't want me to have anything to back up my kooky story."

Abigail dropped the coat on a chair. She couldn't dispute that the stains looked like blood, and she didn't want to hold the coat any longer. "What about the note I left you? That note is gone too, and the killer would have no interest in—"

"You sure? Because I didn't see your note, I thought Karen's records would show I was behind on my rent and the police would take that as a reason for us to be at each other's throats. That made me a lot more nervous when I was talking to them. Maybe that's what the killer wanted. The more scared I looked, the better."

"How could he—or she—possibly have known that I left that note?"

"When did you leave it? Last Monday, right?"

"Yes."

"That's the day I got the 'Chapman' note. When the killer dropped off the note, he must have looked around my place and taken your note."

"You need to sit down and take a deep breath. Who would create an elaborate setup like that? Whoever killed Karen probably did it in a fit of anger, unplanned—"

"Kemper Park in November is not an 'unplanned' destination. Karen wouldn't have gone there without a reason. Whoever murdered her lured her there somehow, just like they did me."

"Derek—"

"If you think I'm wrong, explain *that*." Derek pointed at the coat. "I tore that closet apart trying to find that coat. It *wasn't there*. And now it shows up stained with blood. Do you think I killed Karen and I'm lying about all of this? That's the only other explanation."

The thought of someone breaking into Derek's apartment and stuffing a bloodstained coat in the closet was so far-fetched that Abigail struggled to believe it. Wasn't it more likely that Derek, distracted and under tremendous stress, had simply missed seeing the coat when he searched? The stains could be something completely innocent—sauce from a takeout meal, a splattered drink—

"You don't believe me." Derek gave a jagged laugh. "You still think there's some harmless answer for all of this."

"I think we both need to sit down and calm down." Abigail realized she was trembling. She buried her hands under her arms, trying to quiet the tremors. *Stay calm. You've already fallen apart once today; don't do it again.*

"Let me guess." Derek kicked at the coat, knocking it off the chair. "You think we should call Turner and tell him about this."

"Are you positive you couldn't have left the coat there? Things have been so crazy lately, it wouldn't be surprising if you forgot—"

Derek kicked the kitchen chair. It fell with a crash that made Abigail gasp. *"I didn't put the coat there."*

"Stop it. Panic is only going to—"

"Someone is *framing me for murder.*"

Abigail took a step backward, frightened by the wildness in his eyes. "If this is a setup, you've got to stop playing along. So far, you've been working overtime to make yourself look guilty. Stop it *now*. Don't even think about hiding that coat. Give it to Detective Turner. Tell him exactly what happened."

"Are you for real? Can you think of a single reason why he'd believe me?"

"Because you didn't do it. Because there's got to be real evidence out there, evidence pointing to someone else."

"Better evidence than a bloodstained coat?"

"You won't know if that's Karen's blood until they test it."

"They're not going to test it. I'm getting out of here."

"Derek! Don't be an idiot!"

"What sounds like the idiot choice to you? Sticking around here while the evidence piles up against me, or getting out before I land in prison for life? You can bet there's more evidence than the coat. What about the murder weapon? I've got a funny feeling that's going to turn up next—with my fingerprints on it."

"Derek, please." Abigail fought down her own rising hysteria. "What you need now is a lawyer, a good lawyer."

"You know I don't have the money. And they won't assign me a freebie guy until—"

"I'll pay, all right?"

"You can bet that note got me to Kemper Park right after Karen was murdered so I'd be on the scene before the body had time to cool. They're going to nail me, lawyer or no lawyer. Why would Turner believe me? I've done nothing but lie to him."

"I'm going to find you a lawyer."

"Knock yourself out. But I'm getting out of here. I'm not sitting around waiting to get arrested."

"Where would you go?"

"Why? Want to tell Turner where I'm headed?"

Abigail wrestled back an urge to slap Derek. Couldn't he see what he was doing? If he fled, Turner would be certain of his guilt. "Listen to me. If someone stole the notes and planted that coat, they've been in and out of here several times. Chase or Hunter might have seen them. And what about that handyman? Maybe he had a reason to want Karen dead. He might have a key to your apartment—"

Derek grabbed the jacket he'd tossed onto the couch. "Tell Mom and Dad I won't be there for Thanksgiving. I'm sure they'll weep buckets."

"I will not let you do this to yourself."

"I didn't ask your permission."

"You don't even have your Jeep here. It's at Janssen's, remember?"

Derek looked taken aback, and Abigail suppressed a sigh of relief. He'd *have* to slow down now, and once he did, he'd recognize the sheer stupidity of trying to run from this. He couldn't elude the police for long. The only thing he'd accomplish would be to make them certain he'd killed Karen.

"Fine, I'll take your car." He picked up her purse.

"Derek!" Abigail jumped toward him, but he swung around so his back was to her and pulled her keys out of her purse.

"Give those back. You are *not* taking my car." With deliberate steps, Abigail moved to stand in front of the door. "If you take off, I swear to you, I will immediately call Detective Turner. I'll tell him about the coat. I'll tell him you're on the run, in my car."

"You stupid, self-righteous little—" The string of words that slammed against Abigail's ears were not ones Derek had ever directed at her, and they brought tears to her eyes, but she stood her ground.

"I will not let you destroy yourself, Derek. We're going to fight this the right way."

For a painful moment, the only sound in the room was their harsh breathing. Abigail blinked savagely at the tears; this wasn't a good time to start bawling.

Derek's shoulders sagged and he turned away. "Fine," he muttered. "Fine, you're right. You're always right. Let me go find the phone book and you can start your lawyer hunt. Sit down." He pointed at the rock-paneled chair.

Shaky now with relief, Abigail collapsed onto the leather cushion as Derek headed down the hallway. How would she go about finding a criminal lawyer? She hated the idea of plucking a random name out of the Yellow Pages. There had to be someone she could ask, some way to get a recommendation.

How much would it cost? She had no idea what kind of fees a criminal lawyer charged. Mentally, she did some quick calculations, trying to figure out how much money she could get her hands on right now. Maybe their parents—

Forget that.

Several minutes passed, and Derek had not returned, but Abigail didn't feel inclined to go after him. He'd left her keys on the counter, so she wasn't worried about his trying to sneak out a window and drive away. Besides, she could hear him opening and closing drawers and closets. He probably couldn't find the phone book. She should call out to him and tell him never mind, she'd use her phone to look online, but it was nice to have a few minutes of respite to organize her thoughts.

Maybe she should call Bob Chapman. He liked Derek, and a man that influential in the community would be able to recommend a good lawyer. Of course, she probably wouldn't be able to afford anyone Chapman would recommend.

What would Detective Turner's next move be? Whatever it was, Abigail felt far better at the prospect of facing it with a lawyer to advise Derek.

Derek walked back into the room. He'd swapped his Janssen's work shirt for a hooded sweatshirt. The circles under his eyes seemed darker and he wouldn't meet her gaze, but he looked calm.

"Guess I'd better call Sal and tell her I'm taking the rest of the day off." He dropped the Yellow Pages in Abigail's lap. "Somehow I don't think I can concentrate on work."

"Go figure." Abigail flipped through the pages, looking for attorney listings. "I'm wondering—do you think if we called Bob Chapman that he could give us some suggestions? He probably knows everyone in town and which attorneys are any good. Do you remember when he was due back from Europe?"

Derek wandered behind her. "I'm not sure I want him hearing that I need a criminal attorney."

"He'll find out anyway, since it was his name on the note. The police will talk to him."

"True," Derek said.

Abigail skimmed the listings as Derek stood behind her chair. "I'm thinking that a recommendation would—" Something flashed in front of her eyes and she felt a sharp tug across her stomach and arms. "What—" She looked down to see a dirty white rope encircling her.

"Derek—" Confused, she tried to tug the rope loose, but it pulled tighter, pinning her to the back of the chair, binding her arms at the bend of the elbows.

"Derek! What are you—" Another rope dug into her shoulders. "Stop it, what are you *doing*?" Abigail twisted, trying to grab the rope before he could knot it, but he was too fast and too strong. The phone book hit the floor.

Derek moved to stand at her side. His neck and jawline had turned blotchy red, and he was breathing fast. He held a roll of duct tape.

An electric burst of adrenaline spread through Abigail as she finally understood. He *was* going to run. And he was making sure she couldn't interfere.

He peeled a length of tape from the roll and reached for her wrist. She thrashed against the ropes, struggling to elude his grasp, but he caught her right hand and pinned it to the arm of the chair.

"Derek, please. *Please*, you don't want to do this." She strained to bring her left arm over far enough to strike at him, push him away, but the ropes were too tight. He wound the duct tape around her right wrist, securing it to the arm of the chair. She twisted her lower body, trying to kick him as he moved to her left side, but he kept himself out of range. With a few deft motions, he bound her left wrist.

"Derek."

He moved behind her, and she heard more tape rip.

"Please, Derek. You know you can't run from this. You'll only make things—"

One hand pressed against her forehead, trapping her head against the back of the chair. His other hand pressed a strip of tape over her mouth.

Now as furious as she was frightened, Abigail jerked her head out of his grip, straining to pull her lips apart, to spit on the tape, anything to loosen it. Derek had gone crazy, he couldn't do this—

Derek drew her head against the back of the chair again and added a second strip of tape to the first. "Here's the thing you never understood." His voice rasped in her ear. "Things don't work out for me. You think if I play it straight, everything will be fine, like your perfect life is fine. That's not how it works. If I stick around here, I'll end up in prison for life."

Abigail twisted violently, fighting the ropes, yanking against the duct tape. Her flesh burned where the ropes dug into her skin and pain tore through the muscles in her arms. The heavy chair remained immobile beneath her; no matter how she tried to throw her weight, she couldn't budge it.

Tears muddled her vision. She didn't bother to fight as Derek bound her ankles to the legs of the chair. She'd already lost.

"I'm sorry." He stepped back, breathing in gasps like he couldn't get enough air. "But maybe you ought to thank me. Didn't you tell me it tore you apart to get trapped between helping the police and protecting me? Now you don't have a choice to make. You *can't* call Turner. Hang in there. He'll be here soon with a warrant to search the place."

He disappeared into the back of the apartment and returned a moment later carrying a duffel bag and a folded piece of paper. "I know you won't feel like doing me any favors, but could you give this to Hunter Conley for me?" His eyes gleamed so brightly they looked glazed, and his hand shook as he shoved the folded paper into the pocket of her sweater. "The kid's going to be frantic."

Helpless, Abigail could only watch as he pulled her car keys off the ring and tossed her other keys back on the counter. He picked up the bloodstained coat and headed out the door.

The doorknob rattled as he locked the door behind him.

CHAPTER 16

SNOW SPLATTERED AGAINST THE WINDSHIELD and rendered the freeway slushy and treacherous. Derek drove as fast as he dared, cursing at the way Abigail's car handled the conditions. He should have stopped at Janssen's and swapped her car for his Jeep, but when a warrant was issued for his arrest, the police would look for his Jeep first. Once they'd talked to Abigail, they'd be hunting for her car, but even a few minutes' delay could mean the difference between prison and escape.

Was Abigail okay? He wished he could stop thinking about her, but it was like trying to ignore a fist while it punched him in the stomach. Revulsion and disbelief at what he'd done to her mingled with anger at what she'd done—and threatened to do—to him. With Abigail, it was all about doing the "right" thing, the good thing, the heaven-approved thing. She couldn't comprehend that this time, her Sunday School answers would send him to prison. Did she expect him to sit meekly on the couch and sing hymns while he waited to get arrested and convicted for something he didn't do?

If there had been any way to reason with her, he would have taken it, but when Abigail got stubborn, he couldn't defeat her with words. She would have called Detective Turner. She would have turned him in.

You did what you had to. Words that had sounded convincing when he was filled with panic and fury grew thinner with each mile he traveled away from Ohneka.

He hoped she wasn't too uncomfortable. Had he pulled the ropes too tight? He'd been scared and rushed, needing the element of surprise to give him a chance to overwhelm her before she fully realized what he was doing. He doubted she could defeat him physically, but if it had come to an all-out fight, he knew he couldn't have subdued her without hurting her.

Would he have hurt her, if it had come to that?

He *had* hurt her. She was in pain now; she had to be. The way she'd fought—she must have rope burns, strained muscles, bruises.

But she did that to herself. She didn't have to fight. This rationalization sounded so pathetic that Derek was ashamed of himself for even trying to shove the responsibility onto Abigail. *Abby, I'm sorry.* He'd left her trapped in misery, her limbs cramping, her hands and feet going numb—

Had she finally figured out that he wasn't worth her trouble?

Guilt swelled until he felt it was crushing his lungs. His own sister—the one person who'd never given up on him, not even temporarily, not even when all he'd cared about was the next party and how fast he could get drunk; not even when he'd humiliated his entire family at his grandmother's funeral; not even when his parents had cut him off. No matter what he did, her phone calls and text messages had kept coming, until finally he'd started answering them. It was Abigail he'd turned to when he knew he couldn't stay with Catrina any longer, when the self-loathing cut so deep that it was slashing him apart. Abigail had enlisted her ex-boyfriend realtor to find him a place in Ohneka. She'd landed him a job at the hardware store.

"And this is how you show your gratitude?" The sarcastic Abigail-angel landed on his shoulder. *"What's wrong? Was Hallmark out of thank-you cards?"*

The urge to turn around and go back tugged at him so powerfully that he felt it would drag him out of his seat, swing him around, and throw him in the direction of Ohneka. *Go home. You can't hurt her like this. Go home.*

Go home and go to prison? A convicted murderer—locked up for the rest of his life . . .

A few hours of discomfort for Abigail or a lifetime behind bars for him? What he'd done to her was horrible, but what she'd threatened to do to him was far worse.

He glanced at the clock on the dashboard. Two hours had passed since he left Ohneka. He should have been to Catrina's house an hour ago. How long until he saw flashing red-and-blue lights in his rearview mirror? Was Turner already at his apartment?

What if Turner *didn't* show up at his apartment today? What if Derek had been wrong to assume that Abigail's information was the final piece they needed to get a warrant? What if Abigail remained trapped all day and all night—or even for a couple of days—or longer? Derek imagined her slowly dehydrating, her flesh raw and bleeding from a futile battle with the ropes.

Stop it. That's not going to happen. Turner's probably already there.

He accelerated but let up again almost immediately as the road curved. He couldn't risk an accident.

The bloodstained coat lay on the passenger seat and he kept glancing at it, as though looking at it enough times would magically tell him who had worn it the night Karen died. Who was doing this to him? Someone who knew that Derek and Karen had clashed, and who thought Derek would fit the role of murderer well enough to keep the police from searching any further. And the killer was right about that—if Derek was the obvious culprit, why would the police keep looking? More evidence against him would soon come to light, enough evidence to convince even the most skeptical juror. The killer wouldn't stop with the coat. If Abigail thought Derek was going to kick back and wait until Turner produced a bloodied murder weapon with Derek's fingerprints on it, she was nuts.

No wonder he'd fled Kemper Park when he saw Karen dead. On a gut level, he'd known instantly that he was in the crosshairs.

Who had killed Karen? Chase McCoy? He was a weirdo, painting those warped pictures and bragging like he was da Vinci. But Derek had no idea why he'd want to kill Karen. What about Karen's ex-husband? From the way Karen had talked about him, clearly she'd hated him. Maybe her ex felt the same. Maybe she'd been hounding him, making his life miserable, trying to squeeze money out of him. Maybe he'd been fed up enough to fracture her skull. And what about that handyman guy who had stirred Abigail's suspicion?

Whoever the killer was, he'd successfully pinned the crime on Derek.

Through the blowing snow, the sign for the exit finally came into view, and Derek let out a groan of relief. His muscles were a collection of cramps and knots. *Boo hoo for you. You feel a lot better than Abigail does right now.*

As he neared the neighborhood where Catrina Hubbard lived, doubts about his decision to come here burgeoned. He hadn't talked to her since he'd moved to Ohneka. He wouldn't have even known where to find her, except that a few months ago, he'd run into Roger Terrance, an actor friend of Catrina's, and Roger had told him Catrina was living in her parents' house. Her parents had retired to Florida and had signed the house over to her.

Nothing to do now but go to the house and see what happened. Derek could have made his way to her parents' house blindfolded. How many times had he snuck over there while her parents were gone, until he and Catrina had finally earned enough to rent their own cruddy apartment? How many hours had he spent in the basement using her brother's old rock polishing equipment, feeling the first stirrings of hope that maybe there was something in the world he was good at?

Would Catrina be home right now? Not a chance. Even if she wasn't at work, no way would she be sitting around home. She'd be off with a group of friends. She loved constant activity.

He wagered he could still get inside the house. He remembered the code to the garage door, and he doubted Catrina would have bothered to change it.

The real question was—how did she feel about him? Would she let him hide out for a few days until he figured out where to go? What if she hated his guts?

Too late to worry about that now. He didn't dare drive around any longer. The police might already have a bulletin out for Abigail's car.

The house was an eye-catching, two-story structure of dark wood and light stone. It suited Catrina—bold, striking, different from anything else in the area. Derek parked in the driveway, stretched his aching body, and went to ring the doorbell.

No answer.

Leaving a trail of footprints on the snowy sidewalk and driveway, he hurried to the keypad that controlled the garage door. With all the footprints and tire tracks he'd made, he'd better hope the snow kept falling long enough to conceal them. If Catrina arrived to see evidence that someone was in her house, she'd call the cops. That would be a perfect end to this whole trip—getting arrested by the Ithaca cops for breaking and entering.

Holding his breath, he punched in the familiar numbers. The garage door rose, and Derek grinned in relief.

The garage was empty. He pulled Abigail's car inside. As soon as he heard Catrina arrive home, he'd run out to meet her before she had a chance to freak out and call the cops at the sight of a strange car in her garage.

The door that led from the garage to the house wasn't locked. Derek stomped the snow from his shoes and stepped inside.

The house smelled the same—cinnamon-scented candles with a faint undertone of stale cigarette smoke. Catrina didn't smoke, but her parents did, and even though they didn't live here anymore, the smell lingered.

He wandered into the entryway. This had always been his favorite part of the house, with the floor tiled in lustrous golden onyx and the ceiling towering two stories overhead. The only new, odd note was a massive silk tree in a steel pot—the tree must be twelve feet tall. Was Catrina going for a jungle look?

He headed into the living room. Everything had changed here; Catrina's taste was far different from her mother's floral couches and crystal lamps. This furniture was all steel and leather with sharp lines. Abstract prints in metal frames decorated the walls. On a lacquered black bookshelf, a collection of photos drew Derek's attention. He stepped closer and felt a twisting in his chest, a stirring of old emotions. Some of the photos were publicity shots of Catrina. She looked even more gorgeous than he remembered, with that lustrous blonde hair, those delicate features, and eyes the rich golden-brown of a tiger's eye stone.

Derek picked up one of the photographs so he could study it more closely. Catrina's skin looked so silky that for a moment, Derek ached to reach into the photograph and touch her. Strange how he hadn't even let himself realize he missed her. He'd been so determined to start over, to put her and everything associated with her behind him.

What if she paid him back for his rejection by refusing to help him? She might. And if he couldn't hide out here for a little while, he had no idea where he'd go.

What if she brought someone home with her? She must have a boyfriend.

What was he *doing* here? He hadn't thought this through at all.

He walked upstairs into the master bedroom and poked through the contents of the closet. Relieved to find no signs that a man lived here, he returned to the living room and stretched full-length on the rug with a couch pillow under his head. At least there was a chance he could face Catrina alone, but just because she wasn't living with someone didn't mean she wouldn't come through the door with a guy.

Derek pictured himself trying to explain his presence to some six-foot-five-inch muscle man. *"I'm wanted for murder, so I'm hoping Catrina could hide me for a while. Not a problem, is it?"*

Another brilliant episode in the life of Derek Wyatt. If they made a movie about his life, it would have to be a comedy. No one could play a role this pathetic and expect the audience to keep a straight face.

* * *

COCOONED IN A FLEECE BLANKET that a uniformed officer with motherly gray eyes had wrapped around her, Abigail sat on Derek's couch with her knees pulled up to her chest, her head resting on them, and her eyes squeezed shut while the police searched Derek's apartment. It had taken four miserable hours for Derek's prediction to come true, but at last a ringing of the doorbell and a *"Police—open the door"* was followed by the click of a key in the lock—Karen Brodie's master key—and Detectives Turner and Bartholomew had entered, search warrant in hand. Too numb and cramped to be anything but relieved at the rescue, Abigail had managed to remain calm as they freed her, until the obvious question came from Turner's mouth.

"Did Derek do this to you?"

He hadn't gotten an answer, not that he needed one. All he'd gotten was a flash flood of tears—tears and silence; Abigail feared that if she opened her mouth, she'd tumble into out-of-control sobs that shook her entire body. She'd never have believed Derek capable of the calculated aggression he'd shown today. What was she supposed to tell Turner now? *My brother isn't a murderer. He could never hurt anyone.* Turner wouldn't laugh at this show of blind loyalty, but he'd want to. Derek was capable of leaving his own sister bound and gagged to keep her from getting in his way. What was he capable of doing to a mean-spirited woman who'd deprived him of two hundred thousand dollars?

What did Abigail think he was capable of doing?

She jammed her fingertips against the sides of her skull, as though she could manually force her thoughts away from a path she didn't want them to take. *Derek did not kill Karen Brodie. He didn't do it. I know he didn't.*

Someone *was* framing him.

Would Turner believe that? Why would he? Why would anyone?

The knot swelled in her throat again and she swallowed hard, forcing her breathing into a soft, steady rhythm. She'd finally managed to stanch the tears, and she couldn't fall apart again. Turner had been kind enough to give her time to regain control of herself—either that, or he realized he wouldn't get anything coherent out of her yet, no matter how hard he pressed—but that reprieve wouldn't last much longer. He'd be at her side with a list of questions. She had to be able to talk to him.

And tell him what? Did she tell him about the bloodstained coat Derek had taken, knowing that if there were any doubts left in Turner's mind about Derek's guilt, this piece of evidence would erase them? How could she hold back such vital information? But how could she share it, knowing she might well be condemning her brother to prison?

He didn't kill her. He didn't kill her. The truth will come out.

Won't it?

She could almost hear Derek's voice in her ear: *"Here's what you never understood. Things don't work out for me."*

How *could* he expect things to work out when he was so intent on self-destructing?

The room seemed chilly, but her face felt hot and achy pressed against her knees. Slowly, she lifted her head. Detective Bartholomew, his gangly body making him look like a teenager, was standing in front of the bookshelf a few yards away. In his gloved hands he held two green marble bookends. Derek must have put the other one back, Abigail thought absently. It had been missing last week.

Missing. Like the coat? Like the note?

Bartholomew turned, and the intensity in his expression sent ice slashing through Abigail.

"Hey, Turner," he said.

Turner pivoted from where he'd been examining a stack of mail in the kitchen. Bartholomew held up the bookends and Turner's eyebrows lifted, his expression mirroring the interest in Bartholomew's face.

Heavy stone bookends. Bookends that Derek had shaped so each one looked like half of a Christmas tree, with sharp, three-tiered triangular edges. Derek's voice, acrid with sarcasm: *"I'm just the kind of guy who could take a rock and smash Karen's head in—"*

Take a rock and smash Karen's head—

Abigail's stomach heaved. Pushing the blanket off her shoulders, she leaped off the couch. Her stiff legs wavered beneath her, and she staggered.

"Ms. Wyatt!" Bartholomew set the bookends down and jumped toward her, but Abigail flailed a clumsy arm, urging him back.

"Excuse me—*excuse me*—" She rushed down the hallway and into the bathroom, slammed the door, and bent over the toilet.

Even after she'd emptied her stomach, she kept retching, as though her body were struggling to rid itself of poison that ran deeper than anything she'd eaten. Finally, drenched in perspiration, she collapsed to the bathmat and leaned against the tub.

A knock came at the door. "Ms. Wyatt?" The woman officer. "Ma'am, are you all right?"

Abigail jerked a towel off the rack and wiped her mouth. "I'm okay," she said hoarsely, using the other end of the towel to mop the tears off her face.

"Can I do anything to help you?"

The tears kept flowing. Abigail shoved the towel against her eyes. She had to stop bawling, stand up, and walk out of here before Turner called the paramedics. He'd wanted to do that already, to make certain she was all right, but she'd refused. A few rope burns didn't require medical treatment.

Bracing her hand on the edge of the bathtub, Abigail pushed herself to her feet. She splashed icy water on her face, rinsed her mouth, and opened the door.

"I'm sorry," she said. "I'm all right."

"Ma'am, we should call a—"

"No. No, I'm all right."

With a firm hand on Abigail's arm, the officer helped her back to the couch. Abigail didn't protest—she was too light-headed and shaky to walk a straight line on her own. She sank onto the cushions and pulled the blanket over her.

Detective Turner gave her a troubled look. Abigail knew what he was seeing; she'd glimpsed herself in the bathroom mirror. Her eyes were fiery red and the rest of her face a bloodless gray. "Abigail, you need medical care."

"No—I'm—"

"It's on the way."

Abigail wanted to object but knew it was hopeless. She lay down with her head resting on one of the throw pillows. As long as she'd already been deemed ill enough to need medical attention, she might as well do what she wanted, which was to collapse, close her eyes, and hope to drift away from all of this before Turner started asking questions she didn't know how to answer.

"You told Derek that we talked to you?" Turner asked.

So much for stalling. "Yes," Abigail murmured, not opening her eyes. "Where did he go?"

"I don't know. I have no idea. Obviously he . . . didn't want me following him." Her lips felt tingly and awkward, and it was hard to shape words. Did they know he was driving her car? Had they noticed his Jeep was still at Janssen's?

If she didn't tell them he'd taken her car, that might give Derek more time to get wherever he was going. To hide.

Deliberately withholding information. Lies of omission. Conspiring with Derek to elude the police.

But he's innocent.

Isn't he?

The pain that cut through Abigail's stomach made her gasp. Her shoulders hunched, and her knees came up as she fought renewed nausea.

A hand touched her shoulder. "Take it easy," Turner said.

"Derek didn't kill Karen Brodie," she whispered.

Turner patted her shoulder and said nothing.

CHAPTER 17

CLUTCHING A STEAMING MUG OF spiced apple cider, Abigail sat at her kitchen table and stared out the French doors, watching snowflakes tumble from the night sky. The plate in front of her held half a grilled-cheese sandwich. She'd had to eat the other half to convince Ellie she was well enough to be on her own. She wouldn't have been able to pry Ellie out of here with a crowbar, but Melissa, who had rushed in to cover for them at the store, could only stay at work until six.

Detective Bartholomew had called Ellie for her while the paramedics were checking her out. She'd tried to protest that Ellie couldn't leave the store, and if someone could just drive her home, she'd be fine on her own. Bartholomew had shaken his head without bothering to answer. Abigail, still feeling so sick that it was difficult to sit up, had abandoned her feeble protests.

The police would be in touch soon. They'd want every detail of what had transpired between Derek and her. What would she say?

Pain pulsed then faded, reverting to an achy numbness. She could still sense the wound—deep, bleeding steadily—but the pain had dulled, as though her nerves were too damaged to register the extent of the injury.

When Derek had left her a prisoner in his apartment, he'd assumed Turner would be there soon to rescue her—but he hadn't really known how long it would take. He didn't know how strong Turner's case was, nor did he know much about the legalities involved in getting either a search warrant or a warrant for his arrest. For all he knew, Abigail could have been trapped there for days.

And he'd left her anyway. He'd been willing to take that chance.

A gust of wind blew snowflakes against the glass and shook the trees surrounding the house. Abigail shivered. Normally, she enjoyed the rustic feel of her home, with trees separating her from her nearest neighbor a quarter of a mile away, but tonight a chilly sense of isolation made her wonder why she hadn't purchased a home in a more populated neighborhood.

Abigail touched the piece of paper that lay on the table. She'd forgotten about the note Derek had given her for Hunter Conley until she'd been taking off her sweater and had felt the paper in her pocket. Though it was Hunter's name and address scrawled on the note, given the circumstances, she'd felt no compunctions about reading it.

Hunter—

I have to go for a while. The police think I killed Karen. I didn't do it, but I need to stay away until they figure out who really killed her. Don't worry about me. I'll be okay. Sorry I can't be around. Don't freak out about your homework. You can do it on your own when you stop and think. If you get in trouble, go downtown to the Words and Sweets bookstore and talk to my sister, Abigail. She's really nice, and she'll help you.

Take care,

Derek

She's really nice, and she'll help you. What a heartfelt recommendation from a man whose response to her attempt to help *him* had been rope and a roll of duct tape.

You shouldn't have backed him into a corner like that. He panicked.

Was she trying to justify what he'd done? Reshape it into something she could live with? The more blame she could place on herself, the less she had to hurt over what Derek had done to her.

At least the fact that Derek had been concerned enough about lonely, troubled Hunter Conley to take the time to scrawl a note to him before fleeing brought a few drops of warmth to the cold numbness inside Abigail. But regardless of what he'd written to Hunter, did Derek really think things would miraculously work themselves out if he stayed in hiding long enough?

The doorbell rang and Abigail jumped, splashing steaming cider on her fingers. Wincing, she grabbed a napkin and wiped her hand. Apparently Turner's patience had run out. Her legs felt heavy and her chest hollow as she went to open the door.

Kyle Stratton was standing on the porch. Snow flecked his wavy chestnut hair and he held a vase of yellow roses. "Hi, Abigail." He smiled at her. "I heard you had a rough day. Just wanted to see how you were."

"Kyle." Abigail couldn't manage more than his name without stammering. He'd come to see *her*? "Come in," she said.

"You sure? I don't want to be a pest."

"No, really, you're fine." Abigail tugged the hem of her sweatshirt, straightening it. After everything that had happened that day, it amazed her to realize she was still embarrassed over something as petty as having Kyle see her wearing an oversized sweatshirt and torn jeans, with her face scrubbed bare of makeup and her hair damp from the shower she'd taken to try to ease sore muscles.

"Yellow." He extended the vase. "The most cheerful color I could find."

"Thank you. You're so sweet." Sweet and bewildering. What was he doing here? How did he know what had happened? She set the vase on the lamp table. "Have a seat," she invited. "May I take your coat?"

"No, you may not. You're supposed to be resting, not playing hostess." Kyle draped his coat over the arm of the couch. "You sit, then I will."

"Fair enough." Abigail sat on one end of the couch. Kyle sat halfway between the other two cushions—not quite next to her, but closer than she would have expected.

"Nice place." Kyle looked around the living room, his gaze skimming the oak furniture, the red-and-blue valance above the window blinds, the braided rug, the willow log basket on the hearth. "I like the country decor. I can see your influence at Words and Sweets."

"That's mostly Ellie's influence. She's more creative than I am." Mentioning Ellie's name made Abigail's throat tighten. What would Ellie think if she saw Kyle and Abigail together like this? For all Ellie's words about how Abigail was welcome to Kyle if she wanted him, Ellie must be hurting.

Don't read too much into this, girl, Abigail berated herself. *He stopped by as a friend.* "So . . . did Ellie call and tell you what happened today?"

"Actually, no. I stopped by the store this evening. I needed to swap that travel book I bought the other day—turns out my secretary already has it; I saw it on her desk. Listen, uh—you must think I'm a heel. Ellie told you we broke up, didn't she?"

Abigail nodded.

"I feel rotten. I hate doing that to someone and that's why I . . ." He shifted uncomfortably, his gaze on the braided rug. "Ellie and I had a lot of fun together, but lately, I could tell it wasn't going to work long-term. Things have been . . . winding down for a while. I've known for a long time that I needed to talk to her, but I kept putting it off. Makes me sound like a real hero, huh? A jerk *and* a wimp."

"Not at all," Abigail said. "You cared about her feelings."

"You're very diplomatic, but if I cared enough, I wouldn't have let it go on even when I knew it wasn't going to work out. Instead, I played the coward."

"You're too hard on yourself."

"I hope I didn't hurt her too much. I didn't want to hurt her, and she seemed to be okay with things. We're just at different stages in life. She's only a few years out of college, and I'm . . . not. I know you don't need the same birth year for a relationship to work, but I just felt this gap between us. It wasn't just the age difference."

"I'm sorry."

"I hope it hasn't been too hard on her. I worry about that. Does she seem okay to you? Does she talk about it? Or am I not supposed to ask that?"

"She's fine, Kyle. She told me essentially the same thing you did—that she could tell you weren't right for each other."

"Really? That's good to hear." He smiled sheepishly. "I probably sound like I think no woman can live without me. I hope you know that's not what I mean."

"I know." Abigail decided to change this uncomfortable subject. "How is your father doing? You saw him yesterday, right?"

"Yes. He's weak." Kyle sighed. "But not too weak to try to micromanage everything I'm doing at the resort."

"That doesn't sound fun." Ellie had mentioned that Kyle's relationship with his terminally ill father included plenty of friction, and Abigail admired Kyle for being dedicated enough to visit every week, his father's attitude toward him notwithstanding.

"Dad is what he is. I'm used to it. And I ought to be grateful that he's on my case. This is the first time in my life that he's cared about what I was up to."

"I'm sure that's not true."

"It is. Running that resort was all my parents cared about when I was growing up. Now that I'm in charge of it, we're a package deal. Tough luck for them."

Kyle was smiling, but Abigail couldn't imagine that his feelings on the matter were as light as his expression. "I'm sure they cared about you more than they let on."

"Nobody hides it *that* well," Kyle said. "At least I had good nannies growing up, so I can't complain." He shook his head. "I'm sorry. This is completely pathetic. You've had a traumatic day and I come sit on your couch and ramble about my childhood. What can I do for you? How can I help? Tell me about today."

With Kyle there, everything seemed less terrifying, and Abigail let the words come. She told him everything, beginning with Derek's admission that he'd been at Kemper Park the night Karen died and ending with the disastrous events of this afternoon.

"I want to know what you think," Abigail said. "I want a completely honest answer."

"This is the second honest answer you've wanted from me in a week. Let me know when I'm free to lie."

"I'll keep you posted." Abigail managed a thin smile. "Given the evidence and the way Derek's been acting, if you were in Detective Turner's shoes . . ."

"Unfortunately, that's not a hard question. I'd arrest him without a second thought. It looks like he killed Karen Brodie, and besides that, he held you prisoner all day. I'm not saying he *did* kill Karen. I'm saying that's what it looks like. The evidence against him is significant, and his reaction to it couldn't be worse."

"Agreed." Every time she shifted position, she could feel where the ropes had dug into her shoulders and waist. "I'll be honest with you. For a while this afternoon—"

The jangling of the phone made Abigail start. Her first instinct was to ignore it—it was probably Detective Turner—but a crazy hope that it was Derek made her jump to her feet. "Excuse me. I'd better answer that." She hurried into the kitchen and snatched the phone off the hook. The caller ID read ANONYMOUS. Her heart sank. It wasn't Derek—unless he was using someone else's phone.

"Hello?"

Nothing.

"Hello? Is anyone there?"

A slight shuffling noise and a click were her only answer. Annoyed, Abigail hung up.

"Who was it?" Kyle asked as she returned to the living room.

"I don't know. Wrong number, I think." She sat down, trying to remember where she'd left off in her story. "I'm sorry. I've lost my train of thought."

"You asked me what I'd do if I were the police. And you said that for a while this afternoon—then you got your prank call."

"Oh, right. I . . . for a little while, I was terrified that maybe Derek . . . that I didn't know him as well as I thought. But Kyle, now that I've had time to calm down, I'm positive he didn't kill Karen. It's not . . . not *him*." That sounded so weak that she expected Kyle to respond either with doubt or glib, insincere agreement. Instead he looked thoughtful.

"Tell me what you mean. Do you feel he's incapable of violence?"

"No . . . not completely, but Derek lashes out at things, not people. In his heart, he—"

"You're not a 'thing,' Abigail." Kyle's voice hardened. "And he hurt *you* today. Maybe it's a good thing I don't know where he is. If I did, I might track him down and try out a little violence myself to pay him back for what he did to you."

"No . . . Kyle, no, I'm not hurt . . . he didn't intend . . . I threatened to turn him in and he panicked . . ."

"Don't try to justify what he did to you. It makes me want to break his jaw all the more."

Realizing she was making anything but a good case for Derek's innocence, Abigail drew a deep breath and started over. "Derek can be impulsive. Sometimes he does very stupid things out of fear or anger. But Karen Brodie's murder was planned. In cold blood. Someone had to lure her to Kemper Park—why else would she be there on a November night? If Derek had killed her—not that I believe he ever would—it would have happened spontaneously, in the middle of a horrible argument. It wouldn't be *planned*. Derek would never *plan* to hurt someone. Does that make sense?"

"It does. You know your brother. If you say he didn't kill Karen Brodie, I accept that."

"Thank you. But I'm afraid a jury wouldn't feel the same way. What do I do now? I haven't told Detective Turner about the coat or the car. Giving him more ammunition against Derek . . . but if I conceal the truth . . ." Her voice died. Would Kyle think she was a fanatical idiot to even consider giving such a damaging report to Turner—or would he think she was a blindly loyal idiot for still wanting to help Derek after what he'd done today?

"You can bet Turner knows about the car already," Kyle said. "So that's a done deal. Remember, the police are looking for him. They would have gone to the hardware store and interviewed his coworkers, hoping for hints of where he's gone. They'll see his car there."

Abigail felt a little better. It was far less painful if the information didn't have to come from her lips.

"As far as the coat . . . here's how I look at it. You said Derek thinks someone is setting him up. Is that what you think as well?"

"I didn't want to believe it. It's so far-fetched. But Derek's right—it's the only explanation that makes sense."

"Okay. So your goal is to convince Detective Turner that someone is framing Derek, and to get Turner to keep hunting, instead of closing the investigation with Derek's arrest. Am I on target so far?"

"Yes."

"You hate lying, don't you?"

"Yes, I do."

"I told you that you were bad at it. When you lie, you look like you expect to get struck by lightning at any moment. If you lie to Turner, he'll know it. If you hold something back, he'll know it."

Kyle was right. She'd already had a taste of Turner's astuteness.

"So don't hold back," Kyle said. "If you want to help Derek—not that I think he deserves it—tell Turner everything. I know that sounds counterintuitive, but you need the police to trust you, to see you as a credible witness to Derek's character. From the way you described this detective, he sounds like a decent guy. He's not looking to hang Derek for a crime he didn't commit. He's not going to take the evidence at face value and then shut off his brain. And he's going to *need* every bit of evidence in order to find out what happened. What if someone saw the murderer carrying that coat into Derek's apartment, but the police never learn that, because they don't know the coat was ever significant, so they don't know to ask the question? Do you see what I'm saying? If Derek is innocent, you're not helping him by concealing things. You're making it harder for Turner to get at the truth."

Relief made Abigail feel like she could finally breathe again. She'd known all along what she had to do, but to hear Kyle put it so logically—and to know he wasn't condemning her for being reluctant to deceive the police in Derek's behalf—made her course much easier. "Thank you. That makes sense."

"Chances are, if someone is framing Derek, they've made a mistake somewhere along the line. They'll get caught." He smiled at her in a way that made her almost believe that everything would be all right. "Derek's doing enough panicking for both of you. You need to keep your head."

* * *

"NEXT TIME, MAYBE YOU COULD call first," Catrina Hubbard said coldly, her face still a little pale from the scare he'd given her when she'd opened her garage door to find an unfamiliar car with Derek standing next to it.

"Sorry to surprise you like this." Derek stood uncomfortably in Catrina's living room, reluctant to sit down without an invitation—which was stupid when he'd already broken into her house and spent hours hanging out here waiting for her to return. At least she hadn't called the police. Yet.

Catrina took off her coat and threw it on a chair. No wonder she'd chosen such a long coat, Derek thought. Her skirt didn't even reach halfway to her knees, leaving plenty of tanned, toned leg visible between her hem and the top of her high-heeled boots. Her silky midnight-blue shirt clung to her chest. Derek's heart rate sped up, an automatic reaction that made him angry with himself. He averted his eyes, but his peripheral vision caught the slight smile on her lips. Catrina knew she was gorgeous, and she liked seeing men react to her.

"I'm guessing you don't dress that way when you're teaching," Derek said. "Unless your school is a lot more fun than mine ever was."

She laughed. "I had a date after work. I changed at my boyfriend's house. What happened to your hair? You look like one of your church missionaries."

Derek snorted.

"Well, sit down. You broke into my house. The least you can do is tell me why you're here. Want a drink?"

"No."

"No? I take it you've already cleaned out my liquor cabinet."

"I don't drink anymore."

"You don't drink? At all?"

"No."

"You really quit?"

"I told you I wanted to."

"I didn't think you'd follow through. What do you do at parties? Sip prune juice?"

"I like keeping my mind clear," Derek said, bypassing the fact that he hadn't been to a party since he'd moved to Ohneka, unless you counted the time Abigail and Ellie had shown up on his birthday with pizza, a cake, and sparkling apple cider.

"This isn't still about that little mistake, is it?" Catrina asked.

Derek said nothing.

"I can't *believe* you, Derek. You overreacted like crazy at the time, but I thought you'd be over it by now. We didn't have to do anything anyway. How can you still be upset about that? Have a drink. You look like you need it."

Derek shook his head.

"Suit yourself, Mormon Boy."

"It's not a religious thing."

She winked. "The apple doesn't fall far from the tree. Even the rotten apple."

Derek refused himself permission to respond to this jab. Catrina strolled out of the room and returned a moment later with two wine goblets. Cautiously, Derek took the glass she offered him. Ginger ale.

"Thanks." He took a sip.

Catrina sat across from him. "You look awful. Not the hair—I mean, you look totally trashed. If you're not drinking, what *are* you taking?"

"Nothing. Hey, you, uh—you seem to be doing well. I was looking at your pictures."

"Yeah." Her face brightened. "Things are good."

"I thought you'd be on Broadway by now."

She laughed. "I'm having fun where I am. Did a couple of shows over the summer. Love teaching."

"Yeah, I ran into Roger Terrance not long ago. He told me you were teaching drama now in addition to your own theater stuff. I never pictured you as a teacher."

"That's because acknowledging that I'm more than a pretty face makes you feel stupid." She raised her glass. "To me."

"Cheers," Derek said.

"Why are you here?"

"Listen, Cat, I'm . . . in a lot of trouble."

She arched her eyebrows. "This sounds fun."

"I'm kind of . . . wanted for murder."

"Murder! You're kidding, right?"

"Yeah, I'm kidding. I drove all the way here in a snowstorm and broke into your house to have a laugh."

She leaned forward in her chair, and Derek averted his eyes from the view right down the front of her shirt. "You really killed someone?"

"*No*. But the police think I did. Someone's framing me." Derek told her the story. She listened, eyes wide, until he reached this afternoon's conflict with Abigail, which set her giggling.

"I don't see how it's funny," Derek snapped.

"Come *on*. Your preachy sister is lecturing you and threatening to turn you in, and you finally lose it and tie her to a chair and run." Catrina threw her head back and laughed. "I'll bet you've wanted to gag that girl for a long time. Too bad you didn't have a video camera! I'd pay big bucks to see that."

Catrina's laughter at Abigail's expense made Derek grit his teeth.

"She probably likes the idea of you locked up," Catrina said. "You'll be a captive audience for her preaching."

"She doesn't preach at me." Derek's voice was so sharp that Catrina recoiled.

"Excuse *me*. You're the one who was always griping about your family. I didn't know you and your sister were all lovey-dovey now."

"Listen, Abigail's been good to me."

"Fine, whatever." Catrina rubbed the stem of her wine glass between two fingers. She had beautiful hands—long, slender fingers, perfect nails. "What do you want from me? Cash to get you to Mexico? Forget it."

"I need a place to hide for a few days until I can figure out what to do. They won't track me here. I never told anyone in Ohneka about you."

"Not even your holy sister? She'd be the first to rat on you."

"She knows that we were . . . that I had a girlfriend, but I don't think I ever even told her your full name."

"Too bad. Maybe we could have been best buddies." Catrina ran her fingertips through her blonde hair, tucking a few strands behind her ear. It was a gesture that reminded Derek of Abigail, but it looked different when Catrina did it. It was artful, almost a performance—the graceful, languid motion of her hand; the way she trailed her index finger along her jaw.

"I know this is a lot to ask," Derek said. "Especially since you probably . . . don't like me very much."

She rolled her eyes. "Tell me you're not flattering yourself into thinking you broke my heart. You weren't hard to replace. And no offense, hon, but you were getting boring anyway."

Stung, Derek felt himself reddening, but he kept his voice even. "It would only be for a couple of days, or maybe a week."

"That *is* a lot to ask. When I pictured you crawling back to me, it wasn't with the police in tow."

Derek wanted to say he wasn't crawling back to her in that sense, but this would be a bad time to annoy her. Instead, he smiled weakly. "Yeah."

"I could get in trouble. A lot of trouble."

"No one will know I'm here."

"What about Brett—my boyfriend?"

"Uh . . . does he . . . come home with you every night?"

"No." She smiled in the way that used to set every nerve in Derek's body on fire. "Some nights, it's just me. All alone. Like tonight."

"Uh . . . okay, good. Maybe for the next couple of nights you could—keep him away? For old times' sake?"

"Old times. We had some fun old times, didn't we?"

"Yeah . . . sure . . . listen, I really appreciate this."

"You're cute, you know. Even with that silly haircut. I'm feeling cheated that I didn't get a kiss hello. For old times' sake."

Derek thought of how Catrina's lips felt against his and had to battle a powerful urge to cross the room and take her in his arms. He'd wondered if Catrina would hate him. He hadn't anticipated that she . . .

She doesn't care about you. She's playing with you.

Catrina laughed and set her glass aside. "You funny boy. Do you have any idea how freaked out you look? You *have* changed, haven't you? No more fun for Derek."

"I'm on the run. It's hard to think of anything else right now."

"I don't think that's the problem. I think you don't want to disappoint Sister Abigail. Oh, quit squirming and turning red. You're embarrassing yourself. I'm not going to maul you." She rose to her feet. "Have you already raided my kitchen, or do you need something to eat?"

"Uh—I'm pretty hungry."

"Go boil some water for pasta. I'm going to change my clothes."

Derek headed for the kitchen, struggling to shake off the unsettled feeling that coming here had been a serious mistake.

You need to get out. Go now.

"Great idea," Derek whispered to himself as he banged a pot onto the counter. What options did he have? Drive around like a fool until the cops spotted Abigail's car and arrested him? Go back to Ohneka and turn himself in? His best shot was to hide out here.

Then why did he keep getting jabbed with the impulse to grab his coat and run?

CHAPTER 18

Detective Turner shifted position on Abigail's couch, leaning forward with his elbows resting on his knees and his fingers interlaced. This movement toward her seemed to increase the intensity of his next question. "You're certain you have no idea where he might have gone?"

"No idea at all," she said, relieved that, for once, the answer to his question was painless. She'd been candid with Turner and Bartholomew about everything, including the bloodstained coat that had caused Derek to panic, but at least she wouldn't have to carry the burden of directing the police to his hideout.

"A girlfriend, maybe?" Turner suggested.

"He's not seeing anyone, as far as I know."

"Friends?" Turner asked.

Abigail blinked, realizing her gaze had strayed from Turner to the gray morning sky outside her window. It was a mild day, and melting snow dripped from the trees in her yard. "He mentions coworkers now and then, but I've never gotten the impression that he was close to anyone. He . . . as far as I know, he's pretty well kept to himself since he moved here. He's usually in his rock room working on something or on his computer fixing up his website."

"He moved here from Ithaca a year and a half ago."

"Yes."

"Do you know of anyone in Ithaca he might go to?"

"I don't know a lot about his life there. He wouldn't answer my calls for the first couple of years after he left home, and he'd only occasionally answer a text message. After a while, he'd communicate more, but he never said a lot about his private life."

"Why did he move there in the first place?"

"He went there after my parents cut him off. He'd met an actress from Ithaca when she came through town on tour with a theater group, and after things blew up at home, he left Syracuse and went after her. She helped him find work—he did janitorial work at a local theater and worked for a landscaping business."

"Do you know the names of the places he worked?"

"I don't. I'm sorry. Eventually he moved in with this girl, but in the end it didn't work out. He wouldn't talk about it much, but I had the feeling it was a very painful breakup. I think getting away from her had a lot to do with why he came to Ohneka. I can't imagine he'd go to her for help now."

"What's her name?"

"I don't know her real name. He just called her Cat. I don't know if that was short for Katherine or Kathleen or Katelyn, or if the nickname came from something else. I don't know her last name. I never met her. And I don't know the names of any of his other friends there. Like I said, he never told me much about that part of his life."

"Thank you for your help," Turner said.

Abigail moistened her lips. "You have a warrant for his arrest, don't you?"

Turner nodded.

"I'm sorry, ma'am," Bartholomew said in his deep voice. "We know this is difficult for you."

"Someone is setting him up," Abigail said. "He didn't kill Karen Brodie."

"We're investigating all possibilities, ma'am."

"Karen Brodie was divorced. Derek said she seemed very bitter toward her ex-husband. Have you looked at him? Maybe he had a reason for wanting her dead."

"We've checked him out," Turner said. "He has an alibi for the night of the murder."

"There was a handyman who did odd jobs for Karen," Abigail tried again. "I can't remember his name, but I've seen him around Karen's house a couple of times, and he seemed a little strange. The first time, he asked me questions about the house but said not to tell Karen he'd been there. Then I saw him there yesterday."

"What was he doing?"

"I don't know. I saw him walking out the front door. He seemed to be in a hurry. I didn't say anything to him."

"We have a list of everyone who worked for Ms. Brodie," Turner said. "What did this man look like?"

"Black hair, maybe six feet tall or a little shorter than that, kind of—" The phrase that came to mind was "ruggedly handsome," but if she said that to Turner, he'd think she spent too much time reading romance novels. "Kind of outdoorsy-looking," she amended.

"Ah," Turner said. "That's Ethan Hanberg."

"Oh, that's right. He told me his name, but I forgot it."

"Mr. Hanberg is Karen Brodie's ex-husband."

Surprise and disappointment seemed to flatten Abigail against the couch cushions. Ethan Hanberg was Karen's ex? So much for offering the police some alternate suspects. She should have known Turner would have already ruled out other obvious possibilities. *But he'd look harder if it weren't for Derek. He'd dig deeper and wider.*

What had Ethan Hanberg been doing at the house yesterday? Maybe going through Karen's things. He might be in charge of her estate. Had Karen been so isolated that the only person she could ask to care for her property in the event of her death was a man she'd hated?

"What about the witness who saw Derek's car at Kemper Park?" Abigail asked. "That seems convenient that someone would notice his car. Maybe the 'witness' was part of the setup."

"He's a man who jogs along that route every night, weather permitting. He noticed the cars because it was unusual to see anyone parked there. When he heard about the murder, he called us. We checked him out thoroughly. Is there anyone else you'd like to ask about?"

Abigail shook her head.

"Abigail," Turner said. "In Derek's apartment there were two green marble bookends. You reacted very strongly to the sight of them. Why?"

She'd thought no remaining question could shake her, but at Turner's words, her flesh turned icy. If she repeated what had been going through her mind—Derek's comment about being the kind of guy who could smash someone's head with a rock and the fact that one of the stone bookends had been missing from the shelf a couple of days ago and the terrible fear that had seized her when she saw Bartholomew holding both the bookends—

If she admitted that she'd doubted Derek, even temporarily, it would cancel out every assertion she'd made of his innocence.

Not that her faith in Derek counted for anything with the police.

Turner waited. He was good at that, Abigail thought bleakly, asking a question and then waiting until awkward silence pried the answer from Abigail's mouth.

"One of the bookends was missing from Derek's shelf a couple of days ago," Abigail said. "When I saw it was there yesterday afternoon, I wondered if it was like the coat—someone had taken it and . . . used it."

"You thought it might have been used as the murder weapon?"

"It's heavy. It has angular edges. It could be lethal."

Turner studied her, waiting. He knew she was holding back.

But if she told them what she'd been thinking at the time, it would only mislead them. Derek's words had been meaningless sarcasm, and it wasn't significant that he'd comment about a rock being used to murder Karen. Naturally, if he was thinking of something heavy that could be wielded as a weapon, the first thing that would come to his mind was a rock. He worked with rocks constantly. She'd just been overemotional and overwhelmed after spending hours tied to a chair. She'd panicked, reading meaning into a meaningless remark.

"Will that be all?" She finally broke the silence, hoping to nudge Turner and Bartholomew from her house.

"No," Turner said. "Tell us the part you left out."

At that moment, Abigail hated herself more viciously than she'd ever hated anyone or anything in her life—hated her transparency, hated her confusion, hated her conscience, her guilt, and the fact that no matter how she tried to do the right thing for Derek, all she did was hurt him. If she'd been physically ripped in half, it would have hurt less than this.

And now, no matter what she did, she'd make things worse. If she refused to speak, Turner would assume she was hiding something huge, and his certainty of Derek's guilt would solidify. If she did speak, she'd give them one more arrow to fire at Derek during his trial.

"Abigail, you'll make yourself sick again." Turner spoke gently. "Take whatever time you need. Breathe slowly. Don't panic."

She must look as awful as she felt. Taking Turner's advice, Abigail leaned her head against the back of her chair and forced her jagged breaths into a deep, steady rhythm. They both seemed so kind, Turner and Bartholomew. If she slumped here long enough, silent and pale, Bartholomew would bring her a glass of water and a blanket, and Turner would call a doctor. So kind, as they dug the information out of her that would allow them to send Derek to prison for the rest of his life.

She wanted to scream.

Go ahead and scream. Scream, cry, make yourself sick—how does that help Derek?

She didn't know how to help Derek, and at that moment, part of her didn't want to. She wanted to jump on him and batter him with her fists until her arms were so tired she couldn't lift them. Maybe then she could finally stop remembering what it felt like when Derek had yanked that rope tight and knotted it; maybe then she could stop remembering that he'd left her there with no idea how long it would be until she was rescued.

"Ma'am, do you need to lie down?" Bartholomew sounded worried.

"No." Rallying, Abigail pushed the hurt and anger to the back of her consciousness. The issue right now was not what he'd done to her. It was what he had—or hadn't—done to Karen Brodie. And Abigail needed Turner to keep his mind open to the possibility that Derek had been framed. If she refused to answer his question, he'd assume she was concealing a vital piece of evidence, not an off-the-cuff remark that anyone could have made.

The dryness of her throat made her words hoarse as she repeated Derek's statement, along with the context. "It didn't mean anything. When Derek's scared, he gets sarcastic. But when I saw the bookends, it reminded me of that reference. After everything that had happened that day, I wasn't thinking straight."

"You were afraid Derek was guilty after all."

"I didn't know what I thought. But I do now. Derek didn't kill Karen." She swallowed. "The bookends. Did they . . . was one of them used . . ."

Turner gave her a long, thoughtful look, and she could tell he was debating what to say. "It's a possibility."

A possibility. It was probably far more than a possibility, but Turner wasn't going to say so. The bookend with its distinctive three-tiered shape—Abigail imagined a crime lab technician taking meticulous measurements of the wounds on Karen's head and comparing them to the bookend. And blood—the unpolished portions of the stone would probably hold traces of blood, even if the stone had been cleaned.

Especially if the murderer *wanted* Karen's blood found on the bookend.

Abigail swallowed again, feeling as though her mouth and throat were lined with glue. "If Derek had planned to murder Karen, he wouldn't have used something as distinctive as his own bookend. Can you check to see who else had a key to his apartment?"

"Of course," Turner said, but despite this reassurance, Abigail didn't feel any better. She had the feeling the murderer wouldn't be careless enough to be in possession of a key traceable to him or her. And the lock on Derek's door wasn't exactly designed to guard Fort Knox. He didn't even have a deadbolt, and anyone with an Internet connection could probably figure out how to spring his lock.

"If someone has been in and out of Derek's apartment several times, Derek's neighbor might have seen something," Abigail said. "Or Derek's friend, Hunter Conley—"

"You can trust us to do our jobs." Turner spoke mildly, but Abigail realized she must sound ridiculous, advising Turner on basic police work.

"Abigail, I want you to listen to me," Turner said.

Abigail nodded, not meeting his gaze. *What now?* Soon, the police would find Derek. He wouldn't have the resources to keep himself hidden for long. They'd arrest him. A trial would follow. If *she* were on a jury, listening to all the evidence offered by the prosecution and contrasting it with the defense's feeble assertion that Derek had been framed—how would she vote?

It can't get that far. I won't let it get that far. It's like Kyle said—whoever framed him must have made a mistake somewhere. Maybe Chase or Hunter did see the killer entering Derek's apartment. There have to be hints, clues— some thread to grab that will unravel this whole setup.

"Abigail!"

Startled at the sharpness in Turner's voice, Abigail focused on him.

"If Derek comes to you, tread cautiously," he said.

"He wouldn't—" The phrase *he wouldn't hurt me* sounded so idiotic that Abigail couldn't finish it.

"People do crazy things when they feel cornered," Turner said. "If he contacts you, be careful, don't tell him you confided in me, and call 911. Don't take foolish chances. This is as much for Derek's sake as yours. He won't help himself by creating more trouble."

Abigail rubbed absently at the muscles in her forearm that she'd strained yesterday struggling to break free of the duct tape. "I would bet my life that he didn't kill Karen Brodie."

"I understand," Turner said. "But before yesterday, I imagine you would have bet your life that he couldn't harm you."

* * *

A FULL MINUTE PASSED BEFORE Ellie released Abigail from a rib-crushing embrace. "I am so, so, *so* sorry about everything. And what in the world are you doing here? Melissa and I can cover the store. Go home!"

"Sitting around at home by myself is a ticket to insanity," Abigail said.

"At least come vent a bit. Melissa, hold down the fort."

Melissa nodded. "Abigail, I'm sorry too."

"Thanks," Abigail said, knowing chatty Ellie would have given Melissa the scoop. Ellie would never gossip to strangers or customers, but she kept her friends well informed.

Ellie took Abigail by the elbow and towed her into the office. "Sit down. I'm going to make you comfortable."

Within five minutes, Abigail had a mug of cinnamon-laced hot chocolate in her hand and an assortment of Ellie's chocolates in front of her.

"So how bad was it with the cops this morning?" Ellie asked, sitting on the edge of the desk.

"It was . . . awful."

"Pretty high pressure?"

"No. They're very polite. But Detective Turner has this way of—very gently—wringing me dry. Every time I think I've told him everything, he twists a little harder and I blab out something else that they can use against Derek. Derek's going to hate me. How can he not hate me?"

Ellie narrowed her eyes. "After what he did, *you* ought to be the one hating *him*. And if he wants to hate someone, he can hate himself. If he hadn't been lying his head off from the beginning, I'm betting the police wouldn't be nearly so focused on him. Maybe they would have kept looking and found the real culprit. Instead, he's done everything he can to make himself look guilty. The nitwit."

Abigail rested her elbows on the desk and rubbed her throbbing forehead. The Tylenol she'd taken hadn't kicked in yet. "I know. But he's still going to hate me."

"Abby, what were you supposed to do? Keep up his stupid lies? Tell the police he wasn't at Kemper Park when they already had a witness who saw his car? Maybe you could have tried telling them he wasn't the one who tied you up. 'Oh, officer, it's just a coincidence that I'm in Derek's apartment. Honest, it wasn't him. I got attacked by a troop of Boy Scouts working on their duct-tape merit badge.'"

Despite herself, Abigail laughed. "Okay, you've made your point."

"Have you . . . talked to your parents?" Ellie asked.

Abigail shook her head. Before Detective Turner had shown up yesterday morning and everything had fallen apart, she'd been planning to call while her father was at work so she could talk to her mother and try to find out why she'd visited Karen. Now, talking to her parents was the last thing she wanted to do.

"Have another chocolate," Ellie said.

"Thanks." Abigail picked up a raspberry truffle.

Ellie stood and wandered to the water cooler in the corner. In a breezy tone, she asked, "So did Kyle call you last night?"

Abigail cursed the blush that heated her cheeks. At least Ellie wasn't looking at her. She was focused on getting a drink of water. "He stopped by for a few minutes to see how I was doing. It was nice of him."

"Yeah, I could tell he was taken aback when he came to the store expecting to find you and found me instead." Ellie's tone was still light, but when she turned toward Abigail, her cheeks were pink.

"It was nice of him to worry about me." Abigail tried to match Ellie's light tone. "He's always been a good friend."

"Oh come *on*, Abby! Considering how guilty you look, I *know* you're not naive enough to think he was just there as a friend."

"Ellie, it's not what you think. He didn't . . . we just talked for a few minutes. That's all." It wasn't so much what *had* happened with Kyle as what Abigail *hoped* would happen that made it difficult for her to meet Ellie's gaze. "Besides, he kept talking about *you*. He's worried that he hurt you and wanted to know how you were doing."

"What a sweetie. He's interested in you, okay? It was obvious, the way he acted when he found me here instead of you. I've never seen Kyle act so bumbling and embarrassed."

"He was just worried, after what—"

"Abigail, when he stopped by the store last night, he didn't *know* what had happened to you. *I'm* the one who told him that. He just wanted to see you. I think that's what he's been wanting for a long time."

"Ellie—I promise—he never said anything to indicate—"

Ellie set her still-full paper cup on the desk and came to stand next to Abigail. "Brought you flowers?"

"I—yes, but, that doesn't mean anything—"

"Listen to me, girl." Ellie gripped Abigail's shoulders. "I'm only saying this because I *know* you, and I know you're going to feel all guilty, so I want you to know it's okay. I told you yesterday that if you wanted Kyle, you were welcome to him. He's a free man. I'm not the whiney, clingy type who thinks it's backstabbing if my friend dates the guy I used to date. I don't own him and I don't want to own him. Got it?"

Abigail nodded, but the grim glint in Ellie's eyes didn't match her smile. She *was* bothered, but she wouldn't admit it.

Ellie opened her mouth, shut it, and turned away. What had she stopped herself from saying?

"This has been quite the roller-coaster week for you, hasn't it?" Ellie said. "I'd better get back to work. You take it easy for a while, okay? And I'm not mad about Kyle, so cross that off your guilt list. But I'm guessing Brendan might be disappointed." She winked at Abigail, but it looked more mechanical than mischievous.

After Ellie walked out of the office, Abigail pushed the plate of chocolates aside and rested her head on the cool surface of the desk. Ellie was reading way too much into Kyle's visit last night.

Wasn't she?

Coming alone to her house, bringing flowers, staying to comfort her about Derek . . .

Stop. The last thing she needed right now was to muddle her head with fantasies. Kyle was just a nice guy, visiting a friend who'd been through a traumatic experience. To read more into it than that was wishful thinking on her part—or jealous thinking on Ellie's part.

She needed to focus on Derek. How could she help him? Her effort to point the police in another direction by mentioning Karen's ex-husband had been a dead end. He had an alibi.

If it wasn't him, who was it? This wasn't a random crime, or a crime committed in the heat of the moment. It was a careful setup. Someone had wanted Karen dead for a specific reason. What was that reason?

Find it.

Abigail sat up straight in her chair. She needed to know more about Karen. The answer was somewhere in Karen's life.

Whom could she talk to? Karen's ex-husband? Why would he be willing to talk to her? Did he know the police had a warrant for Derek's arrest? No matter how strained Hanberg's relationship with Karen, her death still must have shocked him, and she couldn't imagine he'd be eager to talk to Derek's sister.

But what did she have to lose by calling him? Nothing. And contacting Ethan Hanberg was a place to start, a concrete act toward helping Derek. If she failed, at least she'd know that she'd done everything she could.

She doubted Hanberg would be home right now. She'd find his number and call him tonight. Abigail reached for the computer keyboard and opened an Internet browser.

CHAPTER 19

Aᴼᴛᴇ ᴀɴ ʜᴏᴜʀ ꜱᴘᴇɴᴛ ꜱɪᴛᴛɪɴɢ at the kitchen table and staring at her phone as she tried to figure out what to say to Ethan Hanberg, Abigail gave up trying to plan. She wouldn't know what to say to him until she had some idea of his attitude toward her. *The worst he can do is yell at you or hang up on you. I think you can live through that.* But she hoped that a man who'd insist on paying for a broken vase that wasn't his fault would also be courteous enough not to attack her verbally for being related to an accused murderer. Thank goodness he didn't know she'd pushed his name at Detective Turner this morning as someone who might have had reason to kill Karen.

Offering a silent prayer, Abigail dialed the number she'd jotted on a notepad. Her heart thudded as she listened to the ringing on the other end of the line. She shouldn't have called from her home number. The name Wyatt would show up on the caller ID, and if he did know about Derek, he wouldn't even pick up the phone. Her mind raced as she tried to figure out what to say if she left a message. *I need to talk to you? Please call me? Despite a mountain of evidence, the police are wrong?* Abigail's mind jumped ahead to a scene where Detective Turner told her Ethan Hanberg had accused her of harassing him, and if she contacted him again, he'd take legal action to—

"Hello?" The male voice sounded guarded, but not curt.

"This is Abigail Wyatt. Is this Ethan Hanberg?"

"Yes."

"We met briefly outside my brother's apartment at Karen Brodie's house."

"I remember," Hanberg said.

"I'm sorry to bother you. This must be a difficult time."

"What can I do for you?"

Relieved at the politeness in his response, Abigail got right to the point. "The police think my brother killed Karen. He didn't. Someone is setting him up."

"What makes you say that?" His tone was cautious, as though he wasn't sure how big of a kook he was dealing with and didn't want to set her off.

Abigail spoke calmly. "I know Derek. He couldn't have done that to Karen, or to anyone."

"I'm not judge and jury. Your brother's fate isn't in my hands."

"I know." Abigail switched the phone to her other hand and wiped her sweaty palm on her skirt. "I want to meet with you. Talk to you. Whoever killed Karen is someone who knew her well enough to know she was in conflict with Derek. It was someone who wanted her dead for a reason and who planned things in advance. The answers must be there in Karen's life, but I'm afraid the police aren't looking for them anymore. They think Derek killed her."

"Karen and I had been divorced for seven years. I'm not an expert on her life."

"But you were still in contact with her. You worked for her at the house. All I'm asking for is an hour of your time."

He was silent for such a long moment that Abigail had to clench her teeth to keep herself from repeating her plea. *Don't hound him. Give him time to think.*

"I already told the police everything I thought was relevant," Hanberg said.

"Maybe there's something you didn't think was relevant at the time." The words sounded uncomfortably arrogant, like she thought she knew better than either Hanberg or the police. She tried to soften the statement. "Maybe if we go over things again, something new will jump out."

His voice was gruff but still not cold or angry. "You're grasping at straws."

"Then I'll grasp until the straws are gone. My brother isn't a killer. I'm asking for one meeting, in a public location. After that, you'll never hear from me again."

"I'm not worried you're planning to stalk me," he said dryly. "A couple of weeks ago, I had the impression I was the one giving you the creeps."

Abigail wished abruptly that she'd been friendlier when she'd encountered Hanberg. "I'm sorry. It had been a stressful evening, and I was on edge."

"No apology necessary. I apologize for approaching you like that."

"It's fine. And—you really didn't need to pay for that vase."

"It was my fault you dropped it. I'd like to help you, but I don't know anything that could explain why someone would kill Karen. The best thing you can do for your brother is find a good attorney."

"I will. But first—"

"Has he been arrested?"

"Not yet." If she admitted Derek had fled, Hanberg would think her even more of a fool for believing in his innocence.

"If they haven't arrested him, they don't have enough evidence against him," Hanberg said. "You're worrying prematurely."

Trying to dodge the facts was useless. "He knows someone is framing him. He panicked and ran. I don't know where he is."

Hanberg said nothing, not that he needed to. Pointing out that Derek was acting guilty was about as needful as pointing out that snow was cold.

"Please," Abigail said. "One hour."

"If it will make you feel better. Where and when?"

"As soon as possible." Abigail couldn't keep the relief and eagerness out of her voice. "I'm flexible on time and place."

"Tonight?"

"That would be wonderful."

"Do you live in Ohneka?"

"Yes."

"Have you eaten dinner yet?"

"No."

"You know Ginny's Steakhouse on Errol Street?"

"Yes."

"I'll meet you there at eight. Is that all right?"

"Yes. *Thank* you."

"Don't get your hopes up. Like I said, I already told the police everything I thought might matter. I'm sorry—" He paused. "I'm sorry, but I told them the only person I could think of who might want to hurt Karen was your brother."

Fear gouged deep into Abigail's chest, but she said simply, "I still want to talk to you."

"I'll see you at eight."

After hanging up, Abigail sat quietly until the spasm of panic abated and her tight muscles began to relax. Hanberg might not think he knew anything useful, but his knowledge of Karen might include some crucial fact he hadn't considered yet.

Eight o'clock. She had time to take Derek's note to Hunter Conley before her meeting with Ethan Hanberg.

Stepping carefully, Abigail made her way down the steep porch steps. A thick layer of clouds blocked the moonlight, rendering her yard so dark that Abigail glanced at each of the lights illuminating the path to her garage, checking to see if any bulbs had burned out. The temperature had dropped sharply, and she was shivering by the time she reached the garage. At least a dozen times every winter, she cursed herself for not buying a house with an attached garage. The freestanding shed-turned-garage that had looked charming when viewed in summer sunlight filtering between emerald leaves was not so charming once temperatures plunged and the trees turned to skeletons.

Hunter's address turned out to be a shabby, gray-shingled duplex a block away from Karen Brodie's house. Apprehensive about what kind of greeting she'd get from Hunter's father, Abigail walked slowly to the door, hoping Hunter would be the one to answer the bell.

She rang the bell and waited. Streaks of light showed through bent window blinds, and she could hear the faint noise of a television.

No one came to the door. Biting the inside of her lip, Abigail debated whether to ring again or leave and try another time.

She'd better try again. Hunter might already be worried, wondering where Derek was. She pressed the doorbell.

An angry shout from inside the house made her cringe. She couldn't make out all the words, but the phrase "stupid kid" was definitely included.

Bad decision, girl. You should have come back later.

Thudding footsteps approached the door. It swung open and Hunter stood there, panting.

"Hey!" he said. "Sorry . . . sorry . . . I couldn't get to the door fast enough. I was in the bathroom. And my dad doesn't like to answer the bell."

"I'm sorry to bother you," Abigail said. "I just wanted to give you this note from Derek."

"Thanks!" Hunter snatched it out of her hand. "I went over there today, but he wasn't home." He unfolded it and read it, face taut with concentration as though it took considerable effort to decipher the words.

"Wow," he whispered. "Wow. The cops think he . . . they think he . . . wow, he didn't tell me anything about this when I talked to—"

"What are you *doing*? Heating the whole outdoors?" The yell from the back of the house made Hunter jump. "Get rid of whoever's there. We're not buying anything."

"Um—" Hunter glanced over his shoulder. "Do you want to—um— maybe you'd better not come in. My dad doesn't like visitors. I just— um—"

"Do you want to come talk to me in my car for a minute?" Abigail suggested. She knew she couldn't drop this bomb on Hunter and immediately speed away.

"Yeah!" Hunter's face brightened. "Dad, I'll be back in a minute," he hollered, and stepped out the front door so quickly that he nearly pushed Abigail off the porch.

"Hey, you have a different car," he said as they approached the rental Abigail had parked at the curb.

"Derek borrowed my regular car, so I rented this one." *Borrowed. Try "stole."*

"What happened to his Jeep?"

"He—didn't want to take his Jeep."

"Because the cops will recognize it?"

"Yes."

"Wow." Hunter settled his tall body into the passenger seat. Abigail switched on the engine to heat up the car.

"Hunter, I'm sorry about this," she said. "I know Derek feels bad that he can't be here to help you."

Hunter fiddled compulsively with the sleeve of his sweatshirt, and Abigail realized he must keep the toy turtle hidden there, even at home. It was little wonder he didn't keep it in plain sight—his father would probably be the first to mock him for it. "Why do the cops think he killed Karen?"

"Sometimes it's hard for the police to figure out who committed a crime," Abigail said carefully. "And some of the things Derek did—like having trouble with Karen over the rent—made it look like he might want to hurt her."

"He wouldn't hurt her! He says violence is stupid."

"I know he didn't hurt her. But the police aren't sure yet."

"Where is he?"

"I don't know."

"He didn't even tell *you*?"

Abigail wondered what Hunter would think if she told him about her last confrontation with Derek. Would Derek's actions make him less of a hero in Hunter's eyes—or would he think Derek had done what was necessary to stop traitorous Abigail from destroying him? Probably the latter.

"He didn't tell anyone where he was going," Abigail said.

"Did he say when he'd be back?"

"He doesn't know."

"I knew he wouldn't tell your parents." Hunter nudged the heating vent on the dashboard, tipping it up, then down. "He said that dinner the other night was a mess, that it was just like when he was a kid, with your dad jumping down his throat and telling him he was a loser."

"That's not exactly . . . he doesn't think Derek is a loser. He just . . . has trouble believing Derek isn't doing the same things he used to do in high school."

"Yeah, Derek told me about it. Smoking pot and skipping school and drinking a lot. He said it was all really dumb and he messed up bad and I should stay away from that stuff."

"He's right."

"My dad drinks beer all the time," Hunter said. "I hate it. How come your parents don't believe Derek's different? He doesn't want to drink again, not after the baby."

Baby? Startled, but not wanting to spook Hunter into thinking he'd said something he shouldn't, Abigail asked casually, "What did he say about it?"

"You know, that booze shuts your brain down and you do dumb things and hate yourself for them later. I know *that*. I live with my *dad*."

Her mouth dry, Abigail asked, "What did he say about the baby?"

"That he wasn't ready to be a dad, but they'd been drinking too much and they got careless, and he was totally *freaked* when he found out. He said *don't drink*. And don't make babies until you're married."

Abigail kept her expression calm. "That's good advice. Did . . . Derek tell you what happened to the baby?"

"Yeah. Sad, kinda, but Derek said it all made him realize he was messing up big time, so he left. I'm glad he came here."

"So am I." Abigail searched for a way to prod Hunter into saying more without revealing her ignorance. "Did Derek say he was sad about the baby?"

"He was relieved, because if they'd gone through with the plan, he said your mom would have *hated* him forever."

"The—plan?"

"You know, the abortion. He was really relieved it—you know—ended on its own. He said he's *not* going to mess up like that again, that he's not putting some innocent little baby in danger because he's dumber than rocks."

Abigail's thoughts raced. So Derek had gotten his Ithaca girlfriend pregnant, they'd planned to abort the baby, but she'd miscarried. And the experience had finally kicked Derek in the face with the realization that he needed to change. That was why he'd left Ithaca; that was why he'd given up drinking and had fought to get his life on track.

And he'd confided all of this to Hunter Conley and none of it to Abigail.

Had she been deluding herself to think Derek had ever trusted her? Did he even believe she loved him?

If he ever had, he didn't anymore. Abigail touched her shoulder where rope had chaffed the skin.

"You could talk to the police," Hunter suggested. "Tell them Derek didn't kill Karen."

"I've talked to them. But they have to figure it out themselves. I'd better go. I have an appointment tonight, and I don't want to get you in trouble with your father. If you need anything, call me." She pulled a notepad out of her purse. "Let me give you my numbers."

"I already have them, where I wrote them down when Derek called. I'm glad you're not mad at him anymore."

This statement caught Abigail by surprise. "Why do you think I was mad at him?"

"He told me. When he called. I—" Hunter squirmed and yanked at the sleeve of his sweatshirt. "Sorry. He said I wasn't supposed to tell you, because you were mad at him, but if you're not mad anymore, I thought it was okay, but maybe that's wrong . . . sorry. Don't tell him, okay?"

"No, it's fine," Abigail said quickly. "You can tell me. Derek won't mind. And I'm not mad at him. When did he call you?"

"Last night."

Abigail's heartbeat lurched into a runaway rhythm. Derek had called Hunter after he fled. "What did he say?"

"He needed my help. I'm good at a lot of stuff. People think I'm stupid, but I'm not."

"What did Derek want you to do?"

"He needed me to call you to see if you answered your phone. Or your cell phone—he gave me that number too. He said he was worried about you, that you hadn't been feeling good, but if you answered your phone, he'd know you were better. He couldn't call you himself because you were mad at him. So I called you."

"But I never talked to you—"

"I wasn't supposed to *talk* to you. He wanted to know if you answered your phone. Then I hung up. Sorry—were you mad? It was kinda rude, I guess, to hang up like that, but Derek said it was important."

The call she'd gotten while Kyle was there, the one she'd thought was a wrong number. That had been Hunter.

"Then I was supposed to call Derek and let him know, so I did," Hunter continued. "And he said was I sure it was you, and I said yes, because I'm really good with voices and I remembered yours. You have a pretty voice, really smooth and, you know, nice. I've tried to call him a bunch of other times, but he never answers. I didn't know what happened to him until you showed me this note." Hunter flapped the paper.

"I think he's keeping his phone off." Abigail said, the pain she'd felt ever since Derek had turned on her in his apartment finally beginning to ease. Derek *had* been worried about her, worried she was still trapped, worried enough to have Hunter check on her. He must not have planned to call Hunter, or he wouldn't have written the note, but it comforted her to know that given a few hours, his anger with her had switched to concern. Of course he hadn't dared call her directly for fear she'd feel obligated to report the call to the police. If she were to tell Turner about the call now, it wouldn't do any good—Derek would be far away from the location he'd called from.

"He hasn't called me either," Abigail said. "But don't worry. I'm sure he's okay. Hunter—over the past couple of weeks, have you seen anyone around Karen's house?"

"Hey, that's the same question that cop guy asked me. Weird, huh? He already asked me once, like a couple of days after Karen died, but he wanted to know if I'd seen anyone since then."

"He talked to you today?"

"Yeah."

"What did you tell him?"

"I didn't see anyone. That house is way quiet most of the time. Nobody even, you know, plays loud music or anything. He asked me if I saw anyone near Derek's apartment, and I said just Derek. I didn't know they thought he killed Karen. He didn't tell me that."

"Thanks, Hunter. I'd better go."

"Derek won't be gone very long, right?"

"I hope not," Abigail said softly.

* * *

AT FIRST CERTAIN SHE WAS too nervous to eat a hearty meal, Abigail changed her mind at the savory aroma of grilled steak that filled the restaurant. She hadn't eaten well for the past few days, and sirloin and a baked potato had never sounded so good. The restaurant was busy enough that background sounds provided a hum to help mask her conversation with Ethan Hanberg, but not so crowded that they were in uncomfortably close proximity to other diners. High-backed booths offered additional privacy. Hanberg had chosen the location well.

He greeted her pleasantly and was gracious during the small talk they exchanged while awaiting their food, asking the usual conversation-starter questions about her work and how long she'd lived in Ohneka. Somehow she'd expected Karen's ex-husband to be a lot more like Karen, though the incident with the broken vase should have told her otherwise. But negative personality traits didn't always expose themselves immediately. Maybe that attentive, slightly shy exterior was a mask, and beneath it, Hanberg was cruel or cold.

Not until the server was setting their food on the table did it hit Abigail to wonder if Hanberg had remarried. She wished she'd thought of that earlier. She would have invited his wife to join this conversation. She sneaked a glance at his left hand and saw no wedding band, but some married men didn't wear them. How old was Hanberg? Mid-thirties, maybe?

After the server left, Hanberg returned to the topic of the book they'd been discussing. He was an avid reader, though he'd admitted—in an awkward, apologetic way that made Abigail smile—that he'd never been inside Words and Sweets. He'd moved to Rochester five years ago, the year before Abigail had moved to Ohneka, and though his office was still here, he hadn't yet made his way to her bookstore. The realization that he'd driven from Rochester to meet with her embarrassed Abigail—she should have asked where he lived and offered to meet somewhere close to his home, rather than letting him drive to Ohneka to do her a favor.

He seemed to be waiting for her to turn the conversation to the purpose of their visit whenever she felt comfortable doing so, and Abigail appreciated his tact. After a few bites of steak and potato to take the edge off her hunger, she plunged in.

"Mr. Hanberg, I want to apologize for being so callous when I talked to you on the phone earlier. I never even told you how sorry I am about Karen's death. And it's beyond generous of you to meet with me, when you think Derek was responsible."

"Call me Ethan, please. And you have nothing to apologize for. Like I said, judging your brother's guilt or innocence is not my job." He focused on the piece of steak on his fork, dredging it back and forth in the juice on his plate. "Karen's death was a shock, but our relationship was dead long ago."

Abigail didn't know what to say, so she nodded.

"You want to know more about her," he said.

"Yes."

"You wonder why I married her."

It didn't seem tactful to admit that he was right. "I didn't know her very well."

"You knew her well enough to get stung by her. She told me about you."

"About me! What did she say?"

His dark eyebrows drew together as he studied her, and she suspected he was debating how candid to be. Apparently, whatever Karen had said had been harsh.

"Don't worry about my feelings," Abigail said. "It's not news to me that Karen didn't like me. I can't figure out what I did to offend her, but she was rude to me from the moment we met."

"I think she didn't like what you were."

"What I was?"

"The good Mormon girl."

"I thought she was—used to be—Mormon herself."

"She was. Her family joined when she was seventeen. In fact, I first met her at a singles activity. I was a new convert, brand new, and she'd recently moved back to Ohneka. She grew up here, but went to college in California and spent a few years working out there before coming back."

"What was she like when you met her?"

Ethan looked away. His expression was remote, and Abigail couldn't read his emotions. Pain? Sadness? Wistfulness?

"She was fun," he said. "Witty. Very funny."

The only humor Abigail could picture coming from Karen Brodie was caustic humor meant to hurt someone. She tried to think of something positive to say. "She seemed like a strong, smart woman."

"Smart, yes. Pretty. We got married five months after we met."

Abigail sipped her water. She wanted to ask Ethan how the relationship had fallen apart, but the question was so intrusive, she didn't dare ask it. She opened her mouth to ask if Karen had done anything unusual over the past few months, but Ethan spoke before she could.

"Things were good for the first couple of years. I thought we'd be sealed in the temple as soon as we were able, but when I'd bring it up, she didn't seem to want to talk about it. After a while, the topic just made her angry, so I dropped it. I thought maybe she wasn't ready, that she needed time." He shifted position and looked around as though locating the nearest exit in case he decided to bolt. His uneasiness made Abigail doubly grateful he'd agreed to come talk to her. Obviously, this was outside his comfort zone, and he'd had every right to turn her down.

"I'm sorry to put you through this," she said. "This must be hard for you."

"It's all right." He turned his attention back to the steak on his plate, and when he didn't resume his story, Abigail assumed that was all he was willing to offer about his marriage. She was mentally framing a question regarding the names of Karen's friends, when Ethan said abruptly, "It wasn't long before I couldn't do anything right. My job—I run a small construction company—was too blue collar, never mind that I made good money at it. Our house was too small. I didn't dress well enough. I was defective all the way around. After a while, she wouldn't even go to church—said the people there were judgmental hypocrites."

Abigail wanted to say that if anyone was an expert on being judgmental, it was clearly Karen, but she kept the remark to herself. Karen was dead. How would it help to criticize her?

"I know everything has two sides." Ethan spread more butter on the remainder of his baked potato. "I don't claim to be perfect, but I swear to you, I *tried* to work things out. I don't bail out on my commitments." He grimaced. "I thought I didn't, anyway."

"How long were you married?"

"Five years." Ethan's mouth was flat and his eyes shadowed. "She despised me so much that I thought she'd file for divorce, but she didn't seem to want it. I finally . . . left her."

"I'm sorry it didn't work out."

"Yeah. So am I. My parents were divorced—so were hers—and I'd sworn I'd never let it happen to us."

"She sounds like she was determined to be unhappy."

"Yeah . . . something like that. I could never figure out why. There seemed to be something . . . buried inside her. Something hard. Something hurting her."

"Something painful from her past?"

"I don't know."

"Did she have a tough time growing up?"

Ethan tore a piece from the sourdough bread on his plate and studied it as though he'd take any excuse not to look Abigail in the eyes. "Like I said, her parents were divorced—her father moved out when Karen was seven. They didn't have much money, which she resented. Her house, where your brother lives—that's her grandmother's house. She lived there with her mother after the divorce. Her mother remarried while Karen was in college—which Karen never forgave her for—and moved away. When her grandmother died, she left the house to Karen."

"Does she have any family besides her mother?"

"She has a couple of sisters, but she wasn't close to them. She wasn't that close to her mother, either." He tore the bit of bread in half, then in half again, and Abigail wondered if he was going to eat it or just shred it. "I *did* try to get Karen to come with me to counseling. I tried everything."

It was interesting, Abigail thought, how intent he seemed on convincing her—or himself?—that he'd done everything possible to save the marriage. Considering the way Karen had treated him, she wondered why he seemed to feel so guilty for divorcing her. "She refused counseling?"

"She said no way would she let some witch doctor crawl around in her head. Like I said, I always had the feeling there was something inside her she didn't want anyone to touch."

"Out of fear?"

"I don't know. I'm not a psychiatrist. But she wouldn't consider counseling of any kind—wouldn't even talk to our bishop. She'd flip out if I even mentioned it. Finally, I couldn't take it anymore."

He looked so miserable that Abigail instinctively tried to comfort him. "I think you endured her behavior a lot longer than anyone else would have."

"Maybe. I tried to make her happy, but I couldn't—or wouldn't—become whatever it was she wanted."

"I don't think anyone could be what she wanted. It sounds like the problem was inside her."

He said nothing.

"Even after your breakup, you kept helping her," Abigail said.

He gave a small, lopsided smile. "Yeah, she'd call me when she needed some handyman job done. She figured I owed it to her."

"You don't know of any recent problems in her life?"

"No. But for the past year or so, something *was* different. She seemed more—more angry. She didn't want me around. She'd just call me and complain."

Something was different. Abigail latched onto the words. "Do you have any idea what in her life might have changed?"

"I don't know. The change in her isn't something I can nail down. She just seemed . . . more excitable, maybe? More agitated?"

"In what way?"

"She started getting hyper and angry and would ramble on when she called me. I even asked her once if something was wrong, like a medical problem. I was afraid she'd gotten some kind of bad news from the doctor that had shaken her up. She laughed and accused me of wishful thinking."

"When she'd call you, what would she complain about?"

"Everything. Lately, she'd gripe that the house was falling apart and she needed money to repair it. I was . . . fed up with her demands. The divorce settlement was more than fair, and I'd already given her a lot of money beyond that. That's why I was there skulking around when I ran into you. I wanted to see if the house was in as bad of shape as she claimed."

Ethan Hanberg's guilty sense of obligation must have made him child's play for Karen to manipulate, Abigail thought. He claimed to be fed up with her demands, but he was still on the scene, worrying she really did need help. "She told you about Derek's rent problems?"

"Yeah, she told me a lot about Derek. I think she was infatuated with him at first."

"He did mention that he caught her watching him sometimes. What did she say about him?"

"She liked that he was the rebel, the black sheep, the lapsed Mormon. Like her, I guess. And she'd go on and on about how 'cute' he was, and how she wasn't *that* much older than he was, and after the dull men she'd known—another dig at me—she'd like to snag herself someone who knew how to have fun. But she got annoyed with him after a while, even before the rent problems started. Said he thought he was too cool to give her the time of day."

Abigail puzzled over Ethan's words. "According to Derek, *she* was always abrasive and rude to him."

"Yeah, that's Karen. Getting ticked because someone returns rude for rude. She called me the day after you and Derek had your parents over for dinner, and she was laughing—said that Derek was kissing up to your parents in a big way, trying to worm money out of them, and she'd trashed the whole thing. 'Put the brat in his place' is how she described it."

Abigail poked at her grilled vegetables, her appetite gone.

"She also . . . I'm sorry, Abigail . . ."

"Don't apologize. I'm here for the truth."

Ethan set his fork down and sat up straighter on the padded bench. "After Karen rattled on about Derek for a while, she said she needed money for plumbing repairs, and I'd better cough it up, that she was good at wringing money out of stuck-up little boys who think they're men. Then she said she'd need money to replace her car windshield too, since she figured Derek was going to put one of his rocks through it—if he didn't knock her on the head first. Then she laughed."

Horrified, Abigail tried to speak calmly. "Clearly she was joking."

"I thought so, but I was concerned, because I knew how provoking Karen could be, and from what she'd told me about Derek, he—I'm sorry—didn't sound like the most upright character. I asked if Derek had threatened her. She said he was trying to play tough guy, but it wouldn't work on her. That's all she told me."

Abigail sat feeling as though she'd turned to stone. She could imagine how this story must have sounded when Ethan told it to Detective Turner.

"I'm sorry," he said again. "I'm not trying to interpret what she said. I told it to the police exactly as I told it to you."

Abigail nodded acknowledgment. Ethan might not be offering an interpretation, but that didn't mean he hadn't drawn the same obvious conclusion the police had: Derek had threatened Karen, and a few days later, he'd killed her. *Had* Derek threatened Karen? *Trying to play tough guy* could mean anything from an outright threat to a contemptuous refusal to talk to her.

Struggling to pull free of the discouragement smothering her, Abigail said, "Karen told you she was good at wringing money out of men. Maybe there was someone besides Derek, someone else she was pressuring."

"Maybe. I assumed she was taking a dig at me, but maybe you're right." Ethan sounded more polite than sincere. He'd already told her she was grasping at straws, and why wouldn't he feel that way? All the evidence, including Derek's behavior—*especially* Derek's behavior—indicated that he was guilty.

"Can you think of anyone else in her life whom she might have been hounding for money, or harassing in some other way?" Abigail asked. "Anyone at all?"

"I don't know of anyone."

"Her other tenant, maybe? Chase McCoy?"

"She made merciless fun of him—he was always trying to interest her in his artwork, telling her if she had a McCoy original, she'd be rich someday—but she never complained that he owed her money. I think he was reliable with his rent."

Abigail felt a little guilty at the way she'd hoped Chase had been fighting with Karen.

"I wish I could tell you more, but if Karen was having trouble with someone else, she didn't tell me about it," Ethan said. "She was very private in a lot of ways. I never felt like I could get into her mind."

"Does she . . . did she . . . have any boyfriends?"

He shook his head. "If she did, I never knew about them."

"On the night she was killed, she was dressed up like she was going on a date. She'd gotten her hair cut and dyed, and her clothes looked new. Doesn't that sound like she was meeting someone she was romantically involved with?"

"Could be. But . . ." Ethan twisted his fork in his fingers. He couldn't have looked more uncomfortable if Abigail had taken the fork and twisted it into his flesh.

She pushed her plate aside; she couldn't eat any more. "But what?"

"Look, I don't know what the clothes meant, or why she'd get all dressed up when she hadn't bothered to fix herself up for a long time, as far as I know. But remember, I think she had something of a crush on Derek when he first moved in. If she thought that he . . ." Hanberg ended the sentence by picking up his knife and finishing the last few bites of his steak.

Abigail knew what he was thinking. Maybe Derek had abandoned a confrontational approach and had lured lonely Karen Brodie to the park by buttering her up, flirting with her, hinting that he was interested. Abigail wanted to insist that Karen was too smart and too cynical to fall for that kind of manipulation, but she couldn't. Ethan Hanberg had known Karen well. Abigail had barely known her at all. And Ethan plainly thought it was possible. Maybe beneath Karen's spiny shell, she'd been far more vulnerable than Abigail thought.

Derek hadn't lured her there, but *someone* had.

"What is Karen's mother's name?" Abigail asked.

Ethan frowned. "Why?"

The server approached their table and cleared away Ethan's empty plate. Abigail surrendered hers as well, though it was still half full.

"Can I interest you in some dessert?" the waitress asked.

"We'll look at the menu." Abigail didn't want dessert, but she feared the instant the check arrived, Ethan would make his escape and she'd lose her chance to ask any more questions.

They both opened their dessert menus, but Abigail could feel Ethan's eyes on her as she feigned interest in descriptions of caramel apple pie and fudge cake.

"I don't think Karen's mother would be able to help you," he said. "She and Karen weren't close, and I don't think Karen talked to her at all in recent years."

"I'd still like to talk to her. Do you have her phone number?"

Ethan's gaze was wary. "I have it, but I'm not going to give it to you. It won't do you any good to talk to her. You'll just upset her."

Abigail's cheeks burned. Ethan must think she was a monster to want to hound the mother of a murdered woman on the tiny chance that she knew something crucial about Karen.

"Ready?" The blonde ponytailed server was back at their table.

Abigail stared at the menu. *My brother isn't a killer!* What would the young server, Ethan Hanberg, and the entire population of the restaurant think if she stood up and yelled those words? She imagined a horrified hush, all eyes focused on her, her throat raw as she screamed out Derek's innocence—

"Abigail?" Ethan said.

"Yes . . . um . . ." The menu quivered in her hands.

"How about the molten fudge cake?" Ethan suggested.

Abigail nodded, set the menu on the table, and hid her shaking hands in her lap.

"We'll both have the fudge cake," he told the server.

"Great choice. I'll get that right out to you."

When the server was gone, Ethan said quietly, "Are you okay?"

Abigail nodded a lie.

"I'm sorry," he said. "I'm sure this conversation didn't go like you hoped, but I warned you on the phone that I didn't know anything that would help."

Abigail drew a deep breath. "Thanks for meeting with me anyway."

"You're fighting for your brother. I understand. If I didn't have an alibi for that night, I'm sure the police would be treating *me* as a suspect. I'm sure Karen never said a nice word about me to anyone."

Abigail couldn't tell if the emotion edging his voice was pain or anger. She tried to think of something tactful to say, but her mind was blank.

After a moment of silence, Ethan asked, "Do you have any idea where Derek is right now?"

Abigail shook her head. "The police asked me, but I don't have a clue."

"Hiding out with a friend?" he suggested.

"Probably, but who? I never knew the names of his old high school friends in Syracuse—he's six years younger than I am, so I was already in college when he started high school." Had Detective Turner asked their parents about Derek's friends? The thought of that conversation made Abigail cringe. *"How would we know the names of the losers he used to get drunk with? They never dared show their faces here."* Had Lillian admitted to Turner the real reason she'd gone to visit Karen Brodie? What *was* that reason?

"After high school he moved to Ithaca, but I don't know much about his life there," Abigail said to fill the silence. "The best I could do was tell the police he used to live with some actress named Cat. Really helpful."

"I'm sure they'll find him."

Was that supposed to be comforting? At least Kyle was willing to believe in Derek's innocence. Remembering the look on Ellie's face this morning, Abigail felt a flash of guilt at how much she wished Kyle were here to comfort her right now.

"I hope you're all right with the cake," Ethan said. "I figured anyone who works at the chocolate bookstore must like chocolate."

"It's fine. Thanks for the suggestion. I—choked under the pressure there."

"I'm sorry about everything."

"Thank you." Abigail picked up her water glass. "What—was your alibi for the night of Karen's death?"

"I was at my mother's house—I live just a couple miles away from her. I was doing some painting for her. Her health is lousy, so she needs a lot of help. That's why I moved to Rochester in the first place."

Abigail sipped more water, feigning thirst so she didn't have to respond. He had been with his mother the night Karen died? Was she the only witness to his whereabouts? How much of an alibi was the word of your mother?

Ethan Hanberg's relationship with Karen had been riddled with conflict. She'd tried to wring a lot of money out of him. He'd known about Karen's clash with Derek.

What was the real reason Ethan didn't want her to talk to Karen's mother? Was he protecting a grieving woman—or was he afraid she might paint a starkly different picture of Karen's marriage to Ethan?

Abigail set her glass down and said as casually as she could, "I saw you at Karen's house yesterday."

"Yeah." He shrugged. "She'd asked me to repair a broken window latch. I figured I owed it to her to finish the job, since the house will probably be on the market soon."

Abigail fingered the salt shaker, pretending she hadn't noticed the sudden blotchy redness in his neck.

CHAPTER 20

As Abigail reached to unlock the back door of Words and Sweets, the sound of rapid, heavy footsteps made her turn. Brendan was striding toward her.

"Good morning," Abigail called. Was Ellie right about Brendan? He certainly *had* been around more lately.

When he got closer, she realized he wasn't smiling. "We need to talk," he said curtly. "Open the door."

Annoyed at his brusque tone, Abigail unlocked it. "What's wrong?"

Brendan didn't respond. He followed her into the store.

Abigail tried to think what she'd done to offend him. With her head aching from lack of sleep and her emotions in knots over Derek, the last thing she wanted this morning was a confrontation. She'd spent most of last night staring at the ceiling, reviewing her discussion with Ethan Hanberg. Why had Ethan looked so nervous when she'd asked what he was doing at Karen's house yesterday? How good was his alibi really?

And what was Derek doing right now?

Abigail hung her coat on the coat tree in the office and turned to face Brendan. The anger in his expression made him look older and almost haughty, as though whatever error Abigail had committed had knocked her onto a lower plane than he. Brendan was generally easygoing, but when he did get angry, his emotions could rapidly come to a boil. A heated argument sounded like torture at the moment, so Abigail tried to set a civil tone. "Please, have a seat. May I take your coat?"

He remained standing. "You made a fool of me."

"I'm sorry, but I don't know what you're talking about."

"Your recommendation," he said. "It was *your* recommendation. That's why I told Bob about your brother's work. That's why I encouraged him to contact Derek. You vouched for Derek, told me how good he was. And now he turns out to be a creep who drags Bob's name into the mud in an attempt to weasel out of a murder charge. *Murder!*"

Understanding jolted Abigail. The note that had lured Derek to Kemper Park, the one purporting to be from Bob Chapman. The police had gone to ask Chapman about it, and now Chapman had told Brendan.

Brendon's tone went from angry to venomous. "And when I came here to see if Derek needed help finding a new place after what happened, you didn't say one word about the fact that's *he's* the one accused of murdering Karen."

Abigail kept her voice quiet. "At that point, he *hadn't* been accused of anything. And he was telling the truth about the note. Someone wrote it and signed it with your stepfather's name. Derek thought it was legitimate."

"Did you ever see the note?"

"No," Abigail admitted. "Derek was sure he kept it but couldn't find it. It seems likely that whoever wrote it stole it back before he could hand it over to the police."

"It seems *likely*? You're kidding, right? There was no note. Your brother panicked and grabbed at the biggest name he could think of to throw in the cops' faces, hoping that would somehow save his neck. That's how he pays Bob back for the work Bob gave him. That's how he thanks him for that solid-gold endorsement. If it weren't for Bob, Derek's business would have gone under before it got started."

She almost told Brendan that Derek *hadn't* told the police about the note—she'd done that—but realized that wouldn't mollify Brendan at all. "Derek would never have used—"

"Where is he? Where's Derek now?"

Wishing she could shove Brendan out of the office and lock the door, Abigail said, "I don't know."

"Because he's on the run. You lied to me. You praised your brother to the skies, knowing he was unreliable, twisted, potentially dangerous—"

"That's not true." Abigail let her voice go icy. "Derek did not kill Karen Brodie, nor did he invent that note—"

"Bob blames *me*. I'm the one who got him mixed up with Derek. Thanks a lot."

"Brendan, can we please back up a little? You're jumping to a lot of conclusions. Derek is under suspicion, but he has *not* been convicted of any crime. Innocent until proven—"

"How naive can you get? The business world doesn't work that way. You should know that. Perception is all that matters. And Bob's name was plastered all over the website of an accused murderer. You can bet that website is gone, by the way—Bob pulled a few strings and got it suspended."

"*What?* He can't—"

"Want to fight him in court? Go ahead. We've been good to you, Abigail. Prime location, great rent. There are a lot of business owners who'd be willing to pay a lot more than you do for a sweet location on Main Street, but Bob had a soft spot for 'the pretty girls and their bookstore.' That spot's not so soft anymore. Bob doesn't like dealing with people he can't trust."

Abigail's throat was dry and her stomach cramping. "We've been good tenants. We haven't given you any cause to—"

"You tricked him into doing business with a murderer. And this isn't about the legalities of the lease. Do you think your business would keep thriving if Bob decides he's had enough of you? He has a ton of influence around here. He could drive you into bankruptcy in a month. If he decides he wants you out, you'd be better off to shut your mouth, cut your losses, and go elsewhere."

Abigail feared she'd burst into tears. Arms folded, she dug her fingernails viciously into her forearms, using the pain to divert her body's attention from the knot in her throat and the stinging in her eyes. "I'm deeply sorry this has caused trouble for you and Mr. Chapman," she said. "But Derek did not—"

"Yeah, he's a great kid, isn't he? Drugs, booze, getting kicked out by your parents—and *you* claimed he'd changed."

"He *has* changed."

"Then why is he off hiding under a rock instead of sticking around to prove his innocence?"

For an instant, the urge to strangle Derek for his idiocy overwhelmed the urge to defend him, and Abigail wanted to snap, *"Because he's an immature twit, that's why."* "Someone is doing a good job of framing him," she said instead. "Someone wanted Karen dead and figured out Derek would be a good person to blame—"

"Look at you. All wide-eyed and naive, too pure to believe your brother could do anything bad. I don't buy it, Abigail. You're smarter than that."

"Instead of jumping to condemn Derek, maybe you could let a jury decide whether or not he's guilty."

"Whether or not he's guilty isn't the issue. The *fact* is that his name is a barrel of mud and he's flinging it all over my family. And you *knew* he was trouble and you still pushed us toward him. First you come to me to find him a place to rent, and I take him right to Karen's door. That looks great to Bob, let me tell you. His stepson taking a murderer right to the door of a helpless woman. Not that anyone who knew Karen could say she was helpless, but Bob's old-school-chivalrous when it comes to lone women."

"Brendan, please. I never would have—"

"Oh yeah, the sweet brown eyes. I remember that look. You think you can suck anyone in with the innocent routine, don't you? And when they're not looking, in goes the knife, right between their shoulder blades. You know what's crazy? Lately I'd been thinking I made a mistake and maybe we should try again. Now I can't believe I could ever stand being around you."

Abigail's self-control fractured. "I never wanted to try again. And I can't believe you're low enough to think referring to our past—"

"Save it." Brendan stalked out of the office and slammed the door behind him.

* * *

FOOL, BOZO, NUMBSKULL, IDIOT—PICK any insult, and it would fit him, Derek thought, pacing for the hundredth time around Catrina's living room.

He'd been here for two days and what progress had he made? Zip. Add *surviving as a fugitive* to his list of failures. His mom probably tracked his failures in a lacey notebook, line after line of disasters recorded in purple calligraphy. It's not like she'd have any college graduation photos or missionary snapshots or wedding pictures of him to scrapbook instead.

He'd hoped Catrina might know someone who could get him a phony ID and license plate for Abigail's car. Catrina had asked a few careful questions to see if any of her friends knew anything but had come up dry. She feared making people suspicious, and Derek didn't blame her. What he really wanted was a different car altogether, but he had no way to buy one. He didn't dare withdraw so much as twenty bucks from his bank account. The instant he used any credit or debit card, the police would know where he was.

Not that there was much money in his account anyway.

At least Catrina hadn't thrown him out yet, but her amusement at his plight had frayed, and her harsh questions rocketed around in Derek's mind as he paced. *"What's your plan? Don't you have a plan? You didn't think you could hide here forever, did you? Do you even have a brain, Derek?"*

No, he didn't have a brain, or a plan either. He'd never had a plan—he'd panicked and fled. Had he thought that once he was at Catrina's an escape hatch would magically open and he could jump through it and land in Mexico? Or that a few years of pot-smoking and underage drinking had given him the criminal qualifications to survive as a big-time fugitive? He didn't have a clue.

His last hope had been that Catrina, desperate to be rid of him before the police tracked him to her place, would shove a pile of cash at him and get him a car somehow, but when he'd hinted at that, she'd laughed. *"Whatever we had, Derek, it wasn't worth* that *much. You decided over a year ago that I was dirt, and you think I'm going to throw money at your problems now? Go ask your sister the nun for help."*

Derek sank into the recliner in front of the television, but within seconds he was back on his feet, too restless to sit still.

Ask your sister for help. Sure. Even before he'd attacked her, her idea of help was turning him over to the cops.

There *was* one way to get a little money. Catrina always stashed several hundred bucks in her drawer upstairs. She liked having cash on hand. And she had a lot of jewelry, a perk of being the only granddaughter of a rich old woman. He could picture the gleaming contents of her velvet-lined jewelry box: that triple-strand pearl choker, a bunch of gold chains, an emerald bracelet, that sapphire and diamond pendant. None of the individual pieces were extremely valuable, but it was better that way. They'd be easier to pawn, less likely to draw attention.

And Catrina wouldn't miss them. She hardly ever wore her grandmother's gifts. She liked big, flashy, eye-catching jewelry, not classic herringbone chains and pearls.

With a little money, he could catch a Greyhound and head across the country. Once he was in Arizona or Nevada or wherever he decided to stop, he could figure out what to do next. Without Turner and Bartholomew breathing down his neck, it would be easier to think.

Catrina wouldn't be home for several hours. She had a rehearsal tonight.

Derek's legs felt weird—weak and almost numb—as he walked toward the staircase. The chandelier hanging from the ceiling far above him was dark. Catrina had asked him to keep the use of lights visible from the street to a minimum. Shadows filled the balcony overlooking the onyx-floored entrance hall, and in the dimness, that huge tree in a steel pot looked like a freaky Halloween decoration.

His footsteps thudded on the tile and he resisted the urge to walk more quietly. No one could hear him. He didn't have to sneak. He wasn't even sure he was going to take anything. He only wanted to look. Slowly, he climbed the stairs, running his fingers along the chilly, wrought-iron railing.

In Catrina's room, he switched on the light. The cash was in a bank envelope in her top drawer. Creature of habit, that was Catrina. He flipped through the stack of twenties. Eight hundred forty bucks. Not bad.

Her gilded jewelry box—another gift from her grandmother—sat on top of the dresser. Derek stared at it, but didn't move to open it. His arms hung at his sides, heavy and awkward, his palms sweating. Paper crinkled as his fist tightened around the bank envelope.

Go on. If you're going to do this, do it right.

Betray Catrina. Like you betrayed Abigail.

"Abigail betrayed me first." He spoke through gritted teeth, his voice rasping through the empty room. If he'd stayed, he'd have ended up in prison. No way was he getting locked up for something he didn't do.

Yeah, well, guess what, hotshot? Now you can go to prison for something you did do. Like imprisoning your own sister. Like making yourself a fugitive. Like being a stinking thief.

Was this what he was? Was this *all* he was?

Derek stared at the sweaty envelope in his hand. Abigail hadn't betrayed him. She'd just wanted him to face this mess head-on instead of trying to run from it. But he didn't have the guts.

When had he *ever* had any guts? When had he ever done anything except run and hide—in a can of beer . . . a cloud of pot smoke . . . in Catrina's bed . . . *anywhere* he could deaden his mind, deaden his conscience, deaden the realization that all he'd ever done was disappoint himself and everyone around him. Why was he such a waste?

Why did Abigail care about him? He tried to tell himself that she must hate him now, but he knew it wasn't true. She was probably praying for him right this minute, trying to nudge God into grabbing him by the collar and dragging him out of this mess.

"I don't think God's in the business of rescuing people who are determined to be stupid." The Abigail-angel was back on his shoulder, whispering in his ear. *"Why don't you show Him you're willing to stop acting like an idiot? Get out of Catrina's house. Now. Come home and deal with this. Get a lawyer."*

But if he went home, he was going to prison.

"You don't know that. Maybe the police have other leads you don't know about."

"Fat chance," Derek whispered. He flipped open the lid of the jewelry box, but the thought of reaching in and taking a handful of gold and pearls made him feel like throwing up.

"Come home and deal with it, Derek. Pretend you're an adult for once."

Derek stared at the gold chains coiled in neat little velvet compartments, wondering if there was some exorcism ritual he could use to boot the Abigail-angel off his shoulder.

There wasn't. Abigail wouldn't leave him alone because she loved him. And she was right. If he'd done the honest thing from the beginning— calling the police the instant he found Karen's body—maybe they would have seen that it was a setup. Instead of acting like an innocent man caught in a bad situation, he'd acted like a cowardly murderer, burying himself in lies in an effort to avoid punishment and then, when the lies crumbled, running away. In every way possible, he'd played right into the murderer's hands.

Now, he could steal from Catrina and keep running—a coward, a liar, and a thief. Or he could go home and go to prison.

Derek sat heavily on the edge of the bed, still clutching the envelope of money. His legs shook and his eyes burned.

No wonder his parents hated him. What was there to love? All he'd ever done was hurt them.

But Abigail loved him. And he'd paid her back by viciously . . . by grabbing a coil of rope and—*Abby, I'm sorry . . .*

The tears escaped, spilling down his face in hot, humiliating streams. At least no one could see him right now, cracking apart. No one except

God, maybe, though Derek was pretty sure God had averted His eyes in disgust years ago.

I'm sorry. God, Heavenly Father, if you're listening—I don't know why you would be—I'm sorry . . . sorry . . . I've ruined everything, hurt everyone . . .

He didn't intend to end up on his knees, but something pulled him there—instinct, years of childhood training—to his knees, then facedown on the floor and he was bawling like a little kid, his face buried in Catrina's carpet, his body seized with remorse so painful that it seemed to slice all the way through him.

He had no idea how much time passed before he sat up again, drained, weary, but calm. Stiffly, he rose to his feet and dropped Catrina's money into the drawer. It was time to go back to Ohneka.

The thought should have horrified him. Instead, relief made him feel like he could finally breathe after spending a week with a sack of rocks on his chest. He'd call Abigail right now. She must be insane with worry. He'd tell her where he was—which would erase the possibility that he might chicken out and stay holed up at Catrina's. Then he'd drive home and face Detective Turner.

Derek pulled his cell phone from his pocket, switched it on, and dialed Abigail's home number.

After six rings, her voice mail picked up. Her recorded message followed by a beep jarred words from his mouth. "Hey . . . Abby . . . it's me. I . . . uh . . . I don't even know what to say." Pain twisted his throat into a knot. "I'm so sorry . . . I can't believe I . . . you were right all the time. I never should have—" What was he doing, babbling a message? After what he'd done to her, did he think voice mail was a good way to apologize?

He hung up. He'd call her cell phone. He had to apologize to her *now*; even a few minutes' wait would be excruciating. Fingers trembling, he dialed the number—and got her voice mail.

He gave a tired laugh, loud in Catrina's silent house. So he'd have to wait to talk to Abigail. The final challenge, to see if the coward in him could follow through, even with a delay.

He stood for a moment, toying with the phone. Several times, he almost put it back in his pocket, but he couldn't. Abigail wasn't the only person he needed to apologize to. And once he was in police custody, there might not be another chance to privately say the things he needed to say.

Shaking so hard that he could hardly control his fingers enough to push the buttons, he began entering the number he'd tried for five years to forget.

Would his parents hang up on him? If they did, he'd call back—he'd leave messages—he'd do whatever . . .

A noise from downstairs made him jump. Footsteps? But Catrina wasn't due home for a couple of hours, and he would have heard the rumble of the garage door opening. Must be his imagination, or the house settling—

Footsteps. Soft footsteps, but even rubber-soled shoes made enough of a noise on the tiled entryway that Derek could hear them.

His heartbeat accelerated. It wasn't Catrina. He had a perverse urge to laugh at the thought that a thief might have shown up to deprive Catrina of her stash of money and jewelry so soon after Derek had defeated an urge to do the same. *Nah, I decided I don't want it. It's all yours. Cheers.*

A thief? At eight at night, without so much as ringing the bell to check to see if anyone was home? Maybe it was Catrina's boyfriend coming to pick up something he'd left here. Derek had noticed a couple of men's jackets in Catrina's coat closet.

Wrong. Catrina's boyfriend would have come in either the garage door or the front door, and Derek would have heard him enter.

The footsteps echoed in the entrance hall. The police. Had to be. Turner had finally tracked him here.

Derek groaned softly. After cooling his heels for two days, he'd finally decided to do the right thing, and what happened? The cops showed up before he could act. Now, instead of surrendering with dignity, he'd get caught like the cornered rat he was. Served him right.

He closed his phone and shoved it into his pocket. There was no time to call his parents now.

Footsteps made muffled thumps on the carpeted stairs.

Go meet them. You can do that much, instead of cowering in here playing hide-and-seek. It wasn't as thought the cops would wonder where he was—Catrina's bedroom was the only room upstairs with a light on.

Steeling himself, Derek stepped into the hallway.

Surprise froze him in place. It wasn't the gun that startled him—it was the ski mask. This guy was no police officer.

Derek stuck his hands in the air. "There's jewelry and money in the bedroom. Take it, it's yours. I don't want trouble."

The intruder twitched the gun in the direction of the staircase. "Come downstairs into the living room."

"Fine, okay." Keeping his hands aloft, Derek hurried down the stairs and into the living room. "I told you, the money's in the bedroom. She keeps it in the top drawer of her dresser, and she's got a bunch of jewelry, it must be worth several thousand—"

"Open the liquor cabinet."

"Uh, sure, okay." Derek swung the glossy black doors of the liquor cabinet open. "Take whatever you want."

The intruder waved the gun to indicate the rows of bottles. "What do you want to get drunk on?"

"Huh?"

"Take your pick."

Bemused, Derek grabbed a bottle at random and held it out. "Here, take it."

"Pour it."

"Sure, whatever you want." The guy must be high on something. Derek slopped scotch into a glass and offered it to the intruder.

"It's not for me, Derek. It's for you. Drink up."

The sound of his name startled him. How did this guy know who he was? "I don't get it. What do you—" Relief sloshed through Derek, followed by anger. "Funny. Real funny." He sank into a chair, glad to take weight off legs that had turned to mush, and clacked the glass onto a nearby table. "So this is how she decided to stick it to me. You're one of her actor pals." He gestured at the gun. "Nice prop. I didn't know it bugged her so bad that I'm trying to clean up my act." Or maybe Catrina was just mad at him for showing up here demanding help, after the way he'd rejected her. He couldn't blame her for wanting a little revenge. "Good joke. Tell her I said bravo. I'm leaving tonight, by the way. I won't be a problem for her anymore."

The gun barrel remained pointed at him. "The night Karen Brodie died, she was wearing a long, ivory dress coat, and a blue scarf. Her body was directly in front of the stone fireplace in the Henning picnic pavilion at Kemper Park. She was lying on her stomach with her face turned toward the fireplace."

Derek's mouth hung open, but he couldn't draw breath. He hadn't told Catrina those details. He hadn't told anyone those details. The only people who'd know them were the police, the dog-walker who had found Karen—

And the person who had killed her.

"Have a drink, Derek. You need it."

Derek's dry lips stuck together. He swallowed hard. "You killed Karen."

"Drink."

"Why? Who are you? How did you find me?"

The man took the bottle of scotch in a leather-gloved hand and set it on the table next to the filled glass. He aimed the barrel of the gun between Derek's eyes. "Pick up that glass."

"You framed me."

"Tonight, in a fit of drunken remorse, you're going to call the police and turn yourself in."

"I was planning to turn myself in anyway. Give me a minute and I'll call right now."

"Sure you were."

"I swear—"

"Fine. But let's play it up a little. Pick up that glass."

"Look—I don't drink anymore. It's a religious thing—"

"You're drinking tonight. Pick up the glass."

With the muzzle of a gun six inches from his forehead, Derek didn't dare disobey. He picked up the glass. "You don't need to invent any more evidence against me. The cops have plenty."

"I'm offering you a choice. You can get drunk, you can make that call, you can babble out a confession. Or you can let Catrina find you here in a few hours with a gun in your hand and a bullet in your head. Suicide would work as a confession, too."

"They won't—they won't believe—I don't even own a gun, they'll be able to trace—"

"Not this gun, they won't. They won't know where you got it, but a dirtbag like you shouldn't have trouble getting his hands on a weapon. Make your choice. I'd rather not kill you. Cooperate, and this will work out for both of us."

The muzzle of the gun touched his forehead. Derek quickly raised the glass and swallowed. The liquor scorched his throat.

When the glass was empty, the man flicked the barrel of the gun toward the scotch bottle. "Pour yourself another one."

* * *

ABIGAIL STOOD FOR A MOMENT on the sidewalk, staring in disbelief at the fake stone facade and the neon lights flashing in the windows of Peppy Pete's Pizza and Pizzazz Palace. The name alone was enough to make her eyes cross, and the thought of setting foot in this bright, noisy children's party place was about as appealing as the thought of a marching band practicing in her living room. It had suddenly become a lot easier to understand why Derek hadn't even blinked when someone claiming to be Bob Chapman had left a note on his door telling him to come to Kemper Park on a November night. Chapman was more than eccentric when it came to choosing locations for meetings. He was certifiably insane.

Shaken by Brendan's angry accusations, Abigail had spent the day trying not to show Ellie how worried she was. If they lost their prime downtown location, that could be the end of Words and Sweets. She had to talk directly to Bob Chapman. If he felt she'd betrayed him by recommending Derek, then she needed to attempt to make amends, not let Brendan play angry go-between.

Half certain Chapman would refuse to meet with her, she'd called Chapman Properties, given her name to the receptionist, and explained that she needed to speak directly to Mr. Chapman. The girl had tried to refer her to half a dozen other people, and when Abigail held firm, she'd said—in a dubious tone—that she'd give Mr. Chapman's secretary the message.

Fearing that was the end of it, Abigail was contemplating other ways to get in touch with Chapman when her phone rang fifteen minutes later and Chapman's secretary told her Mr. Chapman would meet with her, if she would go to Peppy Pete's tonight at eight.

Abigail opened the door and stepped inside. At least it was warm in here. Warm and busy: lights flashed on video games, bells clanged, children squealed, and a carousel churned out an obnoxious electronic tune. Why couldn't Chapman have selected the library as a meeting place?

It was still twelve minutes to eight, so he probably wouldn't be here yet. Abigail started toward a bench near the door where she could wait, but a hand clamped around her elbow, startling her.

"Early. Good for you." Bob Chapman gave her a wolfish grin, keen eyes looking her up and down. Lean, with wild white hair that added a couple of inches to his small stature, he exuded energy and strength.

Abigail doubted she could have pulled her elbow out of that iron grip without an all-out struggle.

"You like banana splits?" he asked.

This was far from the opening Abigail had expected. "Yes."

"Nut allergies?"

"No."

"Good. Let's go sit down." He steered her past the play area and into one of the private party rooms. At the end of one of the bright yellow tables were two glasses of ice water and a pitcher. Fake flames danced in what Abigail supposed was meant to resemble a stone fireplace out of a medieval castle. Cartoonish coats-of-arms decorated the walls.

"Allow me to take your coat, my lady." Chapman deftly helped Abigail out of her coat and scarf and hung them on the rack near the door. "Have a seat. Ah, the banquet cometh." A college kid dressed like a court jester entered the room carrying a tray with two dishes heaped with ice cream.

He set one dish in front of Chapman and the other in front of Abigail. "How are you folks tonight?"

"Hale and hearty, my good man," Chapman said. "Here's a bit of treasure for a job skillfully done." He handed the server a fifty-dollar bill.

The server gawked at the money. "Hey—thanks! If you need anything else—"

"Peace and quiet, my lad. Bar the door behind you."

"Enjoy your ice cream, sir. You too, ma'am." He retreated and closed the door.

Abigail looked at the cherry perched on top of a Mt. Everest of whipped cream. "Thank you for the ice cream," she said, wondering if this was a strange dream, or maybe a hallucination signaling an oncoming mental breakdown. From what Brendan had said, she'd thought Chapman was furious with her—not in the mood to buy her a banana split.

Chapman dug his spoon into his bowl. "As wondrous as it may seem, Peppy Pete's Palace of Putrescence, or whatever they call this establishment, has the best banana splits in three counties. If you're still hungry after you finish that, you should try their strawberry shakes."

"I won't be hungry for a week after I finish this," Abigail said. "They must use a backhoe to scoop this ice cream."

Chapman laughed.

Abigail ate a couple of spoonfuls, waiting for Chapman to show some sign of the anger Brendan had ranted about, but he sat enthusiastically eating his banana split.

Time to jump to the reason she was here. "Mr. Chapman, thank you for meeting with me. Brendan talked to me this morning and told me you were upset about my recommending Derek's work, now that he's in some trouble."

"Ah, yes. I did skin young Brendan alive. It's his job to protect me from fools and knaves, and he's outrageously overpaid."

"I'm deeply sorry that this has proven embarrassing for you. I would never have recommended Derek if I thought there was a risk that the association could damage you in any way. I'm certain Derek is innocent of murder, but I can't dispute that he's acted foolishly."

"A polished yet sincere speech," Chapman said. "*Foolish* is an apt word for your brother's actions. That noble knight of the realm, Detective Turner, informs me that Derek has scampered away rather than answering the charges against him."

"He . . . panicked," Abigail said.

"An explanation, not an excuse. I don't hold you responsible for your brother, Lady Abigail, nor do I blame your crystal ball for malfunctioning and not revealing that your brother would one day be facing a murder charge."

This was so opposite from what Brendan had told her that Abigail was baffled. What had happened to Chapman's fury at her betrayal and his threats to throw her out?

Or had those been Brendan's threats? It sounded like Chapman had erupted at Brendan, and Brendan had in turn lashed out at Abigail. Abigail felt suddenly guilty that her recommendation had made Brendan the target of whatever temper hid beneath Chapman's genially eccentric facade.

"I apologize for all of this," Abigail said. "And I don't think Brendan had a crystal ball either; it's not his fault—"

"Ah, my dear, don't feel sorry for Sir Brendan. He needs a dressing-down every now and then. I enjoy watching his eyeballs bulge as he struggles not to counterattack and risk his potential inheritance. If I was a tad rough on him, I'll sure he'll forgive me, or at least pretend to. I'm entitled to some irrationality."

Abigail was fairly certain that when it came to irrationality, Chapman had claimed more than his share.

Chapman plucked the cherry off of his banana split and tossed it into his mouth. "You are a lovely and gracious lass," he said. "I can't figure out why knavish Brendan let you get away. He's something of a dunce about women. Specializes in breaking hearts."

Not sure what would constitute an appropriate response, Abigail offered an uncertain smile.

"A shame indeed," Chapman continued. "Mel and I were hoping for a wedding, what with you sharing her and Brendan's quaint and friendly religion. Alas!" Without warning, he switched gears. "Karen's death was a shock. I knew her mother."

"Brendan said she used to work for you."

"Yes, indeed. She worked as a receptionist in my office a good few years ago. Karen was a pretty lass back then. Even young Brendan had eyes for her at one point."

Abigail tried to imagine a younger Brendan pursuing a younger Karen. Brendan had never mentioned any relationship with Karen. Maybe he'd just admired her from a distance.

"Karen's mother worried a lot about her," Chapman said. "She was always afraid Karen was veering off course, heading for trouble."

"What specifically was she worried about?" Abigail tried not to sound like she was pouncing on Chapman's information, but if Karen had been in trouble, maybe that was a clue to—

"Dear girl, you look so eager. Are you perchance hoping that a murderer is about to leap out of Karen's past, confession in hand?"

Abigail blushed.

"I don't recall the specific content of her mother's laments," Chapman said. "Just worrying that Karen wasn't happy, that she was chasing the wrong boys, and so on."

"What's her mother's name?"

"Jolene . . . ah . . . give me a moment. Lassiter. She married a man named Terry Lassiter and moved to Buffalo. Still sends me Christmas cards." Chapman dug into his bowl of ice cream and ate with such gusto that Abigail didn't dare interrupt him with a question. Finally, he paused and picked up his water glass.

"As for you, dear lady of the books, let me explain something. I like your brother. He has immense talent. If he were here defending himself with dignity, I might even believe him innocent. Frankly, I doubt he'd kill a woman for revenge, which is what the situation amounts to, since Karen's death wouldn't have brought him anything but satisfaction. But what he did or didn't do to poor Karen and whether or not there actually was a note signed with my name that tricked him into going to Kemper Park is not something I can determine. What I *can* determine is that in running away, he's shown a serious deficit in his character. I don't deal with people like that if I can help it. His website is down and will remain down until all traces of my endorsement are removed. And even if he does wriggle out of this situation, I will never do business with him again."

It surprised Abigail that this statement would bother her so much when right now the success or failure of Derek's business was the least of his concerns.

"It's obvious that you're loyal to Derek, and I admire loyalty," Chapman said. "But I don't lend my name to cowards, and neither should you, my dear. If you're smart, you'll hack that branch off the family tree and go on with your own life."

* * *

SWEATY FROM THE EFFORT OF pushing and dragging Derek up the stairs, Philip lifted Derek's arm from around his shoulders and sat him next to the railing that ringed the second-story hallway overlooking the entryway.

Derek flopped backward onto the carpet and held up the empty glass he still clutched in his hand. "Your—your turn, buddy. Have one on the houssh." He tipped the glass upside down so the last few drops hit the floor.

Philip hurried into the master bedroom, threw back the silk comforter, and stripped the top sheet from the king-size bed. Carrying the sheet, he returned to the hallway, where Derek lay on his back, mumbling something about Karen.

Using the scissors he'd found in a kitchen drawer, Philip cut two strips from the sheet. He didn't have to work hard to make the edges a jagged testament to poor coordination; he wasn't soused like Derek, but his gloved hands were shaking. He fumbled as he twisted the strips around each other to form a rope. *Calm down. Do this right, and your worries are over.*

He wanted to get out of here. This was taking way too long, much longer than Karen, much longer than Leslie. Finding an unlocked window in Catrina Hubbard's dining room had been such a bonus that he'd gotten cocky, assuming everything else would be easy as well. But even while wallowing in an alcohol-induced haze, Derek had been stubborn about writing the note. It had taken Philip half an hour of threatening and coaxing to get a few words scrawled on the paper.

Philip took the note and set it on the floor near Derek. He'd locked the dining room window. When he left, he'd slip out the back door. That door could be locked from the inside and pulled shut, leaving the police the impression that the house had been secured the entire time, with nobody but Derek here. Good thing the snow had melted—he didn't have to worry about leaving footprints across the grass, and he'd stepped out of his overshoes before climbing in the window so he wouldn't risk getting any dampness or dirt inside. When he retrieved his overshoes, he'd make sure to smooth out the mulch beneath the window so no indentations remained.

Derek's eyes were closed and he'd started snoring. Keeping his touch as light as possible, Philip slipped one end of the makeshift rope behind Derek's neck, brought it to the front, and knotted it. He took the other end of the rope and reached to knot it around the iron railing.

The jingle of the doorbell made him jump. The rope fell out of his hand.

Don't panic. It's some friend of the Hubbard girl. Ignore them and they'll go away.

Not daring to move, he stared at the front door. Curtains covered the tall windows near the door. Whoever was out there couldn't see inside. He'd count to a hundred and then resume—

The doorbell rang again, and a fist pounded on the door. "Police. Open the door."

How could the police—they must have followed the same trail he did. They'd be in the house momentarily. Panicking, Philip grabbed Derek under the arms and heaved him off the floor. He shoved him forward so he dangled with his head and upper body over the railing, then grabbed his legs and swung them up and over.

The crunch of Derek's body snapping the branches of the silk tree and a thud as he struck the stone floor of the entryway made Philip shudder. He yanked off his shoes so his sock-feet wouldn't make noise that could be heard outside, and hurried toward the back door.

CHAPTER 21

"**A**BIGAIL, I'M WORRIED ABOUT YOU." The concern in Kyle's voice brought Abigail warmth, comfort, and a twinge of relief that Ellie was not at the store yet and wouldn't need to find out that Kyle had called Abigail this morning. "You went to dinner with this Hanberg guy? How did you know you could trust him?"

"I was careful, Kyle, really. We were in a public place. There were plenty of people around."

"He sounds like bad news."

"I'm not sure what to make of him." With her cell phone braced between her cheek and her shoulder, Abigail pulled out a cookbook a customer had shelved in Science Fiction/Fantasy. "He seemed like a nice guy. He just—looked nervous when I mentioned seeing him at Karen's after she died."

"If his only alibi for the night of Karen Brodie's murder is the word of his mother, I'd say he has no alibi at all. You're right to be leery of him."

"I'm sure Detective Turner has checked out his story thoroughly," Abigail said, hoping it wasn't true and that Turner had missed something. If Ethan Hanberg's alibi cracked, he'd be the perfect suspect.

Why did she feel so uneasy at the realization that she *wanted* Ethan to be guilty? She usually looked for the best in people, and here she was hoping he was guilty of a horrible crime.

"Maybe he's a really good liar," Kyle suggested.

"Maybe." Abigail stifled a yawn and slid the cookbook into the correct spot. She hadn't slept well last night—again—and she was exhausted.

"You're not going to keep after him, are you?" Kyle's voice sharpened. "I've got a bad feeling about this guy. A bitter ex-husband . . . Karen kept hassling him for money . . . maybe he—"

"I know. I wasn't planning to try to talk to him again, but I will tell Detective Turner he was acting strange."

"Good. Let Turner handle it." Kyle sounded relieved. "Any word from Derek? All right, sorry, that was stupid. You would have told me right off if he'd contacted you."

"No, he hasn't contacted me. Half of me hopes he'll show up at my door tonight, ready to call a lawyer. The other half of me—"

"—hopes he's in Madagascar by now."

"Exactly."

"Abigail . . . if he does show up—and if he gets desperate enough, he might—you *will* be careful, right? I'm not saying he killed Karen, but considering what happened last time you were together . . ."

"You sound like Detective Turner. But don't worry. He wouldn't come anywhere near me unless he's decided to turn himself in. He . . . wouldn't trust me to help him." Strange how small and cold those words made her feel. Derek didn't trust her.

He doesn't trust you to help him bury himself in an avalanche of lies, you mean.

"I'd better let you go," Kyle said. "I know the store opens soon, and you must have work to do. Hang in there, all right? I'll call you later. And if you need anything, call me. Call me in the middle of the night if you have to, even if you just need someone to talk to. You shouldn't have to face this alone, and I know your parents aren't any help."

"I will. Thanks, Kyle."

"Talk to you soon." He hung up.

Abigail slid the phone into her pocket, feeling a little guilty at the way she was smiling. Visiting her . . . calling her . . . it was becoming almost impossible to convince herself that Ellie was wrong and Kyle *wasn't* interested in more than friendship.

She couldn't even begin to pretend to herself that she wouldn't be thrilled if Ellie was right.

But if she did start seeing Kyle, how much of a wedge would that jam between Ellie and herself? How could Ellie help but be repulsed by the way Abigail had swooped in the instant Ellie was out of Kyle's life?

You didn't swoop in. Kyle came to you.

But you're not exactly discouraging him.

Abigail imagined her warm friendship with Ellie chilling to frigid formality as Ellie and she tried to work together while Abigail's relationship with Kyle grew serious.

What relationship? Your brain belongs in the Science Fiction/Fantasy section, girl. Kyle brought you flowers and called to make sure you were okay. Period. He's a friend.

Abigail sighed and finished her walk-through of the store to check that all was ready for opening. Kyle's comment about her parents had stirred the confusion that had been simmering all week. She'd delayed talking to them, fearing to tell them that Derek was on the run, and horrified at the thought of admitting what Derek had done to her.

What if they believed Derek had killed Karen? So much for her hopes that Derek and they might ever reconcile.

But she had to know what they were thinking. At the very least, she had to try to convince them that the manner of Karen's death ran counter to Derek's personality. It was believable that Derek could panic and do something crazy, but the cold-blooded planning involved in luring Karen to the park and smashing her skull with a bookend—her parents surely couldn't believe Derek was capable of that.

She'd call them tonight.

The name of Jolene Lassiter, Karen's mother, drifted through Abigail's thoughts. Ethan Hanberg had withheld her name, not wanting Abigail to talk to her. His motives might be innocent—no matter how estranged Jolene and Karen had been, Jolene must still be mourning Karen's death, and the last thing she'd want to do is face questions from the accused murderer's sister.

But what if Ethan had other reasons for not wanting her to disturb Karen's mother? He'd gone to a lot of trouble to make himself sound like the good guy in his failed marriage to Karen. What kind of story would Jolene Lassiter tell?

She wished she knew a few more details of Ethan's alibi, but Detective Turner would never give them to her. Maybe his alibi was unbreakable, but that didn't mean he was innocent. If he was desperate enough to be rid of Karen, he might have hired someone to kill her.

A rap on the locked glass door made her jump. It was still eighteen minutes until ten—

Through the glass, Abigail saw the familiar figures of Detectives Turner and Bartholomew. Her heart racing, Abigail grabbed her keys off the counter and walked toward the door. Had they come to tell her they'd arrested Derek? She couldn't imagine that they'd have more questions for her. She'd told him everything she knew.

She shoved the key into the lock and swung the door open.

Turner nodded a hello. "May we speak to you for a moment?"

At the somber look on his face, Abigail's heart gave a too-heavy thump, as though flesh had turned to stone. *Derek's dead.* In an instant she could picture what had happened: the police had tracked him down, they'd confronted him, Derek had panicked and attempted to run—

"Abigail?"

She stepped back to allow Turner and Bartholomew into the shop.

"Let's sit down in your office," Turner said.

Her legs felt so heavy that it took all her strength to force one foot in front of the other. Turner waited until she sat in the desk chair before settling in the chair opposite her. Bartholomew remained standing.

"I wanted you to know that we've located Derek in Ithaca," Turner said. "Unfortunately, when we found him, he was injured."

He is *dead.* A chill rushed from Abigail's head to her toes, dragging her remaining strength with it. She stiffened her joints, fighting the impulse to collapse and bury her head in her arms. "What happened?"

"He's going to be all right," Turner said. "He was badly injured when we found him, but he's going to be all right."

Relief brought a flood of tears to Abigail's eyes. Blinking, she fumbled across the desk to grab a tissue from the box. "He's—okay?"

"He's hurt. He had a bad fall. But he's stable. And I want you to know that it's thanks to you that he's alive."

"Thanks to me!"

"We were able to track him using the information you gave us about his ex-girlfriend. When we found him, he was only minutes away from bleeding to death. Without your information, we never would have found him in time."

* * *

DEREK'S EYES OPENED A SLIT. He was so pale that Abigail felt dizzy looking at him. With the blanket pulled up to his chin, the only signs of injury she could see were a number of deep scratches on his face, but from what the doctor had told her, she knew the blanket concealed a multitude of injuries: a number of other scratches and lacerations from the branches of a decorative tree that had been in the entryway where Derek had fallen, a broken arm, fractured ribs, and the injury that had almost killed him—a compound fracture of the femur, an injury apparently sustained when his leg had slammed against the metal rim of the pot holding the tree. A piece of bone has slashed the femoral artery, and Abigail couldn't clear her mind of an image of Derek nearly bleeding to death.

Should she have immediately called her parents? She'd debated that question with herself all day, but each time she reached for her phone, she'd stopped. She'd tell them, but not until she'd had a chance to talk to Derek herself.

Acutely conscious of the uniformed police officer standing inside the doorway and watching her every move, Abigail stepped toward Derek. His eyes were open, but so bleary that she didn't know if he was aware of her.

"Derek?" she said softly.

"Abby." His voice was hoarse, and one corner of his mouth twitched like he was attempting a smile.

She moved closer to the bed. Tubes, wires, monitors—she wished she had some idea what all the numbers on those screens meant. Was he really all right?

"What . . . did they tell you?" Derek asked.

Abigail hesitated. When Detective Turner had told her he would arrange for her to visit Derek, he hadn't given her any instructions about what she could or couldn't say, but she wasn't sure how candid to be.

"Detective Turner told me they tracked you to your former girlfriend's house. And that you—fell—over the balcony and were badly injured."

"Did they . . . tell you . . . tried to . . . kill myself?"

Abigail touched him gently on the cheek. "Do you remember what happened?"

"I didn't . . . I wouldn't . . . I wouldn't ever try to kill myself . . . Abby . . ." Derek's right hand wormed its way out from under the blankets and reached unsteadily toward Abigail.

"Take it easy." She clasped his hand, careful of the IV tubing.

"I didn't try to . . . I wouldn't . . ."

"Derek, it's all right."

"Listen." His fingers quivered and went limp in her grasp. "I know how it . . . how it . . . how it . . . looks." He blinked like he was trying to view her through thick mists of narcotics. "Turner told me . . . the note . . . the sheet . . ."

Chills prickled Abigail's spine at the thought of the picture Turner had painted for her: Derek bleeding on the stone floor of Catrina Hubbard's entryway, a twisted strip of bed sheet knotted around his neck, the other end loose where he'd apparently been too drunk to fasten it securely to the railing before attempting to hang himself. And nearby, a note—*Sorry about Karen. I didn't mean to hurt her.*

"Do you remember what happened?" Considering the doctor's report on Derek's blood-alcohol level, Abigail was certain the answer to that question would have been no, even without the trauma his body had endured.

"Couldn't remember at first, but little bit . . . last thing . . . I was upstairs, I'd decided . . . I was coming back."

"Coming back?"

"Home . . . I called you . . ."

"You called me!? When?"

"Uh . . . don't know . . . last night? . . . kind of mixed up . . . head is mush . . . can't talk right, can't think straight . . . sorry, Abby . . . I wanted to tell you I was sorry . . . left you a message . . . you didn't answer . . ."

A message. Last night? She'd been so distracted after her meeting with Chapman that she hadn't thought to check her messages. Had Derek called right before—right before he—

And she hadn't been there to take his call.

"Sorry . . . Abby, I'm sorry . . ."

"It's all right." Abigail blinked back her tears. She couldn't break down now. She pressed Derek's hand between her palms. His skin felt clammy, and she glanced again at the monitors, wishing she knew if they displayed good news or bad. "Rest now. We can talk later."

"*No* . . . need to tell you . . . didn't tell Turner . . . forgot . . ." His face twisted, grayish lips stretching in a grimace of pain.

Alarmed, Abigail released his hand and reached for the call button. "I'll call the nurse. You're in pain—"

"No—Abby—no . . . don't call . . . I'm okay. Let me talk to you. Someone was in the house. Not Catrina . . . I heard someone . . . went out . . . someone . . ."

Abigail's heart jumped, but she kept her voice calm. She didn't want to risk agitating Derek further. "Who was there?"

". . . don't know. I remember . . . ski mask. He had a gun."

He didn't do this to himself. The hope inside her that had nearly gone cold began to flicker again. "What happened then?"

"Don't know. Can't remember. I saw him . . . then blank. I keep trying . . . not there. Got to remember . . ." Anguish contorted his face.

"Don't try to force it," Abigail said. "You need to rest. It'll come back to you as you get stronger."

"Maybe." Derek's eyes slid shut. "I'm . . . an idiot. Sorry . . . for everything. But I didn't . . . I wouldn't . . . didn't kill Karen . . . didn't do this to myself . . . please help me . . . you always know what to do." His eyelids rose halfway, and Abigail had the impression it was taking all his determination to force them open even that far. "Wouldn't have gotten drunk."

"They found alcohol in your bloodstream," Abigail said quietly.

". . . know that . . . told me. But I wouldn't have gotten drunk. They're wrong." His eyes closed.

CHAPTER 22

"**A**N INTRUDER WEARING A SKI MASK and carrying a gun." Detective Turner's voice was matter-of-fact, and the lack of surprise in his face told Abigail that the officer guarding Derek had already called to report on the content of Abigail's talk with Derek.

"It's worth investigating." Abigail shifted in the padded chair across from Turner's desk. Her eyes burned from too little sleep and too many tears. She'd tried to camouflage her haggard appearance with makeup, but no matter what she did, she knew she looked exhausted and scared.

"Of course it's worth investigating, and we have," Turner said.

"There was—no evidence of anyone else in the house?"

"Nothing we could find. And none of the neighbors saw anything. I can't tell you exactly what happened in there, Abigail. I didn't witness it. I can only go by the evidence."

And the evidence indicated that in an agony of guilt over murdering Karen, Derek had drunk himself into near-oblivion, scrawled a suicide note, and clumsily attempted to hang himself from the balcony railing.

He was telling the truth about calling me, Abigail almost said, but stopped herself. She didn't want to bring up that phone call again. She'd already had Turner listen to the message, and from his sympathetic response, she knew he viewed Derek's apologetic words as part of his suicide note, not as an attempt to tell Abigail he was coming home.

"You look very tired," Turner said. "Go home and get some rest."

Tired. She'd spent half the night sobbing over the fact that she'd missed Derek's call while she was meeting with Bob Chapman. "Derek wouldn't try to kill himself."

"Did you believe it was possible *before* Derek told you about the intruder?"

Abigail sat silent, her throat tight. There was no point in answering. The true answer wasn't the one she wanted to give, and Turner would know if she lied.

Turner watched her, compassion in his eyes. "The best thing you can do now is get some sleep."

In other words, give up, it's over, case closed. The murderer confessed. Abigail felt she was standing at the bottom of a pit, fighting to claw her way out even as the walls crumbled beneath her fingers.

If someone was setting Derek up and had found him at Catrina's, did that mean the murderer had known Derek personally—known him well enough to know about his former girlfriend? Or might Derek have mentioned her to Karen, and Karen told someone?

"The note," she said. "The one found near Derek. Was it—have you had it analyzed? Compared it to his handwriting? I know he was drunk, but—"

"Expert analysis indicates a high probability that Derek wrote that note."

"Can it show if he wrote it under duress?"

"Abigail, you need to let this go."

"The coat," she said. "And the bookend. Have you checked to see who had a key to Derek's apartment or to see if a witness saw someone going in—"

"Yes, we have." Exasperation punctured holes in Turner's politeness. Abigail hoped he didn't know that she'd called Chase McCoy already to see if he'd witnessed anything, but Chase's irritable response had been that the only person he ever saw in the house was "that geeky kid skulking around like a hunchback." The thought of Hunter Conley killing Karen was ludicrous. She couldn't imagine he had the capacity to plan something like that, and even if he did, he certainly wouldn't want blame to fall on his hero, Derek.

Turner started to push back from his desk, and Abigail knew she was about to be dismissed. "Ethan Hanberg." She flung the name out. "Karen's ex-husband. What about—"

"He has an alibi for the time of Karen's death. I already told you that. We've checked out Mr. Hanberg."

"I know. He was with his mother that night. But how much of an alibi is that really? She might lie to protect him."

Turner's brow creased. "How do you know where Mr. Hanberg was that night?"

Abigail tried to sound matter-of-fact but ended up sounding nervous. "I talked to him."

"Why?"

Why was she bothering to attempt a confident mien when her blushing face had already revealed her discomfort to Turner? "I wanted to know more about Karen's life."

"You were looking for someone else who might want to hurt her?"

"Yes."

Absently, Turner straightened one of the framed photographs grouped on his desk. From where Abigail sat, she could see only the backs of the frames, but it was easy to imagine Turner with his arm around a smiling wife, with a couple of kids at their feet.

"You need to trust me to do my job," he said at last. "We checked Hanberg's alibi, and it was solid—and not just because of the word of his mother. Whether your brother is guilty or innocent is now for a jury to decide. Go find him a lawyer. Don't get yourself in trouble—and potentially make things worse for Derek—by bothering Karen Brodie's family."

Abigail bit the inside of her lip. "I understand."

* * *

THE WIND TORE AT ABIGAIL'S umbrella, and sleet slapped her in the face as she trudged up the walkway to her parents' home. More than anything, she wanted to curl up in bed and bury herself in blankets and oblivion, but she couldn't delay talking to her parents any longer.

Derek had nearly died. Would that fact finally break through to them when nothing else had? Or would the circumstances of his injuries make them more frightened than ever of opening up to him in any way?

She knocked lightly on the door before twisting the doorknob. Locked. Usually her parents didn't lock the door until they went to bed. And she knew they were home—she'd called to let them know she was coming, as much to force herself to follow through as to ensure that they'd be home when she arrived.

Abigail flipped through the keys on her ring and located the correct key just as the door opened.

"Abigail." The strain in her father's expression made Abigail wonder if the news she'd dreaded delivering was already old news to her parents.

Turner had agreed to let her personally tell her parents about Derek, but maybe he'd changed his mind. "Come in, honey."

They seated themselves in the living room. "Where's Mother?" Abigail asked.

"She's not feeling well. She's lying down."

"I'm sorry to hear that. I really need to talk to both of you."

"She needs to rest. I can relay any messages you want."

Stiff and formal on the immaculate, cream-colored couch, Abigail steeled herself and tried again. "If she can't come down here, let's go upstairs." She had to talk to both of them together, or she feared Paul's protective instincts would keep him from relaying her full message to Lillian.

"We're not disturbing your mother."

If she marched past Paul and up the stairs to the master bedroom, what would he do? Reluctant to provoke an argument, Abigail decided on a different tack.

"The police came and talked to her, didn't they?"

Paul's jaw clenched. "It's not the first time the police have talked to us about Derek."

"When did they—did they tell you what happened?"

"That they think Derek murdered that Brodie woman? Yes, they told us, and asked if we knew where he might be hiding. How would we know?"

The locked door, Abigail thought bleakly. Her parents had locked the door out of fear that fugitive Derek might come here to steal a few valuables to pawn for cash.

"The only reason your mother went to visit Miss Brodie is because she wanted more accurate information about Derek than your rose-colored reports provided," Paul said. "She explained that to the detective, and he understands."

"Detective Turner?"

"That was the name, yes. And a tall, skinny kid with dark hair."

"Bartholomew," Abigail murmured.

"They've talked to you, I take it."

"Yes. Dad . . . they found Derek."

"Did they?" Paul spoke gruffly, as though a rough tone might be enough to keep Abigail from hearing the relief—and the worry—in his voice. "The dumb kid should have known better than to run."

"When they found him he was—badly hurt."

A soft gasp from the direction of the hallway drew Abigail's attention. Paul jumped to his feet as Lillian came into view. She must have moved with deliberate stealth to make it down the stairs so quietly, Abigail realized.

"Honey, you should lie down," Paul began, but Lillian moved to sit next to Abigail. Her face was as pale as her white bathrobe.

"What happened to him?" she asked.

* * *

"It's so late . . . you must be tired, you must have work early tomorrow . . ." Abigail's protests faded into silence as Kyle stepped through the doorway and wrapped his arms around her. The embrace felt so natural that it took Abigail a moment to realize that this was the first time he'd done more than shake her hand.

When Kyle had called earlier this evening to check on her, she'd spilled everything as fast as she could get the words out, so grateful for Kyle's support and understanding that if he'd been present, she would have cried on his shoulder. Kyle had even offered to come with her when she told her parents about Derek, but Abigail had refused—Kyle's presence would be comforting, but it would make her parents less willing to talk freely and would give them the wrong idea about Kyle and Abigail.

"Thanks for letting me come see you," he said. "I just wish I could have talked you out of driving to Syracuse in this weather."

"The roads weren't bad, and the rain stopped before I left to drive home."

"How are you holding up?"

"I don't know. I feel . . . dazed, I guess." She wanted to let her knees give way and lean on the strength of Kyle's arms.

"Let's sit down." Kyle stepped back.

With her shoes off, a fire flickering in the flagstone fireplace, and Kyle's arm around her shoulders, Abigail felt some of the knots inside her begin to loosen. Untangling them altogether was too much to ask, but at least she didn't feel on the verge of a breakdown.

"How did it go with your parents?" Kyle asked.

"I'm not sure. They didn't say much. They're in shock."

"Did you tell them everything?"

"I . . . left a few things out."

"Like what Derek did to you?"

"What does that matter compared to the rest of it?"

Kyle's mouth quirked in a smile that was more melancholy than amused. "You've asked me before to be candid with you. Do you want candor now?"

Not really, Abigail thought, as she said, "Yes."

"It might hurt."

"I'm braced."

"Okay." Kyle touched her cheek, a gesture that made Abigail want to bury herself in his arms and forget about everything except what it felt like to be close to him. "It worries me that you want your parents to trust Derek, but you're not willing to tell them the full truth about him. Do you want them to trust the real Derek—or your own sanitized version of him?"

The words *did* hurt, but they were so accurate that Abigail couldn't even pretend to be offended. "Derek almost died. I wanted them to see how close they came to losing him. They don't have to trust him. But maybe they can reach out to him before it's too late."

"Did you tell them about the . . . about the note the police found?"

Abigail shook her head, not meeting his gaze.

"Do you want me to stop being candid?" he asked. "If you want me to be quiet, I will. Or we can talk about something else."

"You think Derek killed Karen Brodie. You think he tried to kill himself. You don't think there was any intruder."

"Abigail, I don't know what happened. I'm not psychic, and I'm not the police. I'm just worried about you."

"What do you mean?"

"I mean that . . . is it okay to keep being candid?"

"No," Abigail said tiredly. "Right now, I'd like you to lie a little."

Kyle chuckled. With gentle fingers, he drew Abigail's head onto his shoulder. She rested there, her eyes closed, the tightness in her muscles easing in the soothing warmth of Kyle's nearness. She wanted to fall asleep, yielding to exhaustion, blocking out questions she didn't want to cope with. But what had Kyle stopped himself from saying? She had to know.

"Okay," she murmured. "Be candid."

Kyle stroked her hair. "It worries me that even as you defend Derek, you refuse to deal with what he did to *you*. You don't dare be frank with your parents, because you're afraid of how they'll react. I think you don't dare be frank with yourself. You try to downplay what he did, justify it, minimize it—Abigail, it's one thing to be loyal to your brother. It's another thing to be a martyr."

"I'm not—"

"Shh. I can feel you tensing up. Stop fighting for a minute and let me talk. Okay?"

Abigail nodded and let her eyes slide shut again.

"I think you're afraid to look at this too closely," Kyle said. "It's less painful to declare Derek innocent and refuse to examine contradictory evidence."

"You think he's guilty," Abigail whispered.

"I don't know what happened. But I think you need to consider the possibility that he *is* guilty. After what he did to you, it simply isn't rational to refuse to even consider that possibility. Am I offending you?"

Abigail shook her head.

"I can't tell you how much it scares me that you went to Karen Brodie's ex-husband," Kyle said. "You admitted you thought he might be the one who killed Karen, but you went to dinner with him. The guy could be Jack the Ripper for all you know. And if he did kill her, and he thinks you suspect him—what might he do to you?" Kyle's arm tightened around her. "You've got to back off. You've got to leave this to the police. I'm scared for you—scared that if Derek didn't kill Karen, you're going to spook whoever did, and they'll come for you. Scared that if Derek *did* kill her, you'll never be able to accept that, and you'll drive yourself insane with the obsessive need to prove—at least to yourself— that he's innocent."

Kyle withdrew his arm from her shoulders and turned to face her. "Abigail, I can see how this is wearing on you. You look so tired. Are you sleeping at all?"

"Kyle . . ." Everything he'd said made sense; she couldn't break his logic. For an instant, she imagined how it would feel if she surrendered and accepted the evidence of Derek's guilt, along with the realization that the rift between Derek and her parents would never heal. This driven, panicky feeling that time was running out would ease. She could concentrate on finding Derek a lawyer and doing whatever else she could to help him through the trial. And if he did go to prison, she could take care of practical things, like cleaning out his apartment and putting his rock equipment in storage—

In storage? Why bother? If Derek was convicted of murdering Karen, he might never get out of prison.

"Help me." Derek's raspy voice sounded again in her ears. *"Abby, I didn't do this to myself . . . someone was there . . ."*

"I'm sorry," Kyle said. "I'm really sorry. Maybe candor wasn't such a good idea."

"No . . . I want you to be honest." She'd rather know what he was thinking than hear empty words defending Derek.

"I think you need to be honest with yourself. Derek showed you that he's capable of aggression—even violence. Admitting that it's possible he did something terrible doesn't mean you can't love him anymore. You can't let this destroy you."

"That . . . seems a little extreme. I'm not destroying myself."

"Emotionally, you're tearing yourself apart. You take so much responsibility on yourself and feel so guilty when you fail at the impossible."

Abigail didn't know what to say. She didn't dare pose the question she'd planned to ask Kyle—his opinion on her contacting Karen's mother, Jolene Lassiter. It was obvious now what he'd say. He'd tell her to leave Jolene alone, to leave it all alone, to stop fighting a lost battle.

"I'm sorry," Kyle said. "You must think I'm intruding where I should be minding my own business. It's just . . . I care about you. I know my timing isn't the greatest, but . . . I think I've been waiting for you for a long time."

Kyle ran his fingertips over her cheekbones. Abigail's skin prickled. "You're so beautiful," he said.

She couldn't decide whether to respond with something self-deprecating or to simply thank him, but before any words came, Kyle's lips were on hers.

Too soon, he drew back. "I should be sorry I did that, but I'm not. If you want to punch me, go ahead."

"I don't want to punch you. But . . . Kyle . . ."

"I know." He took her hand. "Bad timing. You're exhausted and scared for your brother. And you must think I'm a heck of a jerk—I just broke up with your friend, and here I am, kissing you. I know this must seem very sudden to you, but it's not sudden to me. I've been thinking about this—about you—for a while now."

"You—you have?" Abigail remembered Ellie's comment that Kyle had been pulling back from her for a while.

"Truth is, I would have acted sooner, but I was scared," he said.

"Scared! Of what?"

"Of hurting Ellie, for one thing. Like I told you, I hate doing that."

"Kyle . . . you do realize that no woman wants to get strung along by a guy who's no longer interested. That only makes the pain worse."

Kyle grimaced, looking boyish and embarrassed. "I know. Intellectually, I know that. I did it all wrong, trying to cool things down gradually, hoping things would end on their own or she'd dump me . . . I know. It was rotten and I'm a coward. No wonder Ellie wasn't that sorry to lose me. But my other problem was that I was scared of *you*."

"Of me!"

"You're so . . . *everything*. Beautiful . . . intelligent . . . a savvy businesswoman . . . kind . . . witty . . . classy from head to toe. I kept telling myself to forget about it, you were out of reach."

Abigail tried to fathom how someone like Kyle Stratton could be so insecure.

"I couldn't help hoping you'd show some spark of interest in me," Kyle continued. "But you never did. It wasn't until this trouble with your brother started that I finally saw how vulnerable you were under that perfect facade, and maybe you *could* use a knight in shining armor after all . . ."

"I've been interested in you ever since I met you," Abigail said. "More than interested. But you started dating Ellie, and I wasn't about to try to steal her boyfriend . . . not that I didn't want to . . ." She leaned toward Kyle. He took her face in his hands and kissed her again. Thoughts of Derek faded out of her mind; all she could think of was Kyle, his lips on hers, his fingers trailing through her hair and drawing her more tightly against him.

"Wow," he said when they pulled apart. "I'm sorry about my tacky timing, but . . . wow."

Abigail gave a shaky laugh. "You'd better go home before I get in trouble for breaking curfew. But Kyle, if we're starting something here, we need to make a deal up front. If you *ever* start feeling like—"

"I know. I'll be honest with you. It feels good to know I *can* be honest with you—that you expect it, that you can take it. Not that I'm worried I'll be wanting an exit." Smiling, he lifted her hand and kissed her fingers. "Are you sure I can't stay a little longer?"

"I'd love it, but I'm so exhausted I can't keep my eyes open. Call me tomorrow."

"I will. If you need anything, call me anytime, day or night. And Abigail, I don't want to create problems between you and Ellie. It might be easier on you two if I keep a low profile for a while. I'll steer clear of the store."

Abigail nodded gratefully. If Ellie asked about Kyle, Abigail would tell her the truth, but it would be much easier if Ellie didn't have to see Kyle at all, let alone see him with Abigail.

"Tomorrow night, we'll get together and talk about a lawyer for Derek," Kyle said. "You don't have to handle this alone anymore."

Warm, dazed, Abigail lay on the couch after Kyle left, watching the flames twirling gold and orange and blue. She wanted to fall asleep right here by the fire, glowing in the memory of Kyle's words and his touch. She *had* done what she could for Derek, and Kyle was right—what he needed now was a lawyer, not Abigail chipping uselessly at a mountain of evidence. Kyle would help her . . . she wouldn't be alone . . .

But through the haze of excitement, the same thought kept repeating itself. She needed to talk to Jolene Lassiter.

CHAPTER 23

TRYING NOT TO THINK ABOUT the condemnation she'd see in Detective Turner's eyes or the worry she'd see in Kyle's if they knew what she was doing, Abigail folded the directions she'd printed off the Internet and slid them into her purse. Given Bob Chapman's information that Jolene Lassiter lived in Buffalo and was married to a man named Terry, it had been a simple matter to locate her phone number and address.

Abigail had gone to bed planning to call Jolene Lassiter in the morning, but by the time the sun rose, she'd changed her mind. She couldn't imagine that Jolene would welcome a visit. If Abigail asked permission to visit, Jolene would say no. But if Abigail showed up on her doorstep, maybe Jolene would be too polite to slam the door in her face. At least Abigail might be able to squeeze in a question or two before Jolene set the dog on her.

Ethan Hanberg had claimed he didn't know anyone who would want to hurt Karen—except Derek—but Jolene might.

Could that person be Ethan himself?

Despite Turner's insistence that Ethan's alibi was solid, Abigail wasn't ready to dismiss the possibility that he was guilty. Maybe he *had* been with his mother that night—but that didn't mean he hadn't paid someone to kill Karen and frame Derek. With the way Karen had rattled on to Ethan about Derek, he would have known enough about Derek to frame him.

Abigail still felt stunned by the horrifying connection that had struck her in the middle of the night—Turner had tracked Derek to Catrina Hubbard's house using the information Abigail had given him: Derek had an ex-girlfriend in Ithaca, nicknamed Cat, who was an actress. A little investigation in the local theater community had led Turner to Catrina.

Abigail had given that same information to Ethan Hanberg at the restaurant when they'd been talking about where Derek might have gone. What if Ethan had followed the same trail Turner had?

What if Abigail had led a killer to Derek's hideout?

The guilt that chewed at Abigail over this possibility hurt far worse than her guilt at the thought of how painful her visit might be for Jolene Lassiter. She *had* to talk to Jolene. This afternoon, she'd leave work early, drive to Jolene's home and get her opinion on Ethan Hanberg. She'd already checked with Melissa, and Melissa was fine covering the rest of Abigail's shift at the store.

What would she tell Kyle? He'd said he wanted to get together with her tonight, and if she went to Jolene's, she wouldn't have time to see him. Did she have the confidence to tell him the truth, or was she too embarrassed imagining him thinking she was obsessing to the point of endangering her health? After the way he'd agreed to be honest with her, holding back seemed unfair—but his promising to be honest about the status of their relationship didn't mean she was obligated to immediately start sharing every detail of her life. They were barely moving past friendship; she didn't have to tell Kyle about Jolene if she wasn't comfortable doing so.

Was that rationalization? Maybe. She'd worry about it after she talked to Jolene.

The thought of Kyle evoked a sense of breathlessness. How did she feel about Kyle? How did he feel about her?

"I think I've been waiting for you for a long time."

Could Kyle be that serious about her? Abigail imagined herself taking Kyle to her parents' home for dinner and couldn't help smiling at the delight she knew would appear in her mother's eyes.

Derek's in the hospital and you're all goofy-headed over Kyle Stratton? Impatient with herself, Abigail buttoned a thick hand-knitted sweater over her turtleneck before putting on her heavy coat. The temperature had plunged overnight, and it was twenty degrees outside.

Later, she'd have plenty of time to think about her budding relationship with Kyle. Right now, she needed to plan how she'd approach Jolene Lassiter so as to maximize her chances of getting in the door.

Bitter wind stung her face as she locked her front door. Shivering, wishing Santa Claus would bring her an attached garage, Abigail started down the porch steps. She wasn't looking forward to shoveling all these stairs for the next five months.

Her foot skidded on the second stair. With a jolt of adrenaline, Abigail flailed to steady herself, but as she brought her other foot forward, it seemed to catch; legs tangling, she lost her balance and pitched forward down the stairs.

She threw her arms forward to break her fall. The impact knocked the air from her lungs. Unable to breathe, unable to stand, she slid down a few more inches. Both arms were ablaze with pain, and her right knee throbbed so violently that acid rose in her throat.

Finally able to suck a breath of air into her lungs, Abigail twisted, sliding her legs down the stairs so she was sitting on the sidewalk. Afraid that if she tried to move more than that, she'd lose her breakfast, she sat motionless, hoping the pain would ebb.

She heard the clang of a bike hitting the driveway, followed by the scrape of footsteps. Tentatively, she turned her head to see Hunter Conley approaching.

"Whoa . . . are you okay?"

"I—think so." Abigail tried to work some humor into her voice. Hunter's eyes were wide and his left hand squeezed what looked like a mangled lump of gray-green fabric. The turtle, Abigail thought. He finally trusted her enough to bring it out in the open.

The cold of the sidewalk seeped through her coat. She needed to stand up, but she wasn't sure she could. Had she broken anything? Gingerly, she flexed her arms. They seemed to work. Her forearms had taken the brunt of the fall, and her thick sweater and padded coat had—she hoped—cushioned them enough to prevent broken bones. Her legs—blood was seeping through the right knee of her slacks. Abigail prodded gently at her injured knee. It felt numb.

"You'd better call 911," Hunter said. "The ambulance guys will take care of you."

"I'm okay. I'm just bruised."

"You're bleeding."

"It's not serious." *I hope.* She put her gloved hands on the ground to push herself to her feet, but the pain that flared in her arms made her gasp. She drew her hands back into her lap.

"There's a lot of ice around after that rain and stuff yesterday," Hunter observed.

Abigail nodded. But what had—it had almost felt like she'd tripped in addition to slipping on the ice, but tripped over what? She looked up at the stairs but could see no obstacles.

Clumsy.

"You shouldn't sit on the ground like that," Hunter said. "You'll get frostbite."

"Could you help me up?"

"Sure." Hunter jammed his turtle in his sleeve and took a tentative step toward her. He stretched his hands forward then lowered them like he didn't know where to grab her.

"Come around behind me, put your hands under my arms, and lift," she said. "My arms are hurting, and it's hard for me to push myself up."

He stepped behind her, slid his hands under her arms, and heaved upward. Her left leg throbbed slightly as she rested her weight on it, but when she tried to rest her weight on her right leg, the pain in her knee made her cry out.

"What do I do?" Hunter sounded panicky, and his hands twitched like he didn't know whether or not to let go of her.

Abigail tried not to let the pain show in her voice, but the words came out choppy. "Just—come—around next to me and let me hold onto you." Her left arm hurt less than her right, so with her left hand, she clutched Hunter's arm.

"You'd better call a doctor," he said. "Or call Derek. Has he called you yet? Do you know where he is?"

Gazing at the icy stairs, Abigail tried to figure out what to do. Trying to climb them, even with Hunter's help, sounded not only painful, but like an invitation for a two-for-the-price-of-one accident as she and Hunter both went head over heels.

"I looked up your address," Hunter said. "It wasn't hard to find. I ride all over town all the time."

"That must be difficult in winter." What if her knee was broken? *Did* she need to call an ambulance?

"It's hard when it's really snowy, but I'm tough," Hunter said. "See how I pulled you up? I'm strong. I'll bet I could carry you if you need me to."

He probably could, Abigail thought, glancing at Hunter's tall, broad-shouldered build. "You *are* strong. Thanks for helping me. But I think I can walk."

"I saw you fall. You went, like—" To illustrate, Hunter pinwheeled his arms, including the arm Abigail was clutching. She staggered, gasping at the pain that exploded in her knee.

"Sorry!" Hunter stilled his arms.

"It's . . . all right. Could you help me around to the back door? I don't want to go up these stairs. They're too icy."

"Your face is a weird color," Hunter said. "Kind of gray."

Perfect. "I just . . . need to sit down."

"You ought to call Derek. Have you heard from him? That's why I came, to ask if you'd heard from him. I looked up your address. I didn't know if you'd be at work or what."

"Aren't you supposed to be at school?" Abigail asked.

"Yeah, I guess. But my dad doesn't care if I miss classes. He thinks I'm too dumb for school anyway. Is that your purse and keys on the stairs? I can get them for you."

Abigail released Hunter's arm so he could gather her belongings. He handed her the purse and keys and offered her his arm again. "You'd better hold on tight."

Gripping Hunter's arm, she limped around the side of the house. Her knee burned like a mass of live coals had replaced bone and cartilage, but the fact that her leg worked seemed like good news.

The wooden stairs to the back deck were free of ice, but climbing them felt like hiking Everest, and cold sweat was dripping down her back by the time they reached the door.

"Thank you for your help," she said. "I'll be all right now. I just need to get cleaned up."

"You shouldn't let your stairs get icy like that. You could have broken your neck."

"I know. I didn't realize they were icy."

"I can fix them. You got ice melt? A shovel? Sand?"

"Yes, it's all in the garage."

"I'll take care of it."

"Thank you. That's very nice of you."

"I did all that stuff for Karen. I'm good at it."

"The garage is unlocked. I can make it into the house all right if you want to go take care of the stairs."

"Okay." With an eager grin, Hunter turned and rushed down the stairs, moving so rapidly that Abigail held her breath, afraid he'd trip over his own feet. When he was out of sight, she unlocked the back door and limped into the house.

In the bathroom, she examined her injuries. Her forearms both sported purpling welts that would soon darken into massive bruises. Her left knee was bruised, and her right was swollen and bleeding where the edge of the brick stair had gouged it. Why hadn't she paid attention to the condition of the stairs? She could have killed herself.

Shaky with pain and adrenaline, she cleaned the blood off her knee, changed her stained slacks, and limped into the kitchen. She filled a Ziploc bag with ice, wrapped it in a towel, and sat on the living room couch with the ice pack on her knee and her foot on the coffee table. At least Ellie was scheduled to open today. Abigail had intended to be early to work anyway, but now, she'd rather take some time to ice her knee before leaving.

She closed her eyes and leaned her head against the back of the couch. It would crush Hunter when she told him what had happened to Derek. Was there any way to delay telling him? Probably not, unless she was willing to flat-out lie to him.

Forty minutes passed before the doorbell rang. Abigail moved slowly to open the door.

"Done." Hunter grinned at her, his cheeks cherry-red. "You had some thick ice out there. How'd you get so much ice? You have to keep your stairs cleared."

"I thought I had," Abigail said. "I'll be more careful next time. Thank you for your help. I would have been stuck if you hadn't come along." From her pocket, she extracted the twenty-dollar bill she'd taken from her purse.

Hunter eyed the money eagerly but put his hands behind his back. "You don't have to pay me. I think Derek would want me to help you for free. You're his sister and all."

"I know you didn't help me for money. But I want you to have it."

"Okay." Hunter snatched the bill. "So has Derek called? He hasn't been home. I keep checking, but he's never there."

"He . . . yes, he did call."

"He did?" Hunter's face lit up. "He's coming home?"

"Come inside," Abigail said quietly.

"You—you sound sad. Did something bad—"

"Come inside."

Hunter squirmed on her couch, squeezing the turtle so frenetically that his entire right arm twitched. "The police caught him, didn't they? They still think he killed Karen."

"They don't know who killed her." Abigail touched his shoulder. When he didn't pull away, she rested her hand there until his frantic movements slowed. "They think he did, but I don't believe it. I'm trying to talk to people who knew Karen to see if any of them know of someone else who was mad at her or wanted to hurt her. I'm going today to talk to her mother."

"Cool. Derek told me you were smart." Hunter sounded relieved. Clearly he thought she could solve this problem, and Abigail couldn't bring herself to tell him that the odds that she could help Derek now were miniscule.

"You probably ought to get to school," Abigail suggested.

"Yeah. Hey, that guy had a coat like mine. Weird, huh? I think his hat was the same color too."

"What guy?"

"The guy. The one by the side of your house."

"I'm sorry, I don't know who you're talking about."

"Didn't you see him?"

"See him when?"

"Today. After you, you know, slipped on the ice—" Hunter whooshed his hand down and outward, ski-jump style. "He ran away."

A chilly tingling shot along Abigail's nerves. "A man was here?"

Hunter looked down. "Sorry. I won't tell anyone if you don't want me to. I can keep secrets real good."

Abigail blushed in response to Hunter's assumption. "No, it's nothing like that." Feeling she'd better be more specific, she added, "I don't have a secret boyfriend or anything. I'm just surprised because I didn't know anyone was here. What did he look like?"

"I don't know. I was just coming up your driveway, so I couldn't see him very good. He had dark hair—I could see it sticking out below his hat, and at first I thought it was Derek, but it wasn't Derek, right? I need a haircut too."

Abigail tried to keep the confusion out of her face; she didn't want Hunter to know how unnerved she was. Someone had been here but had fled when Hunter approached?

Hunter's arm was twitching again. "Derek's in jail, right?"

"No," Abigail said. "He's . . . he had an accident, and he broke his leg. He's in the hospital right now. They're taking good care of him."

"Oh." Hunter grimaced. "I broke my arm once. I fell off my bike. So once you find out who really killed Karen, they'll let him come home, right?"

* * *

"SIT DOWN, ABBY."

"Ellie, I—"

"Sit! Sit down *now.*"

"I'm not your dog."

"Oh, I know *that.* My dog has better sense." Ellie's blue eyes were all but smoking as she pointed to a chair. Abigail wanted to rebel, but the walk from the parking lot into the store had left her knee throbbing so painfully that she wasn't willing to aggravate the pain to defy Ellie's tyranny. She sat down.

Ellie took the empty wastebasket from the corner, flipped it over, and set it on the floor in front of Abigail. "Rest your foot there. No, wait, it's not tall enough." Ellie grabbed two phone books and set them on the bottom of the wastebasket. "There."

Meekly, Abigail rested her foot on the makeshift ottoman.

Hands on her hips, Ellie glared at Abigail. "Now, *stay put.* I'm going to get you some ice for your knee."

"I already iced it."

With a light touch, Ellie probed at the injured knee. "This thing is swelling like crazy. You're going to ice it some more. And if you try to stand up, I swear to you I will take a leaf out of your brother's book and tie you down." Ellie marched out of the room.

Suppressing a hysterical urge to laugh, Abigail sat with her eyes closed, waiting for Ellie, wondering if the ibuprofen she'd taken had kicked in and if this was as good as it was going to get. So much for thinking she could get away with coming in to work and making her way through a normal day. It had taken Ellie ten seconds to notice the limp Abigail was trying to hide, and another two minutes to extract the entire story from her.

Who had Hunter seen at her house this morning? She'd tried—as delicately as possible, so as not to alarm Hunter—to pick any other observations from his mind, but he hadn't noticed anything other than the intruder's dark hair and the fact that his hat was blue and his coat brown.

She thought of Hunter's description of the thick ice on the stairs. After yesterday's storm and last night's freezing temperatures, ice was anything but remarkable, but water shouldn't have pooled on her stairs—certainly not enough water to create ice so thick that it took Hunter forty minutes to get rid of it all.

So you're thinking someone sabotaged your stairs? Why don't you call Detective Turner and report this? "I slipped on the ice. I think it was attempted murder." Abigail remembered the feeling of something catching on her ankle when she fell. But there had been nothing on the stairs. She'd asked Hunter about that too.

Who had been at her house this morning?

"Here you go." At the sound of Ellie's voice, Abigail opened her eyes and accepted the bag of ice. "But what you need is a trip to the emergency room. You might have shattered your kneecap or something awful like that."

"I shattered my pride," Abigail said. "It'll heal."

"You look pale. You're in a lot of pain, aren't you? Let me see your arms."

"They're fine," Abigail said. "Just bruised—"

"Show me!"

"You are the biggest little bully—"

At the sound of the door chime, Ellie turned reluctantly away. "Stay put," she said.

For the next half an hour, Abigail remained obediently in the office, listening to Ellie interacting with customers. She ought to be out there helping, but she could only imagine the look Ellie would give her if she limped out onto the sales floor.

What if someone *had* maliciously iced her stairs, hoping to injure her—someone edgy at the way she was trying to figure out the truth behind Karen's murder? Kyle had worried that this might happen.

Dark hair. Ethan Hanberg?

Ellie poked her head into the office. "Okay, girl. Go home and rest. Melissa's coming in now."

"I'm really fine."

"I can tell by the way you wince every time you move. Go home, or better yet, go get some X-rays."

"If the pain worsens, I will."

"Call me, okay?"

"Deal."

Ellie disappeared. Stiffly, Abigail rose to her feet and picked up her purse. She wasn't going home. She was going to visit Jolene Lassiter. Now more than ever, she wanted to know what kind of picture Jolene would paint of Karen's ex-husband.

As she limped toward her car, she caught sight of Brendan's car pulling into the parking lot. *Wonderful.* Just what she wanted right now—another run-in with Brendan Rowe. But chances were he was here to visit another of Bob's Main Street properties; he wouldn't want to talk to her any more than she wanted to talk to him.

Abigail reached into her purse for her keys—and didn't find them. She checked her pockets—no keys—and checked her purse again. Where would she have . . . dismayed, Abigail pictured herself entering her office, the phone ringing as she came through the door, her dropping her keys on the desk as she picked up the receiver. She'd left her keys in the office.

The thought of limping back inside made her want to slump to the ground and whimper.

"What happened to you?" Brendan spoke behind her. "You're limping."

So much for thinking she wouldn't have to talk to him. Abigail turned to face him. "I slipped on the ice."

"Are you all right?" He sounded formal, as though he were speaking to a stranger. Apparently his temper had cooled, and now he was presenting his we-can-still-work-together professional attitude.

"I'm fine," she said. "Just airheaded. I left my keys in the office."

"Do you want me to get them for you? It looks like it hurts you to walk."

Surprised, she said automatically, "No, thank you, I can—" She stopped. Forget pride, and forget the way Brendan had talked to her last time they met. If he wanted to save her the trip back inside, let him. "Would you, please? I'd appreciate that. They're on the desk."

"Sit in my car while you wait. It's cold out here." Brendan clicked the remote to unlock his car and headed for Words and Sweets.

Unable to turn down the offer of a comfortable seat, Abigail headed for his car.

A few minutes later, Brendan hurried back toward the car, the wind ruffling his blond hair. He opened his door, slid behind the wheel, and handed Abigail her keys.

"Thank you," she said. "I really appreciate it."

"Abigail, I owe you an apology. I went too far."

"It's all right. I know Bob shredded you over Derek. I understand why you were upset. And I'm so sorry this has caused trouble for your family."

"I heard the police found Derek."

Abigail nodded. She had no idea if anything about Derek had been in the news—she'd avoided checking any news sources. Maybe Bob Chapman was keeping tabs on the case. He probably had plenty of connections to keep him informed.

"He was hurt pretty badly?" Brendan said.

"Yes."

"That's rough. I'm sorry."

Abigail nodded.

"Have you been able to see him? Is he conscious?"

Maybe Brendan was trying to act friendly and concerned to make up for how harshly he'd insulted her last time they met, but Abigail just wanted to end the conversation.

"Yes, I've talked to him," she said. "He's weak, but he's recovering. Thanks for my keys. I'll see you." She opened the door and stepped out of Brendan's car before he could ask her anything else.

CHAPTER 24

THE EARLY AFTERNOON SKY WAS a dreary gray as Abigail limped along the sidewalk leading to the small ranch-style house belonging to Jolene Lassiter. If Jolene was anything like her daughter, she wouldn't be pleasant to deal with. If she flatly refused to talk to Abigail, what would Abigail do? There *was* a good chance Jolene would slam the door in her face, run to the phone, and call the police to say Derek Wyatt's sister was harassing her. But no matter how mortifying that would be, it would be far easier to live with embarrassment than with the knowledge that she'd quit before she'd exhausted every possibility for helping Derek.

Especially if Derek's injuries were partly her fault.

She rang the doorbell. If no one was home, she'd come back in an hour, and every hour after that until someone answered.

The door opened. Abigail knew immediately that she was facing Jolene Lassiter—this woman had the same dark blue eyes and carved cheekbones as Karen. She was shorter than her daughter, but just as thin, and her curly gray hair was cut short.

Abigail swallowed to moisten her dry mouth. "My name is—"

"Didn't see the sign or can't read?" Jolene pointed to the NO SOLICITING plaque near the door.

"I'm not selling anything. And I'm sorry to disturb you. My name is Abigail Wyatt. I'm Derek Wyatt's sister." She waited for Jolene to react to the name.

Jolene's expression didn't change, and her voice was even. "What do you want?"

Abigail drew a deep breath. If Jolene Lassiter was shocked or even surprised at her presence, she hid it well. "I'm sorry to intrude. I know this must be a very difficult time. But I wonder if you would have a few minutes to talk to me about Karen."

"Why would I talk to you about Karen?"

She'd have to be direct if she wanted any chance of eliciting Jolene's cooperation. "I know the police think my brother murdered your daughter. He didn't. He's being set up. And an elaborate setup means this was planned by someone who knew Karen well. You might know something that could help—"

"If the police want to know about Karen, the police can ask me."

"They aren't looking anymore," Abigail said. "They think Derek is guilty."

"I don't know who would have wanted to kill her. We weren't close."

"I'm sorry. But maybe something from her past—anything at all—"

Jolene smiled bleakly. "Let me give you some advice. You can't make people into who you want them to be. You can do everything in your power to help them, but you can't force them to change. Maybe you need to accept that your brother isn't who you wanted him to be."

Abigail's bruised arms ached as she drew her coat more tightly around her. "My brother is not a murderer." Remembering the line she'd used on Ethan Hanberg, she said, "Please. I'm asking for one hour of your time. After that, I'll leave, and you'll never hear from me again."

Jolene scrutinized her. Abigail waited, fighting the urge to beg.

"Now is not a good time," Jolene said. "Come back at five."

Relief filled Abigail. "Thank you. This means a lot to me."

"I'll see you at five." Jolene closed the door.

* * *

ABIGAIL SPENT THE AFTERNOON AT the Buffalo library, checking her watch to see when she could take more Advil and jotting down ideas for how to make the most out of her time with Jolene Lassiter. Boyfriends . . . any trouble with the law . . . enemies, even ones from many years ago . . . her marriage to Ethan Hanberg . . .

Especially her marriage to Ethan Hanberg.

Kyle called in the middle of the afternoon, and Abigail stepped outside the library to talk to him. On the verge of telling Kyle where she was, she lost her nerve and told him only that she would probably be home around nine. He arranged to come over at nine-thirty. Despite everything, Abigail couldn't help but be excited at the thought of seeing Kyle—Kyle, who'd been interested in her for a while, but had been too nervous to act. Kyle, afraid of her? Abigail felt a little judgmental at the way she'd assumed anyone as handsome and charming as Kyle couldn't possibly have problems with confidence or self-esteem. She should have been more perceptive. Remembering the offhand comments she'd heard Kyle make about his parents, now she could easily see where he'd learned to doubt himself.

At five o'clock, Abigail limped up Jolene Lassiter's walkway and rang the bell.

"Come in, Abigail." Jolene's tone was courteous. "Let me take your coat."

"Thank you." Abigail handed over her coat. The entryway was spotless, with white ceramic tile and a rose-patterned rug. "And thank you for seeing me."

Jolene hung the coat in the closet. "Come sit down in the living room."

Abigail followed Jolene along the hallway. The carpet was a blue-and-white Berber, and the walls were a pale blue that seemed both pleasant and somewhat dated. The air smelled of nutmeg and baked apples.

In the living room, a man was sitting on a rose-pink chair. He stood and nodded a greeting at Abigail.

It was Ethan Hanberg.

"I believe you've met Ethan," Jolene said. "Sit down and I'll fetch some refreshments."

Abigail felt the same way she had when she'd slipped on the stairs this morning—stunned, sick, unable to breathe. What was Ethan doing here?

Jolene exited the room. Not knowing what else to do, Abigail made her way to the couch and sat down.

Instead of resuming his seat on the pink chair, Hanberg sat on the couch with her. Abigail gripped her hands together in her lap, and pain shot through her forearms. She loosened her grip, not looking at him.

"I'm sorry." He spoke too quietly for Jolene Lassiter to overhear him in the kitchen. "But somehow I knew you'd track Jolene down."

Abigail glanced at him. The fact that he was apologizing meant he'd read the dismay in her face. He knew she didn't want him here. "You told her to call you if I showed up, didn't you?"

"Yes."

That was why Jolene hadn't been surprised to see her and why Jolene had delayed talking to her—she'd wanted time to summon Ethan. "If you're here to stop me from talking to her, why did she let me in the door?"

"I'm not here to stop you from talking to her. Jolene makes up her own mind, and she wants to see you. I'm here to support her. She's been through enough, and I don't want her hurt further."

"I don't want to hurt her. I want the truth." And she wasn't likely to get it, not with Ethan sitting next to her. How could she ask candid questions about Ethan and Karen's marriage? She couldn't. Was that the real reason Ethan was here? He'd anticipated her move, and he'd outmaneuvered her. Frustration—and fear—left Abigail sitting rigidly on the edge of the couch. What would Ethan do if she stood up, walked into the kitchen, and tried to hold a private conversation with Jolene? He wouldn't allow it. She was sure of that.

"You were limping," Ethan said. "What happened?"

Abigail met his gaze and saw nothing there except concern. Did he already know what had happened? Had he engineered it? "I slipped on the ice."

"I'm sorry. Are you all right?"

Jolene reentered the living room, carrying a tray. She set it on the table and handed Abigail a steaming mug.

"Hot cranberry punch," she said. "One of my husband's mother's recipes. They had it every Thanksgiving."

"Thank you," Abigail said. Jolene took a plate bearing a piece of apple crisp and a scoop of vanilla ice cream and set it on the lamp table next to Abigail.

"Thank you." The situation seemed increasingly surreal. She'd elbowed her way into the home of a grieving woman to interrogate her about her murdered daughter. Ethan Hanberg—who might have killed Karen—had shown up to stand between Abigail and Jolene. And now they were sitting here companionably sipping hot cranberry punch.

Abigail thought of Hunter Conley sitting on her couch, frantically squeezing that stuffed turtle. She had the feeling Hunter was going to show up at her house tomorrow to ask what she'd learned from Karen's mother. At this point, she feared her answer would be one word long: *nothing*.

Jolene sat on the pink chair. "What exactly would you like to know about Karen? I don't know of anyone who would have wanted to hurt her. I frankly didn't know her all that well anymore. We weren't close. I wanted to be, but she didn't, and you can only get shoved away so many times before you quit trying."

Abigail took a sip of the cranberry punch to wet her mouth. "I'm sorry."

"So am I. At least I saw her now and then while she and Ethan were married—he saw to that—but after the divorce, she pretty well cut me off. I don't know what was going on in her life recently, or why anyone would kill her, and I don't know your brother, so I can't weigh in there."

Ethan spoke quietly. "Abigail suspects me of killing Karen."

Abigail couldn't have been more startled if Ethan had shouted out a confession. "I don't—I never suggested—"

"Am I wrong?"

Her cheeks blazed with embarrassment, and her heart thumped so loudly that she wondered if Ethan could hear it. "I never said anything like that."

"Did you think it?"

"No, of course not."

Jolene gave a hard-edged laugh that reminded Abigail of Karen's laugh. "She's not a very good liar, is she?"

"No. I think she was horrified to find me here. I'm guessing she was hoping to quiz you about what I'm really like and why Karen and I divorced." He smiled slightly at Abigail. "Am I right?"

Mortified and completely off balance, Abigail couldn't think of any way to respond other than with candor that matched Ethan's. "Why don't you leave? If you don't have anything to hide then you don't need to stand sentinel while we talk."

Jolene laughed again. "The sweet young lady has claws. Child, you can ask me anything you want about Ethan, and I'll answer frankly. Do I look scared of him?"

She didn't, in the slightest. Still burning with humiliation, Abigail glanced at Ethan. His expression was calm, but his neck was red, and he was twisting his fork between his thumb and forefinger rather than eating.

"Ask me anything you want," he said. "I could tell when you were quizzing me about my alibi the other night that you suspected me. There's probably nothing I can say to convince you I'm innocent, but ask me anything you want."

Abigail took another sip of punch, but her hand shook, and she set the cup aside rather than risk spilling it. She'd walked up to Jolene's house feeling calm and almost optimistic, ready with a list of questions. Now, ten minutes later, she was sitting here trembling, unable to think of anything to ask except, "Were you at my house today?"

Ethan's dark brows drew together. "No. Why?"

Abigail didn't reply. What a fool she was. Had she completely forgotten Kyle's warning about spooking Karen's murderer? If Ethan *had* sabotaged her stairs, what in the world made her think it was a good idea to confront him over it? Was she trying to provoke him into attacking her more directly?

"He asked a fair question," Jolene said. "Answer it. You can't expect us to be frank if you're holding back. And if you're not willing to be frank, you might as well go home, because this is a waste of all of our time."

For a moment, Abigail debated between her two options: tell the story and see if she could read any signs of guilt in Ethan or call the meeting a loss and retreat.

She couldn't even think straight. The emotional and physical fatigue that had started the night of that disastrous dinner party now seemed to thicken, clouding her mind.

"You look sick as a dog," Jolene said flatly. "If you weren't up to this meeting, why did you schedule it?"

Abigail rallied. She couldn't let Ethan's presence rattle her like this, and it was too late to retract her question about his being at her house. She had to go on.

She told the story about the stairs, carefully leaving out Hunter's name. She would *not* put Hunter at risk.

"Are you *sure* you're all right?" Ethan frowned at her, looking her up and down in the same concerned way Ellie had.

"Yes. Just sore."

"A dark-haired man," he said. "Was this witness *positive* it wasn't Derek? Maybe he'd come to ask you for help but then panicked and ran when he saw someone approaching."

"It couldn't have been Derek. He's in the hospital—" The words stuck in her throat as she thought of Derek's ashen face and weak, hoarse voice. Her eyes stung. Abigail blinked hard, picked up her plate and fork, and shoved a bite of apple crisp into her mouth. The knot in her throat made it difficult to swallow. *Calm. Stay calm.*

"What's wrong with him?" Jolene asked.

The knot tightened. *Stop it. What's the matter with you?* The stern self-lecture didn't help. If she spoke, she'd start crying, and the thought of breaking down in front of Ethan Hanberg and Jolene Lassiter appalled her. She breathed slowly, fighting for control. It didn't help. Tears welled in her eyes.

Abigail set her plate down. "Excuse me for a moment," she whispered, starting to stand up. Too distracted to think about what she was doing, she rested too much weight on her right leg, and the pain that ripped through her knee made her gasp.

Ethan jumped to her side and caught her arm. "You need to sit down."

"No—I—" The tears escaped, streaming down her face. This was absurd. She couldn't get what she came for, and she was falling apart. If Kyle were here, he'd take this as proof that he was right—she *had* pushed herself to the point of emotional self-destruction. "I'm sorry . . . Mrs. Lassiter . . . I've wasted your time. I should go—"

"You're not going anywhere," Jolene said. "You can hardly see through those waterworks, and you can't walk. Sit down."

"Another time—"

"Sit down. You're safe. Ethan's too polite to murder you in front of me."

"Jo, you're not helping," Ethan said.

"Of course, it *could* be a conspiracy, with him and me in it together. Ethan, you hold her and I'll get the knife."

"*Jo.* Abigail, I'm sorry, just ignore her. She gets wacky sometimes."

"I get wacky when I'm faced with worse wackiness," Jolene said. "Ethan a murderer? Give me a break."

"Please, sit down. You're in pain." With his hand on her shoulder, Ethan pressed Abigail onto the couch. His touch was gentle but firm enough to make Abigail look at the muscles that curved beneath the sleeves of his shirt and think of how she wouldn't stand a chance against him . . . but Jolene trusted him . . . Detective Turner trusted him . . . was Abigail paranoid or was he extremely clever?

"Prop her leg up, Ethan," Jolene said. "Drag the coffee table a little closer, and pull off her shoe."

Abigail wanted to protest, but the words wouldn't come. Hands over her face, she sat struggling against her emotions, feeling Ethan slip the shoe from her foot and lift her leg so it rested on the coffee table.

"Look at me, sweetie," Jolene said. "I've seen tears before. They don't shock me. And I don't like dealing with someone who won't look me in the face."

Abigail let her hands drop into her lap. Ethan sat next to her and handed her a tissue.

"Did Derek get shot?" Jolene asked. "Did he resist arrest and the cops shot him?"

Abigail shook her head, thinking it was obvious where Karen had gotten her bluntness. "No . . . he . . ."

"He what?"

"Give her a minute," Ethan said.

"A minute won't change the facts. Just spit it out, Abigail, it's easier that way."

How had things gotten turned around like this? She'd come to get information, not give it. "The police think he . . . tried to . . . commit suicide." *Deep breath. Calm down.* "He didn't." Abigail described what had happened and what Derek had told her about an intruder. She kept an eye on Ethan's expression and saw only shock, followed by compassion.

"That story about some masked man with a gun sounds like a load of hooey," Jolene said. "You're smart enough to know that."

"I don't want to argue about it."

"I'm not planning to argue. If you enjoy burying your head in the sand, keep it there."

Ethan leaned toward Jolene. "Someone might have sabotaged her stairs this morning. Someone was lurking around her house. That wasn't Derek."

"Okay, fair enough. Maybe something else is going on here. So the police told me your brother's car was seen at Kemper Park at the time Karen died. If he wasn't there to kill her, what the heck was he doing there?"

Abigail told her about the note claiming to be from Robert Chapman.

"Maybe your brother *is* telling the truth, since it would take a real nitwit to come up with a lie that pathetic," Jolene said.

"I'm glad you think so," Abigail said dryly, and Jolene laughed.

"Okay, sweetheart. You came to ask me questions. Ask them. What do you want to know? You're wondering about Ethan? He's a good man. The best thing that ever happened to Karen, and the day they got engaged, I fell on my knees and prayed a thousand thank-yous. I'd worried about Karen for years. She was a smart kid, a beautiful girl, but she had that attitude that said whatever she had wasn't good enough—she only wanted what was out of reach. She blamed me for the divorce, said it was my fault her dad was gone and we didn't ever have enough money. And when I remarried, you'd have thought I did it just to spit in her eye."

Abigail's emotions began to level out. Jolene's matter-of-fact description of her daughter made it easier to be matter-of-fact in turn. "How about her romantic relationships before and after Ethan?"

"After? She was hardly speaking to me by then. Before? Didn't speak to me much then either, but there was that one fellow . . . can't remember his name. I'm pitiful with names, call Terry 'Tom' half the time, and I don't even know any Toms . . . good-looking kid. Local boy."

"Ohneka local?"

"Yeah, that's where Karen grew up. She'd been pining after him, but he didn't know she existed. I always figured that was why she wanted to go out west for school—CalPoly—that's where *he* was going. Heaven knows she could never give me another good reason for being so set on it." She tapped her fingernails on the side of her mug of cranberry punch. "Now *there's* a weird story. I haven't thought about that one in ages. A girl at the university was found murdered."

A whoosh of adrenaline wiped out Abigail's pain and embarrassment. "Murdered?"

"Don't get your hopes up. This was fifteen, sixteen years ago. It couldn't possibly have anything to do with what happened to Karen. This guy . . . what *was* his name? Philip. Philip something-or-other. Apparently he'd been dating this girl, and she dumped him. Ugly breakup. A month or two later when she was found strangled in her apartment, the police questioned him. But it turned out that sly daughter of mine had been seeing him secretly, even while he'd been dating this Barbie-doll girl. He was with Karen when the girl got killed, so he was off the hook. How do you like that?" She laughed. "After that, Karen and Philip went out openly for a while, and oh my, you would have thought Karen was queen of the universe, the way she acted. She was smitten with him—this handsome, wealthy boy. Prince Charming. But it didn't last. He dumped her eventually."

A girl murdered. Jolene was probably right—a sixteen-year-old murder that took place all the way across the country had no relation to Karen's recent death. What involving a murder from Karen's college days could make someone want to kill her now?

But still, it was interesting.

"Karen was very bitter—didn't have a nice thing to say about any man for years," Jolene added.

"Do you remember anything else about Philip? Anything about his family, maybe?"

"Going to track him down and do some more interrogating? Good luck to you, but you might want to get that weepiness under control first."

"Jo."

"Sorry. I don't know much about him. He was LDS, but his family didn't come much—can't remember if his parents were members or not, and I moved to Buffalo just a year or two after we joined the church, so I lost contact with the people in Ohneka. Philip . . . ah . . . still can't remember his last name. Karen was off at college while she was dating him, so it's not like I saw him hanging around my house. After him, I figured Karen had sworn off men and marriage. When she met Ethan, I was thrilled, and for a while, she seemed happy. But then it was like she decided to wreck things. No matter what Ethan did, she just complained and criticized and ripped him apart, and I don't blame him for finally dumping her. Anything else?"

Abigail quizzed Jolene about Karen's teen years, her college years, her friendships, and anything else she could think of. Jolene talked eagerly. Grief came through in her words, alternating with frustration, pain, and bitterness. Abigail had the feeling it was a relief for her to unload her feelings about her estranged daughter.

It was nearly seven when Jolene rose to her feet. "I doubt this has been helpful, but if you're determined to keep hunting through her past, I've got a box you can take with you. It's got a bunch of old high school and college mementos, pictures, journals, that kind of thing. You're welcome to examine it, but I'd like it back eventually. Don't know why I want it—you couldn't pay me to read her journals."

"Probably you'll want to read them after a little more time has passed," Abigail suggested, but Jolene laughed.

"No, thanks. I already know what she thought of me. I don't need to see it in print. But I'd like everything back."

"I'll return it to you promptly. Thank you for letting me borrow it."

"I'll fetch it from the basement. Be right back." Jolene strode out of the room.

Awkward silence promptly took the place of conversation. Abigail stole a glance at Ethan. He hadn't said much during Jolene's report, and she wondered what he was thinking. He looked tired and tense.

"What are you hoping to find in the box?" he asked.

"Anything. And Philip's last name. Did you know about that girl's death?"

"No. Karen never told me anything about it, or about Philip. But it makes things clearer. I always had the feeling she'd been hurt badly in a relationship. And I knew she was comparing me to some other guy and I was coming up short. Not that I thought she had an affair while we were married—it was all mental."

"I'm sorry," Abigail said.

Ethan's gaze locked with hers. "Do you still think I killed her?"

"I'm sorry," Abigail said. "I've been more desperate than logical lately."

"Which is a roundabout way of saying yes."

"No—Ethan—"

He held up a hand. "It's all right. You're not willing to cross anyone off your list yet. But I'd like to give you the names and phone numbers of the people I was with the night Karen died. Like I told you, I was in Rochester doing some work at my mother's house. A couple of her friends were there—the wife was talking with her, and the husband was helping me. They can all testify that I couldn't have been in Ohneka at the time Karen died. The police are satisfied. I want you to be satisfied as well."

Briefly, Abigail thought of giving some polite protest that she didn't want or need the names, that it was enough to know that multiple people could corroborate his story, but she abandoned that thought. Ethan had already shown he could read her very easily, and there was no point in pretending she had no interest in talking to people who might be able to give her additional insights into his character. "Thank you," she said.

"Of course this won't convince you that I didn't set up your brother and hire the job done," he said dryly.

Weary of getting zapped by his too-astute observations, Abigail turned it around. "When I met with you the other night, I asked you what you were doing at Karen's house a couple of days after her death. You said you were fixing a window latch, but you looked very uncomfortable with the question. I want to know why."

His face and neck turned red. He shifted on the couch, looking at the doorway as though checking to make sure Jolene was out of earshot. "When we were . . . when our marriage was . . . on the rocks, I could hardly get Karen to talk to me—or listen to me. I started—" He looked so embarrassed that under any other circumstances, Abigail would have hastily changed the subject.

"I started writing letters to her," Ethan said. "Letters that . . . shared a lot of . . . private feelings. Private experiences we'd shared. I thought if I wrote things down, if she could read the letters when she was alone, when we weren't in the middle of another argument . . . if she could remember . . . I thought maybe . . ." He squirmed, hands gripping his knees, shoulders hunching. "I thought maybe she'd soften up, that she'd . . . remember why she married me, that she'd be willing to work at . . ."

Abigail bit her lip to keep herself from intervening and telling Ethan he didn't have to say more. His humiliation was so tangible that it hurt to witness it.

"The letters didn't work, needless to say." He stared at the floor.

"Did she read them?" Abigail asked softly.

"She read them, all right. She'd quote choice passages back to me, especially when we were in public. She always told me that someday she'd turn them into a blog. 'The Groveling of Ethan Hanberg' was what she planned to call it. She never did, though." His mouth twisted. "That's something to be grateful for."

"You went to her house to get the letters back?"

"Yes. Jolene was planning to go through Karen's things, and I didn't want her to find them. I wanted to take them and burn them."

"Did you find them?"

"Yes. Strange . . . they were in the drawer of her nightstand, in an old jewelry box."

"She must have wanted them close at hand. Maybe she still cared about you more than she could ever admit."

Ethan shook his head. "Maybe she was planning to write that blog after all."

Abigail felt like dirt for prying into his pain and humiliation. "I'm sorry."

He shrugged. "Add it to your list of reasons why I might hire a hit man."

Abigail's face blushed so hot that she knew she must be as red as Ethan. To her relief, Jolene Lassiter's footsteps sounded in the hallway.

"Here it is." Jolene entered carrying a cardboard box. "And now, you two can leave. Terry is due home in half an hour, and trust me, he won't be interested in talking with the sister of the kid who allegedly killed Karen. Not that he liked Karen much. She was rude to him from the moment we started dating. Didn't want anyone to replace her deadbeat daddy. Ethan, help the lady to her car. I'll bring the box. Abigail, call me if you have any questions. You're a nice girl. I don't mind talking to you."

"Thank you for your help. I can't tell you how much I appreciate it."

"Not a problem. Not many people like to talk to me about Karen, so anytime you want me to ramble, come over. And if your brother goes to prison, you might need a friend to lean on. I'm here. I don't blame you for anything. Trust me, I know that our families aren't always what we want them to be."

"Thank you." Abigail started to rise to her feet. Instantly, Ethan moved to help her up.

"Are you sure you can make it?" he asked.

"Yes."

"Hang onto his arm, girl. Don't be so proud. I don't want you falling on my sidewalk and suing me into the next century."

Not wanting to argue with Jolene after all Jolene had done to help her, Abigail tentatively grasped Ethan's arm.

"Give me the box, Jo," he said. "You don't need to come out in the cold."

"Your call, Sir Galahad." Jolene plopped the box on Ethan's free arm. He balanced it against his chest as he escorted Abigail to the door.

When he'd stowed the box in her trunk, he turned to face her.

"I'll get you those phone numbers," he said. "I don't have them with me, but I'll get them to you tomorrow." He took out his cell phone. "What's your number?"

Abigail told him. He entered it and shoved the phone back in his pocket.

"I'm surprised you were willing to come out here alone with me," he said.

"I figure you're too polite to murder me on Jolene's driveway." Abigail didn't know if her joke was a mark of insanity or of the fact that the more she talked to Ethan Hanberg—and listened to Jolene talk about him—the less she could believe he was a killer.

"I'm guessing you want to know what I was doing last night when your brother was injured," he said.

"It was two nights ago, Wednesday night."

"Oh. I . . . have no alibi for Wednesday. I was home alone all that night. But this morning when someone was lurking around your house, I was meeting with a client. Would you like his name and number?"

"Not now. But thanks."

"Drive safely," he said. "Are you sure you're up to it?"

"Pushing the accelerator isn't much of a strain on my muscles."

"Still—a two-hour drive—"

"I'll be fine."

Ethan nodded and stepped back. "I apologize for giving you such a hard time tonight."

"I think it went both ways."

"I wish you trusted me enough to let me help you. If someone did tamper with your stairs, you could be in danger."

"I'll be careful."

"You need to call the police. Tell them about the stairs. Tell them about that guy that your witness saw."

"It's not much for them to go on."

"If you don't call Detective Turner, I will."

The grim tone of his voice surprised her. "Fine, I'll call."

"Good. I . . . you're going to find this rude, but didn't you used to date Robert Chapman's stepson?"

Startled, Abigail said, "Yes. Who told you that?"

"Karen. Who else? She knew Brendan."

"Why . . ." Abigail couldn't think how to tactfully phrase a "why is this any of your business?" question, so she let her voice trail off.

"When you—" He hesitated. "When you mentioned that note supposedly written by Chapman, it reminded me of Brendan. Listen . . . I know you don't trust me enough to let me go through that box with you, but will you let me have a look at it after you're finished?"

"Yes, that's fine."

"Thanks."

As he started to turn away, she said, "Ethan."

He looked back.

"Did you come here to protect Jolene from me—or to protect me from Jolene?"

He grinned crookedly. "A little of both. Take care, Abigail."

CHAPTER 25

PAUL CLEARED HIS THROAT AND fiddled with the steering wheel. "It's not too late to change your mind."

Lillian picked up her purse. "We'd better lock this in the trunk." Detective Turner had advised her not to bring a purse or anything else with her. They would have to be searched at the door, and the more she carried, the longer that would take.

Searched. Patted down like criminals.

"Okay. Let's put it in the trunk," Paul said, but he didn't move to open the door.

Lillian unbuttoned her coat. She was sweating. How embarrassing would it be when some police officer had his or her hands all over Lillian and she was sticky with perspiration?

"Dear, maybe we'd better do this another time," Paul said. "I'm not sure you're ready for this."

"There might not be another time. He almost died."

"He's stable now."

But he almost died. The police thought it was a suicide attempt. Abigail swore that it wasn't. Whichever of them was right, it didn't change the fact that Derek had escaped death by a hairsbreadth. If he'd fallen a little differently . . . if he'd fractured his skull, or snapped his neck . . . if that ornamental tree hadn't slowed his fall . . . if he'd gotten the sheet knotted correctly . . . if the police hadn't shown up precisely when they did . . .

She'd always told herself that someday things would work out and she'd have her son back. *Someday.* Instead, she'd almost lost Derek permanently. He could be dead now, and she'd be left with her last memory of him—that awful argument at the dinner party.

"We can't back out," she said. "Detective Turner set it all up. They're expecting us."

"I'm sure we could call and say we changed our minds."

"Paul, we have to see him. Whether or not he—no matter what he did—I . . ." She pinched one of her wooden coat buttons between her thumb and forefingers and squeezed so hard that the pain in her fingers helped divert her attention from rising tears.

"We could come tomorrow," Paul suggested. "It's so late now anyway."

Lillian didn't point out that they'd requested the late hour on purpose so fewer people would see them.

"Maybe when he's stronger," Paul said. "After they . . . transfer him."

Paul didn't want to wait. She could tell. If he wanted to wait, he'd put the car in gear and drive away, not dither about it. He wanted to do this, but he was as scared as she was—more scared, because he feared for her emotional health. For too long, she'd cowered behind his protectiveness, letting both of them use it as a wall to shut out things too difficult to deal with.

If this was going to happen, she had to make the first move.

Stiffening her spine, Lillian reached for the door handle.

* * *

BLEARILY, DEREK TURNED HIS HEAD toward the sound of the door opening. Surprise sent a lash of pain across his injuries and he realized he'd tensed his entire body.

You're dreaming, bozo. They wouldn't come here. Pain punched him in the ribs as he drew a deep breath, trying to clear his head. Maybe he was hallucinating, or he was so messed up he'd lost his mind entirely.

No one spoke. His mother gripped his father's arm, keeping well back from the bed as though afraid Derek might spring to his feet and attack her.

In the background, the police officer lingered near the door. For a crazy moment, Derek thought of asking the officer if he could see Paul and Lillian too, or if they were images painted by the morphine dripping into Derek's arm.

His parents edged forward another inch. "Detective Turner said we could have a few minutes with you," Lillian said, her voice thin and quivery. "How—how are you feeling?"

Derek's throat was so parched that his "okay" came as a sound a frog might make. He swallowed. "I'm okay." What could he say to them? "Uh . . . it's nice of you to come."

Silence.

Derek wished he could at least sit up to face them, but he couldn't sit without help. He tried to smile. "Are you two doing okay?"

Lillian took another two steps forward, towing Paul with her. They were right next to the bed. If he wanted to, he could stretch out his good arm and touch them. Without thinking, he drew his arm from under the covers.

Tension seized his body, and he held his breath, waiting for the pain to fade.

"Are you in much pain?" Lillian asked.

He drew a shallow breath. "Some. Not too bad."

"Abigail told us what happened," Paul said gruffly. He was looking at the wall above Derek's bed rather than at Derek.

His parents thought he was a murderer, and he couldn't blame them. But they'd still come to see him.

"I . . . I swear to you, I didn't kill Karen Brodie. And I didn't try to kill myself."

Silence.

Derek stared up at the ceiling, not wanting to witness the condemnation he knew he'd see in their faces. "You . . . don't have to believe me. It's okay. I know I've never given you any reason to trust me."

Silence. Derek realized his hand was clenched white-knuckle tight around a fistful of blanket. He wanted to hide his arm under the covers but didn't want to draw attention to the movement. He loosened his grip, still staring at the lights overhead.

He needed to say something, or they would leave, the door would close behind them, and he might never have another chance. "I'm . . . I'm sorry. I . . . pretty well messed up my whole life, and yours too."

Lillian's fingers brushed his hand, a light, tentative touch. He started shaking, spasmodic trembling he couldn't control. It hurt.

Paul cleared his throat. "You'll need a lawyer. We can help with that."

Tears spilled from Derek's eyes, dripping down the sides of his face, spotting his pillow. "I'm sorry," he whispered. "Sorry for everything."

Lillian's hand closed around his.

* * *

THE BOX IN HER ARMS, Abigail took her front steps slowly, planting both feet on one step before moving to the next one. If her knee still hurt this much tomorrow, she'd go to the doctor.

Ethan's reference to Brendan had troubled her all the way home. She'd had the sense that he'd wanted to say more but had stopped himself. Was he thinking that Brendan might have had something to do with the note—that he of all people would know Chapman's eccentric personality and his fondness for Derek's work, and would think of using his name to lure Derek to the park?

Brendan had known Karen. But why in the world would he want to hurt her?

Brendan? That was absurd.

She thought of Brendan approaching her in the parking lot behind Words and Sweets this morning, acting conciliatory, asking about Derek. If Derek was conscious. If Abigail had been able to talk to him.

A shudder rippled through Abigail. What if Brendan had asked those questions because he wanted to know what Derek remembered? Because he was worried Derek might remember too much?

Talk about jumping to conclusions. You could put a kangaroo to shame. With the box balanced on her hip, Abigail locked the front door behind her. Maybe tomorrow morning she'd call Turner, tell him about the stairs and the man Hunter saw and then . . . mention Brendan's name?

And it would look—to Turner and definitely to Brendan—like she was a bitter ex-girlfriend who, lacking any way to defend her brother, had decided to stir up trouble for Brendan. She needed to know more about Brendan's interaction with Karen before she could consider giving his name to Turner. Bob Chapman had mentioned that Brendan had been interested in Karen at one point. Had they gotten involved? But even if they had, it would have been so long ago—

But this Philip boy was long ago, and you think it's worth investigating him.

Jolene Lassiter had invited her to call if she had any questions. She'd call Jolene tomorrow and ask about Brendan.

She set the box on the coffee table. Kyle would be here soon. She wished she had more time before he arrived—she wanted to sort through this box of Karen's mementos before she did anything else, and she didn't want Kyle to know she'd gone to Karen's mother. She *could* call Kyle and cancel, but she really wanted to see him.

Her sore arms moving awkwardly, Abigail took off her coat and hung it up. Standing at the base of the stairs, she debated whether her vanity or the pain in her knee was stronger. She wanted to brush her hair and fix her makeup before Kyle came, but was it worth hiking the stairs to her bathroom?

It was worth it. A little embarrassed at herself, but determined to look as good as she could, Abigail started the slow climb to the second level.

She touched up her makeup, and spent so long trying to brush her hair to perfection that she finally threw her brush down, amused at herself. How likely was it that Kyle would say, *"Abigail, I really like you, but your hair is a little too flat on top. This isn't going to work."*? She spritzed her good-enough hair with hairspray, and finished up with a touch of perfume.

The fun of getting ready for Kyle faded back into grim worry as she made her way down the stairs. Who was this Philip boy whom Karen's testimony had exonerated? A murder had taken place close to Karen, and the murderer had never been found. That was definitely something to take to Detective Turner. With the case being old, taking place in California, and the fact that Karen's boyfriend was never charged, Turner might not know about it. She'd talk to him tomorrow and beg him to at least find out who Philip was and where he was now.

She still had a few minutes before Kyle was due. With a pair of kitchen shears, she snipped through the tape sealing the cardboard box.

A white plastic sack shielded something soft. Abigail opened the sack and unfolded a raspberry-pink evening dress. It had a long, straight skirt and long sleeves decorated with beads the same color as the fabric. Both the color of the dress and the trim, elegant style would have been very flattering to Karen. Why had she hidden the dress in a box? The style was classic enough that it didn't look too dated, and she was certainly thin enough to fit into it.

Had the dress evoked painful memories? Carefully, Abigail refolded it, returned it to the sack, and set it aside.

In the box, two grocery sacks protected something wrapped in silky fabric. She unwound the protecting fabric and found a dozen dried red roses. The roses were starting to crumble, and bits of dried petals stuck to the fabric.

Roses. Someone—Philip?—had given Karen roses years ago, and she had valued them so highly that she'd preserved them like this.

Abigail felt strange looking at the roses and associating them with the sarcastic, bitter image she had of Karen. She pictured Karen lovingly drying the roses and keeping them displayed in a vase in her bedroom. Then, when she married Ethan, she still hadn't been able to bring herself to throw them away, but had meticulously wrapped them in fabric and stored them in her mother's basement.

A framed photograph was next, a picture of a middle-aged man with a grinning, brown-haired girl on his lap. Karen's father. And Karen as a child.

More pictures—an envelope filled with snapshots. Abigail drew them out. Karen, wearing the raspberry-pink evening dress, one hand resting gracefully on the marble pillar next to her. She looked so beautiful that Abigail stared at the picture. What had happened to turn this radiant girl into the hard, cold woman Abigail had known?

The doorbell rang. Abigail quickly returned the photos to the envelope and dropped the envelope into the oversized pocket of her sweater. She reached for the roses, but as she lifted the bouquet of brittle flowers, she changed her mind about hiding them.

If she was considering getting seriously involved with Kyle, she *had* to be honest with him—including being honest about the fact that despite his advice, she hadn't yet given up on the quest to help Derek. If she didn't trust him enough to tell him that, then why was she getting involved with him in the first place? He might not like what she was doing, but he wouldn't condemn her. He'd probably help her. And leaving the box on the table would force her to acknowledge that she was searching through Karen's past.

She opened the front door. Kyle's smile drew a smile from her lips in response and made her glad she'd endured the stairs in order to look her best. He had the most charming smile she'd ever seen—almost magnetically appealing.

"Hi," he said. "Let me in. I'm freezing to death out here."

"Poor guy." She stepped back. "Come in."

He stepped over the threshold and closed the door behind him. "How are you doing?" He kissed her on the cheek.

"I'm good. Can I take your coat?"

"I can handle it." Kyle hung his coat in the closet.

"Would you like some hot chocolate?" Abigail offered. "Or would you prefer something cold to show Mother Nature she can't beat you?"

He laughed. "I don't need anything." He started toward the living room. Abigail hung back, wanting to walk a little behind him in an effort to keep him from noticing the awkwardness of her gait. Disguising her limp was not an option.

"Cold in here too," Kyle remarked as they entered the living room.

"Oh, I'm sorry. I've been gone all day, and I haven't turned the thermostat back up yet."

"Wearing that sweater, I'm not surprised you didn't notice." Kyle touched the sleeve of her thick, knee-length sweater. "That's gorgeous, by the way. Hand-knitted?"

"Yes. My mother." Her knee throbbed, and the thought of trekking into the hallway where the thermostat was located suddenly seemed as daunting as crossing the polar ice caps. "The thermostat is in the hall— would you turn it up for me?"

"Sure." Kyle disappeared into the hallway. Abigail sat on the couch.

"It's all good to save money," he said as he walked into the room. "But you ought to replace that ancient thermostat with something that has a timer so you can heat the house before you return home." He walked to the gas fireplace. "Emergency measures," he said as he ignited the flames.

He sat on the couch next to her. "What's all this?" he asked, gesturing at the box and the sacks on the coffee table.

Abigail's cheeks were already warming with embarrassment, but the best way to deal with this was as bluntly as possible. "Karen Brodie's possessions," she said.

"Karen!"

"I went to visit her mother today and we talked about Karen. In her basement, she had a box of mementos Karen had saved." Even with her desire to be upfront, Abigail couldn't make herself add that Ethan Hanberg had been there. After Kyle's Jack-the-Ripper comment, he *would* think she'd cracked up if she told him she'd sat there chatting with Ethan.

Kyle was silent. Abigail wanted to ramble on, telling him what she'd learned, but she wasn't going to let herself babble to fill the awkward silence. She wanted to see his reaction first—but, apparently, not bad enough to look at him; she couldn't seem to stare at anything except the flames twisting inside the flagstone fireplace. Normally, an evening fire made the room seem homey and safe, but tonight the flames looked malicious, as though if she turned her back, they'd leap from the fireplace and consume her house.

Kyle reached for her hand. "Abigail," he said, his fingers closing around hers, "you're sorting through a box of Karen's old treasures hoping *that* will somehow guide you to whoever killed her last week? Forgive me, but that doesn't even begin to sound rational."

"As soon as I know I've done everything possible to help Derek, I'll quit trying and leave things to his lawyer."

"You *have* done everything possible. What you're doing now is stalling, putting off the moment when you have to admit this is out of your hands. What's in the box, anyway?"

"I just started looking at it. So far, I've found an evening dress and a bouquet of dried roses. A picture of Karen and her dad—"

Kyle sighed. "How is this helping?"

"I'm looking for more information about a man Karen was in love with when she was in college."

"In college!"

"I know it's a stretch. But a girl was murdered. Her ex-boyfriend was a suspect, but Karen testified that he was with her at the time of the girl's death. The murderer was never found."

"Did Karen's mother tell you about this?"

"Yes. She said she hadn't even thought about it in years, but when I was asking her about Karen's past, it reminded her. Apparently Karen was head over heels for this boy. Her mother couldn't remember his last name but said his first name was Philip."

"I don't understand what this could possibly have to do with Karen's death. You think somehow the guy that murdered this college girl came back years later and killed Karen? Where did she go to school, anyway?"

"CalPoly."

"This happened all the way across the country?"

"Yes, but the boy involved was from Ohneka. And Karen said something strange to me once. We were talking about Derek—she was trying to weasel money out of me and she said she knew what it was like to shield a creep who doesn't deserve it. It's a long shot, but what if she was talking about Philip? What if she protected him at the time this girl was killed? It was *her* testimony that kept him from getting arrested. What if he *did* kill that girl and she lied to protect him? Ethan Hanberg told me that he always felt she was keeping something buried inside, something painful, something she didn't want anyone to see. What if that 'something' was guilt at protecting a murderer? What if Karen was still in touch with him and did something to set him off? If he killed once, he could kill again."

"You're leaping to a lot of conclusions. Have you told any of this to the police?"

"No. I'll call Detective Turner tomorrow. You grew up here—do you remember anyone named Philip? I know Ellie said you didn't really know Karen, but does Philip ring a bell?"

"Abigail, it's not an uncommon name. Yes, I knew a guy named Philip. He had greasy hair, no neck, and liked to get laughs by shooting beer out his nose at parties. Is that the guy you're looking for?"

Abigail smiled sheepishly. "Maybe he *was* Karen's Prince Charming. There's no accounting for tastes."

Kyle laughed.

"I know you think this is foolish, and truly, Kyle, I did take your advice to heart the other night. But I just don't think I've done everything I can do. I want to see what I find in that box. There are some pictures there, and old journals. Do you want to help me? I know it's not how you intended to spend your evening, but—"

"No, I do not want to help you. This is a wild goose chase, and it's not healthy for you. Your brother manipulates you like a puppet, do you realize that?"

Stung, Abigail said, "Just because I'm trying to help him doesn't mean he's manipulating me."

"Okay, now I'm going to be *really* candid. Are you braced?"

"Kyle—"

"There is overwhelming evidence that Derek killed Karen. But as long as he *claims* he's innocent, you'll keep scrambling to prove the police are wrong, chasing down Karen's creepy ex-husband, spending hours on the road for a futile chat with her mother, digging through musty old boxes—and this after Derek attacked you. Attacked you! Don't you have any self-respect?"

"He didn't—"

"This may come as a surprise, but tying someone to a chair and leaving them a prisoner for hours is illegal. Your brother is a criminal. I'm sorry." Kyle lifted her hand and pressed his lips to her knuckles. "I know I sound cruel. Forgive me. I'm only being this candid because . . . Abigail, I think I'm in love with you. I know it's early to be saying this, but it's true. I can't stand seeing you hurt and manipulated."

Abigail's heartbeat took off at a sprint. *He's in love with me?*

"Sorry." He smiled. "I have the worst timing, but when I feel strongly, I have trouble holding back. Listen, this is what we'll do. Forget all this for now—" He waved toward the box and bags on the coffee table. "Let's get out of here. I know a little restaurant that's open until midnight and has the best pie you've ever tasted. It's a bit of a drive—very rustic; you'll think you've gone back in time—but it's very private. Very relaxing. Just what you need right now."

He's in love with me? "That's sweet of you, but honestly I'm too tired to think of going anywhere. Can I take a rain check?"

"Nice try. You don't want to rest. You want to dive into that box, hoping the dust particles will spell out the name of Karen's murderer. Forget it. You need a break from everything."

"Kyle—"

"You amaze me." Kyle brushed his fingers over her hair. "I hope you don't think I've been criticizing you. I think you're Wonder Woman for the way you've been fighting for your brother, but I can't stand seeing you hurt. Get your coat, and let's get away for a while. If you're so set on searching through the box, it'll still be here in the morning."

Abigail wavered. She was tired, but she was also far too wired to sleep. Maybe she ought to go to the restaurant with Kyle. But after driving to Buffalo and back today, the thought of a "bit of a drive" with her swollen knee and aching arms was less than appealing. What she really wanted was a soak in a hot bath.

A bit of a drive. Confusion flickered inside Abigail. Kyle had said she'd spent hours on the road to visit Karen's mother, but how did Kyle know Karen's mother didn't live right here in Ohneka? He'd hardly known Karen—why would he know anything about her family?

What does it matter? He probably heard from someone who knew Karen that her mother had moved away. Are you afraid he's spying on you, checking up to see if you followed his advice? How paranoid can you get?

But she *didn't* want to go out tonight. Trudging back out in the cold, picking her painful way down the steps—"Kyle, I appreciate the offer, but I don't have the energy to go anywhere. I'd rather take a hot bath and go to bed."

"Uh-huh. You'd rather stay here and obsess over Karen's high school yearbooks." Kyle rose to his feet. He picked up Karen's dress and the roses. Dried petals crunched noisily as he shoved both items into the box.

"Be careful!" Abigail exclaimed. "I have to give those things back to Karen's mother."

"She'll never bother to look at a bunch of old flowers. I'll get your coat." He headed toward the coat closet.

Troubled, Abigail rose to her feet. Maybe Jolene never *would* look at the flowers, but that didn't make it all right to treat Karen's mementos so callously.

Kyle returned wearing his coat and holding hers. "Here you go."

Abigail took it but didn't put it on. "I really do appreciate the offer, but like I said, I'm not up to it. If you want to chat for a while, I'm up to that, and I can offer you some hot chocolate and the mint truffles Ellie gave me today."

"So I eat chocolate and you go through that old box?"

"If that bothers you, I can eat the chocolate too."

He didn't smile. "Abigail, you're obsessed. *You've got to let this go.* You need a break—*now.*"

Her frustration growing, Abigail said, "I understand why you think this is hopeless, and I understand why you believe Derek is guilty. I don't fault you for that. But when it comes to deciding how best to help him, that's my decision to make."

"I'm sorry," he said. "You're annoyed with me. If you want to keep trying to dig up evidence to exonerate your brother, that *is* your decision. But I can't in good conscience let a beautiful woman push herself into a nervous breakdown, so tonight, I'm going to insist that you take a breather. I promise I won't keep you out too late. You're not one of those rigid schedule people who can't slip in a little unscheduled fun, are you?"

"Kyle—"

Kyle leaned over and kissed her forehead. "I'll drive. You rest in the passenger seat."

She'd have to tell him the full truth if she wanted him to understand why she was turning him down. "It's more than just being tired. I slipped on the ice today, on the stairs. My arms are bruised and my knee is killing me."

"You slipped on the stairs! Abigail, that's terrible. Are you all right?"

"Just bruised. But I'm not up to a night on the town—or out in the country. Let's do it next week." Abigail tossed her coat onto the couch. "I won't mess with that box tonight. Let's sit down and relax. I probably ought to ice my knee again."

She expected Kyle to remove his coat and make her comfortable on the couch. Instead, he said, "What you need is something to take your mind off the pain. We'll keep the trip short."

It was all Abigail could do not to stare at him in disbelief. "I'd rather do something to *ease* the pain," she said, trying to sound light.

"Their lemon meringue pie will make you forget every pain you ever had. You're not going to make me throw you over my shoulder and carry you to my car, are you?"

At one point, Abigail would have found this teasing charming or romantic, but the sense of being flattered by Kyle's concern was shrinking rapidly. Concern was one thing. Pressure was another. "I wouldn't want you to risk your back muscles like that."

He picked up her coat. "Time for a break."

This was getting ridiculous. "Maybe we should call it a night," she said. "I'm sorry I'm not very good company. I'm sure you must feel you wasted your time coming here tonight."

"Not at all. Time with you is never wasted."

Abigail's relief at his gracious words faded when he held the coat out to her. "Let's go."

Abigail took the coat. She'd never realized Kyle could be so pushy, and she didn't like it. Was this what Ellie had meant when she'd hinted that Kyle was not Abigail's type? "Kyle, I can tell you don't know me very well. When I say I don't want to go out, that's what I mean. I'm not flirting. I'm not playing games. I'm not asking to be persuaded. I'm saying I don't want to go out, and I'd like you to respect that. In fact, I think it would be better if you went home and I went to bed. Call me tomorrow."

She hoped that Kyle would concede defeat with his usual charm and leave—or even stomp out in anger, if that was how this had to end—but he did neither. He stood by the couch, smiling.

"This time, I think I know what you want better than you do," he said. "Put your coat on."

Any remaining fears that she might offend Kyle wilted and died. No wonder Ellie hadn't been heartbroken when Kyle dumped her. Abigail looked at his charming smile, her disappointment cutting deep. So much for the knight in shining armor. She should have known he was too good to be true.

"I want you to leave," she said. "Now."

"I can't do that, in good conscience."

"Then I hope your conscience can keep you company, because I'm going to bed. Good night." Abigail dropped her coat on the couch and turned away. If the only way to end this was with outright rudeness, she'd be rude. She limped away from Kyle, waiting for the sound of him walking out the door. Out the door and out of her life.

That sound didn't come.

She made her painful journey up the stairs and into her bedroom, and still, she hadn't heard the door open and close.

This is wrong. The feeling that nudged Abigail wasn't annoyance—it was fear. Kyle couldn't possibly be as worried about her as he claimed. Why wouldn't he leave?

She closed her bedroom door and locked it. Her heart was racing again, but not with affection for Kyle. Was he so controlling that he'd stand his ground until she finally gave in and agreed to do what he thought was best for her? Was he that big of a manipulative creep? She pictured him downstairs standing guard over Karen's box of mementos, certain Abigail would soon give up and agree to come with him. That went beyond arrogant to pathological.

She'd give him two minutes, and if he wasn't out of here, she'd call the police.

Chilled, she shoved her hands in her sweater pockets. Her fingers touched the envelope of photographs. She pulled it out and flipped through the pictures. Karen in her pink dress. Karen again, sitting on the couch, Karen and her date. Tall, breathtakingly handsome, his smile charming the camera.

It was a younger Kyle Stratton.

Abigail stared at the picture, blinked, and stared again.

He'd lied about not knowing Karen Brodie.

Abigail raced through the rest of the pictures. Kyle with his arm around Karen; Kyle clowning for the camera, kissing Karen on the cheek; Kyle and Karen at dinner.

Was this why Kyle had been so intent that she not look through Karen's mementos? Was Kyle *Philip*—the boy whose girlfriend had been murdered; the boy whom Karen's testimony had saved from a murder charge?

Abigail struggled to grasp facts from the whirlwind of fear that spun through her mind. Ethan had mentioned that Karen had seemed different for the past year or so, like something had changed in her life. Kyle had moved back to Ohneka just over a year ago. And Kyle, like Karen, had grown up here.

Kyle knew a lot of details about Derek's life. Abigail had told Ellie a lot about Derek—including the little she knew about Derek's life and girlfriend in Ithaca—and Ellie talked freely with people she trusted—like she'd trusted Kyle. Kyle had known all about Derek's rent problems and the disastrous dinner party. And about Derek's work for Bob Chapman, and Chapman's eccentricities.

The night Karen died, she'd been dressed up like she was meeting someone she wanted to impress. A boyfriend? Or ex-boyfriend? An ex-boyfriend who had moved back to town, upsetting Karen, who'd never gotten over him? Bitter Karen, who might have felt he owed her something for her silence—something he didn't want to pay? Had he charmed Karen into meeting with him that night, offering her whatever promises she wanted to hear—and then killed her?

Her fingers clumsy, Abigail shoved the pictures back in her pocket and picked up the phone on her nightstand. She pressed 911 and hit the talk button.

There was no dial tone.

CHAPTER 26

FRANTICALLY, ABIGAIL CHECKED TO MAKE sure the battery was inserted correctly and punched the buttons again. No dial tone.

Her cell phone—she'd left it charging on the table in the downstairs hall—the table near the thermostat. Kyle would have seen it there. He'd know she didn't have it with her. And if he'd unplugged the main base station downstairs, none of the landline phones in the house would work.

From downstairs, she could hear nothing. What was Kyle doing? Could she possibly go down, apologize, claim she'd changed her mind and wanted to go out with him, and then slip away when they got outside—

Slip away? You can hardly walk. And Kyle would never believe her if she tried to act casual, like she didn't suspect anything. As just about everyone had pointed out to her recently, she was a poor liar.

Her window—the deck was below it. She could climb out the window and—*and what? Jump ten feet to the deck, break both your legs, and try to drag yourself away?*

The tread of footsteps sounded on the stairs.

A weapon. Something—anything—Abigail yanked open her closet. Clothes, shoes—there had to be *something* she could wield—

A knock at the door. "Time to go, Abigail." Kyle's voice was cold. So much for the pretense of worrying about her health.

"The police are on their way," Abigail said.

"I don't think so. Your cell phone is downstairs."

A weapon—Abigail snatched the heavy wooden curtain rod from her window, separated it into two pieces and shook it so the curtain slid to the floor, leaving the rod bare.

An earsplitting crash made her scream. Her bedroom door flew open. Kyle stepped into the room, a gun in his hand.

"Drop it," he said.

Abigail clutched the makeshift club as though it could ward off bullets. "You killed Karen."

"*Drop* it. Or I'll put a bullet in your head."

Abigail dropped the curtain rod. "You're Philip."

"It's a nerdy name. I haven't used it since college."

"You killed that other girl. Karen lied to protect you."

"Karen lied to protect herself as much as me. Who do you think got me the key to Leslie's apartment?"

"Karen tried to blackmail you?"

"Let's go, Abigail." He used the gun to gesture at the door.

Abigail's tongue was so dry that she could hardly form words. "No. You framed Derek—you want the police to think there's no killer but Derek. I'm not going to make it easy for you to conceal my murder, or make it look like an accident—the ice—the ice on the stairs—you did that, didn't you?"

He shrugged. "It was too much to hope that the fall alone would kill you, but I would have made sure you hit your head good and hard if that stupid kid hadn't interfered."

Hunter. Kyle was the man Hunter had seen. He must have been wearing a dark wig—

A wig. And a coat that matched Hunter's and a hat the same color . . . Hunter was a big kid, as big as Kyle. Hunter was the only person Chase McCoy remembered seeing around Derek's apartment.

"You dressed up as Hunter Conley," Abigail said. "That's how you got in and out of Derek's apartment without anyone paying attention to you."

"It's not hard to do," Kyle said. "Just slap on a dirty coat, a greasy wig and hat, and walk like this—" He hunched his shoulders, stared at the ground and took a couple of lumbering steps forward.

"You tripped me with something on the stairs. What was it?"

"Fishing line. I reeled it in after you went down."

The icy stairs—he'd rigged it so she would trip, and then when she was down and injured, he'd planned to come out and finish the job. While she lay there, dazed with pain, it would have been simple for him to grab her and slam her skull against the stairs, making sure the damage looked accidental. After the rain and sleet and freezing temperatures, the police wouldn't have questioned it if Abigail had had a serious—or fatal—fall down some icy stairs.

He took another step toward her. "Got more questions? Fine. Let's talk in the car."

"I'm not going anywhere with you. Shoot me. Shoot me right now. Even if you hide my body, good luck on getting rid of every trace of blood. And good luck on making sure no one hears the gunshot. And good luck on blaming my death on Derek."

"Don't be a fool," Kyle said.

Hands soaked in sweat, Abigail removed her sweater and dropped it on the floor. She hoped Kyle would ignore it—and when the police searched her house, they'd find the envelope of photographs in her pocket.

"Good luck on getting both Jolene Lassiter and Ethan Hanberg to forget that I came home from Jolene's excited about searching through a box of Karen's mementos to figure out who Philip was," Abigail said. "No matter what you do to me, the police will still be hunting for you."

Kyle moved closer. Abigail would have backed up, but she was already nearly pressed against the window.

He stopped a couple of feet away from her. "Let's go."

"No."

He smiled. "Fine. You win. You're right. I don't want to shoot you. Noisy and messy." He dropped the gun into his coat pocket. "But there's something I need to teach you. You hurt your leg on the stairs today, right? Your knee? Your right knee?"

Abigail said nothing.

Kyle's leg lashed forward. His foot smashed into Abigail's right kneecap.

Abigail screamed. Her body slammed into the window then crumpled to the floor. Pain choked her as she writhed, wanting to grab her leg but afraid to touch it, sure multiple bones had shattered.

He stood over her. "Lesson learned? Maybe not. You're a slow learner. And I'm not stupid, by the way. I know this has fallen apart. I also know it's your fault. Everyone else was willing to believe your scum-of-the-earth brother was guilty. The cops were satisfied. Everyone was satisfied. Except you." His foot slammed into her stomach.

It hurt more than Abigail had fathomed anything could. She couldn't breathe; she couldn't move. Tears of agony streamed from her eyes.

"It's your fault your brother got hurt," he said. "I never would have hunted him down, but I needed you to back off—and if he were dead, you wouldn't keep stirring up trouble trying to help him."

Kyle nudged her arm with his foot, and she tensed, awaiting another blow. "I like it here in Ohneka," he said. "I like running my dad's business. I never visit him, by the way. He's too sick to stop me from doing whatever I want, and my mother's too worried about him to care. I don't like the fact that I'll have to leave now. And you're the one who ruined things. Do you enjoy making trouble for me, Abigail? Would you like to make more trouble? Say the word, and we can continue the lesson."

Abigail tried to shake her head, but pain seemed to have stolen her ability to control her muscles. All she could manage was a small twitch.

"Okay, good enough. You're learning. Now, your job is to hold still. If you struggle, you know what will happen."

Her vision a blur of pain and tears, Abigail watched Kyle bend over her, drawing a coil of rope from his coat pocket.

"I hoped I wouldn't have to do this," he said. "If you'd taken my advice and left things alone, we could have had a nice, peaceful evening. I do enjoy kissing you. But, no—you had to go to Jolene Lassiter."

He'd come tonight to check up on her, Abigail realized. He'd brought the rope and gun in case he needed them, but if she'd concealed the fact that she'd been at Jolene's, would he have left without hurting her?

And she'd trusted him. She'd wanted him to know what she was doing. So blind—

He reached for her hands. If she let him tie her up, it was over. With all her thoughts focused on one desperate prayer for strength, Abigail threw herself to the side and grabbed the wooden curtain rod where she'd dropped it. With all the force she could manage, she swung it upward, aiming for Kyle's head.

Kyle jerked backward. The curtain rod slammed into his arm. Off balance, he staggered to the side. Abigail rolled over and swung again, aiming for his legs, but Kyle leaped out of reach. He snatched the other piece of the curtain rod from the floor and swung it at her. Abigail met his blow with her own half of the rod, but Kyle's strike was far more powerful than hers. The curtain rod spiraled out of her hands and crashed against the window. The glass cracked.

"That was . . . stupid." From the tightness in his voice, she knew he was in pain. "Really stupid."

Abigail turned, straining to reach her rod, but Kyle swung his rod forward, crashing it against her ribcage. A sickening wave of dizziness sent the room spinning around her. Abigail focused on the dizziness, wanting it to drag her into oblivion before the next blow.

"Any more bones you want me to break?" he asked. "We'll do them one at a time if that's the way you want it. Or are you ready to cooperate? Nod your head if you've learned your lesson."

Abigail nodded. Struggling to breathe through a firestorm of pain, she couldn't do anything but lie limp as Kyle drew her arms behind her and knotted the rope around her wrists.

With his hands under her arms, Kyle lifted her to a sitting position and propped her against the side of the bed.

"Your brother's an idiot," he said. "Anyone dim enough to act *that* guilty deserves to get convicted of first-degree murder. Too bad he's in the hospital, or I could pin this one on him too. I think we'll stay here after all. I wanted to do this somewhere else, but knowing you, you'd find a way to make trouble for me on the trip. Why take the risk?"

She was going to die. There was no way she could fight Kyle off, no way she could summon help. *Please let the police figure out what happened,* she prayed. *Let Derek go free, let him be safe.* "You won't get away," Abigail rasped. "Even if they can't—find me—they'll know—they'll figure out—"

"They might figure it out," Kyle said. "But that doesn't mean they'll find me. And they won't ever find you."

He drew another piece of rope out of his pocket. "Rope's not a very classy weapon. I hope you're not offended. For Leslie, I used one of her belts—a skinny, metallic thing that she probably paid two hundred bucks for at some designer shop." He fingered the rope. "I didn't *plan* to kill Leslie. Trashing her stuff was good enough, but when she caught me at it—well, panic makes people do strange things. And Karen—that was a matter of practicality, an unpleasant job to get out of the way. But you—after the trouble you've made, I'm going to enjoy this." He smiled at her. "Don't get me wrong. I do like you. More than Karen, less than Leslie. I'll leave lilies on your grave. Or maybe tulips. Do you like tulips?"

Fury mingled with Abigail's terror. It wasn't enough to kill her—he had to toy with her first. She glanced at the cracked window, bare of curtains. No neighbors lived close enough to look in her window, but if she screamed, there was a miniscule chance someone might hear her. Abigail sucked in every molecule of air her damaged muscles could gather and screamed, *"Help me!"*

The mocking smile left Kyle's face. "Okay, you're in a hurry. Fine, let's finish this." He grabbed her by the hair and yanked her down so her face was pressed against the carpet. With his knee digging into her back to keep her pinned to the floor, he slipped the rope around her neck.

The sharp, crystalline sound of breaking glass came from downstairs. Kyle dropped the rope and sprang to his feet, bringing the gun out of his pocket. Abigail heard the familiar sound of the front door swinging open.

"Abigail!" A male voice shouted her name. *"Abigail!"*

Was that Ethan's voice? *"He has a gun!"* Abigail screamed. *"Kyle has a gun. Get out of here!"*

Kyle charged out the door. His footsteps thundered on the stairs.

Terrified that a gunshot would come momentarily, Abigail used her bound hands to push herself to a sitting position. "Ethan, *run!"*

From downstairs came eerie silence. Unable to stand on her injured leg, Abigail scooted clumsily along on one knee until she reached the top of the stairs.

A thud from downstairs made her cry out in fear. Another thud, and a crash like a lamp hitting the floor. Ethan must have jumped Kyle; had Kyle dropped the gun? Gritting her teeth against the pain, Abigail sat and pushed off the top of the stairs, letting herself slide to the bottom. She couldn't help Ethan fight Kyle, but she could distract Kyle.

The front door stood gaping open. Abigail pushed herself toward the door, ignoring the broken glass scattered on the floor, and screamed with all the power she could muster. *"Kyle Stratton is killing us. He killed Karen Brodie—"*

Another crash from behind her. Abigail threw herself through the doorway and onto the porch. *"Kyle Stratton—"*

Headlights. Headlights and flashing red-and-blue lights and blurry figures—

"Be careful, he has a gun—" Abigail's warning cry was hoarse.

"I've got it, it's okay." Ethan leaned over her. He was breathing hard, his face tense with pain.

A shout came from an approaching police officer. "Drop the gun!"

Ethan immediately let the gun fall to the porch. "I'm Ethan

Hanberg. I'm the one who called you," he shouted back. "He's in the living room. He's unconscious, I think. And we need an ambulance."

"*Ethan.*" Abigail sobbed his name as his arms slid beneath her and lifted her off the porch. Blood streamed from a cut beneath his eye. "How did you . . . know to . . . come?"

"I was worried about you. Abigail—are you okay? What did he do to—"

"But—your car—I didn't hear—"

"I parked out on the road. I wanted to come have a look around, see if I could find any evidence that someone rigged the accident on your stairs. I should have called you, but I knew you didn't trust me. I heard you scream—"

A police officer took Abigail from Ethan's arms; another officer drew Ethan back. Abigail wanted to explain to the officers about Kyle, about Karen, about Derek, but as the flood of adrenaline began to ebb, her injuries caught fire with new pain, and all she could manage was a moan. The faces around her zoomed out of focus.

"Abigail!" A familiar voice. A hand touched her shoulder. Detective Turner.

"Derek didn't kill Karen Brodie," she whispered.

CHAPTER 27

"I'M SO, SO, *SO* SORRY." Ellie's eyes shone with tears. "I was afraid if I said anything you'd think I was just acting jealous, and I thought maybe I was. I didn't really have any *evidence,* you know. He just seemed kind of cold sometimes—arrogant cold—but he was so charming and so sweet most of the time that I told myself it was no big deal. If I'd warned you—"

"Ellie—" Abigail reached over to Ellie sitting next to her on the couch and squeezed her hand. "Stop it right now. There's no way you could have known."

"Besides, apologizing is *my* job," Derek said.

Ellie wiped her eyes and scowled at him. "I hope so, you punk. Do you have any idea how dumb you—"

"Ellie," Abigail interrupted, but Derek shook his head.

"Let her say it. I deserve every word."

"I'm glad you realize that," Ellie said. "Someone's got to skin the hide off you, because I know Abigail won't. Lucky for you, she's insanely stubborn. And insanely forgiving."

"I know." Derek looked at Abigail. He was grinning, but remorse was marked on his haggard face.

Ellie dug into her bag and took out a silver-wrapped box that she handed to Abigail. "There's a little health food to help you recover from that wretched knee surgery. I wasn't going to bring anything for *you*—" she glared at Derek "—but I figured if I didn't, Abigail would just share hers, so what was the point? I know you're not a big chocolate fanatic—which is another strike against you—so here." She handed him a box of caramel-covered cashews.

Derek looked startled. "Uh—thanks, Ellie. You didn't have to do this."

"I put chunks of glass in them." She looked from Derek to Abigail, both lounging on the family room sectional with footrests extended. "A matched set of invalids," she said. "You must be keeping your mother busy."

"I'm afraid we are," Abigail said.

Ellie grinned at her. "Brendan stopped by the store. He seems very worried about you."

"That's thoughtful of him. He sent flowers." She gestured at the bouquet on the lamp table.

Ellie's eyebrows shot up. "I *told* you he was—"

"Flowers with a card signed by him *and* Mira," Abigail added. She would have laughed at the look on Ellie's face, but laughing hurt her ribs. "Ellie, it's okay. I honestly have no interest in resuming a relationship with Brendan Rowe. I hope he marries Mira and they live happily ever after."

Ellie sighed and stood up. "I'd better get back to work. Everything's fine there, by the way, and like I said, Melissa can come in for as long as you need her."

"Thanks for taking care of everything. And thanks for driving all the way here to visit us. You didn't need to do that."

"No problem. I like to see you in person so I can believe you're all right. Just take care of yourself, and call me if you need anything." Ellie hesitated for a moment, awkwardly switching her bag from one shoulder to the other. "I know Abigail doesn't want to testify against you," she said, looking at Derek. "But I also know it isn't her decision what they decide to charge you with. What's going to happen?"

"I don't know yet," Derek said. "But whatever happens, I won't fight it. If I go to prison . . . write me, okay?"

"Look who's grown up," Ellie said. "The Fugitive, reformed."

"It's not that," Derek said. "It's just that I tried running away on this leg, and a posse of snails caught me."

Ellie smiled. "Take care, okay?"

"Will do," Derek said.

After Ellie left, Abigail picked up the hand of Rook cards she'd set aside. She was about to ask Derek if he wanted to finish the game when she saw he'd closed his eyes. Glad he was resting—Derek didn't like admitting how weak he was—Abigail silently set the cards aside and opened the novel Ellie had brought her in the hospital.

"Abby."

Abigail looked over at Derek. His eyes were still shut. "What?"

"Why?" Derek said.

"Why what?"

He opened his eyes and looked at her. "The big why. You had every reason to believe I killed Karen."

Abigail closed her book. "I couldn't believe you were that organized. If you'd really done it, you would have shown up twenty minutes late at Kemper Park, Karen would already have given up in disgust and gone home, and you would have forgotten the bookend."

Derek snorted with laughter then groaned and grabbed his chest. "Don't make me do that. But seriously, Abby."

"Instinct?" Abigail said. "Intuition? Inspiration? What happened to Karen wasn't something I could fathom you doing. And I don't mean to make light of it—it was a terrible tragedy."

"How about the bigger why?"

"The *bigger* why? Derek, do you want to have a conversation, or do you want to play twenty questions?"

Derek looked at her in silence. Abigail knew what he was asking: *"After what I did to you, why did you keep fighting for me?"*

"Because you needed help," she said.

"I didn't deserve it."

"Because I love you."

"I don't deserve that either. Abby, good grief. You risked your life for me."

"Well, I didn't *mean* to," Abigail said. Derek laughed, clutched his ribs, and glared at her.

Within a few minutes, his eyes had closed again. Abigail picked up her book and tried to concentrate on the words intently enough to keep herself from thinking of Kyle Stratton tightening that rope around her neck.

The doorbell rang. Biting the inside of her lip, Abigail listened to the taps of her mother's shoes as she went to answer the door.

The visitor spoke too quietly for Abigail to overhear the conversation, but she tried to listen anyway, hoping to hear Ethan's voice. He'd come to visit her in the hospital, but her parents had been there, and most of the conversation had involved her mother's tears, her father's awkward thanks, and Abigail's dozing off due to pain medication. He'd called yesterday while she was asleep and asked Lillian if he could come visit sometime this afternoon. Abigail had been waiting eagerly all day; she wanted desperately to talk to him.

Lillian appeared in the family room doorway. She glanced at Derek, dozing, and spoke softly. "Abigail, Ethan Hanberg is here. Do you feel up to another visitor?"

Abigail nodded quickly. "I'll see him in the living room so Derek can sleep," she whispered. "Will you hand me my crutches?"

With Lillian's help, she made it into the living room and settled onto the couch. A moment later, Lillian escorted Ethan in. He carried a crystal vase filled with an autumn arrangement of gold, rust, and yellow chrysanthemums.

He offered her an uncertain smile. A Band-Aid covered the cut on his cheek, and he had a black eye with bruising extending from his eyebrow all the way to his cheekbone. "How are you feeling?" he asked.

"Not bad," Abigail said. "Please, sit down."

"Would you like me to take the flowers?" Lillian offered.

"Thank you." Ethan handed her the vase.

"What a beautiful arrangement." Carrying the flowers, Lillian made a tactful exit.

Suddenly self-conscious, Abigail smoothed her hair behind her ears. At least she'd *brushed* her hair this morning, but napping had disarranged it by now, and she knew she looked pale and ill, with more purple under her eyes than pink in her cheeks. Flannel pajama pants, fluffy socks, and one of her dad's old sweatshirts completed the convalescent look.

"Thank you for the flowers," she said. "And thank you for coming to see me. That's not a short drive."

"I don't mind." He sat on the end of the couch.

"I think you just replaced my vase," Abigail said. "I owe you forty bucks."

He grinned. "How are you *really* feeling?"

"Sore. Tired. But I'm well-stocked with painkillers." Abigail focused on the toes of her fluffy socks, surprised at how nervous she felt. "How are *you* feeling?"

"Good. Except for a little soreness."

"Or maybe a lot of soreness?"

"Except for a lot of soreness."

"Ethan . . . I never really had a chance to thank you, and now that you're here, I don't know what to say. You saved my life. I don't think the dictionary includes any words big enough for that."

"I'm just grateful I got there in time. Answer to prayers. I'd been saying a lot of them for you."

"You had?"

"I thought you could use some help."

"Kyle was . . . he was . . . ready to kill me. Strangle me. Right when you—he'd just looped a rope around my neck when we heard you break that window next to the door. A few minutes more . . ."

Horror flashed in Ethan's eyes, and he reached for Abigail's hand. Looking embarrassed, he started to draw his hand back, but Abigail instinctively grasped his fingers.

"You saved *my* life," Ethan said. "He'd grabbed that big stone vase of yours and I almost took it right in the skull, but when you started screaming his name, it distracted him long enough for me to strike first. Your hands are tied, your ribs are broken, your knee is torn apart, and you're still fighting."

"At that point, I didn't have a lot to lose." Surprised at how reluctant she felt to let go of his hand, Abigail drew her hand back into her lap. "But Ethan . . . thank you. And I'm sorry I didn't trust you."

"There's no reason you should have trusted me. I'm sorry I didn't trust *you* when you insisted your brother didn't kill Karen."

"No reason you should have trusted her," Derek called from the other room.

"I thought you were asleep," Abigail called back.

"I was, until I started eavesdropping. Hanberg, thanks from me too, though I don't know how to thank someone for saving my sister's life."

Red-faced, Ethan looked like any more thanks would send him crawling under the couch. "I'm glad everything is getting straightened out."

"Detective Turner called this morning," Abigail said, figuring Ethan would appreciate a new angle to the subject. "They're building a strong case against Kyle Stratton in Karen's murder—Philip Kyle Stratton, that is." Saying Kyle's name made her want to scrub her lips with antiseptic. "They'll try to nail him for Leslie McIntrye too, but that one's going to be harder, since Karen isn't here to testify."

"Everything about Karen makes so much more sense now. I wish I'd understood in time to help her."

"You tried to help her," Abigail said. "She wouldn't let you."

They fell silent. Ethan shifted position, his shoulders and back straightening. His posture looked a little too rigid, and Abigail wondered how much pain he was in. She opened her mouth to ask if he'd like some extra couch pillows or maybe some Advil, but he spoke first.

"I'm guessing it'll be a few months before that knee is completely healed," he said. "Once you're back at home, you may need some help—repairs, snow shoveling, anything. I'm in Ohneka almost every day. Will you call me?"

Abigail felt herself blushing, which made no sense—he was offering to shovel snow, something any Boy Scout would do. Maybe it was the thought of Derek smirking in the family room and planning to tease her as soon as Ethan left that made her turn red. "Thank you," she said. "I will."

"Good. Do you—mind if I call *you* sometime? I get the feeling you're someone who doesn't ask for help easily, and I want to make sure you're all right."

Derek was going to tease her until his throat was raw, but she didn't care. "Call me anytime," she said. "Even if I don't need help, I'd like to hear from you."

"Not that—I mean—I don't—I wouldn't want you to feel any sense of obligation—"

"Ethan, that didn't even occur to me. I want a chance to get to know you when we're not both under incredible stress."

Ethan's tense shoulders relaxed and he shot her a grin. "Sounds good," he said.

ABOUT THE AUTHOR

STEPHANIE BLACK HAS LOVED BOOKS since she was old enough to grab the pages and has enjoyed creating make-believe adventures since she and her sisters were inventing long Barbie games filled with intrigue and danger or running around pretending to be detectives.

Her novels *Fool Me Twice* and *Methods of Madness* were Whitney Award winners for Best Mystery/Suspense.

Stephanie was born in Utah and has lived in various places, including Arizona, Massachusetts, and Limerick, Ireland. She currently lives in northern California. She enjoys spending time with her husband, Brian, and their five children.

Stephanie enjoys hearing from readers. You can contact her via e-mail at info@covenant-lds.com, or by mail care of Covenant Communications, P.O. Box 416, American Fork, UT, 84003-0416.